THE INSIDE OUT WORLDS

VISIONS OF STRANGE

SOPHIE JUPILLAT POSEY

To Christopher

Enjoy these creepy inside out scenarios!

Sophie Jupillat Posey

Contents

The Angel and the Sphinx

He'd destroyed the world once for her, and he would have destroyed it again, if it had not been for his conscience. For an angel, conscience was a fabricated thing, a useless human concept. But Adiphael was not an ordinary angel. He'd lived among humans, casting aside his majestic wings, casting aside his celestial form to walk the Earth and learn from men. But Adiphael, with his fair visage and translucent hands, had learned of pettiness and battles, ignorance of the heart and of the world. He'd walked among men and clothed himself in his curiosity and disappointment. He'd walked from Aethiopia, Lutetia, Orlivka, Hibera, Kelin, Clysma, Sharuna, the Huanbei, the Zhuxian. He'd lived with palettes of faces, voices, thoughts. He'd brushed by lives that died and lived again even as he never aged.

Despite his many wearisome travels, Adiphael did not know where he came from. He did not know if other angels like him existed. Of his birth, he could remember nothing, only coming to consciousness during the Vedic age in Bharatavarsha, confused and alone next to the Indus River. All he knew was the name of his form and a hazy purpose: angel. As an angel he knew he had to protect, to be a messenger, to fight battles. For whom, or why, he did not know.

He'd sought knowledge of his origins in his travels, but all for naught. He'd known no affection for anything, or anyone, except for the fire of knowledge, which Prometheus had stolen from the gods. Adiphael knew not who his masters were, and so he roamed, seeking but not finding. Gods abounded in the various celestial realms, in their infinite, confusing glory, along with their servants. But nowhere did Adiphael find other angels like himself. He identified with the Greek gods as they were when the great civilization of Athens believed in them, giving them life. As humans gave the gods life, so those humans gave Adiphael a chance to flock and observe gods who had no place for him, no definition of his existence.

He had no master. But what a terrible thing to be a messenger to none but yourself. How terribly lonely, to be constrained, to have a purpose that is unfulfilled. Adiphael could not explain why he needed a master. He yearned to be his own master, but he could not. He felt incomplete, a great abyss in his being he could not fathom. Adiphael felt like a human sometimes, those creatures who had love, talent, and curiosity, but who did not fulfill their complete destiny, because they spurned what they had. Adiphael was a shunned messenger to nobody but the voice inside of him that cried for the dark cradle of the night to bring him to a mother and father he'd never known.

Adiphael was perpetually chagrined by the human race. Why had the gods created such a feeble race? So young, so narrow-minded, so believing of the wrong things, so violent.

Yet he had walked with some of the greats, felt the flicker of power, felt the flicker of fire, the kindling of knowledge, as they tried to impart their knowledge to those who would not understand—could not understand—until millennia had passed, and not even then. Adiphael both respected and loathed the human race. They were children; they needed a helping hand. They acted as foolishly as the gods, yet their civilizations advanced faster than the gods'. The humans destroyed and created faster than the gods could breathe and settle conflicts among themselves.

Adiphael had learned something: the gods were as unscrupulous as the humans they'd created. Wisdom was the key to harmony, the utter union of all species, both mortal and immortal. But even the gods had minute wisdom, except for Lady Athena. It was to her that Adiphael whispered the gods should have the Sphinx—the daughter of Typhon and Echidna— teach the gods themselves. But even she had balked, furious with him, he who had no master, he who implied that she and her kin were flawed. But he'd adapted his suggestion to this: that humans needed to be stimulated, pricked with the titillation of knowledge, so they could evolve and ensure their survival through time.

Without telling anyone, Adiphael hoped that the humans would eventually come to outgrow the gods with their knowledge, surpass them, and come to rule the world wisely. Then Adiphael would have masters he would gladly serve; he could finally fill that peculiar chasm in his nature. Lady Athena did not see the details of his yearnings, and she passed his message to the other gods who, to his surprise, agreed. They sent the daughter of Typhon and Echidna to Thebes, so she could guard the city gates and pose her riddles to those seeking entrance. Alas, the gods subverted the noble intent of teaching knowledge into a cruel punishment for the people of Thebes, for an ancient crime Adiphael did not understand. Adiphael came down to Earth again, to see this reputed daughter of the ancients. He'd heard of her only through namesake—the Sphinx—through the whispered terror of gods and humans alike. When he saw her, asking her riddle, "*Which creature has one voice and yet becomes four-footed and two-footed and three-footed?*" he felt a strange longing in his breast.

Adiphael recognized the budding human emotion of love within himself, as he continued watching her, year after year, contemplating her magnificent head, those luscious, proud features, as she devoured poor ignorants, sliced their heads, or crushed them with her mighty paws. She had eyes of the sheen of the stars, with lashes as dark as an abyss, with a mouth that devoured like one. Her lips, Adiphael wanted to kiss, as softly as a wind does a rose petal. He admired her formidable wings, glistening with a thousand colors, mottled with blood and the dust of knowledge. He adored her human torso, those breasts that hung, ripe and untouchable. He treasured her furry flanks, mighty and strong, flexing and tensing as she paced in front of the city gates. Yes, he realized, he loved this hybrid woman and monster, aviary delight and ferocious feline. She *was* knowledge. She intoxicated him with the seriousness of her mission: for her, knowledge was life or death.

Adiphael never dared talk with the Sphinx. Not because he could not answer her riddles, but because she would not recognize what he was. If the gods could not define what he was, then she would not either. If she did ever realize, he did not know if she'd fear, loathe, or adore him. The risk was too great. Adiphael did not understand women creatures, be they mortal, immortal or in between. They were riddles his heart could never solve. He watched her, though, every moment, as she paced on her hill, respecting her as he'd never respected the gods.

One day, a dusty, brazen traveler came, hirsute, with crimson robes, a staff and an answer to her question.

Adiphael knew the answer, of course: Man. The fools could not even recognize their own race in the form of poetry or parables. Oedipus, like so many others, would fail. Then Adiphael heard the dreaded answer: *"Man, who crawls on all fours as an infant, walks upright later, and needs a walking stick in old age."*

The Sphinx, his beloved, threw herself off the cliff, tumbling down to the rocks, where, broken and injured, she started chewing at her own breast.

"No!" the angel screamed, hurling himself to the bottom of the cliff, buffeting Oedipus with an invisible wind. He soared and tumbled to her, where he revealed his true form, from his gigantic enormous wings, soft as a cloud, to his feet, as strong and sturdy as the ground.

"Sphinx, do not immolate yourself like this. He has bested you once. Nobody else will."

Her large eyes, filled with the bitterness of the River Styx, pooled with tears that fell in her matted fur. Adiphael stroked her tentatively, feeling her erratic heartbeat, willing her to live. She rasped, *"If he has bested me, then others will, too. I am a parody. I am a buffoon of knowledge that any mortal can best. I am not fit to live."*

He looked into her eyes and tried to soothe her, caressing her to sleep. But she fought against him.

"Sphinx, one mistake is not a failure. You should know this. Now you can change your riddle. Make it better. The gods will not smite you for that. We need you to help these creatures get wiser. Do not immolate yourself from shame, it is a foul creature."

"I can hardly help them get wiser if I kill them when they answer falsely," she croaked, leaning upward toward him. *"The rest of the world can learn, but not those of this city. Those who*

come all die, and they cannot gain wisdom. It is a futile cycle, one that cannot be broken. Humans cannot gain wisdom this way. Yet I must kill if they fail. It is my nature. I cannot do otherwise. As I have failed, I must kill myself. It is the best route."

"No, it is not, Sphinx. It can be changed. You can change your ways. Adapt your riddles so they challenge humans, but if they answer wrongly, you do not have to kill them. Let them try again. Learn."

"Do not waste your words, angel. Let me die."

With a swift turn of her head, she rent open her ribcage and chewed her own heart. Adiphael, for the first time, smelled the raw, sweet scent of blood that was neither mortal nor immortal. The angel felt his chest convulse with the desperate sorrow of a universe that never fully finished its quest to termination. He was worlds and time periods clashing together, merging and crashing into each other, squeezing his heart in hideous bereavement. The one he loved was dead. Beautiful, mysterious, fierce, she was now a carcass for the crows. It was unseemly. It was not justice. The gods had sent her, now they had to help her.

Adiphael reared up into the sky and flew to the gods, struggling to contain his weeping. He flew to Lady Athena first, and pleaded.

"The Sphinx is dead. She died of her own hand, for that mortal, Oedipus, discovered the answer to her riddle."

"Why does that matter, angel?" Lady Athena asked, her gray eyes searing, a thunderstorm roiling. *"King Creon shall have his reward. The Thebans will be safe now, their debt is paid. She was never supposed to be the guardian of the gates forever. Have you lost sight of her purpose?"*

"She was our protégée with a mission. Now she is dead. How can the humans evolve if she is dead? Knowledge will forever be just beyond their grasp," Adiphael groaned, anguished.

"Your original plan was changed to suit our needs. Knowledge became secondary. We want it to be that way," said Lady Athena, clenching her spear, alabaster fingers strong but delicate. *"The other gods think we should always be supreme. To me knowledge is power, but I see the wisdom in their decision. If humans were to become more intelligent, they wouldn't need us anymore. We would become obsolete. Your Sphinx was the perfect monster: sent as punishment, she fulfilled our wrath but she held dear tenants we believe in: supremacy of power over mortal knowledge. She was meant to herald her knowledge and kill, Adiphael. That was it. She is finished. Let the humans be. They will learn another way, through the eons. It is not our place to interfere anymore. Ages will come when the humans may no longer need us. Let us not precipitate those ages."*

Adiphael could not believe it. The one goddess he'd thought would support him had turned her back to him, neatly and conveniently washing her hands of the affair. So the gods could meddle with the humans' lives, destroy them, and with them their petty squabbling. But they could not help a being they'd sent to do their bidding and who had failed because of a change in purpose the gods hadn't deigned to inform Adiphael about. Adiphael felt aggrieved, split to the core. They did not care. She had only been a pawn. Arrogant deities, to think they never had any responsibility, and that the world could burn for their errors.

"Do not let your love blind you, angel," Athena said, her eyes piercing through him as surely as her spear. *"Love is the very opposite of reason and sagacity."*

"Angels cannot feel love," Adiphael lied, and he flew up, up, past Olympus into the clouds, to scream his sorrow, his hatred, his thwarted romance. He'd loved her, loved that Sphinx with her molten voice and simmering eyes. He'd never loved anybody else. She was the only being he'd ever felt a connection to, who'd made him feel something angels should

never feel. She'd imparted to him, without meaning to, a kind of knowledge: a human emotion. Athena was wrong. Love was a human emotion, something new, and thus was an acquirement of knowledge and wisdom.

Adiphael kept screaming, and soon his scream turned to song, a song scintillating and arching with dying stars, abysses opening and reversing, lightning shattering dimensions in the future and in the past. He sang and screamed for his Sphinx, and as he did, time and reality seeping through his body, he cracked the silvery egg of the divine Aether. He cracked its solid, silver shell, and he sang to Chronos himself, that serpentine being with heads of a bull, lion and man; Time himself.

"You have cracked the egg, and now the ordered universe is changing. Time itself is changing. What are you, that you can influence my power so?" Chronos said.

"I am Adiphael, angel in a man's body, and a man in an angel's form."

"You weep for your love. A powerful thing. You are willing to see the world burn for her."

"I simply want her to be alive again. I wish that Oedipus had never solved her riddle."

"You already have the power to change time. You are an angel, a creature that will not exist until after these gods fall. Angels will not exist for centuries yet. You have come back in time. How do you think you arrived in Bharatavarsha? You aren't a creation of that culture. You must have been spawned during the birth of Christianity, and somehow, you found your way here, during what will be called the Hellenistic era. You are existing before you were even born, Adiphael. You must be my progeny, an aberration that slipped through the cracks. No one could exist outside of his time like you do; no one could have cracked that egg except for a child of mine."

Adiphael was stunned. There was the answer to his question. After years of searching, of wondering where he'd come from, if he'd ever been a child, or always been a sentient creature, he had his answer. He was a child of Time, a creature belonging to Christianity, which did not exist yet. He had the power, had always had the power, to change time. He hadn't known it, of course. Now he knew his origins went beyond that lonely, gurgling Indus river by which he'd come to himself.

A thought surged into his mind, shoving away the elation of knowing where he came from. With his power, he could reverse Oedipus's ill-fated answer and change the timeline so the Sphinx could live. He could change the timeline so that the gods would fall, and the humans would be ruled by no god whatsoever, neither in the Western nor the Eastern spheres.

Chronos spoke to him again, serpent's tail flicking, curling around the egg of Aether.

"You are determined to save the one you love?"

"Yes."

"Then I will let you try your experiment. I will let you meddle with Time. As your father, I will not stop you. But I will let Ananke, my wife, exert her power. She is unstoppable. Time can change, but the Inevitable will happen, one way or another. The Inevitable wins over Time. What you may do, what we may do, will be crushed by Inevitability. We, the gods, will change and vanish, for our reality depends on human perspective. That human perspective shapes the power and existence of more than deities, however. If you were a normal angel, you would surely be affected. You might be exempt, as you are my child. A child of Time isn't affected in the same manner. As my child, your effects, your power, might linger. It is an enormous burden, a potentially catastrophic power you hold in your hands. If you fail, you will shatter the fabric of reality, you will destroy those you want to protect, and yourself. You, and only you, shall be responsible for the annihilation of your existence. Not even Ananke's power will save you if your demise is what was meant

to be. Choose wisely, angel. Do not make the world burn for the Sphinx. Things are not always what they seem. You have the power of Time, but it is its own master in the end, with the resolute courtesan of Inevitability."

Adiphael bowed his head. He felt the world, the universe, shiver and quake under his hands. He had the power. He might as well do it. He might as well try. If he failed, the world would burn and he with it. If he succeeded, then he could live with the Sphinx forever, among the humans, in peace. Live and love, in a world harmonized by knowledge and awareness of each other. Hopefully, that was where Ananke would lead them.

Adiphael turned his back to Chronos and let time coil and surge around his hands. His hands thrummed with the rawest energy, and he conducted all his anger, all his sorrow into Time. It writhed under his hands, roiling and snapping until Adiphael directed it specifically to that moment he wanted erased—Oedipus answering the Sphinx. He felt the world shudder, but he continued, forcing time to rewind, until that specific moment came. Adiphael flew down from the heavens and plummeted to Earth, to Thebes, to see Oedipus walking up to the Sphinx.

He flew to the Sphinx, cloaking his presence from the mortals. He whispered in her ear, savoring the scent of soil and grass, her musk:

"Change the riddle. You will need to change the riddle."

"Why?" she asked, her proud eyes pinning him under his invisibility.

"Your life depends on it," Adiphael said.

The Sphinx's eyes widened and she turned to Oedipus. She cocked her head, gaze boring from Oedipus's feet to his curly head.

"What is a fool and a child, an adult and a seer, that comes and goes, and is replaced anew as seasons pass?"

Oedipus fidgeted, toying with his staff. Adiphael could see him start to sweat. Good. He would never find the solution. Adiphael knew what it was of course: a god. Oedipus finally opened his mouth and croaked, *"Mankind?"* But his voice trembled.

The Sphinx drew back, fully erect, almost purring as she regarded him.

"No. Foolish mortal, that is not the answer."

Oedipus opened his mouth again to say something, and she leapt on him, to the horror of his fellow travelers. Adiphael watched with something close to delight as she devoured Oedipus, first swallowing his head, then chewing down to his legs. He listened as he heard the crunching of his bones, the ripping of his tendons, the squelching of his organs. Blood pooled around her paws, and the travelers fled. They would not get King Creon's throne now. Adiphael thought the dark red blood around her smooth, milky skin made her look beautiful. Formidably beautiful. When she'd finished, she licked her lips, loping to him and sitting in front of him.

Adiphael reached out to her and put a hand on her head. The Sphinx did not move.

"It feels like I've known you before, although I have never seen you, I think. But I have felt you. Sensed you. What do you want with me? Not my riddles, I know. They are easy to solve for an angel."

"I can give you unlimited power, where you will never die. But I also want to be your messenger, to help you spread knowledge around the world."

"Everything dies, angel."

"But they are reborn, too," he said. *"Just think, a society where you are queen, and I will be your consort and messenger. Both of us helping humans evolve, becoming enlightened so soon they can rule with us. Unlike the gods, they will be wise. We can all live in peace together."*

She purred under his hand. She started to say something, and Adiphael felt himself shrivel internally. He heard, or felt, a crack, and before he knew it, time drew from his body and tugged him in a dimension that sped past him, shimmering and thrumming, making him witness shadows of things that would happen, had happened. Adiphael thought he was being tugged toward the future. He thought he saw himself a few times, the people of Thebes still terrified, the once true prophecy of Oedipus now having never come to pass, and the Sphinx in that heady sprint through time, but he was not sure. Time had control of him.

When time ground to a stop, Adiphael lurched, and what he found made his heart hurtle into despair. The world lay in ruins and smoke around him. A pall of burning gray, the world wept around him, as he tried to understand what had happened. The humans wept through throats sore with age-old screams and despair. What had happened? Why so much suffering? And where was she who had his heart? Had something happened to her?

He flew to the top of the world, where he reached out with his senses and *felt*. He felt the Sphinx pacing on her throne in the continent now known as North America. She stood at the pinnacle of power, her throne as mighty as her giant paws. She looked natural up there, her slender, powerful figure dominant, preying on her subjects, asking them riddles that most could not answer. They came to her at her beck-oningof all ages: the youngest, the young, the elders, and the eldest, they came to her, and kneeled at her throne. Near their death, and at each stage of their life cycle, they came to her for judging. He could smell their fear. Almost none could answer her riddles. They all quaked as they answered, and she devoured them with her hungry mandibles. Adiphael felt a ripple in the fabric of reality. The cycle of mortals was at risk. They were reduced to whimpering slaves, unable to reincarnate, because she devoured them and their souls if they could not answer her riddles. Soon, the human species would be extinct.

Adiphael drew on the power of the egg and reversed time by increments, breaths taking eons, eons taking seconds. He saw himself flying around the world, helping out the humans by teaching them knowledge of history, the cosmos, the mythology of the gods, the philosophy of self. He taught them all he knew, all he'd learned from his wanderings so long ago.

As Adiphael traveled forward in time again, he realized that the Sphinx became more inflexible, she made her riddles spinier, more obscure, as labyrinthine as possible, so that Adiphael could not keep up with teaching the humans around the world. She exhausted him.

Landing back where he'd originally appeared, Adiphael closed his eyes and felt a maw open in his heart. His goal had been to teach them, to enlighten them, as he and the Sphinx protected them, while challenging them. She had destroyed what he'd tried to work for. He felt the humans' desperation, expansive as nothing, shriveling like the lattices of Time. They did not live like sentient beings should. Their whole meager, so-short existence lay in terror and preoccupation with what awaited them when certain death came, or when they had to progress from one age to another. It defeated the purpose of their existence. Gone was their curiosity about the world, their breathless anticipation of the next step, the thrill of understanding themselves, the gift of creating. The humans were breathing in a sarcophagus of mocking knowledge, a whip of subjugation and terror. What had he done?

Adiphael flew to the Sphinx, alighting at her throne, tall and stern, refraining from staring too deep into her alluring, savage eyes.

"We need to discuss your methodology, Sphinx," he said,

seeing her flanks ripple as she strode down from the throne, her tail whipping viciously.

"*There is nothing to discuss,*" she said proudly and coldly, smears of blood marring the marble exquisiteness of her chin and her cheeks. She bared her fangs at him, trying to edge him away. But Adiphael stood strong, clenching his fists, baring his strong chest to her. He was her servant, but she was his Queen, and his Queen was now a tyrant, a tyrant to her subjects.

"*When we started this together, I wanted the humans to have knowledge. I wanted you to challenge them, to be their judge, to ask them riddles so they could learn. I could counterbalance your killing by teaching them myself. Fewer and fewer humans would have answered falsely, the species would be at the apogee of its existence. You could be their Queen, their god! But instead, they fear you, because you are no longer a Queen, you are a monster, a tyrant.*"

"*How very human you sound, Adiphael,*" the Sphinx sneered, circling around him, her breath stirring the feathers of his wings. "*You think you gave me riches, but you gave me a corrupted apple instead, a teasing morsel that can never wholly satisfy me. Teaching the humans knowledge is commendable, indeed; I thought it would work, me judging them, you teaching them. But I have to live, Adiphael. I need to eat. How can I eat if the humans all answer my riddles correctly? In your hubris, angel, you have deprived me of sustenance. You have failed me, messenger.*"

Adiphael felt shame coursing through him, and his wings drooped.

"*It is in my nature to kill. You should know that. Cease being so lenient with your humans. It is better this way anyway. You and I want an elite, a supreme race comprised of few. We do not need this Earth to be overrun by rustic, unknowing humans. Those types of humans are my feasts. I become hungrier and hungrier, angel. There are fewer and fewer humans to feed on, because I eat so much. I must eat, Adiphael."*

Adiphael stared at her, seeing the bloodlust in her eye, the rounded form of her stomach. She did indeed feast well. Her hunger had surpassed her desire to enlighten the humans. He had created a monster. A beautiful, ravenous, uncompromising monster. She'd been right when she'd been killed the first time. It was a futile cycle. No matter what he did or she did, the humans or the Sphinx would suffer.

Adiphael felt temptation brush him with its fetid fingers. He would rather see the humans suffer than her. He could make them breed, keep a portion of them ignorant and dull, and feed those to her. The other portion would be those he taught, those he enlightened, and those who could pass the Sphinx's judgment and reincarnate. Adiphael and the Sphinx could have their elite, their golden minuscule society which they'd preside over. He would not fail her then. He would be her messenger, her consort, her lover. She would be his, and he would be hers.

But as Adiphael felt his mind churn with those thoughts, he heard the anguished cries of the world around him. The very Earth herself shuddered and groaned, her body defaced by war, sullied by blood, ruined by the anguish of the human species. Her very core thrummed, disturbed by the unnatural proceedings. She thrummed because what Adiphael had done was unnatural. He had broken the cycle of evolution and enlightenment with his meddling. The only way he could fix it was to erase the effects of his meddling. He could try to turn back time. He drew on his power, but the air seemed to immobilize his gestures. He tried again, but it was like he had no power left. In his entrails, he seemed to hear the cavernous growl of Chronos.

"To fix what you have done, you must die, and she must die too. It has gone too far."

So it had come to this. He had to die. The inevitable had happened. Except now, he was to die too.

Adiphael could not kill himself. But he also could not kill her. The world could burn, but he could not kill her. He had a duty, a conscience. He had to do what was right for all of them. He had failed too much.

"Sphinx, I challenge you to a contest of riddles. If I answer falsely, you must kill me and kill yourself too. That is how it must be."

"What are you playing at?" she asked, stunned, sitting down heavily next to him. *"This is an easy game for you, Adiphael."*

"Listen to me," he growled, looming over her, letting his frame expand and become taller. *"Those are my conditions. Do it, or you will end up dying anyway. The fabric of reality is fraying. Do it! You must swear by the Phlegethon River. I shall swear that I will not fight if you win."*

The Sphinx shook her head. She regarded him, cold eyes of arrogance and defiance pinning him. He fought against her pull and repeated himself:

"You must swear by the Phlegethon River. This is no time for pride. Are you a creature of honor? Have I served a greedy master without honor all these years?"

The Sphinx shuddered and came to him, her mane bristling. Good. He had hurt her. Now she would listen to him. Adiphael extended his wings, she wrapped her paws around him, warm, soft, and he flew to the underworld. The underworld's terror and misery of old waned sharply next to the state of affairs in the mortal world. Without the active influence of Hades, his kingdom had fallen into faded dreams, archaic nightmares. The only things that held true were the five rivers. Adiphael veered to the river opposite the River Styx. There lay the Phlegethon River, searing and potent, river's embers coiling into Tartarus. Adiphael alighted and folded his wings. The Sphinx unwrapped herself and strode to the river, its fire finding home in her dark pupils.

"We must swear and honor our pact. This is beyond our mortality, our pride, our ideas of grandeur, our history, our everything."

"If it will make you content," she said her voice echoing in the gloom.

Adiphael was taken aback. Since when had she ever expressed such a sentiment?

She coiled her tail and extended it to him. He grabbed her tail and spoke tremulously. *"We swear on the Phlegethon River to honor our contest of riddles. If I answer falsely, the Sphinx must kill me and kill herself too, to preserve the world. Swear, please,"* Adiphael begged, staring at the Sphinx.

She tightened her tail's hold on him and whispered, *"This is what it comes down to. I shall kill you, and kill myself so the world cannot burn. It seems like a waste. Yet there is wisdom in what you say. Ego is nothing next to the obligations of Time. I shall hate to kill you. You are the only creature who has been my companion for so long, who has been my messenger. You wanted a master and I was yours. I'd be a poor master to not honor our bargain now."*

Gazing fiercely at the river, she intoned, *"I swear on the Phlegethon River to honor our contest of riddles. If the angel answers falsely, I will kill him and kill myself too, to preserve the world."*

Adiphael picked her up again and flew them to Thebes, where it had all started, so many eons ago. The Sphinx drew a sharp breath and launched into a volley of riddles. He answered as fast as he could, but waiting, knowing he would have to answer falsely eventually. The game would keep him alive, enflame his veins, keep him locked in a tarantella of wits and tension, for just a few more moments. A few more moments was the best he could hope for, even though she would be the one to kill him.

"What glistens and gleams but can never be touched in the inkwell of the earth?"

"The moon," he replied.

"What is painful to search for, but once gotten is still as painful, but brings joy as well?"

"Understanding."

"What is all things that can be, will be, will never be, and what was?"

"Infinity."

"What burns as a brand and cannot be forgotten unless desired, spawned from whence it came?"

"Hatred."

"What is sweeter than remembrance, but bitter as hemlock intertwined in a trance that cannot be shaken?"

"Nostalgia."

"What is man's deadliest emotion, born of illogical rumination and infatuation, that no immortal can truly feel?"

Adiphael knew the answer to that one. But he did not answer, watching as the Sphinx purred, her eyes glittering at him. The answer was love. But he did not know if he agreed with her definition. She was wrong. He was immortal and yet he could feel love. A shadow perhaps of what the humans thought of as love. Maybe a form of love too majestic, too ancient for them to understand. But regardless, he could love, he had loved, and he would pay for his folly. And so would she. It was unjust that she should pay for his delusions. But the reality of time left no room for compassion, no room for such silly emotions as love.

"Anger," he rasped, and braced himself for the Sphinx's giant paw. But it did not come. She stared at him, her eyes narrowed, her mouth open in a derisive snarl.

"You play with me, angel. That was the easiest riddle of

them all, and yet you failed to answer it properly? I thought you wiser than this. Maybe it will not be such a loss to dispose of you after all."

"If you reach into yourself and remember what you know of me, you would understand why I answered like this. Kill me now, Sphinx. Remember the conditions."

After a long moment, the Sphinx said, "I wish I did not have to smite you. You aren't as wise as you think, Adiphael, for you love. You have always loved me, haven't you? Foolish angel. I was the poorest recipient for your love. But I was a good master to you. I know that is what you always craved, your nature wouldn't have been satisfied otherwise. It is better than nothing. Consider it my thanks to you for what you've done for me. Farewell, angel, farewell, Adiphael, bringer of knowledge, oxymoron of nature."

She reared up and slashed with her claws, ripping through his robes, into his ribcage. Adiphael didn't feel pain, but he felt himself weaken, some energy, some form of vitality escaping from him with each breath he shuddered. The world seemed to pulse, sideways, up and down, snarling his reality. He sank to the ground, flopping across the cliff. His grappling fingers hooked into the rock, his wings fluttered, to keep him from toppling completely over. His whole vision was filmy, coated in a haze of silver. He reached out to the Sphinx, arm trembling and he gurgled, "I've always loved you, Sphinx. I destroyed the world for you, and would do it again. But it has gone too far. Forgive me."

She strode to him, cradled him to her, putting a heavy paw on his frail shoulder. Adiphael leaned into her touch, nestling his fingers in her hair and headdress, clinging to it with the last vestiges of his strength.

"Remember the conditions," he whispered.

For a moment, he thought she would walk away, even though he knew she was bound by their pact. But she reached down her torso and ripped open her flesh. Adiphael smelled her blood splatter across the cliff, down his robes, into his wings. He closed his eyes and slowly felt reality stabilize. He felt her shudder around him, and then he jerked. Her thoughts became his, and his thoughts became hers. He felt her mind meld with his, breathe with his.

He truly did love her. He had worked against the impossible to bring her back. And she'd ridiculed him, scorned him, dominated the world till they were forced to this. Even if he had not asked her to kill herself, she would have anyway. Even though Adiphael had always baffled her, she enjoyed working with him, having him as her messenger. Always deferential, always noble, he'd spread her knowledge for millennia. He was the closest creature she'd ever been with that she hadn't eaten. As much as she loathed the concept, how very human it was, Adiphael had been her friend. Her unknown lover. He had saved her from death, prolonged her life for more than it had ever been worth. She had become greedy. Now she had no place anyway in a world that was disintegrating through her own making. It was time to go. In another world, in another dimension perhaps, one day, she would pay back the unimaginable debt she owed her angel.

They each expired in the other's arms, the Sphinx looking tenderly down at her angel, her paw firmly on his shoulder. He, looking rapturous, still had his hand burrowed in her tresses. His mouth lay open, waiting for a kiss that had come only from death.

The skies rent in a deafening explosion, the egg of Aether quaked and sang as it healed and formed itself again. Chronos and Ananke worked together to repair reality, and soon, the world righted itself again. Destruction, war and lamentation came, hand in hand with hope, enlightenment, though subdued, joy and curiosity. The gods fell and the humans arose, as they were meant to do. Nobody remembered anything about the Sphinx and the angel known as Adiphael. But on a certain cliff in Thebes, the rocks, the sands, the winds and the light still hissed and whispered of the angel and the Sphinx. Time had erased and looped back, but their union had been as elemental as they. Immortal, their strife and love had been.

PROPHECIES OF THE GREAT MOTHER

On the 400th anniversary, Mother Tepaki drew on the walls of Kwaligha, the cave home of all the tribes, which had once been the New Athos Cave. With dark red paint on her fingers she drew two lines together, then one line, and another, and then two more together.

2112.

The year the Apocalypse began.

We all knew how it started. We'd heard tales within the first few years of our lives, from our parents, extended families, and other tribe members. But the details were always nebulous. Only the Elders knew the details for sure, some of which they showed during the Retelling. Sometimes they showed the events out of order. But today, it seemed they would start correctly.

I glanced around the cave, the torchlight throwing shadow blobs on all our faces. I sat with my Keeso tribe. All of us boys and men huddled together. Our girls and women huddled in their own group, cross-legged, their attention focused on Mother Tepaki.

Brother Makate appeared in a suit and white mask. He would play the part of the Antichrist.

Mother Tepaki took out a worn book whose pages fell apart as she read. She held it up and started reciting.

"The Apocalypse dragged on for centuries. But it began with the plagues, super resistant bacteria creating super diseases for which there were no cures."

Brother Makate took off his suit and mask and folded and bent his fingers, casting shadows on the walls, moving his fingers to make it seem like little bacteria were crawling on the cave wall.

"Then came the storms, heat waves, floods, and droughts: Russia, Southeast Asia, the rest of North America. Then came acid rains, so intense, so lethal, they burned away most of the vegetation on Earth." Her voice rose, and as it did, we started ululating, emulating the agony our ancestors felt, so long ago.

"To finish off a limping mass of civilizations, came the arrival of the Antichrist, a puppet who pretended to be a uniter of religions. He came from the West, the land once known as America. He united Europe by whispering that the plagues, the environmental problems were because of the Middle East and Asia."

Brother Makate drew on the cave wall, continents merging together, and he put a hand over his face to cover his mouth. Torchlight gave a red glint to his eyes and turned his face orange. Then he drew flames on the continents and made hissing sounds.

Mother Tepaki continued.

"War started between factions, countries once allies, now terrible enemies. All fighting for resources, all fighting for a better planet. But their weapons, their weapons destroyed the Earth. They created earthquakes, land-shattering earthquakes that swallowed entire countries, like India, Mexico, New Zealand, Peru, Chile, and so many more. Despite warnings and surviving technology that could have helped, nobody escaped in time."

Mother Tepaki and Brother Makate started stomping hard, their steps echoing loudly. Drawn in, we also stood up and started stomping. No one stopped pounding their feet as Mother Tepaki continued.

"The sea life died from plastic pollution, acidification, and overfishing from the elite who stubbornly managed to survive. In 2500, the heat had increased so much that more countries disappeared under the ocean waters."

Brother Makate pulled a rock container over to him and dabbed his fingers in it. He spread the dark gray paint over the ruined continents, with angry scribbles that looked like what I thought waves would look like. I'd never seen any.

"Then came a plague of bioengineered bees gone rogue, created because the true bees had died in 2040. The last gasp of a society where natural resources had to be manufactured." Some of the Saplings in the crowd made buzzing sounds with their lips, stopping as Mother Tepaki continued. "The major rivers never turned to blood, but they did become sludge, full of cancer-causing chemical currents."

I dug my fingers in the hard clay and closed my eyes. I knew all this. I snuck a glance at Ikewa several rows down. She winked at me, bored by the anniversary ritual too. Her large dark eyes in her tar-colored skin hinted to me, *Let's sneak out of here and do something fun.* But I shook my head, my hair dragging on the cave floor. It was blasphemy to miss the Retelling. She knew that, she just didn't like it. She had crazy theories that the Great Mother Kiseta had given a prophecy sometime in the last century that the Apocalypse could be reversed. Supposedly, there was a sacred book, the Book of Watahaca, that had steps to reverse it. Tribes had fought with each other over its authenticity and over the prophecy itself.

The Keeso thought it a myth. No one knew who had

written it. No one alive had ever even seen the book, though Ikewa's tribe was still trying to find it. I wondered if, one day, it could be found. I believed, I guess.

My thoughts were interrupted by two men of the Anemoa tribe rushing into the cave and bowing hastily.

"May the Great Mother forgive us," the taller one said, "but this cannot wait. Brothers Nep and Hep have gone missing. Their weapons have been found scattered on the plains, and there was blood on the ground. We have scouted as far as we could before the Abyss, but we have not found them."

Mother Tepaki sighed and put a fist to her heart, then her lips, and then her forehead. "They keep disappearing. More and more. Maybe it *is* time to consult the Prophecies of the Great Mother." Her expression became one of resolve and she raised two fingers into the air, signaling the Ceremony was over.

"So, what do you think is taking our people away, Wakataka?" Ikewa asked me

"Maybe there's a new predator out there we don't know about," I said, sharpening my spear.

She leaned back on the rope bridge, and it swayed with the wind and her weight. The mountains behind her were small and cracked, like our newborns. Here and there I could see tiny specks of green. I wondered, not for the first time, if other parts of the world had recovered better from the Apocalypse. Were there other societies like ours, holed up by the constraints of our species' terrible legacy?

"You have that look on your face again." Ikewa said. "You want to get out of here and explore."

I nodded. She knew me so well. "I can't wait till my seventeenth nameday."

Ikewa raised her eyebrows. "Too bad. I get to go out when the moon waxes gibbous."

I put my index finger on top of my fist, the Keeso sign for "damn you."

"Do you think they'll let you do your Trial with so many people going missing?" I asked, squinting my eyes and scouting for thrushes.

"They have to," she said. "If people are going missing, we need Roots of the Great Mother more than ever."

"Aren't you afraid at all? Do you even know where you'll be going? What you're going to do?"

She crossed her arms, silent for a while, then spoke. "I want to do something no one has done before. All our current Roots have gone beyond this cave, yes, gone as far as Mount Tebulosmta. But nobody has gone beyond that. I want to, and I want to find the Book of Watahaca." Her eyes shone. "Oh, to see clear blue skies, to have huge oceans like there used to be, or be able to swim, or eat sea creatures. To have animals, not just to eat, but to love and have as friends. To have all the original Commandments instead of just three. We can have all that, if I find it and bring it back."

I bowed my head. I knew what she wanted was close to impossible. But I didn't want to discourage her. And I did want her to find the book.

"What are you going to do on your Trial?" she asked.

"That's a full cycle away," I answered.

"Yeah, but what are you going to do?" she pressed.

"I will go out as far as I can, and never come back. I want to travel to ruins of other cities, maybe go as far as the Old World."

Ikewa's eyes bugged out. "You never want to come back?"

I shook my head.

"But part of the Trial is coming back and showing that you survived. If you don't, you will have to do a spiritual penance. The Commandments are clear. Also, you could die. There could still be rogue technology out there. You have no way of knowing."

I shrugged and put a fist to my mouth, squeezing gently. *Don't expose me.* I didn't want to stay in this cave forever. I didn't know how the Elders did it. Surely there was more to life than scrimping and surviving in a cave. If there was radiation out there, then I would have to pray to the Great Mother and hope she would keep me safe.

Ikewa sighed and put her hands behind her back and wiggled her shoulders in Keeso fashion. *Your secret is safe with me.*

I was about to suggest we go hunting for thrushes when Brothers Une and Unu called to us. Two loud and strident hoots, followed by a softer final one.

"The Great Mother is about to prophesize," Brother Unu shouted. "Come, now."

And we did, Ikewa running ahead of me.

———

When we entered the Pondering room, the Elders were already there, blindfolds over their eyes, vertical stripes of white face paint adorning their lips and their foreheads. They sat in a square formation, just as they had the last time I'd been witness to a prophecy, during my fifth cycle. Hollowed rocks glowed with the lights from captured lightning bugs. As we came in, Mother Tepaki greeted us and gave us each a rock chalice full of Psilocastagma, a concoction made from mushrooms that grew in our cave. They were hard to reach, growing high in the stalactites. I swallowed nervously, then drank it down, the acrid taste sticking to my tongue. The whole cave quivered instantly, an amber sheen filming my vision. A visceral humming rose from the floor and reverberated through my bones. My eyes rolled in the back of my head, and I stumbled to where the Elders sat. I joined hands with one of them and let the sudden chill and the scent of rot fill every sense. Vaguely, I heard Mother Tepaki's high voice chanting.

"Great Mother, we are ready to hear your counsel."

I started to shake, and I clenched my hands as hard as I could, feeling the Elder's hand twitch in my grip.

A droning noise, like a thousand insects frantically buzzing all at once, resounded in my ears. Foreign scents, chirpings of birds I'd never heard before, and the cracking of thunder mingled together, making no sense to me.

Dangerous times are coming. A new threat targets the human species. But the Earth shall renew again. One of you will be the Savior of this world.

Slowly, the droning noise, the strange smells, and the anxiety left me, and I came to. My vision refocused, spots dancing in my line of sight. The Elders murmured together and the other Saplings stared around in a daze. Hanae, Cheke, Abiama, and so many others puffed up and started talking about how they were the Savior, and they would prove it once they passed their Trials. I'd never seen them this excited.

Me, well, like any other prophecy, this one perplexed me. I thought all prophecies were disappointing. Full of ominous, grand words that might relieve the boredom of everyday life but in the end, either didn't apply to us, or promised something much different than implied. Though this prophecy was actually more specific than any I'd heard. One of us would save the world. But how? What threat was looming over us? Would the Savior take care of the new threat? I heard Cheke say, "I tell you, it's going to be me! I've slain the most beasts, I've gone to the Black Sea and survived, I've seen things nobody would believe. I will save us."

Hanae, Abiama, and the others laughed. I got up and

approached them, but before I could jump in, a hand tugged at me. Ikewa. Her face grave.

"What do you think?" I asked.

She shook her head.

"It must be what my tribe has always believed. Someone will find the Book of Watahaca. It is our mission, our calling to find it."

I gave her a look. "You mean, you think you'll be the one. You'll be the Savior."

The principles of her tribe were strange to me, valuing the spiritual purpose of an individual, rather than seeing people as links in the chain of our society.

"If not me, then someone from my tribe, the Ahsotes" she said, her brow furrowed. "I bet the disappearances are related somehow."

Just then, the Elders thumped the ground with their hands and clacked their tongues. We grew quiet at once.

"The Great Mother has spoken," the oldest among them intoned. "We face a new threat. What it is, we do not know. But we will have to make a decision for the unity of our entire tribe. For now, until we know for sure what this threat is, all Trials will be delayed."

Ikewa's shocked, angry "What?" was lost in the din of other Saplings' indignant cries.

The Elders stripped off their blindfolds, revealing their white sightless eyes, then they stood up and stomped the ground with their feet.

"Our decision is final. We will follow the will of the Great Mother until she tells us more."

Ikewa was silent, although the other Saplings groaned and grumbled loudly. But I knew that slant of her jaw, that set brow.

I had finished making bamba paste. Now I gathered various plants and pressed them to get the precious edjol, the replacement for fresh water we drank and cooked with. It had been my turn to hunt for the ingredients and make the edjol supply for us all. I served all our tribes at the feast as they ate bamba paste, beetles and ants ground up and mixed with herbs that grew on the cave walls. It was musky and crunchy, a good prelude to the ox meat and strips of mangha fruit. We hadn't eaten a beast that big for many moons. I worked my way around the passages of the cave filling cups and hand bowls, bowing to the Elders, and smiling at Saplings and Fledglings as the tantalizing scent of fire-grilled meat made my mouth water.

After my rounds and sitting down to help myself, I realized I hadn't seen Ikewa.

I asked Nabi, one of the Saplings, if he had seen her.

"No, I haven't seen her all day," he replied. "She was supposed to be hunting today though."

I didn't say anything, and I ate bamba paste. I had a tingling down my back; Ikewa was up to no good. I'd had that feeling twice before. Once, years ago, Ikewa killed a lynx I'd been hunting. It had almost killed me. I had deep scars on my stomach to this day. But she had violated one of the rules of the tribe: Your kill is your own. Though she had saved my life, she'd ruined my honor. I'd begged her to run away, but she refused. I had had to tell the Elders about the kill. For that, we both were punished. Bound hand and foot, gagged, and left outside the cave with no protection for a day and a night. But we'd survived, and were welcomed back, deemed worthy of forgiveness.

The other time, was when we were much younger. She'd snuck out of Kwaligha to try to find her little brother, even though the Elders had forbidden it. For punishment, she had spent five days in one of the cave's cul de sac, in the dark, given only edjol.

I felt the tingling feeling strongly, like the cave was running dry, chill fingers down my back. I stood up and made for the cave entrance.

My eyes immediately adjusted to the dark as I crossed the bridge and walked out to the plains, once a nature reserve. I'd seen pictures of it from the Elders' scant collection of books. I sped up, sniffing the air, trying to hone in on her scent of acrid perspiration, limestone, and mica, from the clothing she fashioned for herself.

I crouched down looking for tracks. But she was good, having swept away her tracks with a branch to obscure her path. I knew her scent, though. So, I followed my nose. An acrid wind that burned my nose rustled across the plains and made my eyes water. Through my tears I discerned a figure laying on the ground, muscles taut, spear aimed directly at me.

"Ikewa," I said gently. "It's me."

"Wakataka," she said flatly.

She drew herself off the ground and stood up. I could sense her glare in the darkness. "Are you trying to get me caught?"

"No! But I didn't know where you'd gone. I thought..." I didn't want to say, *I thought you were getting yourself in trouble*.

"Whatever you're thinking, you're probably right. And you should have known better than to follow."

"The prophecy is going to your head."

She shook her head, her heavy hair swinging.

"I know I must do this. My Trial is to find the Book of Watahaca. I am meant to do something important. Whether it's being the Savior or not, I don't know. But I must go. Alone."

I opened my mouth.

"Don't even think about asking," she said.

I closed my mouth, then tried a new tack. "You will be in so much trouble if they find you."

"I know."

I sighed. "Then go. I will head back." I put my hands behind my back and wiggled my shoulders. *May fortune be with you.*

She smiled and loped off, muttering, "I *will* see you again. I promise."

She did come back eventually.

I was telling a story to the Fledglings, the oldest having just celebrated his seventh nameday. The actual book lay in the Elders' quarters, falling apart, and I didn't know how to read anyway, but I knew the old stories told to me by heart. I would have to, to make sure I told them accurately to my young one day. I wondered how many books we would keep losing to time, and how many Elders would pass down details to younger generations.

Today, the Fledglings had picked a children's story from the twenty-first century. I recounted it as best I could, making hand motions and faces. I was interrupted frequently because there were words or concepts they just didn't know. Though the interruptions were aggravating, I could understand.

"While the ship was yet in stays, the mate lowered the jolly-boat and jumped into her with the very two men, I believe, who spoke up as having seen me at the helm. They had just left the lee of the vessel (the moon still shining brightly) when she made a long and heavy roll to windward, and Henderson, at the same moment, starting up in his seat bawled out to his crew to back water. He would say nothing else—repeating his cry impatiently, back water! black water!

The men put back as speedily as possible, but by this time the ship had gone round, and gotten fully under headway, although all hands onboard were making great exertions to take in sail. In despite of the danger of the attempt, the mate clung to the main-chains as soon as they came within his reach—"

Mother Tepaki rushed into the passage, almost tripping over the children seated in front of me, her face white. "Ikewa has returned."

"Where is she?" I jumped to my feet.

Mother Tepaki's mouth trembled. "You must rely on the Great Mother's fortitude."

My excitement dimmed.

"She... She... She is in the hands of the Great Mother. It is up to her if she lives or dies."

"Life or death? What is happening?"

But Mother Tepaki breathed deeply, wringing her hands.

"Tell me!" I shouted.

"Let me take you to her."

When we arrived at the healer quarters, Brother Makate and the Elders stood over a stone table in the center of the room. Upon it was a huddled mass, somewhat misshapen, glowing with a strange fire. It thrashed and turned, a guttural moan escaping it, followed by shrieks of pain that went through me like the steady, prolonged lancing of a barbed spear. I approached slowly, but paused as a wall of heat hit me. Heat more intense than our sun radiated from the thing on the table.

"Ikewa?" I whispered in horror.

"What happened to you?" I asked. Brother Makate steered me away, blocking my view, holding a finger to his lips.

"We will ask the questions," he said sadly.

Another Elder started the line of questioning.

"What happened, child?"

"They called to me... They were nice at first... But they trapped me. Hurt me. They stuck me with long sharp things."

"What happened after they stuck those long things into you?"

I moved closer, quietly avoiding the distraught eyes of the Elders. Ikewa wailed.

"Pain. Pain everywhere. Body changing. They kept doing it."

Brother Makate moved agitatedly. As he did so, I got a good look at her. Her body had ridges all over it, segmented like a worm. Her legs quaked, and one of her hands was deformed, flabby with no fingers. Her dark skin had a mottled orange tinge to it, and every so often, embers shifted through her body. But her eyes... Her eyes were Ikewa's, unchanged except for being filled with an agony I wished I could unsee.

"Who is they?"

"There is a group of people... People from before the Apocalypse... Their descendants still live. They want us... people like us... for their plan. Our people... Our people and more are trapped. They are meant to be... Monsters to survive in this world... To do their bidding... They are so powerful..."

A flash of fire coursed through her. She screamed again.

"Monsters? Plan? What bidding? What did they want you to do?"

She thrashed violently and the Elders backed away.

"They... they want more people to... go into places they don't want... to go."

"Where? Into the sea? Into the earth? Into the skies?"

"Everywhere," she moaned.

"Other tribes trapped... people dying. People transformed into monsters... Those long things, they do something. For me... the woman said devil worm..."

Brother Makate shook his head.

"A devil worm? How? You met a devil worm? They can

survive pressure, lack of oxygen and high temperatures. But they are microscopic."

"That's what... she said. Fusing. Transforming? Good for plan. For humanity."

She coughed and gasped.

"Something's wrong... It hurts!" she shrieked, her voice shrill with agony.

The Elders conferred quietly among themselves. I heard whispers of needles, experiments and secret societies. I edged closer, but just then she called my name.

"Wakataka! Help! Please help. They won't stop..."

The Elders panicked and started shoving at me.

I focused my gaze on her, ignoring the monster and seeing past it to my friend. "I will find who did this to you," I said to Ikewa, reaching out a hand before realizing that touching her would burn me severely.

"Leave her," Mother Tepaki said, her face still white. "She needs to rest."

I walked away, and heard Ikewa say, "Please ... don't let them find you."

I left her side only to do the duties imposed on me. The Elders came and prayed over her, and the healer tried all kinds of curatives. The first day, her other hand lost its fingers. The second day, her legs fused together, gathering ridges like the rest of her body. The third day, her mouth disappeared into her face, which lengthened and shrank. The fourth day, her eyes disappeared. The fifth day, she died.

I was too angry to weep.

A funeral was held. First, we prayed to the Great Mother and asked that Ikewa's soul find peace in the next life. Then we put all of her possessions into an ornate leather pouch and sewed it to her clothes. But she was not placed on the bier and shown to all the tribes, as is usually the case. Gossip about her final appearance had reached the tribe and some thought she had been struck by a curse, and they might catch it if they looked at her body. The Elders seemed okay with allowing this because it helped explain why she was not displayed as custom dictated.

But because she had come back and given warning to the tribe, that honorable act erased her previous sin of sneaking out of the cave without permission. So, her body was carried to the bridge outside the cave. We didn't know what lay at the bottom of the gap the bridge spanned. A river, a chasm to the center of the earth, or a void in the realm of the Great Mother.

I put a hand over my heart as her body fell out of sight into the darkness, whispering, "May you find eternal peace, my friend."

Some of the women ripped hair from their scalps and sprinkled the torn strands down after my friend. The men and boys put their hands over their hearts as I did. My throat grew even more tight. "I will avenge your death," I swore, and I prayed the Great Mother would hear my call.

Sadly, Ikewa was the first and the last to come back to us. More disappeared; it was assumed that they had met the same fate as she.

The five of us were hunting, our eyes trained on a creature we'd never seen before. It was a mammal, so it was edible. I hefted my spear and closed one eye, taking aim, when I was hit with an agonizing headache, and as I fell to the ground I heard screaming that wasn't mine.

I woke up and found myself in a strange room. It was tall enough for me to stand in, and long enough for me to lie down, but only just. The walls were strangely smooth, cold, and a dead sort of gray. There were no doors, no windows. What little jewelry I'd possessed was gone, and so was my spear. And, I couldn't get out. No matter how much I pushed, shoved, kicked, beat on the walls with my fists, nothing happened.

I saw no one.

But things were done to me somehow.

A soothing gas wafted into my cell. I teetered and fell over. My legs, my arms wouldn't move, no matter how hard I tried. The needles came, relentless rows of them, coming down into my cell and piercing into my neck, my spine. Other times, a blunt paddle came from the wall and hit my skull. Scrapers appeared magically from the walls and raked at my skin, hair, and tongue while the gas kept me immobile. I couldn't even scream.

How long had it been? Had it been a few days? A month? A season? Or years? Time meant nothing. Without the rhythm of the Great Mother's sun, I could not know.

A blinding glare of light greeted my eyes as my cell, opened up like an eggshell being cracked. It was unlike any light I'd ever seen, so strong, so pure. I stumbled out and covered my face with my hands. A dull roaring surrounded me, alien, forbidding. When I was able to see again, I was in a space where the walls were clear. Struggling to remember the knowledge of my tribe, the old books that had been recounted for generations, I realized I must have been surrounded by glass. This room I was in was shaped like a circle, and through the glass I could see nothing but a deep dark blue; the closest blue I had seen in my life was the blue of the entrails of some slaughtered beast. This blue had a mightiness, a pressing presence that quickened my pulse. What was it?

Another beam of light hit me, and this time I saw the source: a small black tube pointed at me like a spear, the light coming out from one end. A woman held this object. She had short hair that didn't gleam with sweat or oil, her face was unmarked by weather, her skin smoother than anything I'd ever seen. I had never seen a human like her. She had eyes the same blue as the terrifying blue thing that surrounded us, impenetrable and faceted. Her skin was the lightest I'd seen. The woman stopped and pointed the tube down. The light disappeared.

"You are a sight," she said, in a gentle voice. "What is your name?"

"Wakataka. Who are you?"

I felt naked in front of her. I needed my spear. I needed to touch something familiar. I needed answers.

"How old are you?"

I refused to answer. She cocked her head. "Never mind. I can tell from your bone structure and your teeth what age you are."

She wrote on some kind of tablet, one not made of stone. Finally, she raised her eyes.

"You can call me Mrs. Milloy. Have you ever experienced physical trauma?"

I didn't answer.

"How do you quantify pain?"

Again, no answer.

"How fertile do you think you are?"

I blocked my mind and refused to answer any of her strange questions. When she saw I wouldn't talk, she said in a steely voice, "Back to your cell you go until you learn some manners." She pressed a turquoise jewel on her bracelet. Slowly, the world swam and my mind shut off.

I kept getting stabbed, hit, and Great Mother knows what else in my cell. My body would quake then relax. Then it would go numb and I'd lay still, against my will, for what seemed like an eternity. I couldn't stop from making a few grunts. One day, a familiar voice spoke inside my cell, although I couldn't see anybody.

"You are an interesting specimen. Your tolerance for pain is quite high. Higher in fact than some of my colleagues'." A faint laugh made her voice tremble, then Mrs. Milloy steadied and resumed in a curiously flat tone I hated. "Definitely higher than that of your tribe. Wow, they gave up so easily. Weak, weak specimens. I am happy to say you are the only survivor of your tribe. Regrettable that we don't have more specimens to experiment on, but I'd rather they be strong physically. Some of my colleagues don't agree, of course. But I've always preferred quality over quantity." There was a long silence. Then she spoke again. "I think it will soon be time to get more acquainted. See what your mental strength is. For all I know, I might learn from your primitive thinking." She laughed again and I was left alone for a while, no talking, no needles, no pain or anything else molesting me.

When we talked again, it was face to face, although she stayed across the room with the strange blue thing pulsing in the background. She smiled at me, a quick stretch of her lips.

"Now, I know you have questions, Wakataka. But you can't ask them all at once. So I will answer what I can."

I looked around me again, a sense of foreboding rushing through me as the blue mantle around us surged.

"What is that?" I asked, pointing at the blue thing.

She turned and laughed.

"Oh, that? I should have known. The others had the same reaction. That's the ocean, dear. We are deep in the Pacific Ocean."

The ocean? That vast blue thing was the ocean? Why did it surround us like that? There were so many questions I wanted to ask. But one of her comments puzzled me.

"What others?"

"Other people we've secured. Your tribe. The ones who are dead."

"Our people. What have you done? Who are you? Who do you—" my voice echoed loudly.

She cut me off with a long "ssshhhh," a finger on her mouth. "I will not tolerate that tone. We have been acquiring subjects for some time. We finally have the technology to find you, to do it, you see. We've had a lot of test subjects. A lot of them became monsters. A lot more of them died. It's unfortunate, of course. But it's the cost of doing business."

I clenched my fists and hissed, "Let me out. What evil spirits do you worship?"

"So primitive," she sighed. "Really. As if we worshipped anything. We are doing you a favor. You aren't that far removed from monsters. You are animals. And animals serve a purpose. But because of the Apocalypse, we need to transform you a little. We need people to get out to the barren regions, to oceans still acidic enough to melt bone, to rifts so deep and hot only bacteria can survive down them. We don't want to do that. It's far too dangerous and we're too valuable. It will be *your* purpose to gather the materials we need to complete our technology, so we can go to Mars. You see, Earth is going to get worse over time. And we want a better planet, a planet where we can rule again. Once we progress from living in artificial quarters to living on the planet's surface, it will be easier to rule openly, to create division with technology only a select few will understand. So tedious, having to rule from the shadows, watching the poor scuttle about trying to survive. The Apocalypse killed most of you. That was unfortunate. But you are resilient; so convenient for us. You will serve a purpose again in making Mars habitable for us. Oh, and your descendants, eventually."

My mind whirled. The room spun and I had to plant my feet to stop the dizziness. Who was this monstrous woman? I rushed at her. A shock went through me, as if I'd been struck by lightning, and I bounced off something I couldn't see. I writhed as tendrils of agony coursed over my skin, under my skin, into my flesh. I kept my mouth shut and my teeth absorbed my muffled screams.

Mrs. Milloy shook her head and clucked her tongue. "Oh dear. Someone still needs to learn manners."

I spat, and stuck two fingers deep into my bellybutton, our sign for *I hate you*. But the woman only raised her eyebrows quizzically.

"Who are you?" I muttered through clenched teeth.

"Consider me your Master. I think it is time to go back in your cell. You are a simple creature and I want you to process what I have said. We will continue our conversations later. You may be strong, but you are stupid."

She snapped her fingers, and an invisible force gripped me, sliding me backward until I was back in the cell and couldn't get out. I slammed myself over and over against the walls, until the mist spread in my cell, making my eyes flutter. I fell to the floor and went to sleep against my will.

Mrs. Milloy and I did have more conversations. It was always the same; my cell would open, I would step out, and she would be across from me, separated by the unseen thing. I couldn't attack her. She always had a smile on her face, her copper hair clean and unnaturally still. I slowly got answers to my questions, but it took several conversations, and several agonizing stints with the barrier.

One day I asked her what she'd done with Ikewa.

"You keep mentioning that name like it's special. Who is that?"

"She was my best friend," I said tightly. "When she came back, she was unrecognizable. She was fused with a devil worm."

Mrs. Milloy paused, then chuckled. "Oh, the devil worm subject? That would have been subject number twenty-one! She showed promising signs, we could have released her in the San Andreas fault to find materials for us, deep in the Earth's crust. One of my colleagues decided to mix her DNA with a devil worm, thinking it would improve her chances of weathering the heat. But it didn't. Should have listened to me." Again, her face hardened, and the coldness in her eyes struck me like a knife.

I bowed my head and made a prayer to the Great Mother, whispering fiercely over and over, "Please deliver me from this hell, I will do whatever it takes, a thousand Trials if need be, anything to avenge my people."

Her incredulous laughter skated past my awareness. But I was forced to look up as I felt myself sliding back into my cell. I glared at her as hard as I could, wishing for the Great Mother's worst punishments for this woman. How had this creature survived the Apocalypse anyway?

"You are praying? Really? How quaint. I think I know what I'm going to do with you. You're obviously not very bright. But you are strong."

"Just how many of us have you killed?"

She cocked her head and pursed her lips.

"Hmm. Since we started finding tribes around the world, two hundred. Your people are remarkably weak."

My stomach lurched. I stared hard at her, but there was not an iota of compassion, of empathy. She could have been talking about vermin. And I reminded myself that indeed, we were vermin to her.

"We are not one tribe. We are individual people."

"It doesn't matter," she said, not skipping a beat. "A spider and an ant are still the same thing. A bug. Bugs that are meant to be squashed."

"Don't you worry we will all die? That your experiments will fail?"

"No," she said, jiggling her leg. "There are always some who make it. That's the thing about people like you. The Apocalypse can occur, and like rats, you still manage to survive. So I'm sure we will find more of you. Plus, I am harvesting your sperm. Maybe your offspring will survive our experiments better."

A snarl escaped me, and she tsked. "You should be thanking me. You should be honored you are serving a true purpose, instead of running around like imbeciles, praying to a mythical nature spirit. If left to your own devices, you would evolve sometime in the next millennium, and there is no time for that. Thanks to us, you are reaching the next stage of evolution much more quickly. You're welcome." She smiled primly, her lips the color of wet clay.

"Who is this 'us' you keep mentioning? How many more of you are there?" I asked, and I paced in a circle, unable to bring myself to look at her anymore.

"More than you think. We are resilient, too. We prepared for the Apocalypse just in case. We had bunkers and deep-sea pods and some of us had capsules ready to fly us to Mars. But few of us made it. The Apocalypse destroyed more of our resources than we thought. So many of us got cocky and didn't make it. Rocke-locke, Rainheim, Ophental... Oh, and the Dulacq family thought they were invincible. But they got sloppy." She grimaced.

"Your ancestors could have stopped the Apocalypse. Why didn't they?"

She snorted.

"We could have, yes. But you could have done stuff on your end, too. Instead, you were too busy squabbling over religion, over fake gods. It is so easy to have the poor victimized, abused, fooled by the elite narrative." She snorted again. "The world is much grayer than you think. But you are right. We could have helped stop the Apocalypse. But we didn't. My ancestors knew they would die before it happened. So they enjoyed the time they had before all went to hell. Maximized their profits to enjoy all life had to offer. That was smart. Instead of wasting time and resources fixing a world where everyone would get along. How boring."

"Why would you want a world where people don't get along?" I truly couldn't understand. If the tribes back in Georgia hadn't gotten along, we would have been weak, divided, picked apart by predators and Nature's harsh conditions a long time ago. And back when humanity lived in an organized society, before the world had cracked apart and become a ruin, it must have been in humanity's best interests to be united and look out for each other."

"If people got along and everything was rosy, there'd be no need for us, would there?" she asked, no mirth in her voice at all.

"Maybe you need to find another pastime that doesn't involve profiteering off people's suffering," I hazarded. "You could still be powerful. But instead, use that for the greater good."

She regarded me flatly and she tossed her head. Meanwhile, the ocean murmured around us, plaintive, low—an eerie song I was learning to appreciate.

"Idiot boy. Thank goodness your offspring won't be bright. Some might even make good food. The rest will follow in your footsteps."

"Yes," she said after a while, her eyes scrutinizing me from the tip of my head to my toes. "I know what I'm going to do with you. You will be adapted to a CO_2 atmosphere so you can fly around the world and scout for other tribes that may still be hiding. We need as many subjects as we can get. I want to get off this rock so bad. If you adapt to that atmosphere well, then your progeny will have a likely chance of doing so on Mars."

I was so numb and shocked I didn't try to fight as I was dragged to my cell.

My prayers to the Great Mother became jumbled with Mrs. Milloy's conversations, and my agony.

The needles came again and this time they didn't stop. The pain. It writhed like a snake, black and loathsome, settling in the deepest parts of my being, a flail of liquid torture, scaly and cold, clinging to my soul. My mind felt like someone had shattered the mountains of the Earth against my temples, vast, colossal mounds cracking, echoes rattling my sanity.

My body started transforming; strange tentacles sprouted from my fingers, long and soft. Every so often, I heard Mrs. Milloy's bubbly voice announce what they were doing.

"Right now, we are putting loriciferan DNA in you. That will make you able to breathe CO_2. Then we will fuse Accipitridae or eagle DNA with yours. Don't forget to breathe! We need you alive and well for this to work."

But the worst was when she would talk about human life.

I called her a monster when I had enough breath left to yell. But she would override me with arguments that made sense, barbaric as they were.

"You say I'm a monster. Yet I have given you tools to serve a purpose."

"But you hurt and kill people to do it."

"Humans have done that since the beginning of time. Don't you kill animals to eat food?"

"Mother Nature gave us animals to eat so we could survive," I mustered, from the increasing tightness in my chest.

"Ah yes. Using religion to justify killing. Just like your ancestors killed each other over religion. Who are the real monsters, Wakataka?"

My body hardened and shortened, my legs curling up and disappearing inside my frame; my manhood disappeared. I couldn't stand anymore. I rested on the floor like a top, teetering one way, then the other. Radiating flares of stabbing pain, in two distinct spots on my back, bore into me constantly. I barely had energy left to stay awake and talk. But Mrs. Milloy delighted in talking to me.

"What makes life valuable?" she asked me, ignoring my grunts and thrashing against the walls of my cell.

"Our connection to the Great Mother. Our purpose on this Earth. We all make this society."

Mrs. Milloy sniggered. "You really disappoint me. Have you learned nothing yet? You are a puny cog in the great scheme we live in. A human's first urge is survival and that means doing anything to ensure that. Societies fall apart. People war. People always want more. You can't kill everybody who doesn't agree with you. But you can use them. Then they actually have purpose. That is what makes life valuable."

I couldn't answer her. Instead, I prayed silently to the Great Mother, wishing again the worst of punishments on Mrs. Milloy.

"You'd better not die," she said sharply. "My colleagues would love nothing more than for my experiment to fail. You are my prize subject, lowly though your intellect is, saintly though you think you are. I will not have you fail me."

Mrs. Milloy made my humanity die. My face eventually extended until I could see my mouth, like a cone, jutting from what had once been my face. The worst part was I couldn't even scream anymore. I couldn't fight. I couldn't hear, I couldn't feel. I was this creature, with horrible tentacles, who couldn't stand upright, couldn't feed itself, couldn't see the world well anymore. The world was spots of darkness and splashes of lighter darkness. The only thing I could do was pray in what was left of my brain.

I prayed hard, praying with every molecule of the torment that was me, to wreak revenge on those who had transformed me.

Pain continued, an unbearable heat roasting me beyond souldom. Vibrations tearing at me, thunderous maws of destruction descending on me like the Apocalypse. If only I had power, if only I had something to stop all this. If only I could be as strong as the Great Mother who endured so much for so long.

Wakataka...

The voice reached me, and I clung to it. I was Wakataka. I had a purpose. But not to be a slave to the elite who created the Apocalypse.

I was Wakataka and I would burn to set the world right again.

I exploded, and the world exploded, and the world had no concept of existence. My tentacles expanded and stretched over seconds, minutes, eons, bundled together and pulsing, like a womb, pain flickering through it all. Wings erupted from my back, and they lengthened to the limits of the Earth, wrapping around it, squeezing tight. Squeezing hard. Old, old tales from the Elders said that the universe one day would squeeze into a tiny ball and be reborn. Oh, to squeeze and reverse the cycle of time. Reverse it, reverse it all, that was what needed to be done.

The power of the Great Mother, I felt it, I was it, she was me, and I was her, she and I, Mother and Child, we were...

Squeeze the universe and time, the Earth, the present and the future. Our conscience shriveled and then exploded, liberated completely, at last, from physical constraints, from any sensible law of nature.

We went back to the start.

We were a mass of lava and fire, spinning, erupting, swirling in molecules of death, pelted by asteroids, meteorites, and comets, denting us into life. Rage and pain, creators of an abode for all life, stretching across time. Then we became spherical, forging our way, and the atmosphere became poisonous, helium and hydrogen blanketing us in scorching toxic fumes. Our crust stopped bucking and thrashing, rage cooling into solid surfaces of rock. Clouds bloomed and flowered through our skies, water refreshing and eliminating the toxic remnants of the atmosphere. Oceans, huge, limitless, pushed their way around us, gasping to breathe, thrilled with their existence. In their pregnant bosom, life wriggled, ready to develop. They sighed as land encroached on their territory, resistant, dry land forming into mountains, valleys, plateaus, plains, canyons, basins. All potential cradles of life.

For the next step, we could allow oxygen-forming photosynthetic organisms to emerge. But should we? The children of that life will become humanity. Do they deserve to exist, only to render us back to our primal form, lava and death the only states of existence? We hesitated, and time froze.

Humans were forgotten children. They needed to be retaught to worship and value the Great Mother. Could they be retaught? Or would their free will be their downfall, always?

But we are a cycle, and if we are to be destroyed by mankind, so it will be; it will be our destiny. But we will guide them as best we can, for children lose their way. They will need records and sources to guide their evolution for eons to come. We boom across the mountains, the oceans, the volcanoes, and the islands, we boom, and make sure all current living creatures and our innards echo our pleas, pain from memories in other times lending raw power to our voice; our Book of Watahaca immortalized in the New Commandments:

You shall have no other gods before Me.

You shall protect the Great Mother always.

You shall not make false idols.

You shall not take your or others' existences in vain.

Remember the day of creation, to keep it holy.

Honor the creatures above and below you, and those you cannot see.

You shall not murder.

You shall not steal.

You shall not covet the misery of others for your own gain.

Remember, we boomed, and our voice echoed and dwindled plaintively, waiting for the day mankind would be born again.

Inside Out

You are the most infuriating person I've ever had the misfortune to meet!" Elise shouted, wringing her shawl in her hands, no doubt wishing it were Andelion's neck instead.

"You're letting your emotions cloud your judgment," he said, smoothing his mustache delicately. "You could have just said no, instead of losing your mind at the fundraiser like that."

Her lips trembled in rage. She spat out dark hairs that had escaped from her chignon into her mouth as she launched into a tirade.

"It's not enough that you think we're even ready to be engaged when I've told you, repeatedly, that I want to take things slowly. You keep mentioning ring makers and ring styles despite my telling you no over and over. And then, to top it off, you ask me to marry you, in front of everybody, at a fundraiser for children with disabilities? It's beyond tacky. It was rude, egotistical, low class—"

"What was low class and crass was you having a meltdown in front of everybody. You get a marriage proposal and start screaming and shouting. Do you have any idea how that looks? People will judge me based on your behavior. They know you're a beautiful, talented artist and teacher, but after tonight, they'll wonder what ugliness hides inside. And why I'm with you."

Elise snapped her silk shawl around her as if it were a snake's mandible. She posed a striking figure, bristling at him in front of his home bar, the expansive wall of liquors and wine shining softly in the background. Her multicolored dress blended well with the ochre and red tones of the mural around the liquor cabinet.

"I see. It's all about image to you. Like it always has been. Fool me for thinking you were a deep romantic of old, trying to woo your way into my heart with grandiose gestures. No, it's all about appearances. Damn emotions! If it makes you look bad, you don't do it. Your courtship of me, if we can even call it that, was pure theatrics. You taking me on a cruise, taking me to those fancy charity balls and dinners, taking photographs of our dates at fancy restaurants, all part of the pristine image of Andelion Brighton. He thinks he's so important, he thinks the entire world is watching him and judging him."

"That's because it's true. You know how important my family line is—"

"Oh, I know. If you remind me one more time I am going to vomit here and now. I know I am with a trust-fund billionaire brat. And I sorely regret it. I thought we could do great things together. Two spirits from different worlds helping society. Instead..." She bit her lip. Was that a tear he saw in her eye?

"That is not fair. Get ahold of yourself," he said, taking a sip of water to hide his mounting anger. "I have given you everything you needed and more. I have been more than patient with your unusual hobbies and strange desires, like going on a safari in wintertime, or starting a school for deaf children in the middle of Harlem. But you're not from the same... social standing as I, so I tolerated it. Yet despite having it all, you whine and complain all the time. You wear your heart on your sleeve. You know how vulnerable that makes you look? How vulnerable that makes *me* look?"

He stopped, worried she would hit him. She spasmed like she might, but instead she held a death grip on her crossed arms. She laughed low and slow, making goosebumps crawl on his skin.

She rubbed a hand on the bar countertop, squeaking nonstop, back and forth. The noise made him uneasy.

"That is all that matters. Looking good. Appearances, appearances. Your family did a great job with you. Bravo. In a child, the effects of trauma are to be expected and handled. An adult needs to be responsible for their reactions. But instead of doing some self-analysis, cutting toxic behaviors and getting better, you are burrowing into your own little hellhole. I can't believe I put up with this for so long."

"What are you saying?" Andelion asked, hoping she wasn't about to do what he thought she was. The medieval portraits of saints being tortured suddenly jumped out at him from their prominent positions on the living room wall.

"I am dumping you," she said, some color returning to her cheeks.

He winced. "That is such a vulgar expression."

"Yes. So be it! Hit the road, Jack! You are done. I am done being with a pompous ass, a hypocritical bastard, a selfish twat, a—"

"Ok, ok, we get the point," Andelion said, keeping the snarl out of his voice. Thank goodness for his upbringing. A part of him wanted to rage at her, beg her, anything. But it wouldn't be proper.

"Do you? Because I don't think you do," Elise said, grabbing a flute of champagne from the bar and pouring a generous dash of sherry in it. Andelion winced again.

"What are you going to do when I leave?"

He didn't have to think twice. "I am going to take a walk, then read a book. Then I am going to tell my family we broke off our relationship. I'll apologize about the blowup at the fundraiser. Then I'll probably have to bribe some journalists to keep that out of the press, or spin the story to show something else—"

She slammed her glass on the counter so hard it shattered.

"Watch it! That was part of my grandparents' special set." His voice was steady.

"You're done. You're a robot in human flesh. I can't believe I thought you were better than this. You know what I wish? That just once you'd get angry. Or sad. Or anything!" The flush in her cheeks intensified. "You keep all your feelings and emotions on the inside. I wish, with every fiber of my being, with the conviction of the entire Holomek line, that everything you have on the inside would be on the outside."

She pointed a finger at him and he flinched. She'd once mentioned she had gypsy ancestors, or shamans, or something, and he'd swept it under the rug. It could be exotic or it could be low class, depending on the audience. She'd even said she would keep her name if she married him one day, to which he'd thought he'd need to extirpate that out of her mind. But having her stare at him so intensely, pointing at him, a vague feeling of foreboding prickled at him. How strong were those gypsy roots? His nannies had filled his head with myths and tales of terror as a boy.

Elise lowered her arm. Nothing happened. Andelion breathed an imperceptible sigh of relief.

"Is that all?" he said stupidly, wiping the sweat off his brow.

"I wish that for you, with every fiber of my being," she said in a low voice.

Taking another long sip of sherry straight from the bottle, she wiped her mouth with her hand and went upstairs.

She called out, "I am staying in the guest room until tomorrow, when I can catch the earliest train out of here."

Andelion flopped onto a barstool. He guessed he could suffer her to be in his brownstone home for one night, even though it wasn't proper now that they were officially broken up. True to his word, once the roaring in his ears had stopped, he went for a walk, then returned home and read a book. He almost called his father to apologize—he'd seen the entire disaster unfold—but decided against it. He needed sleep. Maybe things would work out. He would wake up and Elise would be back, apologizing for all the absurd things she'd said. With luck, he wouldn't need to contact any journalists about tonight's fiasco. Everything would settle into place, as it always did for Brightons.

Andelion shifted in his sleep fitfully. He reached out a hand and the sheets wrapped around him, sticking to him. Half emerging from sleep, he rolled again, and the silk covers hungrily clung to his abdomen. The next time he rolled, a squelching sensation jerked him from sleep. He went to rub his eyes and gasped as his nails tried to find eyelids but couldn't. His fingers came away wet and pain throbbed in his eyes. He opened his eyes all the way and reached for the sheets. They came away with a wet rustling and a pseudo pain blossomed from his intestines. A metallic aroma wafted in the air. He frowned. Blood? Why would he smell blood?

A clacking sound echoed as his hands brushed against each other. Disoriented, he fumbled for the light on his bedstand

and turned it on. On the bed, between the sheets, lay two trunks of muscles and bones. They looked like bones seen in science exhibits in museums, the stereotypical tibias and femurs cocooned by muscles, streaked with veins and arteries. The colors, the texture... looked so real. Not blue, as on a model, but dark red. Stripes of orange, pink and red laced the muscle-looking things. As he squinted harder, the muscles became transparent and the bones became more visible.

Had he inadvertently gone to bed with the life-sized anatomy dummy Elise had gifted him after he'd spoken at a medical panel a few years ago? Had grief rendered him so stupid? Or had he accidentally consumed a poor vintage that had been spiked with something? Nothing made sense.

His gaze traveled up the bed, and a gargled scream burst from him, growing louder and louder. Genitalia laid as a floppy pale bulge, with veins exposed. A sheer wall of muscle went up a certain distance only to reveal a panoramic view of intestines, kidneys, liver, bladder, stomach, and pancreas. Rolls of tissue of different textures snaked around in someone's abdomen. An abdomen that was exposed to the air. *His* abdomen. He strained to see more of his torso, but horror overwhelmed him. He knew on an instinctual level what he would find.

He closed his eyes and breathed hard, throat hoarse from his earlier scream. Maybe he was just imagining things. Perhaps he was dreaming. Experimentally, he tried to poke his cheek. A bony hand came toward his face and he flung it away. He looked down at his abdomen again and tentatively prodded at the intestines, the stomach. He pressed gently on the stomach and felt it roil queasily. The sensation traveled up his exposed esophagus. An esophagus he could now feel. Shaking, he threw out his hands to his sides and refused to look anymore at his body. What abomination was this? How had this happened?

Had Elise's words held actual power, through the intensity of her gypsy line? Had she somehow actually cursed him?

He was going to have to get up and make sure he was seeing properly. But the task was daunting. He didn't want to leave his bed. If he stood up...

With Herculean effort he fumbled for the mirror on his nightstand. He always had it in case he needed to freshen his appearance for a morning video call. People liked seeing the just-awakened look these days. He just manipulated it a little.

Hands shaking, he took the mirror and aimed it at his chest. His pectoral muscles draped over his rib cage, stark and clear to his eyes, before they shimmered away to reveal his furiously working lungs and heart. It could have been an animal's heart and lungs, so similar were they in shape and color. He'd gone to enough butchers when he was a boy, helping his private cook find a good cut, to know how organs looked: ugly, brown and gray with some red. As he relaxed his focus, the wall of muscle and ribcage reappeared. Forcing every atom of will inside of him, he raised the mirror to his face. Gone were the fine features: the impeccably groomed mustache, the sandy, wavy hair, the Roman nose. Instead, buccolabial, nasal, epicranial, auricular and orbital muscles wreathed what had once been his face. As he stared, haunted, the muscles blinked away again, revealing his skull. For a fraction of a second, he thought he saw his brain sitting in the cranial cavity. Out of morbid curiosity, he poked at his brain before the skull rematerialized. It felt like ribbed gelatin, wet and spongy.

He dropped the mirror and let out an ear-splitting scream. In normal times, he would have chastised himself for that. A gentleman always has decorum, even in adverse situations. He certainly never screamed loudly enough to bother his neighbors. To hell with it!

As he prepared to scream again, wondering how he would return to normal, how he was even going to get up and function, his bedroom door swung open, and Elise rushed in, red in her cheeks.

"What is this screaming, Andelion—"

She gasped and screamed herself as he shifted, trying awkwardly to cover himself with the tangled bedsheet. She put a hand over her mouth, closed her eyes and gagged. He lay there in shame, his heart beating faster; he could see it pumping noticeably more swiftly. As he tried again to cover himself, this time leaving lurid wet stains on the sheets, his anger rose as a vengeful cobra, swift and dark.

"Get out! You did this to me!"

He pointed a finger at her and she dashed out, not giving him another glance. Trembling, he collapsed on his bed, sobbing like a child. His eyes burned.

A few hours later, Elise knocked at his door.

"Go away," he snarled.

"You need help," she said slowly, not entering the room. "That... isn't normal."

"No kidding," he said.

"I can call an ambulance or something," she started.

"No! I am not letting anybody see me like this!"

"You... This is going to kill you. You can't function like this! I don't know what, but something needs to be done!"

"Elise, for the love of God, leave me alone. Leave! I swear if you call anyone and expose me... you will be really sorry," he ended quietly.

He heard a sigh. Then footsteps retreating from the door.

It took him most of the day to emerge from his bed. He did so only because his bladder was full to bursting. As soon as he finished, he rushed back to his sanctuary, hiding under the covers like when he was a boy and his tutor told him scary stories.

His stomach growled. He needed to eat. He might have leftovers from a Greek restaurant he'd gone to with Elise. Her idea, not his. He hated leftovers. Everything should be served fresh.

He attempted to put on clothes. But everything clung to him, and he left bloody stains everywhere. Fine. He would try remaining naked. He almost fell down the stairs, he was so busy staring at his exposed guts. He caught the banister in time and painfully righted himself. He tottered to the kitchen and checked the fridge. The cold hit him immediately and he started shaking uncontrollably. He grabbed the dish with the leftovers and turned to place it on the counter. The fancy marble edge of the counter hit him solidly in the stomach and he retched. He recovered and searched for a pot to reheat the lamb kleftiko, wincing as he saw the hideous reflections taunting him in the spotless surfaces of the stainless steel kitchenware. In his haste to find the proper pot and stop seeing his reflection, he jostled and upended the tidy rows of pots and pans. Everything clattered harshly, a cacophonous orchestra to grate his ears.

More utensils clanged as he dropped them, too revolted to look at his hands. He tossed the lamb and the rice into the same pan and turned on the gas burner. He sat on his glass designer chair and groaned as the hard edges dug into his muscles. He stood up and his muscles peeled away reluctantly from the seat.

Every sharp edge, every corner, every shiny gewgaw, bauble, and trinket seemed a foe. His lavish home, bulging under the weight of accumulated acquisitions from meticulous travels and elegant hoarding, seemed out to get him, to hurt him in ways he couldn't anticipate. He stood there miserably, not waiting long enough for his meat to reheat, so unused was he to cooking for himself. His valet, Charles, always did it for him.

His phone rang and he ignored it. He was not talking to anybody today.

Over the next few days, he almost killed himself in too many ways to count, in the stupidest ways possible. Everything was a hazard. Everything was an obstacle. He burned, stabbed and pinched himself, dropped things on his head and on his feet, banged his elbows, knees and ribs on everything, and got ghastly stuck to everything else. The most dangerous places were the kitchen and the bathroom. Each too much a playground of danger, a plethora of methods to harm his tender organs and muscles. He donned Wellington boots to try to minimize the ooze he constantly discharged.

He avoided calls, not trusting his voice to betray him. He wrote emails and texted to his family and his valet, assuring them that everything was all right. He canceled every upcoming event—charity balls, fundraisers, concerts, a trip to Singapore—under the guise of "personal self-care."

He longed to call Charles. The man was a godsend. But there was no way he was going to let his valet see him like this. Until he found a way to reverse his condition, if indeed it was reversible, he was going to avoid interacting with anybody. Except he was going to have to, much sooner than he wanted. He was running out of food. He could do delivery, he supposed, but he didn't trust other people with his food. And because he lived in such an affluent town, where ordering deliveries was commonplace, it would take forever for the food to arrive. Like his parents always said, if you wanted it done right, you had to do it yourself. So that meant he had to cook. Even though he didn't really know how.

As he contemplated how to acquire food without revealing his secret to the world, pacing to and fro in front of living room mirrors he had turned to face the wall, his thoughts turned to Elise. No. He wouldn't denigrate himself and ask for her help. She had done this to him somehow, and he wanted her to leave him alone. Perhaps he should search his library to see if there was a tome somewhere that talked about a rare condition like his, where someone's insides became external... Surely there was a precedent for this somewhere in history.

After all, he wasn't a superstitious sap. There had to be a reasonable explanation for what had happened to him.

Andelion thought he'd done a great job disguising himself. Taking a leaf from *The Invisible Man* novel, he'd chosen to wear a black trench coat and fedora, a mauve silk scarf, a striped necktie, silk marching gloves, his best Oxford shoes, and black slacks. He'd chosen his darkest Louis Vuitton polarized sunglasses, which did a good beginning job of covering his face. He considered wrapping his face in bandages; after all, people in this day and age could conceivably be burn victims and want to hide their scars. But it seemed to him much too much like cosplay; he didn't want to be mistaken for one of those insufferable geeks. He had a face mask that had his likeness, from the pandemic a few years earlier. It always looked like he was smiling, even as his true expression was hidden. He could wear that. Combined with the sunglasses, no one would suspect a thing.

He grunted as he felt his ubiquitous wetness seeping into

his fancy clothing. It would have to do. He couldn't bring himself to wear anything more casual. With luck, he'd be in and out of the grocery store fast. What could go wrong, besides his newfound clumsiness and sensitivity to everything? He called Charles to let him know he wanted to drive, insisting the chauffeur drop the car off. To his credit, Charles didn't press him on the issue. Andelion could fake it. With enough luck, his condition would reverse sooner than he thought.

Things went wrong much too quickly. First, he constantly had to pull aside his sunglasses in order to see items. The glasses were much too dark, and his vision wasn't the best, though he refused to wear glasses or contact lenses, much to Elise's exasperation. A few times he dropped them or the item he was holding. His gloves and shoes were squishy already with his bodily moisture. He tried to get as much canned food as possible; it was easier to cook. But he was tempted by what he saw in the rotisserie aisle and meat section. He couldn't bring himself to actually buy any meat, though. It reminded him too much of his condition. He was a slab of meat now, just as disgusting, just as raw.

If people passed too close to him, he shuddered. He shrank against his cart, his lungs feeling deflated, his heart beating faster with every passing minute. Every kid who skipped by, every frantic couple who raced past, every straggler who paused in front of him, every two minutes, it seemed, would have made him sweat, if his condition had allowed it. Finally emerging from the crowds of people, he rolled his cart, relieved, to the dairy aisle to get some cream for his coffee. He grabbed a carton, but it slipped from his agitated hand. It bounced on the open door, hit the cart, and fell on the floor. When he picked it up, frothy cream started pouring from a hole in the carton. He juggled it, trying not to spill more, but it leaked urgently, creating a bigger and bigger puddle on the not-so-clean floor. He tried to catch the attention of a worker, but there were only shoppers around. In a panic, he tried putting it back on the shelf, but it fell again and hit him in the chest. A flare of pain struck his lungs and he doubled over, clutching his chest and coughing uncontrollably. His wet coughing mingled with the ruined sound of the carton splitting open and fountaining out onto the floor. He grabbed his cart for support as he struggled to straighten up, but the cart rolled in the wetness, and he lost his footing. He fell on his back and howled in agony as a crunch came from his left elbow. His sunglasses flew off and his hat landed a few feet from where his head rested in the leaked cream. He heard a few people gasp, hurried footsteps darting by. As he woozily tried to sit up, his scarf unwound and his trench coat threatened to slip off his shoulders. His elbow throbbed.

A crowd had gathering around him. Concerned faces peered at him, a clutch of college kids briefly giggled, young teenagers screamed in fright. One with cropped teal hair said, "That's some sick cosplay, dude."

Andelion fumbled quickly for his glasses and hat.

A woman ventured, "Are you ok?"

But an underlying ugly whisper hissed and roiled around him.

"Freak! Freak! He looks like a monster. You can see his brain, so gross!"

Out of stupid habit, Andelion pulled off his sopping gloves and scrabbled ferociously for his disguise. He couldn't gain purchase. Some children started screaming, others pointed at him and hid behind their parents.

A couple of construction workers grunted disapprovingly,

as one added, "It's the wrong season for Halloween, weirdo. You're scaring people."

A portly boy, no more than nine or ten, walked over to Andelion, his hand raised. Foolishly, Andelion raised his, assuming the boy was reaching to help him up. But the boy giggled instead and yanked off Andelion's mask. The giggle cut short, and the boy screamed, shoving Andelion back onto the floor.

"Monster!" people started hyperventilating.

"Someone call the police! There's a freak in here!"

The crowd danced maddeningly around him, willing to look, to gawp, but not to help. A few got out their phones to record him or take pictures. He staggered back, putting out his hands to shield himself. Shrieks and laughter eddied around him. Blindly, Andelion abandoned his cart and stumbled in search of the nearest exit. A few shelf stockers cried out in alarm as he careened past them. The implacable lights in the store bore down on him; the quickening footsteps of the crowd behind him intensified. His pursuer's shouts became louder, and he hurried on desperately.

He needed to leave. Find his car. Safety.

He bumped into a couple looking at flower selections and they screeched at the sight of him. The woman threw a bouquet at him; it bounced painfully off his arm.

He went straight through an emergency exit, the klaxon started to wail. Yellow lights flared and he clapped his hands over his earholes. He ran faster, hunting in his pockets for his car keys. The mob was hot behind him. Suddenly he realized that if he got into his car, they might report the license plate number. Instead, he veered off into the settling dusk, the yellow and orange in the sky punishing him with their glare like the alarm in the store.

Thankfully, he knew the town well, and he soon lost the chasing horde by sticking to the shadows and zigzagging through neighborhoods with copious shrubbery. At one point, he stopped and crouched, panting, in a bush of pink azaleas. It was uncomfortable, the branches poking him in all the sensitive spots. But he stayed there until he heard no more screams, no more running. His elbow continued to throb. Only later, as he walked home in abject shame, did he realize that he could have let them record him. After all, he was a being of bone and muscle; everyone's skeleton looks the same. Inside out, everyone would look the same. But he was still Andelion, and the spirit in him didn't want to be a spectacle. Didn't want to be a creature to be pitied. No one had tried to help him. Perhaps if they'd known who he was, they would have. He was now just another bag of walking meat in a world full of ambulating flesh bags. He wept long and hard and stumbled into his home, his stomach growling, his spine hurting, his elbow most probably fractured. There was no use denying it. He was useless, incompetent. He was trapped in what was left of his own body.

Andelion was lying in bed, pitying himself, mummified in the same sheets he'd woken up in, when the doorbell rang. He checked the security app on his phone to see who it was. An older woman stood with her head bowed, one hand holding a valise. She wore light blue hospital scrubs, but she also wore a colorful head scarf; it looked like a *ghoonghat*. Bangles hung from the scarf; he could hear them tinkle in the breeze as the dark-skinned, slightly wrinkled Indian woman waited patiently.

Through the app, he asked, "Who are you? What do you want?"

On her end, she heard his voice as a deformed rasp. But not intimidated by it, she responded.

"Hello sir. I'm Dayamai."

Stupefied, Andelion dropped the phone. She looked as traditionally Indian as they came. And yet she had a thick Southern accent.

"Elise sent me to check on ya. Yer inside out, right?"

Elise had sent her?

"I am inside out, yes," he said at last, picking up the phone warily. "But nothing can be done about it. Leave me alone. And tell Elise I am done with her. I can do just fine on my own."

"Rilly now? I think yer mistaken. Arncha the one who were in tha store? Made uh spectacle of yerself? Elise thinks there might be uh fix, she's tryin' to solve yer condition. In th' meantime, she asked me to check on ya. Even if she hadn't sent me, I think ya need help. Ya need proper care. Ya need to go to uh hospital, be observed, izza dangerous world out there."

"I'd noticed," Andelion said chillingly. Then he softened. So Elise still cared about him, in her own strange way. Yet she had sent a stranger to look after him instead of coming herself. She was a coward, while he was forced to relearn to survive in a world that tried to kill him just for existing. He stomped on his anger. "I do not want to go to a hospital," he said firmly. "Someone will notice and make an experiment out of me. News of my identity will spread. I can't have that."

"Ya need to be looked after. Ya could accidentally kill yerself in yer condition." Dayamai stood firm. "I'm not leavin' until I git uh sensible answer out of ya."

She stood there, resolute, holding her medical bag. Andelion was tempted to let her wait, hoping she'd leave. She did not. And with every passing minute, his proud heart wilted. What could it hurt? He needed help. He was starving. His elbow still hurt badly. He was a hazard to himself. He needed supervision. If somehow a cure was found, it would be even better. But he'd be damned if he would go into a hospital where he could be gawked at by strangers.

"Fine. I accept your care. But on the condition that you take care of me here in my home. You need to respect my privacy and not share anything of what you see with anyone. I will have you sign a contract."

"I've my medical privacy," she said wryly. "I don't need no contract, sir."

Andelion toyed with his phone, hoping he wasn't making a mistake. Could he trust her? Could he trust this eclectic specimen of a woman, obviously Hindu but raised in the Southern U.S.A.? Would she be capable of taking care of him properly? In his mind, he could see Elise's disgusted face. *Your inner biases are working against you*, she'd say.

"All right. You will come every day to take care of me. I will have specific requests of you; I have strict routines and rigorous demands."

"I can work with that. Yes, Andelion, sir. Ya gonna let me in or not?"

If he still had skin, he would have flushed. "Of course. Where are my manners?"

He let her in through the app and prepared to dress himself.

"I knew ya would see reason. Elise said yer uh lotta thangs. But ya ain't stupid. Pleasure to look after ya, sir."

Andelion groaned, sure he'd regret his decision all too soon.

Dayamai proved to be a firm, but gentle caretaker. She came every day like clockwork and stayed the entire day with him. Sometimes she stayed the night. She never once looked at him with revulsion or disgust. She fussed at him and plucked at him like a mother hen. She swooped on his elbow the first day, and determined he had a simple fracture. She iced it and immobilized it in a sling. "Same principles whether yer orgins is out or in, dearie," she said.

When he asked for painkillers, she gave him over-the-counter ones.

"I'm not uh licensed doctor, my dear. Just uh retired nurse with too much time on 'er hands."

When he asked about the equipment that she would use to monitor his vitals and make examinations, she looked faintly abashed.

"Elise is in th' process of donatin' new vital sign monitors from yer foundation to them hospitals and urgent care centers tha suffered from th' pandemic uh few years ago. They was sittin' there gatherin' dust! She decided to go ahead an' donate 'em. But she kept one aside fer us to use, until yer well again, God willin'. An' when we is done, we can donate it."

Andelion tried not to be a snobbish idiot and correct her accent or cringe, but he couldn't help hating it. It clashed so hard with her appearance it drove him a little crazy. Yet he couldn't fault her care. She checked his vitals and tended to his elbow every day; she helped him shower and go to the bathroom; she cooked for him; did his laundry; and went shopping for him. Every so often, she tried to take tissue samples to see if one of her nurse friends could analyze them, but he refused.

"Ther has to be uh fix, God willin'. Whether spiritual or medical, ther's gotta be one. Maybe is in yer flesh. Or in yer heart."

Andelion shrugged her off when she said things like that. "You're not here for philosophy discussions," he'd say curtly.

A call came in from Elise. Dayamai saw herself out when she saw the number. Andelion toyed with the phone, answering only to lie there stupidly, not saying anything, just breathing.

"Hello?" her soft voice came through, expectant.

He sat in petulant silence.

"Andelion. Are you there?"

Sighing, she hung up.

He stewed there, angry tears in his eyes. She could have... She could have tried harder. She should have known him well enough to know that he needed to be pushed out of his stubbornness. After all, she had fought past some of his barriers when they'd first met in Dubai, when she'd forced him to stop heckling a local for what he perceived as disrespect, or when he'd almost flubbed his public speech, nearly disrespecting his hosts.

Over the next couple of months, he started taking Dayamai for granted. He demanded she cook long, complicated recipes because he was tired of the same old simple meals she made for him. Never mind that she'd cooked many of her family's generations-old recipes. He knew what he wanted. His Sunday market trips with his father as a boy were seared in his mind. Specific cuts called for specific recipes. And in his home, he didn't want peasant food of any kind. He was an invalid, not a beggar.

He gave her money to buy her own food, but not once did he offer her the meals she cooked for him. She was here to serve him, after all. Sometimes when she stayed the night to make sure he didn't hurt himself, he acquiesced to her having a room in the house. Otherwise, he insisted she stay in the rowhouse a couple of blocks down. All paid for, of course; one could never say he was stingy. But he didn't like the idea of having her stay in his home. She wasn't family and she wasn't a friend. All in all, she seemed alright with his demands, even when he got piggish with her. He even started tolerating her horrid Southern accent and the outrageous perfume she splashed over herself.

Elise continued to try to check on him over the phone. She left voicemails and attempted to video call him. Not once did she knock at the door, however. In his bitter heart, he thought perhaps it was her way of staying on neutral ground. Checking on him without having to touch him or see him in person—he was that revolting. Still, he was disappointed with her, a woman who worked with disadvantaged members of the community. So he never answered the phone. She didn't care and left long messages, about what she was working on, that she hoped Dayamai was taking good care of him, and for him to stop being a brat and open up about his feelings.

Sometimes a smile would come over his face when he listened to her messages. She was bossy, even remotely. In his mind, he rehearsed what he would say in case the courage to call her back ever arrived, if his spite ever cooled: *I miss you, dammit. I hate saying it, but there it is. I miss your face, your long letters, your songs that you sing to the kids at the school. Heck, I miss your nagging and prodding me to not be an ass. All you ever talk about is work. You work so hard and so tirelessly. You work for everyone and never complain. But I wish you could see me. Come talk to me face to face. I feel so lonely, even with Dayamai. My life revolves around food, around safety, around telling Dayamai what to do. I'm not self-sufficient anymore. If I ever really was. I hate it. So I give Dayamai a hard time. I am a monster. It doesn't look like that is going to change. I tried to deny it at first. Had faith that there would be a cure. Then I raged against it.*

He had, in his anger, broken a collection of precious Ming vases during the first few months of his infirmity. He'd dropped his razor while walking out of the bathroom. He'd slipped on it and lost his balance, cutting himself. So he'd hurled the vases against the wall, also damaging his vintage record player.

Rage didn't do anything. Plus, it isn't proper. Now I just hope if I somehow keep surviving, eventually some poor godly entity will take pity on me and reverse the curse I am under. Because I've tried, Elise. I've tried so hard to research in every tome, every library I can get access to. I've sent Dayamai out scouring for material. I've forced her to sit with me on the computer and search through archives late into the night. We can't find anything about my condition, how to solve it, how it happens. I still think you cursed me. But would you admit it? No. You never mention it in your insufferably long messages. The guilt should be eating you up. Who's avoiding their feelings now?

He practiced this in absolute silence, and so not once did Dayamai have any clue about the struggle that raged inside him. He tried to tone down his demands with her, but it was hard. His frustrations about her accent, her not so great cooking, her constant doting, slowly ebbed.

Until one day, she decided to bring her grandson with her. A twelve-year-old skinny stick of a thing, with big soulful eyes that couldn't stop staring at him. The boy sat in a chair and watched his grandma mutely as she cared for Andelion, replaced and cleaned the sheets. After a while, the boy took out a wooden yoyo and started swinging it, chewing his lip in concentration. In a rhythm that didn't waver, he continued swinging the yoyo, then glancing at Andelion. Eventually, Andelion couldn't stand the boy's gaze.

"Can he go somewhere else?" he burst out petulantly.

Dayamai, in shock, stopped tucking Andelion in.

"Is he botherin' ya?"

"Yes. I mean," Andelion swallowed his lie, "no."

Dayamai nodded. "We're 'bout to go to th' kitchen. He'll come too."

She gestured at the boy, and he wordlessly put away his yoyo. He stared longingly at a ship model Andelion had on the bedroom dresser. He approached it and waved his hands, emulating waves. Andelion flinched, expecting him to pick it up. But he didn't. His grandma shooed him from the room, and he scuttled out.

———

She brought him over every single time after that. Andelion tried his best to ignore the child. The boy never spoke, just looked at Andelion from the corner of his eye. Dayamai had brought a bag from which he took out a few Lego toys, some coloring books, and gaming cards. He usually went into the living room and sat on the suede sofa. He put his toys on the floor or on the glass table. Andelion kept his grumbling to himself at first. Then one day it burst out of him. The boy was putting his Legos on the glass table and leaving prints on the surface! He was displacing magazine collections from fine art museums Andelion had visited. Worse, the kid was touching his centuries old pine bonsai tree, which he'd narrowly acquired at auction for 2.4 million dollars the previous year.

"Hey, you!" he shouted. The boy looked at him but didn't answer. "You! I'm talking to you. Put your Legos somewhere else. Play in a corner or something. You're going to ruin my table and my bonsai tree. Do you know how much they cost?" The pedestal table alone cost twenty thousand dollars.

The boy took away his Legos and put them in the bag. He stared at Andelion with his big mocha eyes.

"Stop staring at me like that!" Andelion snapped. "Go play! Don't you have something else to do? Answer me when I'm talking to you!" he cried in exasperation, unnerved by the silence.

The boy's grandma stopped pouring pasta in the pot.

"Be nice to my boy. He's mute, in case ya hadn't noticed."

Andelion stopped fiddling with his silver fork and knives at the oak dining table. Mute?

"I... I didn't know," he said softly. It still didn't make him like the boy more. In general, he didn't care for children. They were disruptive, emotional, and loud. And terribly dirty.

"If ya bothered to pay attention to anyone but yerself, ya would've noticed. Haven't ya noticed us signin'?"

If Andelion racked his brain, he could vaguely recall them gesturing at each other. But he'd thought it was playing or something. It never occurred to him that it would be American Sign Language.

"Do ya even know my boy's name?"

Andelion lowered his head.

"It is Dhairya," she said fiercely, proudly. "He may not tawk, but he smart as uh whip. Ya should try tawkin' to him sometime."

Andelion thought the possibility of that quite remote. He didn't know American Sign Language. It wasn't useful. None of his patrons or clients used it. He already knew English, Spanish, French, Chinese, and Russian. He certainly wasn't going to add sign language just for some sad little boy.

"Why do you bring him? Dhairya, I mean. You didn't always," he said, trying to be polite without explicitly saying, *Stop bringing him.*

Dayamai sighed and stopped stirring the pasta. "Family troubles. Too complicated to explain. Until thangs is resolved with his mommy an' daddy, he stays with me. An' comes with me as uh package deal. Understood?"

Andelion sighed but didn't push her on the point.

"Ya rilly should try communicatin' with my grandson. Would do ya both some good."

"If I don't know how to sign with him, how can I?"

"Ther's other ways to communicate besides tawkin'. It's mighty high time ya learned that."

Suitably abashed, Andelion tolerated her cutting slices of cheese and spreading them on bread for him. She gave him his eating gloves, and they both avoided looking at each other.

His first attempts to communicate with the boy were disastrous.

"Why can't you talk? Why are you always staring at me? Do I disgust you?"

Silence as ever. Dhairya regarded him impassively and lapsed into his middle school homework.

"What is going on with your parents?"

Nothing.

"You don't want to talk to me, is that it? You think I won't understand your sign language?"

The boy held his right hand up into a fist in front of him, then flicked his pointer finger up. He repeated it several times, but Andelion didn't understand. In the end, Dhairya shook his head and went back to reading his textbook.

Andelion huffed. "You think you have it bad. Look at me." Dhairya's gaze flickered his way briefly. "I look like a monster. I can't go out even with the nifty clothing your grandma sewed for me." She had, in fact, striven to find waterproof fabric and sewed silicone parts into his garments where they covered his abdominal wall to make sure he didn't hurt anything in there. She'd made a mask that fit over his face to protect it. But he still couldn't venture outside without his condition being seen one way or another. Like everything in life, he slowly got used to the horrifying sight of his bones, muscles, tendons and organs greeting him every day. But he loathed it as much as he'd once loathed public displays of emotion.

"My life used to revolve around social events. Meeting new people. Now I have to keep everyone at bay. I can't see my own family. I wonder how long I can keep hiding this from them."

Andelion flounced in his bathrobe, tossing his own book to the side.

"Being mute must be hard. But try looking like a science exhibit."

He rubbed his facial muscles tiredly. What was he doing unloading on a mute twelve-year-old boy? But his frustration welled up, despite his best efforts to control it. "Now I have to babysit you, as if being stuck in my own home isn't bad enough. Kids are too much responsibility. I don't trust you not to touch stuff you shouldn't."

Dhairya raised his eyebrows and pointed to his textbook. At that moment, Dayamai came in with a load of unfolded laundry. She placed the laundry basket at Andelion's feet.

"Here ya go. I've mollycoddled ya long enough. Is time for ya to start bein' more independent in th' house. Fold this laundry. Next, we'll tackle cookin' an' cleanin'."

Andelion's breath was knocked out of him as he stood up hurriedly. "What? What do you mean? I need your help. I can't do everything alone." Panic lanced through him. He didn't like to admit it, but he had become extremely reliant on Dayamai. She ran him and his home smoothly, even if she didn't do it precisely the way he wanted, a feeble voice whispered through his conscience.

Dayamai put her hands on her hips. "Yer not doin' everythin' alone. But ya don't do anythin' for yerself either. Ya need to learn to run yer own home. Now tha ya can function without hurtin' yerself, this is th' next step. Ya can rely on me. But ya can't lean on me forever."

Andelion resisted the urge to say *But I don't know how to fold laundry. I don't know how to cook or clean.* All of that had always been done for him. She would have to show him. And a ball of shame grew in his throat, silencing him.

"Ya've got uh chronic condition. Ya have to learn to function with it. Is not worse than other chronic conditions out there. Y'all'll be fine." The steadfast positivity in her hazel eyes, her firm, gentle voice gave him no choice but to quail under her resolve. His childish inhibitions crumbled a bit more. It was better for all involved if he became more independent. Even if it flew in the face of everything he'd been taught.

Over the next few months, his demands became fewer and fewer. He learned to care for himself and run his home, even if he bungled things up terribly at first. His initial attempt at cooking—and he'd been ambitious attempting to grill a sirloin steak—ended with meat charred on the outside and raw on the inside and vegetables a dry, blackened mess. Dayamai had swooped in to rescue him, taming the flames and disposing of the burned mess. Then she'd sat him down and chastised him for trying to cook such an advanced meal.

She taught him how to cook the basics, rice and pasta, and how to steam vegetables. Then she slowly moved on to teaching him to cook poultry, then pork, then beef. In time, he fought to take control of the kitchen. He still didn't like looking at raw meat, but at least *he* was cooking it; *he* was in control. It was his, his possession. He almost called Elise when he managed to cook his first filet mignon. But he abstained, content with listening to her most recent weekly voice message.

Occasionally he lost his temper, which made Dayamai lose hers right back at him. He learned to channel his frustrations better, by working out or by journaling. He ended up being in closer proximity to her grandson. Dhairya often worked on his homework as Andelion ruminated in his massive living room library.

One blustery, gray afternoon, Dhairya tapped on the table. Andelion looked up from his poetry book and saw the boy staring at him, holding his own book. Andelion wouldn't have been caught dead with a poetry book—fluffy, abstract things that poems were—but Elise had mentioned she'd started reading some Mary Oliver and loved it. Andelion had started reading *Dog Songs*. The last poem had found him unexpectedly shedding tears. How could words hold such a profound effect?

Dhairya waved at him. Andelion came over and asked, "What?"

The boy clenched his fists, raised them up and brought them down, and pointed at Andelion. Then he stopped, scribbled in his notebook instead and showed the page to Andelion.

Can you please help me with these vocabulary words?

"Sure," Andelion said.

He sat down next to him and read the words Dhairya gestured to on the page. The book was *Tuck Everlasting*. Dhairya scribbled some more. *I don't understand the dictionary definition. Can you explain?*

Sure enough, a dictionary lay open beside Dhairya, but his puzzled expression confirmed his confusion.

"Battered," Andelion read. "He was thin and sunburned, this wonderful boy, with a thick mop of curly brown hair, and he wore his battered trousers..."

"Battered in this case means old looking, damaged. Does that help?"

Dhairya nodded. They continued like that for about a dozen words. At the end, the boy was grinning, a beautiful buck-toothed grin, neat definitions scribbled in his notebook. Andelion thought this was the first time the boy had smiled at him. To avoid the rising sentimentality within him, he spoke. "It helps to look at secondary definitions in the dictionary. Oftentimes a word has multiple meanings. Choose the one that makes the most sense."

Dhairya gave him a thumbs up, and put his hand to his chin, waving it downward.

"What was that?" Andelion asked.

Sighing, the boy wrote out painstakingly, *Thank you.*

"Oh." Andelion felt dumb. "How do you manage to remember all these signs? It looks so hard. I can't imagine having to learn that to function."

Dhairya grinned. He wrote *It is actually easy. Look it up.*

Secretly, without either Dayamai or Dhairya noticing, Andelion tried to teach himself ASL. After all, if he was already a polyglot, adding one more language wouldn't kill him. It turned out to be even harder than he thought. He struggled, he cursed, he even wept a little. But eventually, he was able to sign some rudimentary phrases. Nothing he wanted to divulge just yet, though.

Meanwhile, he and the boy had grown closer than he was willing to admit. Just by writing notes to each other.

On the eve of Halloween, Dhairya gestured at the paintings on the living room walls and up the staircase. Andelion had changed his autumn collection for his Halloween collection; all gothy masterpieces. He was proud, as he'd done it all himself. At first, he was worried the paintings were scaring the kid. But, after a hastily written note asking to explain some of the pieces, Andelion's fears were allayed.

"This is *The Crucifixion and Last Judgement* by Jan van Eyck. What you see are all those lost souls going down into Hell. See the monster in the corner on the right?"

Dhairya nodded fervently, eyes wide. He pointed to another painting.

"That is *Il Trionfo della Morte*. No one knows who painted it. It is Italian and it means *The Triumph of Death*."

The boy rubbed his chin. He signed *dog* and *straining*, pointing at an emaciated animal in the background of the painting. Andelion laughed.

The next painting was *The Nightmare*. "Painted by Henry Fuseli. People back then thought nightmares were living beings that sat on you and slowly crushed the air out of you. That was what gave you bad dreams."

Dhairya signed, *I don't like it. It is beautiful. But creepy.*

Andelion signed, *I get it.* When he'd been a boy, he hadn't liked that painting either. As he looked now, the helplessness, the fragility of the woman lying there, her head drooped, unnerved him. Perhaps he should switch out that painting. Who cared if it was a masterpiece? He didn't want to feel creeped out in his own home. Or creep out Dhairya either.

Dhairya beamed at him. At that moment, Dayamai walked in, and she also beamed.

"My! Look at ya two signin' together. I knew ya had it in ya, Andelion. Say. I was worried 'bout my boy. We've been savin' up for years to git an iPad that can have software for him to click on an' it'd speak. But it's very expensive. So for now he writes or uses th' computer, or signs. Ya'll signin' together... makes me happy. Makes for easier communication."

Andelion shrugged them off, walking into the kitchen to stave off the pride and joy he felt growing in him.

All Saint's Day marked the one-year anniversary of his transformation. Elise sent him a Zala pentacle talisman in the mail; in a fit of pique, he threw it in a bedroom drawer. Andelion stewed most of the day, avoiding interacting with Dayamai and Dhairya as much as possible. He read and grumbled in his bed, muting his phone.

Until a gaggle of children arrived at his bedroom door.

"What is the meaning of this?" he gasped, anger starting to roughen his voice. He tossed his blankets and sheets over himself, letting only his face peek out.

Dayamai pushed past the kids, apologizing profusely.

"Sorry, Andelion, sir." He knew then she must be really apologetic. She hadn't called him sir in months. "It was Dhairya's idea. He thought he could brin' his school friends to cheer ya up. He knows is uh difficult date for ya. He said his friends have been wantin' to meet ya."

Andelion was stunned. Dhairya waved at him. But he bit his lip, obviously waiting on Andelion's approval. Well, he hadn't been expecting this. However, Andelion couldn't say no. Dayamai had said the kids wanted to meet him. Surely they knew of his condition. Yet here they were. That was enough to let them in. He gestured them in, making sure he was covered properly.

Dhairya came in first, and then the other four followed. They were around Dhairya's age, two boys and two girls. One boy was in a wheelchair, his arms and legs atrophied and standing out rigidly. His head lolled to the side. The other boy had Down syndrome. He waved timidly at Andelion and squeezed a stress ball. One girl had white patches on the skin of her legs, face, and arm, vitiligo it was called; she swept her hair out of her eyes and helped push the boy in the wheelchair. The other girl seemed to have no disability. She looked older and hovered over the boy with Down syndrome protectively.

"Hello," Andelion said awkwardly. "To what do I owe the pleasure?"

"These is my friends," Dayamai said, translating as Dhairya signed fast. "They wanted to meet ya. I wanted to cheer ya up. This is Clara, Tom, Luis, an' Elaine."

"Nice to meet you," Clara, the girl with vitiligo, said.

Tom attempted to wave from his wheelchair. Elaine smiled and so did Luis.

"You're cool," Tom said, his voice a little slurred. With effort he tilted his head so he could meet Andelion's eyes.

"Really?" Andelion breathed. "I look... monstrous. I haven't gone outside in almost a year."

"Everyone has something. I don't look normal either," Clara said, raising her arms so he could see her patches better.

"There's lots of us that look different," Elaine said, translating Luis's (the boy with Down) signing. "You're inside out. Tom is right. It is kind of cool."

"Thanks," Andelion chuckled. Dayamai slowly retreated from the room.

"We have difficulties with the outside world too. But it's ok. There's nothing to be sad about. We brought games and puzzles," Luis said through Elaine.

"Are you her brother?" Andelion asked, pointing between Elaine and Luis.

"Yes," she laughed. "I sign for him because he struggles to speak clearly. Faster to do it this way."

"Ok. We need way more space if we're going to play games. And I need to get properly dressed."

Tom laughed, and the rest smiled. Dhairya signed *Let's go downstairs.*

They had fun playing that afternoon. They worked on a puzzle. They even played ball. It was slower due to waiting on Tom to be able to grab the ball and throw it. But none of the kids minded. After a while, even Andelion didn't mind. What he did mind a little was their incessant jabbering. They vomited words, even those who had difficulty speaking or had to sign. Dayamai had to help Andelion translate; the kids' signing was much too enthusiastic and rapid. As he kept observing, he started noticing their tics, their gestures with personality traits. Luis signed joyously; every gesture had a bounce. Tom took his time and paused every four or five words. Elaine tilted her head when she was happy. Clara talked faster and faster when she became excited, almost wheezing. Dhairya, of course, signed purposefully and slowly.

And amid the children's prattle lay some endearing and insightful gems that Andelion discovered not just that day, but in the months that followed. For every Thursday afternoon after school, Dhairya and his friends came over to hang out and play. Their stories—about feeling included in their charter school, where kids with and without disabilities could learn together; about the battles some of them had fought to be able to talk; about the way their parents helped and fought for them to be included but challenged in social and academic settings—they gave him pause.

Tom bragged about his friends, particularly how they responded after another child bullied him at school. His friends had stood up for him and reported the bully to the principal. Thanks to all of their testimonies, the bully was suspended, and it came to light that other kids had been bullied, too.

Deep down, he knew that these kids, despite their disabilities, and, importantly, because of their disabilities, had an advantage he'd never had. They had unconditional love and support from their families. Their friends were like them and were just as supportive. They had a whole other dimension in their communication and emotionality that he never had.

Andelion knew that if he had had any kind of disability, even the one he had now, his mother would have aborted him. She had proclaimed multiple times her disgust for anyone with a disability. He'd needed to be the perfect heir, physically and intellectually. Yet Andelion's sureness of his privilege crumbled progressively the more he hung out with Dhairya, Tom, Clara Luis, and Elaine. They were truly a family. They helped each other, they shared things with each other, both the good and the bad. Sometimes he was able to see if they were sad or confused before they even started to sign. He made accommodations for them, without having Dayamai help, so they could move around without effort.

These children erased his pretentious airs. Yes, their families had low to middle incomes and resources. They didn't have tutors or valets to tend to their every need, every whim. Regardless, they were able to function in society. Andelion realized that he'd never truly functioned in society. His transformation had only brought to light that particular fact. He'd had a cold, sterile life, he'd worn a mask of arrogance, of superiority, to conceal his paucity of soul. No wonder he'd driven away women, he'd never been able to make long-lasting friends.

He felt ashamed. He was a monster now outside and in, and he deserved to stay that way. But he could try to change. He could try to make a difference, not by throwing money every which way to make himself look good, but by genuinely making a change, by seeing it through.

He wrote to Elise that night and asked her to buy a tablet for Dhairya, the one Dayamai had talked about, using Andelion's money. He also let her know that he was working on a charity for special needs children. He was open to suggestions and advice, he wrote. He avoided writing anything that hinted that he might miss her, or begging her to come see him. After all, one still had to have some pride.

So it was, in the late winter months, as he worked tirelessly on this new charity, still cooped in his house, with Dayamai and her grandson now staying full time, that Elise walked through the front door. He stood there, frozen, holding his phone to his ear, in the middle of refusing any publicity for his organization.

He dropped the phone, gazing at her slender, ethereal beauty, vivid despite the dull lassitude of the winter light behind her. In her hand, she held a tablet. Dhairya's tablet.

He ran to her, all decorum forgotten. He rushed to her and wrapped her in an embrace. She shuddered at first, then took him all in, those discerning eyes raking over every organ, every exposed piece of flesh and tissue. Delicately, she put a hand on his cheek.

"I'm so sorry. I'm so, so sorry. I—"

He cut her off gently.

"I should be saying sorry. I'm sorry I was such a prick. I'm sorry about everything."

She embraced him this time, carefully. He breathed her in. If he stayed like this, it didn't matter. If she stayed with him, so much the better. He couldn't keep his condition a secret forever. Sooner or later, he was going to have to show himself to the world. As she withdrew to smile at him, black circles under her beautiful eyes, he hoped she would be by his side. As a friend or more, it didn't matter.

CLARION OF THE DEAD

T ake me to where people go when they die."

Clarion extended his homemade tickets in his scuffed hands. The people at the front of the bus laughed nervously; the bus driver's non-existent eyebrows climbed up past his widow's peak.

"Joke's over, kid. Where do you really want to go?"

Clarion nodded his head insistently. He extended his hands further, the tickets so close to the driver's face he leaned back slightly.

"No joke. I want to go to the place where people go after they die. Daddy said I could go check it out."

He had, in fact, asked his dad multiple times to travel by train, boat, plane, and car. But it hadn't gone anywhere. It's hard to travel when you're a kid. People get suspicious. His dad had shrugged and put his head in his hands, as he often did, and said, "Whatever, Clarion. Do whatever you like. Go find your place. Leave me alone now, please."

So Clarion had made his own bus tickets.

His attempts to follow the ghosts who came to him, whether at home, school, the supermarket or the park—he never sought them out, they always came to him at random times of the day and night—never worked. Oh, yes, they would come to him and talk and reminisce about their lives, sometimes for hours. Clarion never got bored, even when their stories repeated. Clarion could understand them even if they spoke German, Greek or Chinese. He'd never learned those languages. But when the ghosts left and he tried to follow, they disappeared in a fog. Clarion was the best at hide and seek at his school, yet he couldn't find them after they vanished in that fog.

Clarion's favorite visits were when he talked to his mom's ghost for hours under the lemon hybrid tree in their backyard that always stubbornly gave more tangerines than lemons. His mom told him regularly to keep an eye on his dad. She never said why. But she'd talk at length, about when she was a girl and she left melting ice cream on her babysitter's chair, because she could; her struggles with high school and how painful it was to be the school dork; her love of riding her bike after a thunderstorm, pedaling as hard as she could toward a rainbow; her passion for reading random books and spouting facts to strangers, no matter how uncomfortable it made them. Clarion had tons of memories she'd given him. But she never talked about her death.

He followed her one and only instruction. He watched over his dad when he came home from work, nibbled on his crusty bread and expired slices of ham, and went to bed without saying goodnight. Clarion watched as his dad lost his job, drank too much and fell asleep in front of the tv, weeping at some romantic comedy he didn't know the name of. He tried to remind his dad about friends, and that he should go out and talk to people. He asked his dad to play Ping-Pong like they used to. But his dad never listened. He drank instead. Clarion tried hiding some of the bottles every now and again, but there were too many. And he didn't want to make his dad unhappy. When his dad did drink, at least he didn't cry. Clarion wished sometimes his mom had tips for watching over his dad, but she had none.

Clarion tried following the ghost of his mom many times. He would follow her, and the world would gradually lose its luster, its timbre; he was the only thing that wouldn't change. He'd be able to see his striped shirt, full of mustard stains and chocolate sundae smears, as vividly as he could see his freckled hands, his skinny legs rife with scars. The world around him would turn off like a sleeping computer but Clarion was not afraid. He knew it made him weird, but he didn't know what it was like *not* being weird. He would follow the ghost without fear but after a while his mom would merge with the fog of dimness and he would lose her. If he walked sideways or backward, he would find his way out and end up exactly where he had started following the specter. It wasn't just with his mom; he'd tried following the ghost of his next-door neighbor, the kid at school who'd drowned, the lady at the park who'd crashed her car, the man at the supermarket with the booming voice who'd died from a stroke. All with the same result.

If ghosts could come to him, there had to be a way for him to go to them. Everything had an entrance and an exit. Or so his fifth grade teacher said. Thus Clarion had started his search for the land where people go after they die. He thought he should name it the Land of the Dead, but then it would sound too close to the places he'd read about in his friend Daniel's books—books full of weird beings, monsters, gods and places more exciting than Fiji, where Clarion really wanted to go one day. He wasn't sure his friend's books were accurate.

Instead, he called it the Plaza of the Dead.

It didn't look like today would be Clarion's lucky day. The bus driver did not look friendly and neither did the people on the bus. Clarion said, "I do have tickets, you know." He looked at the ghost of his mom, in the back of the bus. She was shaking her head. Her thick red hair swung and shimmered faintly over her freckled face. She hadn't approved of his plan from the beginning. But she couldn't change his mind.

"Stop wasting our time, kid. Get out," the bus driver said.

So Clarion backed out and huffed miserably as the bus left without him. His mother stayed on the bus.

"Can't anyone help me find the Plaza of the Dead?" he asked the world at large. A few adults walking by eyed him and ignored him. Some said, "Play somewhere else." Clarion sighed dramatically. He had to go and see for himself. Nobody could help him. Not even Daniel's strange, exciting books about cultures and death around the world answered his questions. None of them matched his perception of the Plaza of the Dead.

A few weeks later, he asked the next-door lady's ghost again about that time she wheeled around the countryside on her tractor and drove it into a river but survived. He loved that story. But she frowned, and her rheumy gray eyes blinked like an owl's.

"Clarion, I don't remember that story."

Clarion frowned. "What do you mean? You tell it to me every time you come."

She shook her head. "I don't remember."

"Ok. Can you tell me about that time you threw a teddy bear at your brother and he put spiders in your bed afterward?"

She shook her head again.

"I don't remember."

"I don't remember," a woman who'd cut herself said to him.

"I don't remember," a teenager who'd died in a motorcycle accident admitted.

"I don't remember," a businessman who'd overdosed on Valium confessed.

They crowded around him, sheepish, their forms more translucent than Clarion was used to.

"But you told me just last week that your favorite memory was going to the prom and meeting Derek there. You guys went to an ice cream place and had the best praline ice cream ever," Clarion said to the woman with long blonde hair.

Clarion turned to the teenager with bangs hiding his eyes. "And you, you told me again, just the other day, that you loved going to the beach with your grandma and enjoyed drinking a martini with her even though you weren't supposed to. Your favorite memory was finding a huge conch shell washed up on the shore, and you tossed a coin to see who would keep it."

Finally, Clarion reached out his hands to the businessman with a wine birthmark on his cheek. "And your first time in Osaka. The first time you saw Osaka Castle, almost buried by the skyscrapers but standing proud despite it all. Really, you don't remember?"

The ghosts shrugged, more depressed than alarmed. They sat down and avoided looking at each other. Clarion had never seen them this untalkative. They always talked his ear off. He noticed he had to squint to see them. That was unusual. Clarion asked after a while, "Talk to me. Tell me anything. They can be new stories. I love listening to you talk!" But the ghosts groaned. The ghost of the businessman finally said, "Why do you persist in talking with us?"

"You came to me first," Clarion said, hurt.

The woman who'd ended her life said, "We feel more relaxed than we ever felt. Thank you, Clarion. But now what do we do?"

Clarion didn't know what to say.

Clarion started hearing a lot of *I don't remembers* from the ghosts who'd come to him for years. However, he had newer ghosts, the ghosts of a girl who'd been beaten to death by a drunken father, an old man who'd fallen from his ladder and broke his neck, a young teacher who'd died in childbirth. They didn't forget their memories, and they didn't fade. But his mom's ghost... She was definitely losing her memories. He could barely see her anymore and it scared him.

One night, she came to him and sat next to his bed. She touched him, but he didn't feel it. He sensed her presence, though, and woke up. He had to strain his eyes to see her.

"Mom? Are you ok?"

"I am losing you. I don't know why. It's harder and harder for me to come here," she whispered.

"Can I help?"

She laughed ruefully.

"I don't think so. Maybe, though. You surprise me."

"What do you remember, Mom? Do you recall any of your stories?"

She clasped her hands and frowned. Clarion sat up fully and looked at her, anxiety rising as her form almost melted completely into his bedroom.

"No, I don't."

They both sighed and Clarion was struck with suspicion.

"Do you remember how you died?"

She nodded.

"Can you tell me?"

But she tensed and stood up, her face disintegrating then coalescing together again.

"Your dad is coming. You might find your answers there. Come find me, but try something new."

She walked away into that pathway of shadows and dimness and she murmured, "I love you."

He didn't get to answer her because his dad did come in his room, for once alert and awake, not huddled over with some invisible pain.

"Clarion. Sorry to wake you. But there is a full moon and the tide is high. We might be able to catch some fish."

Clarion gaped at him. His father hadn't gone fishing since Clarion's mom died five years earlier. He hadn't seen his dad this excited in too long.

"Why tonight?"

His dad blinked. "To celebrate! I... I got a job offer. Nothing is confirmed yet, but it's a good step."

Clarion looked up at his dad and smiled. This was the best news he'd heard in a while. If his dad had a job, maybe he'd finally be happier. When Clarion's mom found out, and she would, because he would tell her, he knew she would smile, too.

Clarion wasn't a big fan of fishing, but he remembered that when he and his dad used to fish, he'd sit in the boat and talk with his dad while his dad did all the work. Tonight, he could help his dad celebrate.

"Let's go."

They made it to the bay in just under three hours. The night's domain stayed untouched, with stars and a moon that gleamed so brightly they hurt Clarion's eyes. Even as his dad huffed and puffed from pushing the boat out into the bay, Clarion couldn't stop looking at the sky, so wondrously open and clear. He could see the Milky Way, stretching to infinity over him. He snapped his fingers to himself and took out the fishing poles, the tackle and gear from the car, the smell of the fish bait, salt, and algae curdling his nose. He hauled it all to the boat, where his dad had cracked open a bottle of beer already.

"Come, Clarion. With some luck we can find some good bass tonight, have an actual meal that's not frozen for once."

Clarion nodded. That would be nice indeed.

He and his dad climbed into the boat and paddled together, the swishing of their oars piercing the underlying humming of the night, full of toads and cicadas. As they rowed, Clarion kept glancing at his dad. His dad was smiling dreamily, his face relaxed.

"Why fish with me?" Clarion asked, as they stopped rowing and readied their fishing poles.

His dad shrugged, not meeting his eyes.

"It's a good night. Look, you can see Cassiopeia here. And there! Do you recognize Draco?"

Clarion followed his father's finger. Yes, he could see the constellations, and many more he didn't recognize. So bright, so temerous, so *real*, unlike most of Clarion's life. He contemplated the stars for a bit, as his father guzzled his beer and waited for a fish to bite. Finally, he asked, "Dad, when did you meet Mom?"

He'd heard the story from his mom's ghost already, but he wanted to hear it from his dad. His dad sighed and tapped his bottle on the floor of the boat.

"You always ask the randomest questions. So much like your mom. Ok. I met your mom when she graduated college. We happened to live next to each other. She was an odd duck. She talked to herself a lot. She obviously lived in her head quite a bit. When you talked to her, it was always like you'd interrupted a scene going on in her mind. She'd start to talk to you, and then pick right back up where she'd left off in her head. She was a loner; she kept trying to make friends, but people gave her a wide berth. We got to know each other because we liked going to the same ice cream shop across the street. I never knew what she was going to say. She might say, 'How are you?' one day, and the next, she'd say, 'You know, the biggest galaxy out there is thirty times bigger than the Milky Way and it's called IC1101.' She and I started talking and we could talk for hours about things that were interesting, creepy, weird; it was never anything mundane."

Clarion's dad smiled and reached for another beer bottle. He was teetering slightly. Clarion smiled, too, marveling at how his dad described a memory his mom had described a certain way. His mom had told him that their friendship had been natural and they hadn't even flirted in the years they'd known each other. When they'd decided to marry, it really was because she'd stated one day, "Marrying wouldn't be a bad idea for us." But Clarion had a more pressing question to answer. He had to know...

"Dad, how did Mom die?"

His dad hissed and his hand started shaking.

"Why... why do you have to ask this?"

"I have to know. It's important."

His dad glared at him and then softened. Opening a beer bottle and chugging it down, he said, "It was purely my fault. I was supposed to bring the car in for repairs. It was my responsibility. The airbag had a recall; they asked to bring the car in. I kept forgetting about it. So did your mom. One day she takes the car out to buy groceries. And a damn old fool careens into her, speeding on the highway, and the impact kills her on the spot. The airbag exploded in her face. She... she died... because of my neglect."

Clarion's dad sobbed and looked up at the sky, where light was dawning languorously, pale as a corpse. Clarion sat still, silent, seeing the dimming ripples of the reflected constellations slosh in the water. They still hadn't caught a fish. Bottles rolled around and clinked a song of emptiness as stronger waves lapped at the boat, pushed by a sudden wind, chilly and austere. He wished his mom were here. She would know what to say. Then he brightened.

"Dad. I can see her. Mom, I mean."

His dad stared at him, eyes red and puffy. "What?"

"Mom's ghost comes to me. We talk. I can see other people's ghosts, too. When people die they're not truly gone. That's why I want to go to—"

Clarion stopped short as his dad seized him by the arms and shook him.

"Dad?"

"How dare you?" his dad howled. "Spouting your nonsense and imaginary crap here, now? When people die, Clarion, they die. They are gone. They don't come back."

"They come back to me," Clarion said seriously. "I can't follow them back, but I'm working on it."

His dad passed a hand over his face.

"It... it, it doesn't work that way. Whatever you think you're seeing is not real."

"But it is! They tell me about their lives. I can tell you about our old next-door lady. She had a string of puppies she rescued in Prague when she used to live there and—"

"This isn't a game or a joke, Clarion!"

"Dad, I'm not joking! I can see the dead!"

"No, you can't! You can't," his dad shouted, his voice echoing across the bay.

Clarion murmured to himself, "If you could see Mom, she would tell you to believe me."

"Enough!" his dad shouted, his face pasty, features thin as a blade. He pushed Clarion hard, and Clarion's back thudded against the side of the boat.

"Dad, stop."

Clarion was keenly aware of how his dad's chest heaved as he breathed hard, of the movement of the boat as it steadied against Clarion's impact, of the now shrill sounds of birds hunting and celebrating the rising day. Clarion steadied his own breathing as his dad loomed over him, a shadow of anxiety and tremors. He cleared his voice and tried again.

"I don't know why other people can't see them. I can, I—"

Clarion jumped as a wretched sob came out of nowhere and the next moment he was underwater, a tomb of rushing sounds and gray thick water bubbling around him. He paddled awkwardly up to the surface; he couldn't swim very well. One thing he did know was that his feet didn't touch the bottom.

"Dad, help me up. Please!"

All he heard was water trickling from his ears, his own splashing, and the sound of someone crying deep, jagged sobs. And a whisper. "You're too much like her."

"Please, Dad! I can't swim!" He splashed more and more frantically, struggling to keep his head above water. His heart was beating fast, his legs kicked furiously but water still kept spilling into his mouth. The current was pulling at him, pushing him away from the boat. They were too far from shore. He couldn't swim all the way in, even if he did manage to best the current. The only person who could get him out was his dad. And his dad was crying.

Clarion tried to fan his fingers and propel his arms, remembering to kick his legs, but he kept doing it wrong. Daniel had tried to teach him, but Daniel hadn't been very good. Clarion didn't want to die. Then he thought that maybe, just maybe, this could be a way he could follow the ghosts to where they lived. He forced his muscles to relax and kept his head above water. He let the current gently steer him into the dying night, and as it did, he thought about his mom, about his other ghosts. The stars were still out, the stars of the

Milky Way, so many, just blinking and sparkling down on him. They filled his vision, he could float all day in this nasty water, the stars were his friends. A numbness crept upon him and he smiled. He had to relax. It was important.

"Take me to where people go when they die," he whispered over and over, shivering, snot trickling over his face.

He could see nothing but the stars. Huge, white diamonds that almost had a texture if he could just concentrate enough. And then he realized he was floating in space. Not in water, but in outer space. A pool of black, a black so deep it could no longer be considered black. This black had the depth of eons of reflection. And in that black, Clarion drifted, like a fish, surrounded by stars that glittered coldly. He kicked his legs and he surged forward smoothly; it was the most natural thing in the world. He wasn't cold, he wasn't hot. A strange ringing echoed around him; he couldn't hear his own breathing. He twirled in the void, and he laughed. Clarion was completely lost and confused, yet this didn't scare him. He wasn't drowning. Now he had to figure out where he was and if he was anywhere close to his destination.

He let the darkness and the starlight flow around him, a gentle cradle of universe debris carrying him forth.

"Take me to where people go when they die," he said firmly, thinking of the ghost of his mom and all the ghosts he'd ever interacted with. A cold touch tugged at him, pulling gently on his arms and his legs, and he drifted forward. Still, expectant, he let it take him. It was hard to judge time in this place, wherever he was. He didn't know if he had been dragged along for a few seconds, a few minutes, a few hours, or an eternity.

All at once, Clarion felt a minute vibration around him, an abnormality in the air. His eyes shone as in front of him, a diamond-shaped portal scintillated into existence, pulsing like a heart, a nebulous filigree of silver dancing around its edges. It thrummed and expanded, then shrank down again, still keeping its shape. At each point of the portal, skeins of some silver-white material knitted themselves together and materialized into a praying mantis. Clarion had seen many strange things, but this was something else. Four praying mantises appeared, one at each point of the diamond portal, the vibrant green of their bodies a shocking flash of color in the tenebrous night of the universe. Their mandibles twitched, and their forelegs worked furiously as they spun what seemed to be a web, connecting to the portal. Clarion felt this was right. *This* was the place he had to go to.

As he floated through the portal, blinding light coursed around him and through him. It felt like he was sinking into running velvet. It was warm and comforting and he drifted along peacefully. Clarion pushed through, but then, all at once, he was projected backward. When his eyes focused again, he saw the praying mantises regarding him with their neutral, abnormally clear eyes.

"You cannot enter," a raspy voice echoed, grating against Clarion's ears.

"Why?"

The mantises stopped looking at him, their forelegs not stopping their work.

"Only the dead are allowed to come through."

"If the dead can come through to my world, I should be allowed to come to theirs too."

One of the mantises pointed its middle legs at Clarion.

"It doesn't work that way. The dead are allowed to come to your world, though it is not encouraged. But the laws are clear. A living being cannot enter this portal."

"Oh yeah? What happens if someone living does enter?"

The mantises paused for a moment before resuming their weaving.

"That does not happen. It cannot happen because it is not possible."

Clarion would have stamped his feet if he could have, but instead he floated upside down and crossed his arms.

"Then why was I able to enter the portal? Why was I kicked out?"

The annoying. raspy voices were silent, and Clarion huffed.

"The boy is right. He *was* able to enter. We pushed him out. But he would have entered the portal otherwise."

The mantises conferred amongst themselves, their forelegs twitching madly, heavier webs emerging from them.

"Are you sure you're alive?"

"Yes. But I belong here," he said quietly. "I can see ghosts, they come to me all the time. They find me, whether they're ghosts from my town or across the globe. They talk to me. I have tried following them, but I couldn't. I'm on the right path. This is it. I can sense them. Let me through."

Clarion was sure, beyond a doubt, he would find his mom through the portal. He was also pretty sure he would find his other ghosts. Ghosts, he'd come to realize, had footprints. A particular scent, a particular whiff of memories, a pang of emotions that clung to them. He sensed that and more through the portal.

The mantises squeaked and stopped weaving their webs. Clarion couldn't hear everything they said, only snippets.

"... Could he be..."

"Haven't had one ..."

"Help the situation..."

"... need a Ferryman..."

"...he the one?"

Clarion approached the portal in a few gliding moves. The mantises didn't look up.

"Look, I'm right here. Let me through."

One of the mantises pointed at him again. The others squeaked again and huddled in next to Clarion.

"The dead can come out, but the living cannot come in. This is how it has always been."

One of the other mantises, its body mottling to a darker green, chittered, "But there might be one exception. A blessing for us if it is true. You might be the Ferryman we were promised, many galaxy births ago. What is your name?"

"Clarion."

The mantises scratched their bodies, their weird, creepy legs bending in ways that made Clarion flinch.

"You seem to be the right one."

"The laws are too specific," said one mantis.

"Or too vague," said another.

"While you figure it out, I'm going in," Clarion announced.

He focused on the recognizable scent of his mom. A particular combination of pecan cookies, never-ending mirth, a sense of wonder so much more intense than his, and finally a dagger of regret, so strong it almost hurt him physically.

Clarion glided through the portal: light coursed around him and embraced him almost like his mother did. A roaring filled his ears, then stopped just as suddenly as it had started. When Clarion was able to refocus, he smiled. The Plaza of the Dead was peaceful. Ghosts gamboled in a glade where lakes shone like polished topaz. Trees bowed, dignified, over valleys and prairies, and the sun shone valiantly, never obscured by any clouds. It was beautiful. No screaming, no tears. Clarion recognized a few of the ghosts here and there, and he waved at them. They waved back. He noticed tunnels full of muted light, arching away from the glade. He'd never seen so many ghosts in one place. The ghosts of a woman who'd died from scarlet fever, a young boy who'd died of polio, a man who'd died in his sleep, a girl who'd been run over by a car, twins who'd been strangled by their uncle, wandered about, avoiding other ghosts like there wasn't a crowd.

The ghosts of schoolchildren played together, kicking a ball that vanished and reformed. Clarion saw old couples sleeping, young brothers snoozing, grownups with blank stares on their faces talking to themselves in murmurs he couldn't hear. Clarion strained to hear them.

Clarion closed his eyes and soaked up the presence of the ghosts. A huge, almost overwhelming swarm of emotions and memories rolled over him, but he pushed it away, snatching at a few here and there, trying to focus on one at a time. There. He felt sorrow from a man who'd died after hanging himself. He had lost everything but his wife over such a short time. Once, he had been full of smiles. Clarion detached his gaze and focused on another ghost. There, a little boy who wished he had never followed that strange man in the crowd. A love of dinosaurs, Oreo cookies, playing Scrabble with his mom, enveloped Clarion before terror wiped the rest away. Clarion hurriedly looked for another ghost. There, a woman who'd poisoned herself and her children because she didn't want to keep being unhappy and could find no way out.

Clarion turned around and looked an old man's ghost in the eye, one who'd died from partying too hard. Clarion smiled, the man's presence infectious. He saw ghosts who stared down at the floor, and he focused on their thoughts. Their thoughts chased each other, round and round, suddenly stopping and snarling. Fear and confusion knotted Clarion's stomach. From these ghosts he felt alienation, rage, profound jealousy so intense it took his breath away. Images started forming in his mind and he pushed them away. They made the knots in his stomach worse.

Daniel's books were wrong. Death, the land of the dead, wasn't anything like it was in those books. The good and the bad weren't separated from each other. People didn't get judged. There weren't any adventures or trials the ghosts had to face. What were they doing here, though?

"You truly are the Ferryman," said a voice Clarion recognized as one of the guardian praying mantises. He looked around but saw no one besides the ghosts.

"What is a Ferryman?" Clarion asked out loud, embarrassed at having no idea what was going on. The ghosts looked up as one and gazed expectantly at him.

"Someone who eases the transition between death and the next life. Ghosts here are awaiting their next vessel to be born in a new life."

Clarion thought for a moment.

"How do I help them out? I don't know what to do."

"You already have. What do the ghosts do when they come to you?"

"They talk to me. They tell me about their lives."

Clarion started as he saw his mom in his peripheral vision, waving at him, with tears streaming down her face, yet a smile beaming at him. She looked proud. Sad, but proud.

"Yes. The ghosts have to let go of their memories to be able to go into their next life. People can go insane if they don't—the human species is quite susceptible to this."

Clarion frowned. "I don't understand. Why do they talk to *me*?"

"You are a part of this world *and* the world of the living. Only you have the power to absorb their memories, and so ease their passage into the next life. It is their payment to you for helping them transition. The laws explain this, it's just we've never had a Ferryman before. We've been waiting a long time for you."

"How did the ghosts manage before I was born?" Clarion asked. He understood a little, but he was confused too.

"They transitioned on their own, but the process was

much slower. There would be backlogs in this world, of too many ghosts who couldn't go on to the next life, or wouldn't."

It all started to make sense now. It was like a major traffic jam.

"So I'm the Ferryman." He was starting to like his new title. "Do I have to sign anything?" He knew that's what adults did when they wanted to make something official.

"No."

Clarion saw his mom approaching him, her arms out, beckoning him like she used to when they played hide-and-seek when she was still alive. He could barely see her, but he sensed her more distinctly than ever.

"Every so often, when we have too many ghosts, we will ask you to come here and spend time talking with each of them, relieving them of their memories."

"What happens when all their memories are gone?" Clarion asked abruptly.

"I think you know," the mantis said simply.

Clarion's throat was clogged all of a sudden. A stinging sensation prickled at his eyes, but he forced the tears back. Maybe he did know. He looked fearfully at his mom, but she was still there. Only just. What was holding her back?

"Do you, Clarion, accept your duty as Ferryman?"

"Oh. Oh yes," he replied, focusing. It would be a cool job. Certainly better than the jobs he'd heard about in school. He could be as weird as he liked and help the dead as the Ferryman. That was a win-win.

Clarion sat down and put his knees up. He was starting to feel cold. The scenery around him started to fade.

"Clarion of the Dead, you are now officially the Ferryman of—"

But Clarion didn't hear the last part.

"Clarion," his father gasped, hauling him back in the boat. "I'm so sorry. So sorry!"

Clarion's head lolled as he felt rough hands poking at him. His head swam and he was cold all over. All of his limbs ached. What had happened? Where was he? With effort, he saw the fishing tackle by his feet. The fishing poles were strewn in the boat like broken trucks. His dad hovered over him, his hair wild, his eyes wide and terrified.

"I was drowning," Clarion trailed off.

His dad looked down.

"I pushed you out of the boat. I'm sorry. I'm a horrible person. A bad dad. If you want to call Child Services on me... I understand."

Clarion looked at the beer bottles filling the boat's hull. He stared back at his dad.

"You need to stop drinking. I can't keep watching over you. I have too many people to watch over now."

From the corner of his eye, Clarion saw a child's ghost swimming in the bay, a boy, along with a girl. He focused. They had been brother and sister. They drowned when they snuck out in their parents' boat and capsized.

His dad blushed and sat down awkwardly in the boat.

"I miss her so much. Your mom. The pain... I can't deal with it. I want to join her. I don't deserve to live."

Clarion's throat tightened. The pain in his dad's voice. It rivaled the pain of some ghosts he'd talked to who had had horrible lives.

Clarion gasped as he saw his mom, standing in the boat with them, watching his dad tenderly, a miniscule sigh escaping her.

"Dad. Mom is still here. She is here right now."

"Clarion, come on," his dad said weakly.

His mom sat down next to Clarion and brushed her hands through his hair. Clarion felt her faint touch and he leaned into it. He got a sense of urgency, that feeling he got from people when they talked fast to him, even as they jogged away.

"I know you can't see her. But I can. She... she needs to go."

Clarion's mom nodded her head approvingly.

"You are holding her back, Buckaroo Billy," Clarion said plaintively.

His dad's eyes widened.

"H-h-how do you know that?"

Clarion's mom had told him a while ago the pet nickname she'd given his dad. Clarion knew his dad had never shared that with him.

His mom stood up and paced in the boat, her form passing through his dad's. He shivered and looked around longingly, a frown on his face.

"Mom," Clarion said, his voice cracking. "What is holding you back? I know you're here for a reason."

She paused and crossed her arms.

"I can't leave until your dad promises to take care of you. To live, to be the man I fell in love with. Kind, funny, distracted. Not a man who drowns his own child," she finished, glowering at his dad.

Clarion was about to transmit the message to his dad, but his mom continued.

"Ask him, Clarion. Or I can't give my memory to you. I can't move on."

"What memory is that?" Clarion asked.

"My death," she said.

"Dad, the Plaza of the Dead is real. I have a job there now. You have to live. I miss Mom too. She won't stay here forever." The tears came again, and this time, he didn't wipe them away. "I will miss you if you go too. Please stay. Forgive yourself. Mom isn't unhappy about dying. She's unhappy you almost drowned me. You're a better guy than that."

His dad breathed deeply and started crying again, his hands shaking. "Oh my God. Oh my God. I almost killed you. She is right. Oh my God. Oh my God. I suck."

"You don't suck!" Clarion roared. "But you will suck if you keep treating me like that. If you keep drinking. If you let death get you before your time."

His mom gave him a thumbs up, and whispered, "Go Clarion."

Clarion, surprised at himself, stilled his voice. He sighed. He continued more softly.

"Live, Dad. Stop drinking. For me. For Mom. Trust me. Please?"

His dad looked at him and swallowed hard. The desire for death was still there, buried deep in the pain. But Clarion saw something else. A will to keep going on. A stubbornness that had been for too long repressed.

"I will, Clarion."

Clarion nodded. He could see just faintly the outline of his mom's ghost.

"Clarion, I have to tell you how I died. Now that you have your father's version. Let me give you mine.

"I knew the car needed to be brought in. But I kept forgetting. Your dad had a lot on his mind with work. I wanted to get you guys MoonPies and angel food cake for a little party I was preparing. I was driving, and then I was dead. I never saw it coming. I didn't even feel pain. Death was... easy. I could have moved on. But I wanted to keep seeing you. Your father. The way your father fell apart... That hurt. That hurt more than death ever did." She bit her lip.

Clarion gazed at his dad, who stared at him with fear and awe on his face. Clarion cleared his throat.

"Mom says death was easy. What you did afterward was hard for her. You must keep your promise. Or I will stay in the

Plaza of the Dead, Dad. It's a cool place. Living with you sometimes sucks really bad."

"Clarion... I don't want to lose you too. I will take care of you."

Clarion's mom smiled wide. She got up and cracked her knuckles, although Clarion heard nothing. She held out her hand.

"I want to go now," she said eagerly.

He took her hand. He knew, instinctively, it was for him to lead. He looked at the sky, with its infinite stars. So clear, so bright, so inviting. He stepped out of the boat and so did she. Their feet didn't break the water. He walked with her, out across the bay, focusing hard on the Plaza of the Dead, letting the stars fill his vision. A dull roaring and white light flickered around them.

"I love you," he said, voice tight.

"Why, thank you!" she said, laughing.

And he knew she didn't recognize him at all. And that was ok.

"Go, you can go," he said, as a foggy tunnel materialized in front of them. There was water here too, but their footsteps didn't mark the waves. She walked away from him, her form vanishing completely, just a faint hint of pecan cookies, never-ending mirth, a delightful sense of wonder trailing behind her. No regret, no pain.

Clarion walked backward and eventually found himself back in the boat with his dad. He threw himself at his dad, and they both did what they should have done a long time ago. They cried together long and deep, as the dawn broke over them, lighting the boat with a gentle touch of coral and apricot. While they cried, the ghosts of the boy and the girl splashed around and laughed, edging their way toward Clarion to talk to him.

Full Integration

I was one of the last to be bitten and one of the last to
sire vampires. Over centuries, my brothers, sisters, and
fledglings all died. I was hanging on, but only just. I
was the only one left who had turned. I was made in the
twenty-third century, but it still wasn't enough to survive the
quickening evolution of humankind. They had evolved; we
hadn't.

The death knell has struck. Humans have found a way to
permanently leave the Earth and colonize the Milky Way. I
shall starve to death—the worst death for a creature like me—
complete disintegration. When I was turned, human bodies
couldn't integrate with technology yet. That meant I could
still feed on their blood. But now, even if I follow the humans,
which I couldn't without some adaptive technology that
won't work with my body, I will not be able to feed because
humans don't have blood anymore.

The humans are leaving because they have destroyed their
planet. They can explore the Milky Way; they have already sent
expeditions with zero failure to nearby and faraway planets. I
cannot keep drinking the blood of rodents and other small

animals. There are precious few left, and their blood has become toxic.

I stiffened as a slow, pulsating beat called to my desiccated, dying senses, a beat that I followed around the renovated Franz Liszt Academy of Music. I avoided the random groups of people laughing, or staring straight ahead, immersed in their Neural Neighbor Network, invisible to the naked eye. The pulsing was small, and I homed in on it, ignoring the almost alive feeling of the few old architectural buildings that hadn't been destroyed. I saw the backside of a little girl, her auburn hair down to her waist, a floral skirt brightening the dimness of this manufactured autumn day over the city of Budapest. I gave a secret thanks to the creator of the Bullia technology, who created artificial climate bubbles around the world to give citizens the semblance of natural cycles. For a vampire, that means day holds no threat anymore.

I smoothly trailed behind her, her frame dwarfing mine. I made no sound, taking advantage of my evolution-cheated smaller body, not needing to crouch at all like I used to on my hunts a thousand years ago. I finally felt like a predator again. It had been too long.

The little girl paused and put her hands to her ears. A thrum emanated from her, which I recognized as reception of a message through the Neural Neighbor Network directly into her brain. I scanned around us. No parents, no friends close to her. The few people present stood stock still, the same sound emanating from them. Perfect. My vampire instincts kicked in. The air folded around me and snapped like a clap, though I knew no sound came with it as I dashed to the girl, put a hand over her mouth, and whisked her away to the top of the Medos Hotel.

As soon as I released her, my head spun, and a general tingly feeling prickled my entire body. My fangs erupted, tearing through the shrunken, shriveled flesh of my gums.

Hunger. My stomach clenched ferociously, painfully wracking my abdomen. My lips quivered with anticipation. Before the little girl could scream, I sank my teeth into her soft throat hard enough to pierce her voice box. She twitched violently, arms and knees flailing. My tongue curled as the artificiality of her blood struck, too late, but some actual human fluid was still interspersed in the AI plasma. So I drank as deep and hard as I could, even though I knew the AI plasma would weaken my state and not satisfy my hunger. A little blood was better than none at all. I easily held her down as she continued her struggle.

Her slate gray eyes widened and her pupils dilated as her body went limp. The beating of her heart stopped, and I was seized with curiosity. I punched through her ribcage and reached for her heart. My spirits sank as I regarded the object's silicone walls, its now still chambers. It was the size of a large grapefruit and quite lifelike in my hand. It had fooled me. I'd known there had been complete artificial heart technology for a few decades now, but only adults had been able to enjoy the procedure for transplanting a heart that would keep them alive for two centuries minimum. Children were too young to undergo such a delicate risky procedure. But the tech had improved, and I guess so had the consent laws regarding full artificial conscience transplant. Now I couldn't even feed on children anymore.

Feeding on children. I had promised myself many moons ago that I would never stoop to that. One thousand years ago, I had been young and thought I was God. I'd fed on a pack of young refugee children and a pregnant woman. They were dying and alone. I hadn't needed all their blood, but once I killed one, I couldn't allow the others to live. The guilt stayed with me as my bloodlust lessened over the centuries; they could have survived.

And yet...here I was. I had broken my own code. This girl I

had just killed could have survived. Her death barely served me; my hunger had hardly been touched. I touched the ring on my index finger, with six notches on it. I brought it to my mouth and added one more notch.

I willed myself down to the street level, which came easily thanks to the spurt of actual blood I'd gotten. I walked down the street, evading the ghosts of buildings that had once existed, past the movie theater, beauty salons, restaurants, laundromat, and vintage stores. In this world, none of these were necessary. With perfect bodies that didn't age or fail unless the tech itself did, people enjoyed all these comforts at home.. The price to pay had been the consumption of all of Earth's resources.

I came to the ferry and stared morosely at the Danube, bobbing tranquilly to a rhythm only it knew, its churlish, grey surface reflecting the skylines.

I jerked as a woman's voice floated to me, her high, fast-paced syllables tripping over each other to whoever she was talking to on her Neural Neighbor Network.

I growled, glaring at her, but she didn't notice me. Her bodysuit wrapped around her hourglass figure and as she walked, it merged with her skin so perfectly she could have been made of that ultramarine material. Those suits were typical of hospital workers and scientists. I tried tuning her out, but she kept talking more and more loudly. I was about to scare her with my vampiric gaze, but she cut off my momentum as she snapped at the person on the other end of her call, "Stop treating me like I'm a monster! I'm dying, ok? Whatever horrible things you think I've done, I'm paying for them now. Happy?"

I couldn't hear the response, as the receiver was wired directly to her cochlear nerve, but the woman started sobbing. A pasty and aged face, something I hadn't seen in years, struck me with its raw sorrow.

"I will always love you. You are my daughter. If you could forgive me and see me just once. Once before I go… it would make me happy."

A long silence ensued.

"I will not stop. I will not stop doing what I do. I'm dying, but I'm not an invalid."

Her mouth set, her brow furrowed. I stared more attentively at her. Something about that face. Maybe adding a few more pounds, taking away the lividness and the deep bags under her eyes… Darker, longer hair…

"You have never understood my work. I don't expect you to now. But I'm not going to stop."

Snorting, the woman jerked her head and stopped talking. I had to gaze up to meet her baleful, wet stare. I raised my eyebrows. I knew who she was.

She was Dr. Borbála Farkas, one of the most famous scientists of this era. Famous for her work with the human genome. The older she got, the more she was ostracized from the community for being an anti-progressive. She did not endorse purely artificial improvements and man-made evolutionary enhancements. It was strange seeing her out and about but in such an intimate way. The beating of her heart called to me and I leaned instinctively. I withdrew as I braced myself for the plausible eventuality that the beating I was feeling was synthetic. Strange that humans wanted to transplant their organs yet keep their original design.

Her anger spiked because she deduced that I'd been listening to her conversation. "What are you looking at? Mind your own business," she said as a familiar beat enthralled me and stirred my hunger.

I raised my hand toward her to see if I could hypnotize her.

Her pupils dilated and her mouth slowly gaped. I whisked to her side and bent her down. I smelled her. My fangs grew, that familiar pain stabbing through my gums. There was a pulse, and I could smell the blood just under the surface, the scent of sick blood, true, fatigued plasma. But it was blood. I could not be mistaken twice in the same day.

As I was about to plunge my fangs into her, I remembered an important detail. Her scientific work was all about evolution. Specifically, about manipulating the human genome to make it evolve more quickly. Unlike other scientists, she believed the best of the human genome lay in the past. She had supposedly found ways to make the genome integration and acceleration process happen, but no one who was willing to have her technique tested on them. I'd read many conflicting articles about the scientific community's take on her. Perhaps she could help me. If she couldn't, I would will her to forget me, and I could go back to dying an excruciatingly slow death.

I snapped my fingers and her eyes focused again. By the time she was done blinking, I was standing a few feet away from her, arms crossed like nothing had happened. But her golf ball-sized eyes tracked me warily and she softly said, "Are you a pricolici?"

I chuckled. Just because I was more hirsute than most and had thick features did not make me a pricolici. I didn't even have a tail. "Pricolici? Those haven't existed in centuries! You need more up-to-date folklore."

Dr. Farkas hesitantly approached me. "Then you are strigoi." She pointed at my mouth.

I ran my tongue across my teeth. My fangs were still out because I could still feel the pulse in her. There had to be real blood running in her veins and that precious serum of life called seductively to my senses.

"No. I am not strigoi." For one, I didn't have the ginger hair, blue eyes, or two hearts. And like the pricolici, the strigoi had died out sometime in the twenty-fourth century. And she mistakenly assumed I was Hungarian. I was from the long-forgotten state of Paleslelem, the tiny region forged between

Palestine and Israel after centuries and centuries of conflict. I was bitten on the thumb by a vampire demoness, not even originally from the Middle East. I could still recall her accent even if I'd never seen her face. It had been a foreigner's accent, crisp with tall vowels. I did not know what kind of vampire I was. In the end, it did not matter. I was a vampire who'd survived.

"You must help me if you can. I can persuade your fellow scientists that your work is valuable. But only if you keep me alive," I said, locking my eyes with hers.

"What are you?" she whispered, an almost eager look creeping on to her face. Not at all what I had expected.

"Just a vámpír," I answered, adding, "You are dying too, no?"

Anger flared in her eyes, quick and fierce, then it smoldered, giving her deep ocean eyes a savage tint. "Yes. I am."

"I understand the feeling. I am the last of my kind, the last node. Believe me. I have searched everywhere. You are the only person who might be able to help me."

She stared sideways at me, like she didn't believe me. The Danube River flowed blissfully on behind us in churning wavelets. I now wished whoever had activated the "autumn day" mode in the climate regulator had chosen something else.

"A vámpír cannot die," she said, turning from me and stalking away, her ultramarine clad form slowly disappearing from sight.

"That's what I thought, too," I whispered to myself.

An announcement came over the Neural Neighbor Network, this time in the form of digital strips floating around in the skies:

"A new upgrade is available for individuals with artificial conscience transplanted bodies. Expect faster processing speeds, more acuity, more—"

I dove into the river, to block out the incessant vocal reminder of what I could never be: immortal.

Dr. Farkas left me no other choice. I decided that night to track her down and make her see what I meant. I would have to use a technique I hadn't used in a long time. A form of hypnosis mixed with mental fusion. I'd only used it for sexual encounters between other vampires and myself. Now, for the first time, I would use it as a plea, not a weapon.

I tracked the scent of her blood, sickly, weak, but still pumping, due to the will of its owner, I was sure. She lived in the Turkish quarter, where the Turks had fled in the twenty-second century after Europe bombed Turkey for its support of Muslim immigration. Rows and rows of pods lay in a sinuous line, with Turkish flags raised high. Flags from other countries decorated the doors of some of the pods. I recognized French, American, Vietnamese, and Russian. Some artificial gardens added a spice of color to the dusky backdrop of the night. Occasionally I heard a dog bark or a child sing. Two centuries ago, there would have been stark divides in the neighborhood and the poor and the rich demarcation would have been obvious. But the access to all technological resources and the rebellions from scientific communities around the world had put a stop to global poverty. So it was not surprising that Dr. Farkas would live in the same neighborhood of pods as a plumber or teacher.

People were proud of the professions they had. On the pods, they displayed holograms of themselves at their jobs, working on projects that showcased their best moments. But I didn't need holograms to figure out where my scientist lived. My nostrils flared and the scent of her blood overshadowed the scent of wet dog, plastic flowers, alloys, and rotting cloth. I reached her pod and I let myself meld into a shadow, a shadow that crept up and up to a window I slid through, and then I let my corporeal body flesh out again. I almost banged my legs on her toilet. Confusion filled me as the toilet, shower, and hand sink shone bright in the darkness. These were all old-fashioned amenities. Dr. Farkas may be an evolved human being, but she definitely did not embrace the augmentative tech. These days, humans had bowel parties, where they pretended to urinate and defecate. Their bodies expelled waste-like fluids, giving them the sensations that actual waste expelling would, but augmentative technology and conscience transplanting had gotten rid of most natural bodily functions.

I slipped out of the bathroom and glided to her bedroom, where I felt her deep, rhythmic breathing. Crouching next to her pillow, I placed two fingers on her eyelids. Then I placed my other hand on her chest, above her heart. I locked onto her heartbeat and willed mine to sync with hers. She took a deep breath and almost woke up, but I coaxed her back to sleep, to deep comforts and childhood memories that made her smile. I connected with a memory of a severe-looking woman with an aquiline nose proudly regaling tales of strigoi, which she still believed in. Dr. Farkas as a little girl, wide-eyed, exhilarated and scared at the same time, held on to every word.

I explored that memory more deeply, as it led to a teenage Dr. Farkas going to the library with her class, immersed in the VR experience, where she walked among dinosaurs, among the survivors of the mass extinction, among the first cavemen. Her hawkish eyes swiveled as she focused on details that were passed from species to species, theories blooming in her mind. The seeds of her research lay in those recurring trips to the Hungarian Natural History Museum.

Awe and determination washed over me, equaled by a nagging wave of disgust. Dr. Farkas shifted irritably in her sleep, and more of her thoughts travelled through me: humans made of nothing but synthetic parts, perfect in appearance, almost immortal, but still capable of dying. One little flaw in the tech was all it could take. One little flaw could kill the human race. The human genome was too complicated, and too intrinsically *theirs*, to put in the hands of unfeeling technology.

She thought of waves of humans colonizing the galaxies, their thoughts as one, one synchronized mass, without obstacles, without limitations. True immortality: a mental connection between all beings. No more loneliness, no more selfishness, no more weakness. Collective power. Complete eternity.

I started pulling back, taking my hand off her chest and her eyes. These thoughts... were not mine. If that was what *she* wanted, it meant death to me. I could not prey on a *spiritus mundi* form of humanity.

I am going to die, I thought. Immortality couldn't be a collective power, not for a vampire. Vampiric immortality was the eternal quality of one soul. One powerful being using others to survive. Vampirism had no room for others. Even with each other, when my brethren were populating the world, we backstabbed each other all the time. We never formed communities. Even with our fledglings, we never supported each other, never trained each other. I couldn't remember their faces at all.

What Dr. Farkas wanted was in direct opposition to what I needed. As the dread and panic seared through my senses, Dr. Farkas's eyes flickered and she murmured, "I am going to die." Solitude and degradation until she was a husk of herself. No finished works, no lasting legacy of her existence besides a daughter who scorned her. She would be forgotten in history and having gotten no happiness from her time on Earth.

Dr. Farkas sat up with a gasp, and her huge eyes found me in the darkness.

"You," she breathed, and strangely, there was no fear. "I knew you'd find me."

She smiled, swinging her legs off the bed. "You can turn me," she said, licking her lips. "You can give me eternal life."

"I can't. I can give you a few extra centuries maybe. Maybe a millennium at most. But your body won't keep up. I've lived a thousand years and your species has surpassed mine. That is why all my brethren have died. That is why I am dying."

I paced through her room; regretting having come. She was shortsighted after all. When would humans realize that vampirism was vastly overrated? They wanted eternity but without the consequences that came with it.

Dr. Farkas cocked her head and got up, teetering a little bit as a wave of weakness washed through her.

"You might very well be the missing piece. Yes. You are. I can finish my research! I can—" she continued excitedly, but scientific terms I couldn't discern kept derailing my comprehension and so I disconnected mentally. When she was finished with her tirade, she swept by me and went to the back of her pod. I followed her, past a series of circular rooms that looked unlived in, until we went into a huge chamber filled with nothing but slots on the walls and a huge contraption in the middle.

The contraption, this machine, was arrowhead shaped, and stood about seven feet tall, the size of an average human being. Rainbow shimmers cascaded on its sleek surface, creating amorphous shapes that dissipated as you watched more closely. Walls of slots, thousands of them, glittered subtly. Dr. Farkas turned toward one of the sections of slots, and pulled something out of one. An e-paper sheet the width of a fingernail. Her fingers covered most of it, but I could still see some fluorescent orange liquid rippling on the tablet.

"What is that?" I asked, as it cast a manic light on her tired features.

"This machine? It is a data repository for DNA sequences. Cas9, cRNA and tracrRNA to help modify the sequences. I call it the Fusionner."

I looked at the sheer number of slots in the walls and pondered how many DNA strands could be harbored there.

"This one," she said, pointing to her sheet, "is part of my collection of prehistoric humanity's DNA. I have collected what I feel are the essentials for our next evolutionary step. Some of the adaptations I have decided to keep, from the Mesolithic and the Neolithic Age, for example, are our endurance, running ability, larger teeth and jaws, and our abilities for homeostasis and changing our pigmentation according to climate. I accept that some of these traits we might not need on certain planets. But on those that are similar in makeup to Earth, those traits will be valuable."

"You don't have just prehistoric DNA, do you?" I asked, surveying the glowing slots in the walls.

She smiled, her tiny teeth flashing. "I have *every* kind of DNA. Now, with you, I can add vampiric DNA to the mix. That would give true immortality." Her face lit up, despite the wrinkles, shadows, and bruises on her unnaturally white skin. "Fringe research indicates vampirism is a disease, but it is an organic disease that gives some pretty good adaptations. All this tech to have *perfect* bodies, choosing superficial traits, in the end gives impermanent adaptations. We are messing with our evolutionary process and trusting the tech to work. All it takes is one flaw..." She snapped her finger and angrily thrust her sheet back in the wall slot.

"Is there even a way to test if your samples will work?" I ventured.

Her face darkened and she glared venomously past me, at the machine behind us.

"Have you tested your samples on anybody?"

"No, I have never been able to test my samples. Since

starting my work decades ago, I have tried. But no one was willing. My own colleagues accused me of dragging us backwards, of slighting our evolution. Some have even called me a Dr. Frankenstein saying that such an experiment would kill a human being." She scratched her head and focused her eyes on me. "But you, you are immortal. I can test on you. And I can accelerate the process so you can experience centuries' worth of evolution within only a few weeks. It will be uncomfortable. Probably agonizing. But it's a risk that must be taken. Anyway, you are already dying."

I walked to the machine and laid a hand on it. It was cold, smooth to the touch. But it warmed the longer I kept my hand on it. Bubbles of color surged as I played on the surface, swiping my hands to and fro. She was right. There was death, another kind of death, and potentially life. But at a cost. However, I'd been living with the cost since the twenty-third century. This was nothing new.

"Is this about saving me, or is this about saving the human species?"

A long, brooding pause stretched for her, but passed in a wink of an eye for me. She swayed for a moment and clenched her fists. "Both. You, because you are a unique specimen. It pains me to see anything die from something that can be fixed. I believe I can fix your feeding problem. As for the human species... The human species can go screw itself. If this works, you will be truly immortal, better than any of our species. You will be my perfect creation," she said quietly. "I gave them plenty of opportunity to become better and they refused to see the light. I choose to help you over those humans."

I stared bewildered at her. I had rarely seen humans with that level of detachment.

"Why help me reach immortality when you could have augmented yourself or done a conscience transplant and avoided death?"

Dr. Farkas planted her feet to retort, but started coughing, wracking coughs that bent her elongated back. Once she stopped, she resumed her position. "Very pertinent questions. But I don't want to answer them now. You will find out. For now, all you need to know is that I will work on combining the genomes I have and then I will need you to come in so I can start the infusion process to make you capable of feeding again."

She waved her hand and the lights in the chamber turned off.

"What is your name?" she asked.

"Adolam."

"Just Adolam?"

"Yes. What more do I need?"

She nodded in the dark. "I am Doctor Borbála Farkas."

Another silence hummed loudly as we walked toward the front door.

"So, what are our next steps?" I hazarded, stretching out my hand to confirm our agreement.

She took it, her large fingers enveloping my entire hand, and shook it. The larger hand size was definitely a new human trait I hadn't gotten used to yet.

"Let's go conquer death." She laughed, and she ushered me out of her pod.

———

Weeks passed in a flurry of analysis and isolation sessions with Dr. Farkas. In her downtime, she hunted for behind the scenes reports that were being hidden by the smiling news anchors: secret data reports of random deaths occurring across the world from artificial conscience transplant upgrade failures. Those didn't dim the growing sense of hope for Dr. Farkas and me.

Some sessions we would spend without saying a word. I would just stand there while she waved a wand-like object around my body, and her machine would scan and register my DNA and transform it into code she could visualize and work with. She used the genome editing system that she patented during her research to test the reactions of my DNA to her samples. She tried explaining how the idea was influenced by the CRISPR-cas9 system of the twenty-first century, but groundbreaking innovation had made it more efficient and reliable. In other sessions, we would talk about the possible future of humankind. Every so often, she let me feed from her, just a tiny bit. Enough to revive me, enough to not kill her. She had leukemia, and she was getting more and more transfusions. But her doctor warned her that she was running out of real blood. Because there was no demand, there was no reason to artificially produce it, much less keep actual quantities of it. After her transfusions, she would stare stonily ahead and silent, tears pooling in her eyes.

One evening, I asked Dr. Farkas a question about the past. *Her* past.

"Why, with all the options available out there, are you basically choosing to die? People don't die from cancer anymore, unless there's a breakdown in their tech. Even so, there are ways to strip the cancer away and heal you. So...?"

Dr. Farkas swallowed hard, grimaced, and paused her work over a table as long as her room.

"Why? When I turned eighteen, I decided not to be conscience transplanted, even though I legally could then. I didn't want to be a machine. I did not even want augmentations. I grieve for the children now, who are forced to be conscience transplanted by their families before they can even enjoy their organic body."

Dr. Farkas hugged herself, and I noticed that she was thinner, almost bony. Her breathing was louder than usual. I expected her to faint, but she held herself together, eyes burning with unshed tears.

"I did not *choose* to die. What people are doing now, conscience transplanting themselves into these bodies, is death. Taking unnecessary risks. We are not supposed to physically live for centuries. It is unnatural. It is a drain on the planet.

"What we are doing," she continued, "is also a risk, unfortunately. No great idea doesn't have its set of complications or unexpected outcomes. But I believe it's worth it.

After a while, she spoke again, after fiddling with the Fusionner. "You're different. You were turned. You have a different role in this ecosystem, but you are a natural part of it. Now, stand still."

She waggled her fingers in the air, and a massive holopanel shimmered into existence. A timeline stretched out across it, and the beginning portion turned green. She took out a series of sheets from the wall and started sliding them into slots in the arrowhead contraption, as I liked to call it. Once she had inserted about two dozen sheets with modified data sequences on them, she turned to me and activated another screen. This one hung right above me, and as I watched, it showed my genetic makeup—my blood type, my traits—and then codes began to stream onto it. Code after code I could not understand, but judging from Dr. Farkas's expression, she could comprehend perfectly. Once the screen had finished spewing its information, Dr. Farkas pressed both hands to her temples and her eyes took on the same hue as the screen. She waved me to the machine. I stared there dumbly. This would be my first time entering it.

She pressed an oval on the face of the contraption. Its smooth surface bisected and opened up like a Venus flytrap.

Nothing but white surrounded me, and I touched the too-blank walls. They were soft, like foam. The roof of the machine was beyond my reach. And then the doors closed and the seam vanished into the perfectly white surface. My strange friend's voice echoed around me.

"Stand tall and try not to move. Nanobots are going to descend from the ceiling and crawl onto your skin and into your body to start modifying and editing your genome, integrating it with the ones I've coded into the machine. It might hurt. I don't know. I have never had such an experience."

So I stood still and closed my eyes. Soon enough, prickling sensations erupted all over my body, and then gradually worked their way inside of me. After a while, I could not feel anything. Then, visions started: flashes of memories, flashes of long-forgotten sensations pounding through my head. Roaming in the wild when there were still trees and greenery on the planet. Hunting animals many times my size. Sweat trickling down my brow, my teeth tearing into thick, raw meat. Soon, memory after memory darted through me and it took all my concentration to stand still and not bend from the onslaught. Overwhelming fear of bigger predators, awe at the knowledge I could make weapons. Incredulity at the big world out there, of mystical beings that controlled it. I forced myself to focus on the hope of immortality, of bloodlust, of superiority of species. I hadn't felt emotions that weren't predatory in so long. This wasn't Adolam.

When we were done, Dr. Farkas took me out of the Fusionner. I could barely keep my mind straight. Out of habit, I sought out her neck, to reopen the bites I had left from previous sessions. But she had to guide me and hold my head as I sucked, desperately but carefully. I sucked for exactly 6.7 seconds. Just enough to satisfy some of my hunger. Just enough not to kill her. She was tastier than usual, more fragrant. She must have had a transfusion. The usual sickliness of her blood had some extra punch. After I released her, I made sure to lap up any excess drop of blood that remained on her skin or mine. Her hungry gaze met mine.

"Efficiency. Don't waste any of it. You and I are more similar than you think." Her voice curiously neutral despite the lust in her eyes.

I knew she hadn't had any man touch her since her failed marriage two decades prior. I also knew she wanted to be a predator just like me. But she didn't want to get her hands dirty. Ironic that she would die, while I carried out her legacy.

One evening during the fourth month of our endeavor, Dr. Farkas sat in the experiment chamber, on the floor, drinking synthetic coffee. I, of course, ate and drank nothing. She sipped, and as she did, my heart sank at her bruised, shaking wrists, her increasingly skeletal face, and the scent of decay I could sense in her ever-weakening blood. But the ferocity in her eyes paralleled the degree of physical weakness that was destroying her body. The blue in her eyes darkened as she contemplated me.

"Do you sense any changes since we started this?"

"Some," I said. "I feel better. The pain is less. My instincts are less slow, they are strengthening back to how they used to be. But I still feel the hunger."

"That's because I'm not done giving you the last three centuries' worth of DNA. Once that's done you should start feeling a major difference. In a few months' time, you should be able to get on a ship and survive and be able to drink the artificial blood from the artificial conscience transplants. I have chosen to give you recent traits that will help you settle in the biggest settlement they expect to have on Draugr."

I nodded, but inside I fretted. She seemed so sure that it would work. She didn't even conceive of failure. But what choice did we have? I was desperate. She was desperate. We were both on ticking clocks that grew louder with each passing day. The true question was, would she die first, or would I?

I didn't know if it was worth asking her if she had a backup plan. In the end, the death of one would entail the death of the other.

"Adolam, what was it like? Being turned?" she asked, still sipping her coffee.

"Unlike anything you will ever feel," I said haltingly after a long break. I had never had to think about what it felt like to become a vampire. I became one, and then I had to survive. I rarely thought about my human days or lingered on the past. It was a waste of time. But I could try to answer Dr. Farkas's question. "It was supremely painful, awkward, and orgasmic at the same time. It took time to grow used to new powers you never had. Being so powerful, the first few centuries, was intoxicating once I learned what I could do. I lived for draining the next person dry. Immortality was worth it; I could travel, I could live under different names and identities whenever I wanted; I was better as a vampire than I had ever been as a human. I became assertive, strong, sensual, fast, and permanently healthy. As a vampire, I became *superior*."

Dr. Farkas finished her coffee and licked her lips, leaning her head back against the wall behind her and folding her hands together.

"Did you ever fall in love?" she asked, her eyes closed.

"No." I gazed at her in consternation. "Never."

She frowned, then cracked one eye open. "I don't believe you. Vampires always find love in the stories."

I threw my hands up in the air.

"No. Sorry to disappoint. Your knowledge of vampires is nothing but fairy tales. We are predators. Not lovers. We find sexual pleasure, but not even that is as pleasing as drinking blood. Falling in love with a human would be pointless. You do not fall in love with your food. Besides, even if you can look past that elementary fact, why fall in love when that person will die in a hundred years or less?"

"True, it *is* a waste of time." She set her mouth. "Come to think of it, we don't benefit much from love either." She took a few deep breaths and coughed hard, phlegm rattling nastily. I could have heard it even without my preternatural hearing.

"Why do you persist in helping a vampire? I am a predator that feeds on your race. Why would you help me kill your race?"

I had asked this question multiple times. I wondered if her answer would remain the same. Humans were fickle.

Dr. Farkas stood up and marched to the Fusionner, taking out the empty sheet and smoothing it over and over with her hands.

"Adolam. My species is a cancer. We killed our own planet. We are going to go to new planets and eventually destroy them, too. You are a check on our greed and appetite." She smiled ruefully and slid a sheet back into its slot. She moved slowly, deliberately. "I know you probably won't wipe us out. There are so many of us. But you can cull the population a little once you're able to feed on artificial blood. Remember, you are supposed to be my masterpiece, become something better than what my species can be with all its foolishness and fancy tech."

I seriously wondered in that moment if she was a genius or a psychopath.

"The human race needs culling. People turn on each other. It's the way we are. Even your own children turn on you." Her face became frigid, and I looked down.

A dull thrum billowed from her and she stiffened. She remained in that pose for a few minutes. When her eyes cleared, she fiddled with her cochlear implant settings and motioned for me to listen. A bubbly voice suddenly broke the silence.

This is Chris Walker from NNN with more information about the upcoming Fearless Starfarer Expedition from Earth. In T-minus ninety-one days, six hours, the first settlement of ships will launch for Proxima Centauri B, HR2562B, and Draugr. We are happy to report that new amenities have been added. In addition to the team of the world's best synth-body engineers and conscience transfer specialists, ready to ensure you against any side effects, the ships have been unveiled to be completely integrated with Slo-Mode, so you can extend the experience of travel, as well as offering Neural Music Connexx, so you can share your favorite songs right from your brain. New simulators have been unveiled as well, like the food and toilet sims; experience eating and...well, you know...all over again. Doesn't that sound fantastic? And these are in addition to the spacious beds where you can power down your brain and recharge your body, the expansive compartments allowing you to bring along your condensed home packages with safety and security, and the exciting news that the craft will be entirely transparent to allow for complete and unobscured views of space as you travel to your new home.

"Sounds more like advertisement than news," I said, but that was nothing new. I was cut off as another message came through the NNN.

Make sure your artificial conscience transplant is compatible with the planet you have decided to spend your life on. If you are unsure, get your ACT tested at the nearest lab (click the link now). Also get tested for potential software upgrade failure. This is just a friendly reminder, nothing to be concerned about. Enjoy your day, community!

I didn't think more of it. Humans died all the time and covered it up. But Dr. Farkas's lips drew tightly together.

Dr. Farkas finalized her sessions with me. She worked frantically but precisely, finally finishing my injections. For the last few, I had to stay in her home and sleep on the floor of her chamber. My body swam from so much genetic memory. My features started changing bit by bit. My eyes swelled as big as golf balls. My body stretched as all my limbs lengthened; I lay in agony as bones and cartilage grew longer and longer. I could suddenly tune in to the technology around me and hear conversations from around the world through the NNN. I could know facts about any random thing I thought of if I concentrated hard enough. The world itself felt stark and full of tiny details I could process all at once. If I wasn't careful, people's emotions and voices started leaking through the NNN and I would start responding. Now when Dr. Farkas put me in the Fusionner, her voice would echo in my head, as opposed from the wall in the contraption. Her frustration, her doggedness, trailed with me afterward when I went hunting to train my new body.

I had to adjust my pacing, my stealthing methods, and the killing stroke now. I killed an elderly woman and a teenager with some difficulty. My thoughts had almost given me away. But their blood had left me with a semisatiated feeling, which was a small victory.

Now I trailed a young couple on their way to a boat ride on the Danube. They held hands and laughed as I stayed in the shadows, though the shadows were starting to repel me. I did not like this new adaptation. Vampires relied on shadows to cloak them. I crawled out of the shadows and activated my super speed, focusing on every inch of my body and factoring in the air and space around me. But I forgot that I was taller, bulkier than I used to be. The air folded around me the wrong way, and when I reappeared, I appeared right on top of the couple. They squealed as I squashed them and sent us tumbling into the river.

Fighting the current was like swimming in air; my limbs powered through the water effortlessly. I easily found the man. I caught him and squeezed his skull until I crushed his brain storage unit so he wouldn't be able to send messages for help. I opened my mouth and attempted to pierce his neck, but the skin of his body was too tough and it sent a dull pain up my fangs. I would have to slash him open, using the water as cover, without losing any of his blood. I willed the water away from his neck and peeled it open, sinking my teeth into his jugular. I drank hesitantly, bracing myself for the gross tang of artificial blood, but it tasted effervescent, like bubbles in champagne. I drank faster and harder; his limbs never even had time to twitch.

I let go of his corpse and rushed after the woman, who was flowing downstream. Her panicked eyes met mine, and I quickly crushed her brain storage unit, too. I ripped open her neck and drained her, my mouth frantically digging in her jugular. In the midst of my feeding, I gagged, realizing I was overstuffing myself. But the bloodlust fueled my body, and I couldn't stop. I was coughing up her artificial blood and reveling in the taste, drinking more and coughing up more. When I was done, her corpse also gently floated away. Her husband had fully fed me. She... well, she had been for naught. The muck of the Danube soon hid her from sight, and I emerged from the water, sorrowfully putting two notches on the ring I now wore on a chain around my neck. It did not fit my finger anymore.

I reported to Dr. Farkas the next day, too ashamed to look her in the eye. I still felt queasy from the overfeeding. When I finished talking, she smiled, and said, "It looks like the treatments are working. Hurrah!"

She threw her head back and as she did the wounds on her

neck opened. I smelled her blood. It smelled of rot, of mold, of every putrid thing in the world rolled into one. I almost vomited. She noticed and approached me again, baring her neck for me. I stepped away from her.

"It is truly working. When word of this gets out..."

I interrupted her. "Remember, at the very beginning when we first started talking about this. I said I could influence people's minds and have them celebrate your research. I can still do that. All you have to do is ask."

A flash of relief lit up her face and was quickly replaced by a scowl.

"No. I don't want you to. A few years ago, maybe. But not anymore. My research has proven more effective than even I thought. I don't need anyone's approval. I don't need any fame. My legacy will live on through you."

I was about to interject, saying that creating me as her twisted masterpiece of revenge and justice on her species wasn't really a good payoff of the bargain for her, in my opinion, but we winced as simultaneously our NNN connections flared:

Breaking news from Neighbor Neural Network! An unprecedented number of cancellations for Fearless Starfarer were made after a record number of people died in what appear to be Conscience Transplant Bodies related complications due to malfunctioning brain storage units. As numbers continue to come in, it appears that today alone some ten million people have succumbed to this mysterious software failure. We are advising that anyone with a CTB go to the nearest lab and have your software upgrade checked, even if you are showing no symptoms. Those of you with tickets for the Fearless Starfarer, be aware that the company may change their terms and conditions regarding cancellations; you are advised to hold onto your tickets and honor your reservations.

NNN clicked off.

Dr. Farkas snorted, then sighed. "I knew it. I always knew it. Throwing away everything organic and placing our conscience into a machine was begging for trouble. We are reaping what we sowed. Mark my words, this will be catastrophic." Then, to me, she added, "We need to hurry. We may have even less time than we think."

Her jaw was set, and that fire burned in her gaze. I truly hoped she was dead wrong.

Dr. Farkas was right. The malfunctioning of ACT's brain storage software became an epidemic. By the end of that week, a quarter of Earth's population had died. Nothing could be done. People were scrambling to change their ACTs, but there were no guarantees about the new ACTs, and many people died from the attempted transfer from one to the other.

At one point, I was in the Fusionner when I heard Dr. Farkas talking to someone else.

"They tested me, Mom," a woman's voice said, wavering. "I tested positive for software failure. It could happen any day now. They don't know when. And there is nothing they can do. I just wanted to say... I'm sorry. For treating you the way I did."

"Get out," Dr. Farkas said. "The only reason you're apologizing is because you're dying. Where have *you* been while *I've* been dying? You didn't even come to see me."

I tried pushing away Dr. Farkas's anger, but it was useless. My vampiric telepathy and the new adaptations made it too hard to disassociate.

"I am sorry, ok?" Farkas's daughter said. "I shouldn't have cast you away. It's not an excuse but there's been a lot going on."

"Too much going on to see your mother," Dr. Farkas said flatly.

"It's not just that. I didn't want to deal with your... your weird theories and experiments. You see people as numbers and statistics. You're a people user, Mom. You always have been. But... But I should have accepted that...instead of—"

"You are the user, Meredith. You took and took and took while your useless father ran off and left us alone. I raised you, counseled you, educated you all by myself. And yes, I do see the world differently from you. It's how I have survived for so long."

"Yet you—"

Dr. Farkas raised her voice. "I did what I could for you. And what did you give back? The silent treatment, years without calling, talking bad about me to anyone who asked."

"You've mentioned some pretty unethical stuff, Mom, about—"

"I don't have time for this. I'm not getting lectured by anybody today. I'm on the verge of a breakthrough. I'm sorry you're dying. Oh, well. Death is a lonely process. Death leaves behind loneliness. You're finally learning that lesson, at least."

The voices stopped.

When I exited the Fusionner, I asked Dr. Farkas if she was ok. There were no tears. She responded stonily, "I am perfectly fine."

"Death is lonely?" I said, bewildered. "You're hardly lonely. I'm helping you out. I'm your instrument of justice."

"Who's the idealist now?" she smiled thinly. "Yes, you're helping me. But in the end, I'll be dying alone while you become immortal. The pain will claim me, my body will fail. A body I worked so hard to keep sacred. It won't matter because it will die and rot, and my conscience will be lost."

"I wish I could help more," I said.

"You can't. Move on. Now, let me see how your body is adjusting."

I continued to change, my nose becoming two tiny holes in my face. No need for smell on the planet I would be on. My teeth grew into two long thin needles capable of piercing ACTs' bodies. My skin veered to a dull gray tone and hardened so I could camouflage myself among humans.

Dr. Farkas claimed that the final step was "brushing" all the DNA together in one last sweep in the Fusionner. This, she said, would be the most painful and risky part. The day had come, and delaying would serve no purpose. So I groggily agreed.

I picked myself up from the cold, hard floor and walked unsteadily into the Fusionner. I heard the multiple clinks as sheets slid into all the outer slots. I focused on my own body and my identity. I was Adolam. A vampire about to become truly immortal, if everything worked as it should. I refused to think about the possibility of failure. Or worse, that there would be no one to feed on if more humans succumbed to the ACT defect.

Dr. Farkas's voice trickled through the walls of the contraption.

"It is fighting me today. Strange."

After a pause, she continued.

"I was thinking... If the process goes through smoothly for you, then I could become immortal after all. You could turn me, and I would survive any adaptation. All I'd have to do is take your DNA, which is comprised of your original vampiric DNA and the human DNA I've transfused into you, and inject it into me."

"Oh, no, Dr. Farkas. You do not want to be what I am.

You never had a chance to be a normal vampire. That was frightening in itself. To become the hybrid I am now would be too much for you."

"You think I can't handle it?" she snapped.

"No. Being a vampire is monstrous."

I know that! she yelled, though not aloud.

Do you? I thought back at her.

Yes. I know you kill people. I know how *you kill them. I know how you will kill them after this brushing process.*

It's one thing to say it, it's another thing to do it.

The possibility of immortality is here, Adolam. For you and *for me. I don't see why I should cheat myself out of it now that it's a possibility.*

Death is preferable to the life I lead. I wasn't given a choice.

But you took a chance to continue your immortality when we started working together. You didn't want to die any more than I do. Don't be a hypocrite. Leaving a legacy would have been all right, but now, knowing that you will become the perfect immortal killing instrument and can turn me... I wouldn't have to die. I could become another natural part of the ecosystem without violating my body.

I thought you *said death was natural. You're being a hypocrite, too.*

She tuned me out and yelled, "The brushing process is beginning."

A series of grunts and expletives came to me, but I didn't acknowledge them.

A light pulsed its way into existence around me, slowly flaring to a brightness that would have destroyed a normal human being's eyes. Filaments and clouds of dark matter popped out of the light, flexed and bent around my body, massaging my every limb in ways that left me feeling emptier yet fuller than I had ever been. It squeezed me horizontally and vertically, and a prickling started, in my toes first, then in my head, before working to the middle.

The prickling became pain like that of one being skinned. I knew the sensation. I had fallen on remote populations in Australia once in my early travels and had suffered through part of their torture before I came to full control of my vampire powers. I wanted to mentally reach out to Dr. Farkas and ask what she was doing, but I couldn't think clearly. I tried to rein in the panic, but it spread inside me, as surely as the light that was melting my eyes.

A crack like broken glass echoed loudly, and a piercing shriek surged and peaked. A blast erupted around me, and my body cracked apart like an egg, my innards shockwaving out into nothingness.

I died. My body was no more. Yet... Yet I could think. Better than before.

A bubble of darkness wrapped around me, and I reached out with my mind. The bubble expanded and expanded until I stopped to analyze what I was feeling. Stardust, atoms of every living and nonliving thing in the cosmos, each as precise and clear as a strand of hair, all wriggling in me. It *was* me. I was this nebulous cloud of elements. The dying, carbon-choked atmosphere of the Earth was also me, and the emptiness of the stars throbbing all around me. A new feeling wiggled its way in, and a clinical, awed, familiar sensation burgeoned into being. It was a woman I knew well—her wonder of the world around her; her insatiable romanticization of vampires from memories brought down from generations and generations of overly avid storytellers; her disgust at the useless deaths of the human race and the destruction of the Earth. Anger at her daughter and former husband. Scorn at the nature of the human race. But she was not dying. That acrid, weak scent of her was gone.

Dr. Farkas, I thought, and her mind connected immediately.

Adolam. An accident happened. Terrible. I'm not sure what happened.

Terror and marvel trembled—hers.

Are we dead? Are we alive?

Her thought probed its way across the cosmos and inward. I bobbed along gently, focusing my awareness on the Earth. More humans were dying from the software upgrade defect. Their life essences switched off, as if cut by a blade in swaths. At this rate, there would be no more humans left, besides the paltry thousands who had chosen not to have their conscience transplanted.

Dr. Farkas's awareness was pulled by mine, and said, *We are celestial. We are* everything.

Tiny stabbing sensations flew past us, and her awareness latched onto one. She absorbed it, and a new awareness sprouted into being, an awareness of memories completely alien to me, yet as it became us, it was as if it had always been a part of us. A human conscience, full of rigid beliefs, and small gaps of a childlike mind that had been begging for release for years.

More. More. More. Those tiny stabs hurtled out, and we latched on to as many as we could. Souvenirs, thought processes, visual echoes, compressed and squished into one big cloud. The Earth's humans winked out and were born again with us, as us, like us, they were us. Dr. Farkas's anger, cold efficiency, and rage at death were gone. My individuality, my predatory nature had disappeared. Humans needed to be culled, yes. Humans would never change. Humans were food. Humans betrayed each other. But we were all becoming one. We could all together become a better species. Collective power was uniting. No need for superiority anymore; everyone was invincible. Vampirism was weak. Had always been. There was no power in one.

Which thoughts were mine?

Which ones were Borbála's?

Which ones were the humans we were saving?

I could not tell.

If Dr. Farkas could laugh, she would have. Her awareness glowed incandescent with triumph. *Our* awareness hummed with power. We all thought, *We are all immortal. The human race is no more. Now, a new one begins.*

One that surpassed any physical constraint or body, any boundary of time. We were the species of everything, for all time.

Girl at Sea

I am your mirror, Oneira. Your every thought, dream, and behavior are reflected back at you. Don't forget that," her mom intoned, her eyes focused on the floor-length mirror in front of them in the living room.

How could I forget? Oneira thought. *You tell me almost every day.* She wrapped a coil of copper-red hair around her finger and worried it again and again as her mom continued.

"Everything you do, I will do back to you."

Oneira flinched. She knew that too well. Even as a little girl, she'd known if she threw a tantrum, her mom would throw one, too. If she lied about something, her mom would lie back to her. If she made a mistake in the kitchen, her mom would ruin dinner when it was her turn to cook. The only difference was that strictly speaking, instead of replicating it exactly, her mom would increase the severity of her "crime" by tenfold. It was all a pantomime. A farce to hurt Oneira's feelings. Not that she would ever tell her mom that it was working.

Standing here, in front of that blasted mirror, reflecting Oneira's whey face and her puffy eyes, and her mom's proud upturned face and her saggy body encased in a fluffy bathrobe, Oneira wanted to scream. But she couldn't. She just wished she'd never brought up the idea of going to the store by herself, a store only two miles away from the beach. All she'd wanted was to buy some jewelry and a little something to honor the seventh anniversary of her father's passing.

The few friends who still dared to call, if they could get past her mom's Cerberus-like guard of the telephone, spoke of the things they did, tried to invite her to go places with them. But usually around the time the conversation got interesting, Oneira's mom's five-minute timer would go off and she would cut the phone conversation. House rule.

"You will never speak of this again. Your place is here at home. Taking care of me, as is your duty. Remember, if you whine or get angry, I will simply copy you. Because..."

"You are my mirror," Oneira said sufferingly, her stomach in knots.

"Good." Her mom softened, her onyx eyes losing their predatory glint. "You are an okay kid. Too much of your father in you. But I'll fix that. Give me a hug," her mom said, her arms outstretched.

Oneira took a little too long and her mom shifted, her lips tightening. Oneira hurried and gave her mom a sloppy hug.

Afterward she rushed to her bedroom and threw herself back into mapmaking. Her rough sketches and pens waited for her patiently. She looked in a blur of tears at the paintings of lighthouses on her walls, her collection of nautical ounce coins, ethnic masks and rugs her dad had brought back from his travels. So much for her ever travelling like him. She never got out of the house by herself. Her mom always had to come. Oneira was fifteen. She could go out on her own, she knew it. But it would never happen without her mother's permission.

She pushed the historical maps on her bed away and capped her pens with shaking hands. Seven years. Seven years since her dad had passed away. If he were here, this house would be alive again. Joyful. Semi-joyful at least. Her mother had always had her dark moods. Only her dad had been able to quell those moods, when she let him. But no, he had to get lost at sea and never come back. Transforming her once fairly mellow mother into a husk of her former self. Leaving Oneira stranded in this ancestral home on the beach. Lost at sea while solidly on land.

Changing her mind, she grudgingly pulled her half-finished maps to her and added real-life details: landmarks, roads, and secret treasure troves. This land had had many hidden pirate spots back in the day. People avoided the beach because rumor had it that many a pirate, escaping the Old World, had gotten lost here in the cove and died, either from mutiny or starvation. Odd occurrences littered the cove from as early as the 1600s: bright patches of light in the waves during pitch darkness, almost like St. Elmo's fire, but more ghostly, more translucent and wicked; murmurs and echoes of men's voices floating above the cove like entities; strange cloud formations reminiscent of apocalypses; lava monsters streaking across the volcanic sand in the hours leading up to the dawn. There were more, but these were enough to keep both tourists and locals away. A few deaths took care of the treasure hunters and thrill seekers quickly.

Oneira's mom used to walk on the beach with her. But since her dad's passing, it was as if his ghost had joined the legends and chased her away. Oneira wanted to go on the beach for a walk. She didn't mind the whispers, the clouds, the ghosts. She perused her maps again, noting with despair that her proportions were slightly off. She added some shading and more hidden spots for treasures and booby traps. She closed the historical map books. She only ever needed them to look up some details she wasn't sure of. She liked making her own maps, even if they weren't perfectly to scale.

The house phone rang. Oneira bolted, flying to the kitchen. Before she could reach it, her mom arrived and answered the phone.

"Hello. Who is this?"

After a pause, her mom said, "She doesn't want to talk to you right now. Please don't call back." Her mom ended the call.

Oneira's eyes widened.

"That was Jessica. I don't like her. I guess she hasn't figured out that calling is useless."

Oneira refrained from saying that she liked Jessica, and that her friend was one of the few who still kept in touch after Oneira's dad's passing. Nothing she'd say would make a difference. She'd learned that.

"Go back in your room and play," her mom said, adjusting her bathrobe. She sat down and looked through her address book for someone to call.

Oneira swallowed her ire and stomped to her room. She took one look at the maps and grabbed them like she was going to rip them apart. All she'd ever wanted was to travel. To go with her father on his trips; to sail into the ocean during a storm; to find unique artifacts and spread rumors about their magical nature. She wanted a squad of friends to come with her and be her pirate crew. They would be good pirates. The kind that found and restored artifacts; discovered new populations; cleaned up the ocean along the way. Never having a home on land, constantly looking to the horizon.

Why did her dad have to die?

Too much self-pity, she thought, anger collapsing like leavening bread. *I need to go out.*

She was supposed to tell her mom where she was at all times. But she didn't want to. No. Today she would sneak out and tread in the water, and say a private prayer to her dad, wherever he was in the fathoms of the deep.

She walked across the sand, its sharp brittleness mildly uncomfortable on her feet. The waves roared back and forth, protesting at the gray sky, at the fog that clung to everything like cobwebs. A wall of secrets, hiding the horizon from view. Oneira pulled her hair back to stop it from getting into her mouth. Her rain jacket squeaked against her jeans and latex crop top. The damp tickled her bare stomach. She walked head bowed for a while, memorizing the trail she'd left behind on previous walks. The waves teased her feet, swiping across her toenails delicately. The cold gave her goosebumps all the way up her nape.

She looked up finally and was met with a fog tsunami staring broodingly at her. Its massive girth spread across the sky, vertically and horizontally, threatening if one didn't know better. A wall of slate blue curling and spreading the more she looked. She laughed at it and sat on the beach.

"I miss you, Dad," she said out loud, wishing the tsunami fog would come and claim her. "I am so alone. Mom is alone. I think that's why she gets mad so much."

Oneira swallowed.

"I don't think you're really dead. I think you are an elemental. Like those things that Ariel becomes in Grimm's story after she dies. That's not really death, though. If you're part of the skies and the earth, you're not dead.

"I want to see you. Find you one day. I want to go traveling. Make and keep my own friends. I want to be free. Is that too much to ask?"

She always expected a response. None ever came.

"I drew these." she said, showing her maps to the sea. "I remember some of the secret paths and legends you told me about.

"Here is Grommel's Lair," she pointed. "Hidden behind

the Rocks of Bain. The seaweed and shelves of dried lava cover his stash. And here is the Gynell River, the one that Driv got lost in and where his ship sank."

She kept showing her maps until the endless rumble of the sea washed her voice away.

Oneira hugged herself, clutching the maps to her chest. She should go home. Go home, be an obedient daughter and wait until the next anniversary. Hoping and praying that her life will have improved.

Suddenly the fog was all around her. She couldn't see anything past the tip of her nose. She waved a hand in front of her trying to dissipate the fog, but it did nothing. Wind tore the maps from her hands. She cried out, reaching for them. But the maps were gone.

Bright patches of light danced and twinkled in the fog. It was hard to tell if they were on land or out at sea. They shimmered and waved, like old friends. She reached out, trying to get close to the water.

A force yanked at her, from the inside, like something had hooked behind her heart. She stumbled forward, rasping. The fog trailed away from her in a shining snake of pale green light. She breathed in, and it grew, thickening and sparkling more.

A weight sank in her rain jacket pocket. Before she could touch it, her mom's voice pierced the fog.

"Oneira! Silly girl. Come here. You are going to get yourself killed."

A flashlight glared in her face. Rough hands pulled her away from the water, smoothing away the damp hairs from her cheeks.

"Come home," her mom said, worry blanching her face. "It's dangerous tonight. Storms are coming and so is high tide."

Her mom actually trembled a little as she led the way. Wordlessly, Oneira let her mom lead her back to the house.

Oneria only discovered the bottle a few days later. She was organizing her clothing, throwing out some that were too small. She took her rain jacket off a pile on the floor and prepared to toss it in the closet. Its heaviness surprised her, as did the clink that echoed as it bounced against her hip.

She dug inside the pockets, her hands finding and pulling out a scratched little bottle, its cork worn to a nub. Fancy carved insignias adorned the blue-green surface of what seemed to be a gin bottle. Oneira's eyes latched on to the pearlescent smoke undulating inside. As she tipped it, the smoke shifted, creating patterns and shapes that were almost tangible. She brought the bottle close to her face, and the smoke clutched at the side, grasping at her misty breath. She gently tapped the glass and the smoke disintegrated, before coalescing again shyly.

"What are you?" she asked.

It glittered, dancing a sensuous dance that stretched from the cork to the bottom and back again.

Oneira debated in her head whether to open it, and the smoke recoiled.

She shook the bottle lightly, and the smoke drifted toward her again.

"Should I open you or not?" she asked the smoke.

Again, it recoiled.

I guess not, she thought. *What am I doing? What is this?*

The smoke—how could it not be sentient?—wriggled and started to glow. The glow warmed the bottle, enough that Oneira almost dropped it. The warmth radiated out and pulsed at her heart, the glow morphing from a pearly hue to a cascading gold. That warmth enveloped her, and a force gently yanked her head up. Oneira's eyes fell on a painting of the boardwalk downtown. The bright colors whirled and merged until she had to close her eyes to avoid getting dizzy. The warmth at her chest burned and she gasped, just in time to swallow sea mist. She opened her eyes and nearly cried out. The wooden boardwalk beneath her thrummed from the pressure of the passing waves. People walked all around her, talking to each other, pointing out sights with their binoculars. Little kids thundered around, screeching and playing tag. Someone touched Oneira's arm and she shrieked.

"Oneira!" her friend Jessica said, her eyes owlish behind her horn-rimmed glasses.

"Jessica," Oneira breathed. "You're here?"

"Of course, I'm here, silly. I invited you remember."

Oneira stammered, but Jessica didn't give her a chance to respond. She was off in a blur of pink cargo pants and ash-blond hair. Oneira got dragged all the way to the beach and got handed a bag.

"What are we supposed to do with this?" she asked.

"Collect seashells. Whoever gets the most exotic seashells will get a prize! Oh, and it's timed, so hurry up!"

Oneira took a quick glance at the other people on the beach, bags in hand, looking expectantly at a man standing on the lifeguard chair. He looked at his watch and said, "Get ready, get set, go!"

Everyone threw themselves into a flurry. So did Oneira, though her thoughts jumped erratically. What was this? How was this happening? Was this magic? If it was, it was a whole other level beyond anything she'd ever imagined.

She combed the beach furiously, occasionally bumping into other people. She expected them to yell at her, but they just worked around her, some laughing off the collisions.

Eventually, the man called out, "Time!" and everyone stopped hunting. Neither Jessica nor Oneira won.

"Come on," said Jessica. "Let's go to the ice cream place down the street."

"I'm not hungry—" Oneira began, shoving a couple shells into her pocket, but again Jessica dragged her away.

They arrived at the shop, and to her astonishment, Oneira saw her friends from elementary and middle school in all stages of gangliness, acne, and trendy clothing. They swarmed her and she grunted as they squeezed her in a group hug.

"Oneira! Haven't seen you in forever!" squirrely Martin said, wearing his hoop earrings as always.

"I've missed you all... so much," Oneira said quietly.

They ordered cake batter and caramel swirl ice creams, Oneira with a waffle cone, Jessica with a sugar cone. As they slurped their ice creams, Oneira couldn't get over the situation. To have all her friends together in one place. To be talking about the future like she wasn't going to be stuck with her mom her whole life.

"What are you going to be doing in five years?" Jessica asked Oneira, crumpling her cup in one hand.

Oneira felt her world shrink and tighten. An emptiness that stretched beyond measure. She knew what she wanted to do. "Be an explorer and travel the world. Go to college and use scholarships to go to new countries. But I'll never be allowed to leave town. Never allowed to leave my mom."

She hadn't realized she'd spoken out loud until Jessica replied with, "Why can't you just leave and follow your dreams?"

Why can't I? Oneira thought.

Gray smoke wafted in front of her, snaking to her heart and obscuring her vision. When she blinked, she was back home, standing by her bed.

"What was that?" she asked the smoke moving around in the bottle.

It wasn't until later she found the seashells she'd gathered with Jessica in her pocket.

It took a few tries for her to master the gift of the bottle. She'd found that if she tried too hard, the smoke entity would curl up at the bottom of the bottle and refuse to budge. If she let her thoughts wander, it would become alert, dancing up the sides.

She had multiple adventures.

She was a mermaid, swimming the seven seas; she was a snorkeler off Australia, talking to sharks and whales; she was a lifeguard in Sarasota, Florida, directing people to safety; she was an old salt, weathering storms in the Atlantic; she was a denizen of Atlantis, reading magical texts before the flood came. One time, she even talked to someone who looked so much like her father, she returned crying uncontrollably well into the evening.

Each time she was sucked out of her room, when she came back no time had passed. She started a collection of mementos: spiral shells, frayed ropes, faded colored cloth, and foreign texts. At no point did she ever feel in true danger.

As her joy grew, so did the smoke entity's glow. Seldom gray anymore, it sported the color of crushed up seashells and nacre. Sometimes Oneira fell asleep with it, cuddling it like she would a pet.

Her mom stomped around more and more, casting dark glances at her.

"You look way too happy to be up to anything good," she would say. "Is there anything you need to tell me?"

Each time, Oneira said no.

One bright sunny afternoon, Oneira sat on her haunches and checked the new maps she'd made. The sun dappled the bottle next to her in puddles of scintillating light. Driv had made his detour into the Squayle River in 1790. Rumor had it some of his men had stolen the treasure and thrown themselves off the ship to escape his insanity. With most of the crew gone, provisions low, and the ship barely limping along, the remaining men knew the end was nigh. So, they'd mutinied.

Captain Driv had been a tyrant, a brute with no consideration for his crew. His temper had even killed many of his most loyal men. Oneira didn't know if she'd have had the guts to mutiny.

She leaned back against the bedpost and added reeds along the river, more relief to the surrounding hills.

Her head drooped. A familiar warmth tingled through her, and she opened her eyes to a leering face, dripping sweat, prickly beard inches from her nose.

Oneira recoiled and shrieked.

She looked around wildly, and saw frightened men around her pretending to scrub the ship's wooden deck, angling and shifting away so they weren't in the way of the man standing straight in front of her. She was tied to the mast, thick cords digging into her ribs and wrists. The man growled at her, and she snapped to attention. His ragged flowy yellow shirt, ripped up breeches, and leather sash clinging together by a thread made him look simultaneously pathetic and dangerous.

"Where is it, lassie?" he asked, fingering his dagger.

"Where is...what?" Oneira squeaked out.

"The treasure!" he screamed, foul spit flying in her face. "I know you helped the others escape. When I find them, I will gut them and trail their organs around the ship as a reminder that no one crosses Captain Driv. But first," he unsheathed his dagger and pointed it at her, "I will start with you."

"I don't know where it is," Oneira repeated, still overwhelmed by the circumstances. It was hard to enjoy the slight rocking of the vessel, the smell of dirty crew, or the residual scent of alcohol from the barrels on deck; the living presence of actual pirates, with Captain Driv threatening to stab her.

"Liar! You *know* where it is. You know *where* they went. I will reward you if you tell me." The pirate sank back, returning his dagger to the fold of his sash. But he didn't take his hand away from the hilt.

Oneira yanked at her bonds, but they wouldn't budge.

"More riches than you can imagine once we are out of this accursed river..."

Oneira shimmied around but that didn't help either.

"Or I can cut off a body part one by one," Captain Driv said calmly. He drew his dagger again and placed its blade against her cheek.

Oneira trembled. "I do not know," she whispered.

The blade started cutting into her skin. It stung, but she didn't cry out.

"More?" Driv said, his wrinkles disappearing into his beard.

"No. I will not tell you anything."

He probably was going to kill her. It didn't matter. She one hundred percent knew that if she died now, if the bottle stopped protecting her, this was the way she wanted to go. Better to live and experience, albeit briefly, then to never have lived at all. And even though all of this had happened in the past, integrity was everything. She knew, with her modern-day knowledge, roughly where the treasure had been stashed. But this man didn't deserve to know her secret.

"Very well," Driv said, moving the blade to the top of her ear before starting to cut downward.

Oneira's guts heaved as he sliced and stars danced in her vision, sickening and faint.

When she finally screamed, she screamed to the calm disarray of her bedroom. She stopped screaming and sighed in relief. A whimper escaped her as the pain throbbed along the line of the cut. She touched it and her finger sank in the opened groove in her ear. Ribbons of pain lanced through her ear and face. Oneira reached out and scrambled at the bottle, smearing her blood all over it.

Her bedroom door slammed open, and her mom rushed in. "What happened to you?" she gasped, grabbing Oneira and steering hertoward the bathroom. She bent Oneira's head over the sink and ran cold water over the damaged ear. Oneira flinched and wiggled but her mom kept a firm grip. Finally, she dabbed at the wound and told Oneira to hold the towel in place.

"What were you doing?"

"I'm not sure," Oneira said.

Her mom raised an eyebrow. "Wounds like that don't happen randomly. You were doing something. Were you doing some kind of experiment? Some trick?"

"No! I am not sure how it happened, Mom," Oneira said weakly, her heartbeat increasing.

Her mom's face set and she searched in the cabinet drawers of the bathroom, behind the toilet, patted down Oneira's pockets.

She then went into Oneira's bedroom and rifled through stacks of papers, in drawers, under the bed, in the closet. Her ear still throbbing, Oneira could only watch in mute shock. Her mom's gaze fell on the bottle, and she reached for it. A deep rumble emanated from the bottle as soon as she touched it. The little smoke entity, so often close to white these days, flashed and turned black. Oneira ventured out of the bathroom and stepped back as her mom looked up at her. A thin black thread materialized and connected her mom to the bottle. Her eyes glowed black for an instant, then the thread was gone. Oneira's blood was smeared on her mom's hands, but she didn't seem to notice.

"You have been up to something. I will find out what it is."

She got up, with bottle still in hand, came back into the bathroom to check Oneira's ear.

"It looks worse than it is. I will bandage it and keep an eye on it."

Oneira nodded.

"I am going to keep this," she said, waving the bottle.

"No! Don't. Leave it."

Again, that strange black glow glittered then vanished from her mom's body.

"Why?"

"It's mine."

"I've never seen it before."

"It's still mine."

"What is yours is *mine*," her mom intoned, "Remember, I am your mirror." In the bathroom mirror, veins of black writhed, ghostly. Oneira's breath caught as she lunged and fumbled for the bottle. The smoke entity flared and morphed toward a shade of silver. It stuck to the side of the bottle Oneira was closest to. But Oneira's mom pushed her away.

It started with feeling tired whenever she got close to her mom. At the dinner table, doing chores, when her mom came in the bedroom to rant yet again about how the world was getting more messed up: how people were becoming more complacent with everything; how parents let their kids just roam free doing whatever they wanted; how families were becoming less and less supportive.

Her mom never let the bottle out of her sight.

Oneira caught her mom staring at herself in the mirror, touching her face as if she'd never seen it before. She started talking to people who weren't there.

After a week or two of strangeness, something snapped.

Oneira went to get the mail and her mom raced with almost superhuman speed to close and lock the door.

"I don't want you going outside," she said, jingling the keys and stuffing them in her robe.

Oneira threw up her hands. "I always get the mail. What's the deal?"

"You are not getting the mail anymore. Now or ever. You are staying here the rest of your life."

Oneira laughed nervously. "You don't actually mean that, Mom. I will leave home one day. Go to school, get a job, find somebody. Or get a pet and travel the world."

Her mom stepped toward her and grabbed her face with cold rough fingers.

"You will never leave."

The doors in the house all popped, as if they'd all been locked at once.

She dragged Oneira by her chin to the mirror. The infamous mirror where Oneira always got lectured.

"I am your mirror," her mother said. "A reflection cannot leave its mirror. What will you do without me anyway? We need each other. We *are* each other. But you are the better version of me. The me without loss."

Oneira tossed her head to dislodge her mother's grip. She was talking crazy. But Oneira couldn't break free. Her mother's grip tightened and Oneira gasped as her face shifted and roiled, like manipulated clay. Her round cheekbones morphed into her mom's angular features. Her eyes flashed from teal to the dark brown of her mom's. A humming black aura sizzled around her mother. This had to be the bottle's doing. Why was it making her mom so scary?

Oneira pushed her mom away, her face aching, her vision blurring and sharpening as her skin, her muscles, went back into place. She touched her cheeks, backing away from her mom. That awful black aura vanished, and her mom took a deep breath.

"Go to your room. Now."

Oneira obeyed, afraid the aura would come back.

She lay on her bed, faintly nauseous. What was going on? She knew her mom had issues. Always had. Her dad had been able to soften the rough edges. But Oneira lacked his special touch. She knew the bottle had magical properties. But it had never transformed her into something fearsome. Why was it giving so much more power to her mother?

Oneira jumped as her mom closed her bedroom door and locked her in. Oneira surged up, banging her fist on the door.

"Unlock it! Let me out!"

She got no response.

Oneira banged on the door some more and tried picking the lock. Nothing budged. A cold sweat prickled all over her skin. The nausea increased tenfold, and she breathed as hard as if she'd been running.

"I have to get out."

She looked for other openings, anything. But her room had never had a window. There was no other door to the outside world than her bedroom door. She opened her mouth to scream again, but she yawned instead. Her body sagged, she shuffled to her bed, laid down, and curled up to sleep. Quietly, a voice in the house said, "Stop fighting."

When Oneira woke up, she tried to stretch. She tried to get her legs out of bed. She tried to sit up. Each time, she fell back violently. The lights were still on. And as she craned her head to look at herself, she jerked, a keening sound leaving her throat. Massive black restraints of the same humming, threatening ilk as the aura that had surrounded her mom earlier wrapped around her arms, legs, and chest. She heaved up and down, trying to dislodge them.

But could she dislodge magical restraints?

She wriggled from side to side trying to slide her way out. But that didn't work either. Sweating profusely now, her heart thumping so loudly her head spun, she twisted around desperately. A heady sensation wrapped around her, forcing her eyes to close.

Stop fighting, a familiar voice said.

Oneira wanted with all her heart to listen to it. To just go to sleep and stop fighting. After all, what would fighting against her mom do? Her mom meant her no harm.

No! Her eyes popped open. No. This wasn't how this was meant to be.

She strained, her joints screeching in protest. She had to get out. Oneira thought of her dad, of her newfound confidence, of precious moments given to her by the bottle, of time spent with her friends. That was life how it was supposed to be, meant to be enjoyed, in freedom, in security.

The black vines of horror withdrew a little, wisping away in swirls of smoke. The black tint ebbed into a gray hue. Oneira concentrated harder, slipping free some of her newly loosened limbs. She thought of the feeling of ocean spray on her lips as she fished with her dad; throwing wet sand at her friends before rolling around in the surf; modelling for her mom in costumes made of seashells and fishing nets. Memories of simpler times, before happiness had become a shadow of a dream.

The restraints on her shimmered away, smoke lightening to white, like it had when it was still in the bottle, in Oneira's possession. Oneira vaulted off the bed and the smoke wrapped around her hand. She shoved the door open and tumbled straight into her mom. The smoke left her, Oneira felt it leave her as if it were yanked from her heart, ripping through her muscles and flesh. The smoke slammed into her mom who smiled at Oneira, the smoke, black again, filling her eyes and mouth with gags of dark thoughts.

Oneira stumbled back, horror dawning on her.

"What did you do? You released it, didn't you?"

Her mom shrugged.

"The bottle broke. Whatever was in there is mine now. As are you. You really think you can resist me? I am your flesh and blood. I am your mirror…"

Oneira felt that molesting touch start to mold her face again. She swatted at it and bolted around her mom.

"I am *not* your mirror. I will never be your mirror because I am my own person. Being your daughter doesn't make me your slave, or your puppet," Oneira spat.

The door leading to the beach. Where was it? Before her eyes, the hallway and rooms flexed and shifted as if they were melting into different things altogether. The paintings on the wall bled into each other, the stones in the wall drooped like wilting funeral flowers, the floors slid in a Machiavellian dance. Oneira planted her feet, closing her eyes to withstand the blurring of reality. She snuck an eye open and caught her mom with a frown of concentration, black wreathed around her entire body. The walls bent and groaned, hands forming to grab Oneira. Every trinket, every knickknack from past travels, items her dad had brought back, oscillated on their tables, shifting and lengthening into weapons, aiming at Oneira.

None of this was right. This would never happen. Nothing of her dad's would ever harm her. Her own home would never harm her. Everything her mom touched, she infected with her fears, her traumas, her grief, her vindictiveness. All her life, her mom had bent her reality. It had gotten worse after her father was lost at sea.

Oneira had one thing, and it was her reality. Her mom had no right to take that away.

"No," Oneira stated, and the house stopped buckling and twisting. "No. Not again, not this way."

Her mom let out a snarl and Oneira ran blindly to the door, yanked it open, and dashed out, running... running where? Her mom knew her hiding places. She knew her mom would hunt for her. Her tenaciousness was what had helped her survive the death of her husband, her sisters, her own father. Her mom had been assaulted, beaten, dealt with leukemia as a child. Life had taken Oneira's mom, ground her up and spit her out as a soul-wizened warrior. But it had also sapped her compassion, her trust, her affection. All she knew now was possession. After all, she owned Oneira. Had spent days in labor, which she never failed to remind her.

Oneira ran toward the ocean, not sure what she was doing. A storm was brewing, the clouds and waves gnashing against each other in palettes of black and gray. In a moment of panic, Oneira considered throwing herself in the ocean. Only then perhaps might she be free.

She squared her shoulders. *That was the coward's way out.* Her dad had brought her up better than this. Hell, her mom had taught her better than this, before her warped side had taken over, before her father's death.

Veins of ink bled through the sand, snaking toward her. Her mom was here.

Oneira turned to face her mom. The black haze surrounded her, as a shroud, scintillating with enmity.

"You can't run away, Oneira. You can't leave family. Family is forever."

Oneira squeezed her hands over her ears in pain. Wise advice corrupted by her mom's possessiveness... She couldn't stand it anymore.

"Stop talking about family like you know what that means!" Oneira shouted, her hair a copper tempest in the biting wind.

"Everything I've ever loved leaves me!" her mom bellowed, her face a mask of pain. "My sisters. My father. *Your father*. You want to leave me too. I can see it in your eyes." For a moment, the ravages of hurt streaked across her mom's face as lines of sorrow and grief. Then a rictus deformed it, as the black smoke swirled through her. "I will never let you leave! You are my precious daughter, my life. I need you. Your life is mine to do with as I wish. I will make you see that. Come here, honey," she said sweetly, but Oneira backed into the surf, the waves sticking her sodden skirt to her trembling legs.

As Oneira watched the black smoke, how it pullulated in her mom like a disease, she knew she would suffer the same fate. Her mom had ingested the entity and turning it into something formidable, threatening. She would keep Oneira and turn her into a dutiful pet, a living museum relic confined to the house until her death. Or worse. Corrupt her to see the world the same way she did: a personal faceless enemy that pierced the fake bubble of a haven she'd created out of lies and isolation.

"I will not," Oneira whispered so softly she was sure the wind and the crashing waves had masked her voice. Her mom stiffened and she spread her hands. The black smoke reared like a cobra and struck at Oneira. She flung herself to the ground and the tendril smacked the wet sand, making a thunderous noise. It reared and struck again.

But Oneira caught it with her hand. It vibrated against her, trying to wrap around her arm. She held firm and squeezed. "All my life you made me feel like I was an extension of you," she said to her mom. "I had no free will. That stops now. You are not my mirror. You never were. You are so broken you try to grab everyone else's identity. Keep them all for yourself."

Oneira had flashes of her mom screaming at her dad, trying to hold him back as he left, disgusted with her pleas to stay despite the drama she'd fabricated and lied about. Terminating lifelong friendships in a single phone call if her mom's friend didn't agree with her. Yet stalking them afterward and spreading rumors so they'd reach back out to her. Her mom adopting new personas after watching television shows. Tormenting Oneira as a child for not responding to her sudden mood swings.

The smoke quaked in her hand.

"You never let go of your grief and rage," Oneira said.

She tugged on the smoke, and it swirled out of her mom. Her mom screamed and tugged back. Oneira arched her back and planted her feet. She tugged and tugged, straining, panting, the rocky sand digging into her heels, the sea pushing back against her. Rain started pouring, blinding her vision. Her hands were in agony, her fingers sore, lancing with pain. She'd had practice when she was younger, with her friends, playing tug of war. She was strong. She could do this, though her mom seemed a titan of confidence and fury. That banshee scream continued, but Oneira chose to focus on the tense lullaby of the surf. She pulled and pulled, dragging more of that dark matter out of her mom. Her mom cursed and raved incomprehensibly, then started pleading. Oneira kept pulling. The smoke finally leeched out completely, as a massive black spider with legs so long it stood as tall as a Belgian horse. Oneira screamed once, her arachnophobia in full force, but she tugged the spider by one of its legs. She flinched and yanked it with all her might, tossing the entity into the ocean waves.

"Go away," she shouted.

She looked at her mom, who'd crumpled to her knees, staring with dead eyes at the ocean.

Black smoke exploded from the surf, the spider flailed about, turning gray, then white, then a nacre color as it spread like a puddle in the waves. It became ripples of light, light so bright it was like the reflection of the moon. The light shimmered and jittered, then bounced into the sky like a merry entity, soaring into the clouds, lining them with silver and white sparkles. It flew down again and crashed into Oneira, who fell on the sand, winded, holding her stomach. It writhed around her, an angelic glow buzzing with energy. It seemed to want something. Something more.

Oneira crawled to her mom despite the pain and cradled her to her chest awkwardly. Her mom let herself be handled, wordlessly, her limbs limp.

"Heal," Oneira cried, tears leaking out. The white entity sprung from her and pulsed at her mom's head. It did not change color. Finally, it drifted away and evaporated. Her mom collapsed like a rag doll, her face blank. "You are fear, but you are joy, too. You are confusion, but hope. Excitement, but sorrow. As it should be. Everyone had darkness inside of them. The trick was to remember to triumph over it. You have to. Because the alternative is to drown." Oneira hugged her, rocking back and forth, like the waves, like the lament in her heart.

"Heal," she sobbed, unaware that the smoke had returned, sinking into her from behind, as a gray being rippling, undulating with specks of pure white light.

ReGroup

Today was the day Dhriti, formerly known as Delia Robinson, would post her broadcast of her yoga lesson on social media. She hummed to herself as she cleaned her studio, wiping down mats, turning off the meditative music, and moving tables back where they belonged. Her frosty blond hair clung to her cheeks as she bustled around, winded from the Breath of Fire exercises she'd had her students do earlier. Usually, she worried that some of her students might pass out. Some usually quit and sat back as the others continued. But this time, none of her students complained about the exercise or fainted.

She smiled. She'd given up on the usual social media: Instagram, Facebook, Twitter, TikTok. She'd trashed her blog many moons earlier. But a new social media site called to her: ReGroup. It was a cross between a website/blog and a normal social media feed. It allowed users to stand out, at least, in Dhriti's opinion. It was a classy social media site, where it finally seemed no privacy was violated, and where there were no rules.

Perfect. Rules constrained freedom of speech, and constraint of speech led to misalignment of the chakras.

She needed to prepare her items for her end-of-the-lesson demonstration where she showed what foods and drinks were best for each chakra. Let's see, perhaps she should focus on one chakra per video. Make it easier on the newbie audience. Today, she would choose the solar plexus chakra. After all, she'd only just recently aligned that particular chakra for herself. She lifted her shirt and looked at the flabby skin and stretch marks on her stomach. Then she touched her arms, her neck, her breasts. She had once been morbidly obese. She had been reliant on an electric scooter to move around in stores. Her doctors had given her strict instructions to lose weight asap or she would develop full on diabetes. She had hit rock bottom after her miscarriage four years ago. But by sheer force of will she had overcome, all by herself, even after her partner left. She had succeeded and she could teach what had saved her life: yoga. She would forever be thankful to Yogini Layla for her advice. Well, now it was her turn to save so many desperate lives through the net.

She connected to the ReGroup site through her tablet, a special trapezoidal black unit with USB connectors. She uploaded her video and while it processed, she typed her information on to the "personal" page it showed to her: *@Dhriti: She/Her | #yogawarrior | A tough-as-nails survivor passionate about spreading peace into the community||*

She scribbled on a piece of paper some material she wanted to post in the next few weeks. Mantras, exercise demos, foods, and photos of her daily routines. She opened another tab on ReGroup and scrolled for other yoga influencers. There were a lot. Tough competition. Her lip curled. She would post outstanding content. She had no reason to worry too much. In time, people would flock to her; who knew, perhaps she'd make a living off her social media if she stood out enough in the yoga community.

———

Chef Gilbert cursed as he accidentally hid his profile on the ReGroup app. These icons all looked the same! If it were up to him, he wouldn't even be on the stupid site. He really should learn to say no to his grandson. Then again, if it weren't for his grandson, he wouldn't have half the equipment needed to film his many delightful culinary creations nor the precious 30,000 ReGroupees following his feed that he'd managed to amass in just a few months. Still, Gilbert wasn't comfortable around smartphones, much less the newer social media apps. ReGroup tried to keep its interface simple, so his grandson claimed, but Gilbert didn't agree.

He painstakingly found the setting to unhide his profile and he scrolled through the list of content he'd posted in the last week alone. Flashy photos of soufflés, roasts, soups, and gratins, all saliva-inducing meals he'd spent days buying the perfect ingredients for and setting up for his camerawork. He briefly glanced at the comments, mostly complimentary and admirative. As it should be. He had spent a lot of time perfecting these recipes, a lifetime's worth of time. Occasionally, an amateur would post how he would change the recipe. But pah! What did the younger generations know about these days?

The doorbell rang, and Chef Gilbert hastily put his apron on. That would be Timothé, his grandson. He was running the boy ragged these days; they filmed almost every day, most of the day. They had to film a lot today; twelve pastries and cakes Gilbert had made, ranging from a Grand Cru to a Saint Honoré. He wasn't sure it was the smartest retirement plan, but Timothé insisted it was the best thing for him. Gilbert privately thought he should probably start paying the boy. But each time he offered, Timothé insisted it wasn't necessary.

Without Timothé, he would still have to work for a living. Work himself to the bone and be taxed within an inch of his life. Without Timothé, he would have no retirement.

Abigail counted the carcasses with ease. She'd killed seven wolves today, all menaces to her neighbors' pens. A part of her cringed at the killing, but the logical part of her was proud. Ever since Montana had passed laws allowing open seasons on wolves, the number of livestock deaths had decreased dramatically. Her family's farm, passed through the generations since Great-great-great-grandfather Coulson, had finally managed to come out of the financial pit it had been in.

In his day, Great-great-great-grandfather Coulson had been a wicked shot. It was even rumored the Indians named him "Lethal Weapon," though Abigail surmised it might have been a joke. The men in her family had an interesting sense of humor.

As she went in the house to get the tools she needed to skin the carcasses, her phone pinged. She sighed and picked it up, despite the fur and blood on her hands. If it was Virginia asking her to babysit Lenny again... She loved the kid, but she had other things to do besides babysitting her nephew all week. There were only so many times she could sing the ABCs with him or play with toy trucks before it got old.

No, it wasn't a message from Virginia. It was David and Paul, two of her cousins, posting pics of her with the bucks she'd killed last week. She frowned. This wasn't a site she was on. ReGroup. Was it spam? No. Her cousins had profiles on there, and tons of pics, too. She didn't have a profile on there, though. Somehow, in tagging her, they must have created an account for her. She tapped on the photo. They had copied it over from the PM she'd sent them. Ordinarily she'd be annoyed they hadn't asked if they could share. But she had killed five big bucks, aggressive and challenging to hunt. That was no small feat.

Her eyes narrowed as the caption her cousins wrote jumped out at her: *@AbyGaby does it again. | But can she keep up her streak? | We challenge you. | #Mostkillschallenge.||*

Abigail laughed. She might be younger than them, but she could keep up her streak and beat them besides. Her ReGroup profile would be full of pics of her kills and wins. She clicked on her username and it gave her the option to claim her profile. On it, she wrote: *@AbyGaby | #Montanachick | Loves hunting, trekking, and family. And guns. Lots of guns. | I am joining the #Mostkillschallenge, tagged by @DavyG and @P1985G ||*

———

Akio ReGrouped the pictures of his grandparents. Within minutes, others had ReGrouped the pics, with comments like "Beautiful couple," and "Strong family despite the horrific era this took place in." Akio considered printing out the photos to bring to his class the next day, to show his students the context of World War II and how the Japanese were treated in the American internment camps. His grandparents were two out of many innocent people who'd been trapped in those camps.

As he sipped his coffee and waited for comments to roll in, he remembered his grandparents. As long as he'd known them, they'd been the most positive people he'd ever met. Yet their stories hurt his heart. Having to live with other families in the "Relocation Center," having rations day in and day out, and his grandpa having to travel thousands of miles to do seasonal farm work while his mother worked in the center as a teacher, all were but the surface of the hurt they'd endured. Sometimes, he wished he'd never heard the stories at all.

The racism still lingered. Some of his students still bullied each other over looks and ethnicity. He addressed it as soon as he saw it. But he knew the undercurrents of racism still ran at home. He wondered idly if he shouldn't skip showing the students the World War II Bugs Bunny cartoons altogether. Too much racism and too many stereotypes shown toward his people.

What was he thinking? Denying history wouldn't change anything. Right?

To settle his nerves, he prepared for his Sunday call to Hiroto.

Dhriti alternated between satisfaction and annoyance. Her ReGroup page was taking off, with mostly positive feedback. She had 10,386 subscribers. More joined every minute. She had a number of ReGroupees with stellar feedback:

@Meditateerin: You made my morning with your exercises. I am not sore anymore. I actually feel focused for the rest of the day. ||

@KaylaL23: You make it so easy and simple to find balance in yourself ||

@PeterLugo: I have shared this with my friends and we make it part of our daily routine to do yoga in the afternoons. ||

@WellsOqi: I have never felt as invigorated and relaxed as I have since I started following you. Thank you. ||

Many, many more bolstered her feed. There were a few comments, a few ReGroupees who poked fun at her or made some sexual comments. Those she deleted, but somehow a few always came back. She wished ReGroup had an option to block people, but that was impossible. ReGroup was all for free speech, no matter the content. Dhriti wasn't sure anymore if this was such a great idea.

No matter. She would get more subscribers. She'd already surpassed quite a few of the other newbie yogis who'd recently joined ReGroup. She posted daily as it was, and she intended to videotape her entire daily routine nonstop.

———

Chef Gilbert nodded his head as his page amassed more subscribers. His latest recipe, Tarte Tatin, had garnered him another 75,302 ReGroupees. He'd had the brilliant idea to post his recipe with a prompt: "Have you ever made this recipe? If so, describe the story behind it, or a memory dear to you involving the Tarte Tatin."

@Lovestocook: I made Tarte Tatin once and it was a disaster. We ended up buying a cheap cake at the patisserie. But I made Tarte Tatin again following your recipe. It was a success! ||

@Angelfoodcake: I remember having this as a snack growing up. It was my mom's fave treat. ||

@Yummynomnom: I made this with classmates when we went to France during high school for an immersion trip. ||

@BruceG: This recipe is soooo easy. I love how it follows the traditional recipe closely but you add your own personal touch to it. ||

@KitchenAdventures: Tarte Tatin rocks! I'm making this for my guests tonight. ||

@BoyBoyGirl: My husband made this for my in-laws and it's a hit every time. ||

Good. Cooking bringing people together, as it should. It made him happy so many people loved his take on the old recipe. Of course, he'd gotten a few ReGroupees who complained it wasn't purely traditional, but he ignored those.

He would continue posting his own recipes and adaptations of old ones.

He also ignored the ReGroupees of the ilk:

@LilyHert: A Tarte Tatin? Is that really a fancy dish? ||

@Americafirst: Not American. Support American recipes!!!! ||

@Truedeal: All of you saying you made a Tarte Tatin. You're lying. Only professionals can do that. ||

@Debunker: No room for amateurs here! Your pics r Photoshopped. ||

Abigail was running out of space on her phone. She had taken so many pictures of the tools and guns she used to hunt, it was maxing out her phone. She'd have to ask her mom if she could borrow her phone for a bit. She had killed so much venison in the few weeks since she joined ReGroup, her family was unable to use all the carcasses for food or houseware. She'd started giving her spoils to the neighbors, so as to not let it go to waste. They were quite grateful. She also didn't want to get busted for going over the kill limit. Silly rules. There were too many deer. She was really doing a favor to the environment. She made sure her subscribers online could see the pictures of her charity.

Her cousins had agreed to meet up today so they could all post pics of their guns together, as a family. Abby was excited. She was still winning the challenge Dave and Paul had started. Poor fools. She had the most ReGroupees of them all, too, 334,490.

She was surprised by the number of positive comments she'd received about her kills. Others had even posted some of their pics, in solidarity. Many more people were hunters and pro-gun than the media led one to believe. It was nice to feel supported.

@!Wisconsinrocks77: Awesome job! ||

@Loveguns486: You are a natural! What gun are you using? ||

@BanalHaley: We need more people like you. All these deer ruining things. Sick of running over them. ||

@Family1295756: Take that, snowflakes! A teen providing for her family and community! ||

@2ndAmendmenttree: Guns are our friends. Hunting saves lives. ||

———

Akio felt his lesson had gone over pretty well. The students had pressed for more details about his grandparents' experience, but he'd found himself incapable of providing them. A block had settled in his throat, effectively gagging him. Besides, they didn't need to know all the horrors his grandparents had gone through. Best to leave that in the past where it belonged.

Akio wearily pushed aside his stack of homework assignments and absorbed the after-school silence in his classroom. He opened his ReGroup app and scrolled listlessly through his feed. There were a few heated ReGroupees responding to his views on watering down history. He was starting to believe that first-hand accounts and experiences of history might not be the best tool for educating the younger generations. Families could talk to their children about it if they wanted to. But schools had to stop the cycle of generational trauma by moving forward and not circulating harmful thoughts from the past. Literature was too good a vehicle for propagating accounts of evil. There was no moral in history. Children needed a clear moral compass, and neither history nor literature provided an explicit one.

For his own sanity, Akio logged off. Still, the comments swam in his mind.

@Concernedcitizen1776: Your a retard! History repeats itself with or without your help! ||

@89Mommydear: You're ruining kids' education. Without a textured, detailed view on history, you're teaching lies. ||

@HaydenW: Ur a special kind of stoopid. ||

@LibrarianLilo: Erasing history is never the answer. ||

@Unknown: Resign! ||

@Partyfirst: Japanese freak, go back where you came from. ||

The comments were becoming too aggressive. History did repeat itself. He didn't have time for this negativity. He had too much grading to do. And he had to craft the rest of the lessons for the week. His ReGroupee following was at 200,724.

Dhriti blinked at the flashing neon pinned post that filled her entire screen whenever she logged onto ReGroup.

| Who is the Best Poster on Regroup? |
| Three simple rules:

- *You have to interact with as many users as possible. Keep your ReGroupees, and obtain new ones as fast as possible.*
- *Post new content as much as possible.*
- *You are forbidden from blocking or reporting ReGroupees. |*

| The best poster gets a cash prize of $50,000,000 USD, can be converted to other currencies. |

| The best poster will be the #1 in the SEO for eternity. ||

@gr8t23: Your channel is a sham. Yoga can't cure everything. You don't have a medical license, you aren't a doctor, stop pretending you are one. ||

@Dhriti: @gr8t23 | I am the best at what I do. Just because you're narrow-minded doesn't mean yoga can't help with serious medical issues. ||

@Haley1098: You are not a real yogi. You are not even Indian. You're whitewashing a sacred art, a science. ||

@Dhriti: @Haley1098 | Bugger off with your bullshit. Anyone can practice yoga. India doesn't have a monopoly on yoga. ||

@mommydear15: There are yogis out there with way more experience than you. Just give it up. You're good maybe for children. ||

@Dhriti: @mommydear15 | You are a sad, bitter person. Experience isn't everything. ||

Normally, Dhriti wouldn't have responded at all, but each ReGroupee she replied to gave her extra points on her profile. The point meter lay next to her profile pic, and it kept mounting. She breathed fast, adrenaline giving strength to her fingers. She would show them all, all the skeptics, all the hecklers, she would show them what she was made of. She deserved to be on this platform every bit as much as them. More, even.

She received a message from @KiriTengen1. Expecting it to be creepy or hateful, she pounced on it, ready to eviscerate the person. It started off with *Dear friend, I hope you remember me from school. It's been a while. I haven't forgotten about you. But life gets so busy.*

Dhriti stopped reading. It sounded like spam. Ignoring her habitual meditation, she turned the video camera on, ready to film another exercise.

As she did so, her ReGroupee count surged to 25,445. Her tablet thrummed, the site grew brighter, the light flared as if someone had lit a flamethrower in the dark. As the light grew, Dhriti sagged. Her chakras must have become misaligned again.

Chef Gilbert drank a long swig of Cointreau. It burned his mouth, but he didn't care. He glared vehemently at his computer. If he had to read another comment that he was a snob, that he should be nicer to amateur cooks, that he wasn't being diverse enough, he would explode. His grandson insisted he disconnect from ReGroup for a while. He would be damned if he'd lose all his subscribers and delete weeks' worth of work and time. No. He would stay. His point meter was skyrocketing. No one was going to get in his way. He was now at 195,125 ReGroupees.

He rubbed his sweaty forehead and ignored the pain in his chest. It had been happening more frequently lately. He was getting older. He was used to weird new pains.

In his head, he wrote his next few posts and recipes. A twinge of guilt plagued him as he thought of Timothé, neglecting his wife and newborn to come help him. No. He couldn't think of that. What mattered was that he win this challenge. He promised that once the challenge was finished, he'd disconnect from ReGroup. The ReGroup site flashed, throbbing like a heart, like an ex-lover clinging to a mate who was never right for him.

Abby laughed to herself as she scrolled past the insults and profanities on her posts. The flames weren't even about her hunting anymore. Some people had posted some coherent reasons to stop hunting so much. But the majority were crybabies, part of the anti-gun crowd so rampant these days. She'd figured out a way to keep her point meter high with minimal effort. She just posted memes to the critics on her page. She could keep doing it; you weren't allowed to block or report comments. She could be as offensive as she wanted. She fired off another pro-gun meme to a ReGroupee, as she crunched into a piece of bacon.

A new ReGroupee came in.

@Dhriti: You should be ashamed. Killing those beautiful animals for attention. ||

@AbyGaby: @Dhriti | I don't need your approval. ||

@Dhriti: @GabyAby | I'm pretty sure you're poaching. That is illegal. What you're doing is wrong and illegal. ||

@AbyGaby: @Dhriti | Oh boohoo, cry me a river. ||

She looked at @Dhriti's profile. One of *those* people. New age hack. She wouldn't waste more time. She had to hurry. She had more elk to hunt for the winter. She wasn't going easy on anybody, even her cousins. If they wanted to win, they had to step it up.

Her parents came into the kitchen but didn't talk to her. Maybe it was because she hadn't showered in a week. Or because talking to them took too much effort. Who needed them anyway when she had 825,099 followers? As her pride surged, so did ReGroup. Her phone was constantly hot to the touch. As the heat intensified, Abby's hands grew clammy. Her fingers didn't work quite right.

Akio put on some meditation music to quiet his anger. He dearly wanted to put on some old-school anime to relax. But he had to continue responding to these abysmal comments cluttering his page. Perhaps he shouldn't have said that censorship was a necessary evil to keep society moving forward. Or perhaps it was the petitions he'd put out, calling for the removal of "beloved" classics like *Gone with the Wind*, or *Huckleberry Finn*, or *Uncle Tom's Cabin*. He certainly had not anticipated reactions like these:

@9024Felix: People like u r the reason y our society is fucked. How can u think censorship is ever the right response? ||

@KalV: Sap. You call urself a history teacher? Resign. ||

@JoleneS12: Go back to Japan where you come from. Keep your fascist ideas over there. ||

@Littlestar76: I wonder what your grandparents you harp on about would think. You forget history repeats itself. ||

Akio conveniently blanked out from his mind his own responses, his own insults along the lines of "simpleton" and "racist." He didn't even have the energy to eat. He didn't want to call Hiroto. His friend would probably make fun of him anyway. He hadn't had the energy to call his friend in weeks. His laptop hummed angrily as he walked away to shower, turning up his music instead of logging back on.

Dhriti almost broke her ankle as she spun in her studio, filming every item, every book, every knickknack that helped her do her yoga. She was going to do every single exercise from every single book every day. Her point meter was at an all-time high. She was going to win this competition, damn it.

But first, she needed to respond to ReGroupees. That was where the true satisfaction lay.

@Dhriti: @Lilo24 | Give up yoga. You don't have what it takes. ||

@Dhriti: @JasonR | Women do yoga best. We have the virtues needed to truly practice it. ||

@Dhriti: @OompaLoompaeris | I am the best. The rest of you suck. You don't have my skills, my experience. ||

@Dhriti: @JillWard1 | All my chakras are aligned, thanks. Yours are not. Seek help. ||

@Dhriti: @Paramahansa | Yogananda has nothing on me. I am the best yogi of this age! The one who understands it all. The one with the clearest vision of the universe. ||

Dhriti filmed her responses to the ReGroupees, exaggerating her facial expressions to sell them. Her points and her followers increased. She was at 946,778 followers.

"I will not stop!" Chef Gilbert cried. Timothé glared at him, jangling his keys.

"Grandpa, I can't. I know you really need the money. But you're being a bully. I can't be with you twenty-four seven. My family needs me. Please. Stop. Get off ReGroup! It's unhealthy."

"No! I am not quitting. We came to this country and persevered despite everything being stacked against us. We do *not* give up."

"This contest is driving you insane. All you care about are the points. The followers. You're churning out recipes and videos like some madman. It isn't about the food. I don't want to help you anymore."

Chef Gilbert felt his blood pressure skyrocket, a pulse in his temples throbbing menacingly.

"Don't you dare! Family doesn't quit on each other. You are not allowed."

"Until you get off the app, Grandpa, I am not coming back."

Timothé sighed and walked out the door.

Chef Gilbert threw his pile of recipe books onto the floor. He stomped a few times for good measure and opened the app.

He'd made the mistake of contacting his ex-wife on ReGroup, hoping she'd support his page and help bring in more points. Instead, she'd used his page to rehash old drama. While it pushed his point meter higher, it made his ire grow exponentially.

@ChefGil: @Ada475 | You are jealous. Have always been jealous of me. I was a prodigy and you treated me like merde! ||

@Ada475: @ChefGil | You always thought too highly of yourself. Pompous ass. ||

@ChefGil: @Ada475 | I am the new Escoffier and you have no respect. ||

@Ada475: @ChefGil | Yeah right! And I am the Dalai Lama. Get over yourself. ||

As Gilbert prepared a blistering response, he gasped, and his vision swam. A pain blossomed in his chest. For a moment, his hand disintegrated and reassembled in motes of gray and blue. ReGroup's signature colors. The next moment, the pain was gone.

———

Abigail knew she was winning. After her recent ReGroup post about protecting the Second Amendment, her followers were now at two million! Her point meter was high, but only because of her posts to others. She had no real content anymore. She couldn't bring herself to go out and hunt. An immense lethargy weighed her down, keeping her bedbound. It was an effort to open the app and post.

From the corner of her eye, a blue and gray glow shone. Was it the app? It seemed to follow her whenever she moved.

You're out of control! Hiroto's voice haunted him. After their last conversation a few weeks earlier, Akio hadn't called back.

Remembering his most recent posts, Akio had to grudgingly concede.

@AkioSakio: @Playdohlover | You are losers. ||

@AkioSakio: @Kidally | Save the children! No one cares about protecting their innocence. ||

@AkioSakio: @MuseumofHumanity | Ban all historical books! No exception. ||

@AkioSakio: @ParentsoftheInternet | Protest! March! Go to your school boards, your local libraries, and demand the books be removed. ||

Akio didn't have that many new Groupees. Just a paltry 20,338 more. His point meter was middling. He did want to win, but it was tiring. He couldn't post fresh content all the time. Yet it galled him to see inferior teachers posting their content and getting more recognition. It wasn't fair!

Some deep part of him wanted to quit. He'd tried. He'd lasted four days. But even after deleting the app, he'd heard the whispery ding of the notification in his dreams.

The relapse had started with re-installing the app. Then checking posts. Then replying to ReGroupees. Then posting some pictures. And in no time, he was back in the game. He wished he could summon the energy to grade papers. He was severely behind. And he was oversleeping more and more. ReGroup purred in the background, tantalizing him, beckoning him to come back like the prey he was.

Akio fired off a nasty response to a bunch of his fellow teachers. He didn't care if he got terminated at work. They needed to be cowed into agreeing with him. No one said you couldn't cancel your colleagues.

His triumph evaporated as he stumbled onto his couch, his app dinging as ReGroupee after ReGroupee came on. His hand opened feebly, the phone falling. He sank back and fell into a deep sleep, a sleep so profound he didn't hear his phone ringing, with the country code eighty-one.

Dhriti wanted to weep. She was exhausted, lying on her mat all day, all energy gone from her body. She couldn't film anymore. She couldn't do her basic yoga warmups anymore without nearly fainting. Her point meter was plummeting.

Abigail couldn't get out of the house. She played with her gun, much to the despair of her parents. But she lay there, half awake, half asleep, dreaming of numbers, of followers, of that pleasing repetitive music that was her app notifying her of more ReGroupees. Her hands twitched in the air, as if assembling her rifle, even when her parents came to confiscate it.

Gilbert hadn't gone to the grocery store in more than a week. Timothé's calls went unanswered. He did a video call with his doctor as the pain in his chest intensified. His doctor, his face grey and grave, advised him to go to the emergency room immediately. Gilbert nodded, and slumped over at his desk, nose buried in a notebook of rectified recipes.

| *Hello?* || @AbyGaby asked in an echoing hall of gray fog. Faint blue veins snaked into the fog, flickering feebly. Gray arteries pumped slowly in that fog, gray sludge traveling steadily downwards, like a decrepit circulatory system.

Whispers, like tissue-thin paper crumpled and floating on a nonexistent wind, lent a peculiar flurry to this hall.

Beside her, another avatar formed, sneezing as his apron flew over his face. He had the diamond shape of the profile photo, typical of ReGroup.

| *Allô?* || @ChefGil exclaimed, walking through @Aby-Gaby. She called after him indignantly, but her voice was swallowed by the hungry silence of the hall. It stretched into a murky infinity, billowing like an ominous, sentient mantle. It waited, yearning for more souls, for souls to turn angry and unleash their potential.

An avatar appeared lying on the floor. He didn't stir. The others did not even see him. Blue and gray particles danced in the air, then coalesced into nothingness.

@Dhriti blossomed into existence in a swirl of scarves. She bounced and squealed, flopping on the floor, but as yet no one heard her or saw her.

| *Hello? | Anybody here?* || she called, picking herself up.

| *What is this place?* || she asked, shivering as the minimal warmth she had crawled out of her.

The last place she'd been was her couch. She'd taken a nap after railing against too many ReGroupees criticizing her profession.

Now it all seemed so trivial. What had been the point? Wasting precious time in the day to respond to people just to get points. For a stupid contest nobody would remember in a year. A contest that effectively brought out the worst, pitting ordinary people against each other in a spat for... points? Popularity? Sure, there had been the siren call of sweet, sweet cash, but in reality, with some normal hard work, @Dhriti could have monetized her posts.

For the first time, @Dhriti wished she'd actually read the fine print when joining ReGroup. What kind of social media platform was this?

What she needed was to meditate. She hadn't done that in a good long while. It might center her. As she focused her breathing, she lapsed into a calm state where she let her mind wander, trying to feel this place. This emptiness hid something. She was sure of it.

@AbyGaby wished she had her gun. Those veins of blue flickered again. then disappeared. Try as she might, she couldn't get the fog to go away. She waved her hands, jumped, screamed, but nothing worked. There wasn't so much as an echo. Surely she couldn't be the only person here?

@AkioSakio groaned as he got up. He flinched as the cold air hit him vigorously. Shivering, he stood up and rubbed his cheeks. As if his very skin were fog, it blended in with the chill mist around him. What was this place?

| *Hello?* || he asked. Waves of blue numbers flickered inside of him. For a moment, he saw human-shaped outlines, with those flurries of binary numbers flashing in the fog around him. Then, nothing.

| *Hello?!* || He wavered, his stomach roiling. Huffing, he lay on the floor again. He had been asleep. Of that, he was sure. This was just a dream. He just needed to wake up. Through lidded eyes, he forced himself to relax. Sleep, go to sleep. A vein of light throbbed and he opened his eyes, just in time to see a teenage girl walk into a familiar looking woman sitting cross-legged on the floor.

| *Ouch!* || @Dhriti exclaimed as a girl walked straight into her. She toppled backward and the girl cursed.

| *What are you doing on the floor?* || the girl asked scornfully. @Dhriti knew her username: @AbyGaby. The profile photo and the name were familiar.

| *Why did you walk into me?* ||

| *I didn't see you! You should have seen me.* || @AbyGaby said. |*You're one of those yoga nuts, aren't you? A yoga warrior.* || She rolled her eyes

| *That's on my profile. How do you know—?* ||

| *You're one of those who kept bashing me for my guns and hunting. I looked into you, lady, and you're nothing but a hack who—* ||

@Dhriti, finally realizing why the rude girl was familiar, said | *Abigail Sommers. You are my first-cousin-once-removed's childhood pal. He talks about you all the time.* ||

@AbyGaby looked like she softened, then went straight back into aggression. | *Maybe so. But I don't know you. Besides all the new age shit you put on your page.* ||

| *Listen here, you are going to moderate your language—* ||

| *Yogi Dhriti? Is that you?* || a soft voice said.

Both females turned around.

@AkioSakio pushed himself off the floor. He walked over and stood awkwardly.

| *You are Dhriti, right? My mom started following you recently. She also went to college with you.* ||

It took @Dhriti a moment to remember.

| *You are Akio? Akari's son?* ||

He nodded.

She felt annoyed. She'd tried to keep in touch with Akari after college, but after Akari went back to Japan the letters had gotten few and far between. Sometimes, there'd be a picture in the mail or an email, but that was it. Still. Hadn't she gotten a message from Akari on ReGroup recently? A long and heartfelt message about how positive her yoga was? In all the bustle of the social media aggression, @Dhriti had forgotten to respond. Worse, she'd thought it was a scam.

| *I am a teacher. Who are you?* ||

He turned to @AbyGaby. | *What is this place?* ||

| *I don't know!* ||

Out of nowhere, a figure burst forth, red in the face, yelling | *Anybody here? Help me!* ||

He wore a chef's hat and an apron. Nobody said anything until @AbyGaby exclaimed, | *Chef Gilbert? Is that you?* ||

The man stopped and stared haughtily. | *Who are you? Oh. You are @AbyGaby.* ||

| *How do you know that?* || she asked.

| *I can see it. I can see all your names.* || He turned and scanned the fog, trying to look for more people.

| *You're my grandpa's favorite chef!* || @AbyGaby said, straining to get a better look at Chef Gilbert.

| *Is he one of those idiots who thinks because he has some slight talent in the kitchen, he is a master chef?* || @ChefGil asked without even looking at her.

| *Hey! No, he just likes looking at your stuff and learning—* ||

| *Does he even have the proper tools? Can he make a good sauce? Can he make a perfect roast? Is there one thing he has mastered in the kitchen? No? Then he shouldn't bother.* ||

@AbyGaby flushed. | *You don't have to be an ass about it! You're not all that either! There are plenty of chefs better than you—* ||

@ChefGil and @AbyGaby gasped as they faded almost to nothing. Code filled the spaces where their forms flickered momentarily before snapping into place. Both avatars panted, like they'd run a marathon.

@AkioSakio put his hands over his ears. In agony, he cried | *Can you please just stop?* ||

| *Stay out of it! Who are you anyway?* || @ChefGil asked, squinting at him. Then his lip curled. | *You're one of those bleeding hearts who thinks history has to be sanitized to accommodate your precious sensitivities.* ||

The fog roiled around them all, gray and blue flaring, walls of fog closing in, gorging, expanding.

@AkioSakio jumped. How did he know? Then, as he glared at the chef, he saw a round-shaped blurb spin around @ChefGil | *Michelin Star Chef, bringing traditional French recipes to your dinner table. Cooking is an art, cooking is a skill learned by the best.* || There must be Akio's own blurb around him, touting | *He/Him | Woke teacher protecting the next generation from the horrors of the past* ||

| *Let me guess, you're one of those pompous chefs who thinks he is a god in the kitchen?* || @AkioSakio mocked.

| *I am! I bet you don't even know how to cook the native dishes of your country. I can, and they're not even my specialty.* ||

@AkioSakio blanched. He advanced slowly, wanting dearly to hurt the pretentious chef. As he walked, he stumbled and tripped, feeling his lungs struggle, his breath faltering. He flopped to the floor as he became transparent, code flitting through his form. A pattern was forming. As he struggled to breathe, an image struck him: an image of himself, slumped over on his couch, a book on his lap. Phone calls going unanswered in his apartment.

| *Where was the last place you were at before coming here?* || @AkioSakio asked.

@Dhriti blinked. | *I was in front of the computer. But I think I fell. My legs wouldn't work.* ||

@ChefGil sighed. | *I was talking with my doctor.* ||

@AbyGaby frowned. | *I was arguing with my dad. I think. What is this place? Hell? It doesn't look like heaven.* || She shivered.

@AkioSakio shook his head. | *Every time we fight, we...*

drain. We are code. When I look at you, you are like social media profile pics, complete with blurbs. Not people. ||

@Dhriti observed the fog around her. | *Everything here is gray. Sometimes there's some blue. Those are ReGroup colors.* ||

| *What are you saying?* || @AbyGaby asked.

| *Ever since the contest...* || @ChefGil hesitated. | *People have been falling into comas. Going into deep sleeps. There were news broadcasts about the vast majority being ReGroup users. But what does it* mean? ||

A long pause. | *I don't think this is heaven or hell. If anything, this is purgatory,* || @Dhriti said. | *When I meditated earlier, I thought I felt traces of other people. I felt myself back home, briefly. We need to get out of here.* ||

|*There can't be just us. I only know some of you because you were on ReGroup,* ||@AkioSakio said. | *There's got to be more people here. We've got to find them.* ||

| *How is that going to help? We need to get back to our bodies.* || @ChefGil protested. *This must be a dream. A night-mare, more accurately.* ||

| *We need to work together. I think that's the clue. The solu-tion. Every time we argue, we get weaker. I think we need to try to work together.* || @AkioSakio said.

| *We need to get out,* || @AbyGaby said. | *But trying to get out of here is like a maze. Plus, I can't see! The fog keeps me trapped here.* ||

| *You said when you meditated, you felt something.* || @AkioSakio said to @Dhriti.

She nodded. | *Let's meditate with you.* ||

@AbyGaby rolled her eyes. So did @ChefGil. But @Akio-Sakio followed @Dhriti's example and sat cross-legged on the floor. They held hands. And they meditated, trying to erase negative thoughts from their minds, trying to focus on feeling people, or an escape route.

@AbyGaby tried hitting the fog. She screamed and tried to

touch the walls, but she passed through like a ghost. Sobbing, she staggered next to @AkioSakio and observed, curbing her instinct to scoff.

@ChefGil tried to pinch himself awake. It was only a dream! Yet, he pinched till he was sore. Nothing changed. A rage, similar to the rage he still held for his ex-wife, simmered. The fog whispered softly, gently poking him to stew in that rage. @ChefGil twitched, trying to calm his thoughts.

Blue veins flashed in the fog, brighter and brighter. It could have been minutes, or years. Time had no schedule here in this forsaken place. @Dhriti and @AkioSakio's eyes were scrunched in concentration. If they had been flesh and blood, their hands would have been slippery with sweat.

| *Find others, escape, find peace, go home.* || two thoughts blending together messily.

Like static, a thought buzzed in, incoherent, then materializing.

| *Must let go.* || @ChefGil sputtered.

Then, much later, another, this time acerbic and to the point as a bee sting. | *Here goes nothing. Nothing I've tried works. Let's see if you dimwits can do something better.* || This was @AbyGaby.

The light in the fog dimmed. An imperceptible scream started to form. They couldn't be allowed to work together. It needed their strife, their pride, their anger. Yet the fog buckled under @Dhriti and @AkioSakio's efforts, and even under @ChefGil and @AbyGaby's dubious hope.

Eventually, other figures coalesced out of the fog, children, men, women, everyone in between; dazed, frightened, their first instinct to touch themselves, groaning as some were as faint as gossamer gauze. They reached out in the fog and bumped into each other, recoiling in surprise.

The group of four opened their eyes, seeing usernames flash above disoriented heads. Slowly, they got up, still holding hands, and walked toward the materializing crowds.

A tunnel opened up in the fog, still mysterious, with no end in sight, no illumination. From the corners of their eyes, the reluctant team noticed more people materializing from the fog: co-workers, old friends, previous lovers, distant family, students, relatives of those students, on and on it went.

Most of them were in a silent panic. Some had no voice but gesticulated to compensate.

@AkioSakio kept his ears strained to hear anything that could be useful. @Dhriti was in charge of communicating what they knew to others as they connected with more people.

At one point, @AkioSakio heard two self-proclaimed nerds and nihilists talking about this place as the Slate of Silence. Their theory was that this was a purgatory, too, where personalities came to die, drained of their life essence, due to investing so much of it online.@AkioSakio felt ashamed. They had all come so low. They had all become trolls, hacks, the very worst of themselves. And now they actually might die from it.

More and more people followed. But not everyone. Some decided to stay and argue. As they came across more stubborn avatars, some blinked completely out of existence. Others with more stamina staggered but held. However, to @AkioSakio and his companions' eyes, figures with no faces, squat and corpulent, flew and flitted all over the place, holding sticks no one else seemed to see. The fog formed them, lightning of blue and gray birthing them to life. No blurb, no breath animated their not-quite-human forms.

Wherever they poked, strife came. Strife between co-workers, strife within families, strife between complete strangers.

They swarmed entire groups like a plague, wriggling and squirming, agitating their sticks.

| *Can't you see them?* || @AbyGaby cried, pointing to the monstruous figures. But the other avatar people were too far gone in their arguing.

| *You are an evil person because you don't agree with me!* ||

| *You want the downfall of this country.* ||

| *You are everything toxic in the writing community.* ||

| *You are so stupid. Can't you see you are being brainwashed?* ||

| *I'm going to get you cancelled so hard you will be unable to find work anywhere.* ||

| *You all need to die. You are unredeemable.* ||

@Dhriti, @ChefGil, @AkioSakio, and @AbyGaby flinched at hearing the ReGroupees, seeing avatar people succumb to the ardent poking of the faceless agents. There were so many. So many people were going to die, consumed by their perceived hatred of other strangers, sometimes even family! The only relief was that many more saw the agents, too, and held on tight, following the group to an exit. The more avatars joined them, the more a steady blue light rippled out from the procession. A constant whisper thrummed around them.

| *We must work together, we must stand together. Stronger united, stronger together.* ||

@Dhriti smiled as she held on tight to the hands of absolute strangers: cooks, gamers, politicians, artists, construction workers, and many, many others. As they blindly trusted each other, she felt the whispers of their ReGroupees, their comments and thoughts radiating out into the void. She pushed against them so she wouldn't be consumed. She didn't love all of them, that was utopic, but she could understand they had different lives, and so she'd never be able to step into their shoes. That also meant she didn't get to judge. Her cheeks burned. She would never say to them what she'd said on her ReGroup page.

All at once, she felt a sharp stab and an irrational anger welled up in her. The person closest to her, holding her hand, was a social worker. How useful did they actually think their profession was? There was too much strife and discord within families and society to fix people's mental health. It was useless to waste tax dollars on social workers. Thinking so high and mighty of themselves, thinking they were the world's little saviors. Her social workers had certainly done nothing for her. @Dhriti had had to work it out on her own.

@Dhriti gasped. She looked up and flinched from the wall-to-wall tide of agents. One of them had poked her. Steam wafted off her from where she'd been poked. The social worker glared at her but didn't bother replying.

| *Let us out! Let us out!* || the crowd chanted.

| *No!* || came the raspy response.

| *Why not?* ||

| *What is your goal keeping us trapped in here?* || @Akio-Sakio asked.

The swarm of agents hummed angrily, and they swatted at the lost avatar people with all the strength they had.

| *Why stick up for him? He is a godless sinner.* ||

| *Why care about her? She's a SAHM on welfare. Draining resources.* ||

| *They want the government to be in your business. Take your freedom. You're gonna let them destroy your country?* ||

| *Women. They have all the same rights as men yet still complain.* ||

| *Anyone who doesn't like your opinion is wrong. Fundamentally wrong. Destroy them.* ||

| *POC whine way too much about their past. They need to get up and move on. Tell 'em! Keep the boot on their throat.* ||

| *A burger flipper shouldn't make more than you. They*

don't deserve the same rights as you. Keep hating them, let the policymakers make sure they stay on the ground where they belong. ||

@ChefGil cowered under the onslaught of insults and hatred. Some avatar people let go of his hand and joined the surge of agents, their faces becoming blank, sticks appearing in their hands. But more held on more tightly, fighting against the assault.

It was hard for him to resist the virtual bloodlust. His family had always taught him to look out for himself. Caring for other people completely different from you was extra baggage. Given the chance, @ChefGil wouldn't cross the street to talk to some of the people trapped in this hell with him. Yet here they were, all in the same place. Too easily swept up in seeing the worst of each other instead of seeing the common denominator: they were all humans trying to survive. The world was allowed to be made of different people and different opinions, as long as those opinions didn't kill or endanger anyone.

He should have been kinder to his grandson. He'd been an asshole to his ex-wife. He'd been such a prick he'd isolated his own family. Maybe looking out for himself was the wrong thing to do.

Without the help of that yogi, that teacher, that hunter, he wouldn't be here, close to escape. Cooperation was the key. Like when he worked with Timothé. They argued sometimes. But in the end, they loved and respected each other.

"Why do you want us trapped here? Why do you keep pitting us against each other?" @AkioSakio asked. @ChefGil had to concede he didn't agree with the teacher's worldview, but he *was* tenacious. At last, someone was asking the right questions!

| Strife feeds us! So many emotions! ||

| *Violent emotions are life. We have been stuck here longer than you. Watching. Observing you.* ||

| *Seeing you invest your souls in social media. Your lives give us life.* ||

| *Boredom breeds anger. We need your anger to forget why we are here. Creations of cruel entertainment.* ||

| *Pride is the best trait. People will do anything for pride. Collecting numbers, followers, to feed their own souls.* ||

| *Proving people wrong, that is important. You know best, you know everything! It is vital to prove, to show you're special.* ||

| *Aggression begets aggression. There will never be peace, people are too different.* ||

| *Those people hate... Those people think... Those people do... Those people are worth hating!* ||

| *You are wrong.* || a faint roar formed from the trapped ReGroupees.

| *You want us trapped because you are trapped?* || @Aby-Gaby asked.

| *You create anger as a distraction.* || @Dhriti said. | *If we are distracted by others like us, we can't get angry at the real people responsible.* ||

Gilbert nodded. She was right. More than once he'd taken his frustration with his personal life onto social media. Some were dismissive attitudes from his friends, or communication problems with his ex-wife. Some were bigger scale, like being taxed so ruthlessly he barely had money to keep his business going. The creeping racism in everyday life toward foreigners like him. Screaming against the world was impossible. Screaming at blank faces was not feasible. Finding the exact people responsible for his misery couldn't be done. But social media... It opened the doors wide for stacking all the frustrations with the world on other people who were struggling as much as he was.

@AbyGaby pointed a finger at the agents. | *You are a diseased prey who thinks they are the predators. Not anymore.* ||

She puffed up and willed with all her might that she had a gun. Her beloved Remington 700 rifle. She willed for its existence as surely as she willed for these avatars to escape with her. They all needed to escape this circus before they succumbed to their baser thoughts. She knew these agents preyed on her competitiveness, her hatred for weakness. So, she would show them, and erase their toxic touch on her soul.

She aimed through the sight and released. As she did, a fire-red glow shimmered around them all. Weapons formed out of thin air, pistols and rifles, halberds and glaives, longswords and katanas, clubs, shurikens, and simple sticks used to swat away pesky underbrush. She could have purred in satisfaction. Weapons, in the right hands, in the right circumstances, saved lives. Quite a few avatar people blinked in surprise, but took up the weapons readily available.

Others shook their heads, and the weapons before them vanished. Dhriti, Chef Gilbert, and Akio chose not to use weapons. Chef Gilbert looked like he was tempted, but he raised his hands.

Some of the crowd leapt toward the agents and lambasted them, ferociously stabbing, hacking, slicing, shooting.

The others looked inward, concentrating on themselves, fiercely meditating, ruminating, working past years of brainwashing and emotional confusion. Contemplating, healing, uniting, improving.

As they worked together, the fiery light pulsed like a heartbeat. A heartbeat full of conflicting code and imploding algorithms. Then, letting out a defeated breath, the Slate of Silence pushed out the avatar people who had fought together as one. They winked out like a hastily deleted comment.

Millions of people awoke from their comas as if being born for the first time.

Many kept in touch with each other. Some did not. The ReGroup app was erased from many a smartphone or computer.

People triumphed. But not all.

A great many never woke up.

THE GIRL WHO
TALKED TO DEATH

He towered over the young couple, his emerald velvet cape not stirring in the breeze, his doublet's buttons not shining in the sun. Delilah waved at him. He rolled his iris-less eyes as he usually did when she saw him. Today, death lurked over the young couple. Their laughter, their dreams would be cut short tonight, snuffed out in a car crash. The man and woman did not see him. As they twirled and danced with each other, Delilah saw the babies they had been, their lives' end, and the old couple they would have become. Grim Reaper caught her gaze and glared. She cringed, not at his expression but at what would happen to the couple.

She dashed to them and spontaneously hugged the woman, making the man stagger. A hole, a black hole of nothingness, opened around her. Delilah squeezed her eyes shut and reached into the couple's future. A flick of the wrist, unraveling skeins of life, and she saw them: reincarnated as siblings, several hundred years in the future. She grasped the skeins and imprinted her wish, her destiny for them. When she let go, the woman looked down on her awkwardly, sunglasses slipping down her nose. Her boyfriend edged her away, and they left. The Reaper watched them go, face tense.

"What did you do?"

"I don't know."

"Who are you?"

"Delilah. Who are you?"

"I have many names. I am called Thanatos, Ankou, Hel, Grim Reaper, Osiris, and more. But I prefer Thanatos."

"Ok. I'll call you Mr. Death."

Thanatos's sturdy face paled. "You shouldn't be able to see—"

"But I do! All the time. You are *everywhere*."

"Come here."

But she skipped away, laughing, knowing she had to be home for lunch, or her foster parents would get mad.

Eleven years old

Delilah sulked through her dinner that night, picking at her mashed potatoes and roast chicken, observing her foster parents, heart clenched. They would die tonight. She didn't know how; her vision was clouded this time. She had seen Mr. Death earlier in the day, as her parents made coffee. He'd made coffee with them, brooding quietly, avoiding her gaze.

She smelled his cologne now, a musky scent that let her know he was coming. She responded robotically as her parents talked about the new middle school, the one she'd be going to. They asked her about her wishes, what backpack she wanted, what books she needed. She answered dutifully, trying not to soak in their mannerisms, their voices, the scent of the house around them. Soon, it would all be gone. She went to bed and tossed and turned, toiling laboriously to fall asleep.

Instead she stayed awake, the foreboding feeling

compelling her. She crossed her arms and read *King Solomon's Mines*, reading the same page over and over. Sure enough, Mr. Death came for her, a few seconds before her alarm went off. He stood over her, arms crossed.

"Waiting for me?"

"Yes," she said quietly. "I've been dreading it all day."

"Who are you?"

"I am Delilah. You keep asking this."

He threw up his hands, his business suit crinkling. This was the first time he wore a suit.

"My parents!" she cried, rushing out of her bedroom to theirs. They lay in each other's arms, unmoving. Delilah shook them, crying, yelling, but they did not move. She touched her dad's bare arms and she felt the residue of his passing into death through carbon monoxide poisoning. She traced it to the gas heater, its signature a flare in her mind.

"Why aren't I dead?" she murmured to herself, then asking Mr. Death, tears streaming down her cheeks. "Why do you always show up?"

"Why do you always see me? No one else can."

Delilah didn't know. "Why am I not dead?"

Mr. Death adjusted his silk tie and buttoned his blazer.

"You were supposed to, but you saw me before I could sneak up on you."

Delilah turned toward her parents and kissed them on their cheeks like she did every night. As her lips touched their skin, she fell into that abyss of existence, saw their souls departing. The house around them fell into a cycle of abandon, until her aunt, her foster mom's sister, came and created a foster home for children, a few years in the future. The house would become one of the main refuges for children in the nation. Delilah would be there too; but how, she did not know. As ever, she could never see her own fate.

Mr. Death observed her, conjuring a cup of coffee.

"What are you?"

She didn't answer. She numbly went to her dad's cell phone to call 911. Mr. Death lunged at her, and Delilah gasped. Her hand wrinkled and shriveled where his fingers touched her. A creeping sensation of numbness radiated from his touch. But she fought it, grasping him back, and Mr. Death bowed down in pain, golden light searing him where she touched him. They both let go. After some panting, he crouched to her eye level.

"You are...*something else*. Why do I feel like we know each other?"

She shrugged. "I don't know. I'm tired of seeing you."

"*I'm* tired of seeing *you*."

She ran away with the phone, dialing 911, alerting the paramedics to her parents' fate.

"What will become of me?" she asked plaintively.

Mr. Death shrugged. "You will keep persisting"

He handed her his cup of coffee. When she drank, it was warm milk. When the paramedics came, Delilah knew she would go through a few more foster families by the time she was eighteen.

Fifteen years old

Delilah was tired. The teacher's lecture went on and on, grating every pore of her soul. Her friend, Camila, rocked beside her, fidgeting, dark bags under her eyes. Things had been rocky for her family for weeks—siblings moving out, one in jail for drugs, her father feeling weaker and weaker. Delilah started to snore, but hissed awake as through her eyelids the shadow of Mr. Death passed. He bent over Camila and crossed his arms. Her friend took out her phone and keened. Delilah jumped as her friend dashed from the room without asking for a pass. Mr. Death followed, slowly, languidly, and he rubbed his arms as he walked, tracing the veins under his skin. It was her first time seeing him in a polo shirt. And with a twisting of her heart, she knew Camila would slit her wrists. She would die for sure, since Mr. Death was here. Delilah darted out of her chair and followed. Mr. Death turned around and sighed.

"You, again. Unlike me, you can't be everywhere. But you do a pretty good job of being in my way. You can't stop this."

"Yes, I can. Death doesn't always have to happen."

"Silly child. Death always happens. You cannot stop the cycle of life."

The fabric of time rustled, a pinprick of light glimmered and beckoned to Delilah. She touched it, with her Vision. It gave her an opening, a slight change.

"There's a way. You always swoop in, unwanted. I'm here to stop that," Delilah growled. "You have no bedside manner."

She pushed past him, gasping as even that touch, fleeting as a ghost, made her hand tingle painfully. Mr. Death gasped too.

She dashed to the bathroom, hearing Camila hiss under her breath, sobbing uncontrollably. Mr. Death whirled around her, gesturing her away, a black flare in the anemic walls, lights flickering.

Delilah froze, bombarded by images of death, of Camila's father passing away, in only a few weeks, from stage IV pancreatic cancer. Of her mother pining away, a thread's breath away from ending her own life. And Camila herself, now digging sloppily at her veins, trying to open them with a switchblade knife. Usually, Delilah needed to touch someone for this to happen. Erasing the stray thought, she shouted, "Camila! Stop!"

Mr. Death threw up his hands, leaning against the wall petulantly.

"I can't!" her friend screamed, tears blurring her vision, as she stabbed a grotesque gouache of reds and browns in her wrists.

Delilah reached over and touched her arm. Sorrow and rage, a toxic helix of doom, threatening to overwhelm her. Delilah swallowed and pushed the dark threads away from her soul, trying to find the snag she always found when she touched people affected by Mr. Death. A snag there: Camila's mom rubbing her belly, her belly growing with the seed of a little girl. Delilah laughed through her tears.

"You are going to be a big sister."

Camila stopped, the knife poised like a hawk.

"You're joking."

"No. She will grow up to be a spitfire. Like you. Her name will be Kate."

Delilah staggered back, gold threads from her mental fingers fusing with the dark threads of Mr. Death.

"Whoa," her friend breathed. "Your eyes are gold."

Camila threw herself at Delilah and hugged her. Her friend knew of her strange power now. What that power was exactly, Delilah wasn't sure. She wondered if she would ever know.

"You did it again," Mr. Death said, and this time awe tinged his voice.

Twenty-four years old

"Come on Delilah, let's go party! We've been cooped up here far too long!" Her roommate, Roberto, said, juggling eight beer bottles.

Delilah sat on the sofa, eyeing the remnants of their Monopoly game, little metal tokens strewn about like dead children. Her senses shivered with foreboding, a shadow of a familiar presence in the future. A presence touching her friend, shattering his life, extinguishing it, not mercilessly, but because it had to be.

"We should stay home," she whispered, wrapping a blanket around herself. "Nothing good will come tonight."

"You're too serious," Roberto said.

Delilah shook her head. His dreams of becoming an engineer, starting a large family, his triumph over drug addiction, his success over his dyslexia, all coalesced into a dead end tonight. She just didn't know how yet, because she hadn't touched him.

She couldn't stop him. Her mind cast out and she sensed others with the mark of Mr. Death, most a natural ending, some not. She bore her fingers on her skull, the pain stopping the curse, the expanse of her Vision.

"Here, have some chocolate." He handed it to her and his knuckles brushed hers. He would die in a motorcycle accident tonight. She shuddered. She tried her usual move, pushing aside the threads of death and inserting her own. But he pulled back and she lost her connection. How much had she been able to actually change?

"Come on. I'll drive you to and back," she said.

"Really? Thanks. You may as well come to the party too," he said.

"No thanks," she smiled tremulously.

She drove and stopped one possibility of death. But another came. A few days later, she received a call. Roberto had gone to see his estranged dad to make amends. They hadn't spoken in years. Roberto had reached out to apologize for his behavior during his drug years. His father accepted, forgiving him on the phone, asking him to visit. Along the way, Roberto had gotten in a deadly motorcycle accident.

Delilah sobbed, striking at the sofa with her fists, wishing it were Mr. Death's face.

"No matter what I do, it doesn't matter," she cried angrily. "I'm bad luck. Wherever I go, I see death."

She jerked. Mr. Death strolled into her living room. Today, he wore black slacks and a long-sleeved, button-down purple shirt with black cufflinks. Slender and affable as ever, he said, "Wherever I go, I see the effects of your touch. You may not be able to physically be everywhere. But your ideal is universal."

"What ideal is that?"

He looked down. "You have to find that out yourself. And your power might change."

She had lost the ability to see people at all stages of their past, current, and future lives. But the ability to see *him*, and her ability to do...whatever it was she did had not changed.

"I want to have a normal life. To not be able to see anything."

Mr. Death laughed. "Have some chocolate," he offered, being careful not to touch her.

She declined.

"You know, you don't have to hate me. Death is a part of life. I am as natural as the sun, the earth, the air that surrounds us."

"I know, I know," she grumbled. "I just wish I didn't have my Vision."

"You've always had it. But something is new this time. It's up to you to find out what it is. Your Vision will never go away. So, you can mope about it, or bear it."

He bit into a piece of chocolate. "You're starting to grow on me. It'd be a shame to give up now."

Delilah reached out to whack him, but Mr. Death had disappeared.

Thirty-six years old

She knew before any of them that her mother-in-law was going to die from a heart attack. But she pretended that it came as a surprise, she endured her husband's grief as if it were new. Even he didn't know of her strange gift, her Vision. In fact, she'd known as soon as she'd met her mother-in-law, nine years earlier, that she would die like this: suddenly, dramatically, in her kitchen, alone. That is, until Delilah decided to keep her company. She proposed they make pies together. They'd spent the afternoon making various jams, then had moved on to baking pies. The sunlight filtered through the curtains, a green haze of springtime bouncing around the kitchen.

"You make my son so happy," Leilani said, smiling, her silver ringlets swaying as she rolled out the dough.

"I try my best."

After putting the dough in the pie plate and adding the filling, Leilani spoke again, as she crimped the pie crust. "I wish he had more ambition. He has always spoken about following his dreams. Being a world-renowned musician."

"He is working on it," Delilah told her, fingers stained with elderberry jam, dark spatters under her fingernails, in the ridges of her skin. "He will be a famous singer and guitarist, touring around the world, Gold and Platinum albums selling tons. He will be known as 'The Child,' for reinventing famous tunes from childhood and making them new."

"You sound so sure," Leilani said, beaming. "You have this way of stating things."

Delilah had almost told her about her gift then. The woman was open to a great many things. She might have understood. But having nearly gotten killed by an abusive boyfriend after Camila let slip about her Vision, Delilah had never told anybody else about it. Camila was killed a few months later by him, after becoming his girlfriend.

Delilah was ready when her mother-in-law collapsed. She

gave her CPR, called 911 despite knowing it would make no difference. Mr. Death watched her give CPR, smoking a cigarette, wearing a wrinkled black wifebeater. Delilah worked hard, instilling threads of hope in Leilani's departing soul: the knowledge that her son would become famous, the knowledge that her husband would die a natural death, overcoming his alcoholism down the line. Delilah tried to see when and who she would be reborn as, but she scrambled against the tenacious wall of time. She sagged back and watched Mr. Death through lidded eyes.

"You have stopped fighting against me," he observed, sitting down next to her. The holes in his jeans gaped like open wounds.

"I know you're inevitable. But that doesn't mean I'll let people die without some peace."

She stopped talking as the paramedics burst in. She and Mr. Death watched passively, as the medics searched and failed to find a pulse.

Forty-four years old

Delilah learned to be in several places at the same time, dividing her consciousness into people's slices of despair, impending deaths connecting similar fates. She first learned to do it when she met a homeless man teetering on a bridge, his red beanie a match for his red nose, rendered so by too much liquor. He stood there shakily, knobby knees and hopes clattering around. He hadn't even seen her, swinging her legs on the bridge, reading a book. This close, she didn't need to touch him. Despair, desolation warred inside of him. He had lost his wife, his sons, and his dog in the same month. He had spiraled and destroyed his friendships, refused to continue working, and he had started an addiction to alcohol. All those patches of misery, of anguish had made him think of suicide. There was no way out. There was nothing to live for.

"Hey," she said softly.

He turned his head, face livid, Delilah an unwelcome spectator to his brash decision.

"Sorry. I was already here," she whispered.

He teetered and she grabbed him. His life wobbled, quite literally. In one reality, he threw himself off. In another, he walked away. In yet another, he yelled at her but walked away.

She really did want to go back to her book. She had already seen Mr. Death a dozen times that week and he paced behind her now. She settled on the easiest route. For good measure she concentrated, and saw the man marrying again, and becoming a math teacher; a dream he'd never admitted to, even to himself.

"When you think there is nothing... Remember that death is the ultimate nothing. There is no going back from that."

"What would you know? You are young. You can't preach to me that life will get better," his voice shook, sorrow vibrating him.

"It certainly won't get better if you die now. Besides, who will be left, once you die? You've lost everyone. If you die, your wife and sons' memories die with you. Your love, your dedication to them will be forgotten."

"Who are you?"

"Delilah," she said, though he would never remember.

"How do you know about them?"

"I just do."

He reared back, ready to launch into a tirade. She had talked too much.

"You know nothing about losing people. You're here reading a damn book! You know nothing about my struggles, about grief, about wanting to give up. Life is hard. Existing is pain."

She considered this, remembering what happened when she'd told her secret to someone she thought she could trust. But now she was stronger. If something happened, she could defend herself.

"You have their memory in your hands. You give up living and your tribute to them dies. If you live, you can continue honoring them. You can make them proud."

A deep breath and she continued.

"I have seen death come and take strangers, family, friends. I know how it happens, when it happens. There is nothing I can do." A small lie. "I have lost people close to me more than your years and mine combined. But I do know that when you stop your life, there is no going back. There is no possibility to make it better. You will find new friends. A new wife. A new hobby. Life is like the seasons. This is your winter. You have to find springtime again. You have to not die."

Delilah injected her willpower, pushing the possibility of his death away, shoving aside the other eventualities. Mr. Death stopped pacing and teetered over the bridge. Not tonight. She didn't want a death tonight. She was tired. This man would survive. And he would live to see hope again, to see love and joy.

The man stared at her, lips working. His eyes welled but he did not cry. He glared at her, desperately wanting to believe her but still skeptical. Delilah concentrated, and the dark thoughts shrank to a ball of shivering skeins.

Mr. Death muttered, "Thanks," as he plunged into the river. All she saw was a blur of silk and satin. Was he wearing a tunic?

The homeless man nodded his head and walked away without a backward glance.

She sighed, long and deep, breath misting in front of her. Then she almost fell over as she was hit with others like him, across the country, across the world, with those same suicidal thoughts. She inhaled and accidentally wound up next to a young woman, shaking as she hung a noose around her neck. Delilah inhaled again and she blinked into existence next to a teenage boy adjusting the barrels of a shotgun to his face. The world spun around her, dizzying fractions of humanity calling at her, tugging her every which way. Delilah gasped and focused on the bridge she'd been on. She collapsed, quivering, and curled up on the asphalt. Too much. One day she could help them all at once. But right now, it was too much.

"You will learn to master your power," Mr. Death's voice floated in the wind. Delilah didn't have the energy to respond.

Fifty-two years old

Delilah had a knack for saving the children. A lot of them still got snatched up by Mr. Death. But she empathized and connected immediately with children in need. And she started recognizing when they would die anyway. But she was always there to give what they needed. Now, she stood in a dilapidated home, a drunk, angry father beating his seven-year-old, the child's eyes already swelling shut. Bruises littered the boy's body and his father struck his chest and stomach, a litany of abuse of love and trust. Mr. Death stood behind the boy, chewing his lip.

"I wish you wouldn't do this," she said automatically to him. But it was a tired farce; a memory replayed over and over. He didn't do this on purpose. He came because it was time. Humanity managed to inflict the worst on itself. Death would always come. How depended on everything else. She just couldn't stomach when children died, no matter the circumstances. With her gift she'd touched countless children: sick, dying, accidents, natural deaths. But those that were caused by their parents... she couldn't.

The father hadn't seen her yet. He should have. But every year she became more and more like Mr. Death. Transient in space and time.

Delilah walked through his blows and touched the child. A wriggling mass of darkness pulled at him; he was moments from death from one more blow. The father swung and Delilah scooped up the child, wrapping her arms around him, aggressively shoving away the skeins of death that yearned for him. He would live. She blinked her eyes, and she was at her aunt's house, the foster center she'd created years earlier. Delilah set the boy down and reeled back. He sat up, smiling, bruises fading, eyes opening fully again. Mr. Death popped up next to him, shaking his head.

"You don't do half measures, do you?"

Delilah didn't know what to say.

"You are the other half of me. The one that gives hope, joy, all the positive things to them as they die. But they must still die. You are disturbing the cycle of life and death."

"I didn't do it on purpose!"

"Well, you need to learn to control it. Honestly, woman. You've had over half your life to learn!"

"I can't help what I do."

Mr. Death pointed a finger at her, his blank eyes accusing. He wore black overalls, with a red bandanna wrapped around his throat. It positively bobbed with anger.

"Without you, I die. Without me, you die. Do not undo the work of Time itself. Something has changed this time around. Now instead of painting Grim Reapers, people are drawing a haloed woman surrounded by light. That light is a friendly death. How ridiculous is that?"

"I think it's wonderful," Delilah intoned, looking at the boy she'd saved. "If people learn to not fear death, if more hope is given to them, where is the harm in that?"

Mr. Death sputtered. She had a talent for rendering him like this.

"It sounds like you're jealous. My power is starting to match yours. Maybe that's why you sermon me all the time. Trying to make me give up," she winked playfully.

Mr. Death tried and failed to stop grinning.

Sixty-seven years old

Delilah tried to not stop death. But as she grew older, so did her power grow. She had to pull back when she touched people and gently tug at the skeins of death instead of shoving them aside. That way people died, but a positivity in the universe happened as an equal reaction. Delilah was the balance. She didn't run away anymore. She knew what to do and how to do it. People blurred in her memory; she saw Mr. Death every day and exchanged jibes with him. But he was no longer her enemy. She flitted through the instant before death, heartbeats counting to finality, every second, every moment, sometimes at the same time.

She considered telling Harold about her power. They'd been together long enough for him to earn her trust. But these days he toured with his band, earning the fame she'd predicted so long ago.

Delilah hummed along to Harold's hit single as it played on her phone. He was radiant, beaming at his fans, strumming the melody he'd so laboriously worked on at home, as she watched, silently encouraging him.

The frenetic splashing of her neighbor stopped as he hauled himself on an inflatable yellow raft in the pool.

"Michael's music is one of a kind," he said. His Alzheimer's. It wasn't too advanced yet. But enough to swap people's names. Delilah enjoyed these Sunday afternoons with

Paul. They played table tennis and then swam. These days, they fawned over her husband's music. Paul's family was out shopping and they'd be back in the evening.

She might have fallen asleep or been lulled by the music. A thrum in reality snapped her awake. Paul. He wasn't on the raft. He was sinking in the pool. His reality surrounded him, a death by drowning, alone and silent, an aura around the entire pool. She set her lips. No. She was here. She dissolved this reality where he died alone.

Paul, with his Alzheimer's, had forgotten how to swim. He sank helplessly, limbs akimbo. Delilah jumped after him and tugged him onto the deck, giving him CPR. With every thrust, she pushed away the horrible eventuality of his death. He would die, yes, but he would die at home, surrounded by family, before the Alzheimer's claimed his brain and his soul. In five years. Water burst out from his mouth, a fountain of vitality.

As she waited for him to recover, Mr. Death emerged from the pool, dry as a bone. He wore a black wetsuit this time.

"Delilah, Delilah. Saving someone from me yet again. You know he is still going to die, correct?"

"Yes. But in a better way, eventually."

He tugged at the wetsuit and peeked at Paul.

"It is not natural, what you do. Pushing me back."

"You need to make up your mind. I thought pushing you away entirely was a no-no. But this, what I do now... it is natural. Some people's lives swing from death to life, the deciding factor is arbitrary. If my presence swings the pendulum toward them living, then so be it."

Mr. Death shook his head but did not rebut her.

"You have thought this through," he finally said.

"A lifetime's worth of experience will do that."

They smiled at each other.

Eighty-one years old

It was her time to die. She knew it. Even without touching her heart and sensing that familiar ball of death inside her soul, she knew it. She sat on the veranda, knitting in her lap, her cats playing with a toy behind her. Her husband would come home to find her gone. She'd left him a lengthy note, a profuse thank you letter for helping her find her confidence. He knew that for a long time, she'd kept something significant from him. But he'd just held her quietly and reassured her when she came home, crying over yet another loss. He'd told her over many, many years that she could handle whatever was thrown at her.

She'd also left her wish to continue the foster shelter to her aunt's daughter. A lovely woman, full of promise, like her mother had been. Delilah had said goodbye to the kids, giving them copious hugs. They knew of her Vision, without her telling them.

Delilah got up and greeted Mr. Death just as he materialized in front of her. He wore a bathrobe, pink and fluffy, and he smoked a pipe. He shuffled his slippered feet and puffed out smoke. Even with his blank eyes, he radiated pride.

"Well?" he asked.

"It is my time."

"Yes. your time," he chuckled and put a hand out. She took it, her strength siphoning out. Mr. Death grabbed Delilah, almost in an embrace, and smiled.

His true form erupted into wings of black and silver, a char black fog where his body should be. His eyes two pits she could fall into for eternity, an emptiness of non-existence. He towered over her.

"No reaper or scythe?" she whispered, refusing to show how awed she was.

Delilah scintillated, flexing out in a shower of dazzling

light, golden and black. She couldn't look at herself. She *was* light, the pure embodiment of it. Webs of light appeared and disappeared around her fingers.

"We are partners." Mr. Death said finally, "Death and hope mixed together. Next time, try to stay focused and learn more quickly, will you?"

Delilah laughed, and the golden being that was her erupted in an explosion of sparks. She forced herself back into a human form, a little girl, like when she'd first seen Mr. Death. She took his hand and he took hers back.

"Let's keep going. And this time, I lead."

SLOT OF LIFE

The laughter of the bustling crowd hit them like a slap, rising in the air like their foggy breath. Cynthia, Matthew, and Melanie huddled together, adjusting their beanies and head scarves to squint at the movie display. Times and movie titles blurred together, and Matthew went first.

"Hi, three adult tickets for *A Slot of Life*."

The ticket agent looked at him strangely, counted the group and gave him the tickets. Matthew got the tickets and they staggered into the theater. At the kiosk, the ticket taker said, "One ticket for *A Slot of Life*, one for *My Fair Lady* and one for *A Spot to Play In*."

Melanie frowned. That was not what they'd asked for. But Matthew guffawed and pushed past the stone-faced ticket taker. Cynthia looked around, eyeing the crowds of people wandering every which way. Melanie overheard people also mentioning how their tickets were wrong. She expected an announcement or something saying there was a glitch. But none came. She turned back to the ticket taker, but any desire to correct the issue slipped away. The celebratory beer she and her friends had had was muddling her senses. Tonight, they celebrated their fifteen years of friendship. Or was it fifty-one? No, it couldn't be. She really was too inebriated. Looking at her tottering, giggling friends, they were, too.

"They gave us the wrong tickets," she said.

"Yeah. The times are all weird, too. But that's ok," Cynthia said, sucking on her braid as was her habit. But Melanie thought she'd outgrown that habit years ago.

"I'm hungry, guys. Let's get some food," Matthew said, stumbling forward. For a moment, Melanie saw him in a walker, back bent and twisted. With a shake of her head, he was back to normal, bounding to the counter and asking for some popcorn, hotdogs, chips, and sodas. Melanie drank in the artificial smells, the butter, the sharpness of sodas being prepared, the sweat of people coming in, overheated in their winter coats. A good night to come to the movies, that perfect gap between the fall festivities and Christmas holidays. Melanie couldn't even remember why they'd chosen this movie. This wasn't the kind of movie she and her friends particularly enjoyed. They loved fantasy and science fiction, or lacking that, a good action flick full of impossible stunts and endless explosions.

A Slot of Life. Such a bland literary name.

Melanie was pulled out of her musings by Cynthia tugging on her. "Look!" she pointed to the side, where the arcade games sat.

Melanie expected to see old games like *Pacman* or *Asteroids*. But instead, they had games she'd never heard of before. All the games were crowded (none of the players were children, she noted with amusement), except for one. A tall, yellow and black arcade machine with the words *Slot of Life* blinking on top.

"Have you heard of that game?" she asked Cynthia.

Her friend shook her head. "But it *is* the name of the

movie we're supposed to be seeing. Maybe it's a marketing thing?"

Melanie shrugged.

They looked at Matthew, who had gone back in line to order more food. Cynthia threw up her hands, giving him a warning glare. He pretended he didn't see, of course. Melanie had always thought they would end up together, Matt and Cyn. Instead, they'd married partners quite different from each other and divorced within ten years. Only twenty years later had they found true happiness.

Melanie fell back, holding her head. A throbbing pain sprouted in her temples. None of this made sense. The movie, the times, the memories. They were twenty-one, about to finish college, all single, and all looking for jobs. Why did none of that feel tangible?

"Are you ok, Mel?" Cynthia asked, holding onto her.

"Yeah... Headache. But it will go away."

"Come, sit down at least."

Mel followed her, sitting on a booster seat meant for kids. She massaged her temples, eyeing the gamers through slitted eyes. No one touched the *Slot of Life* game. Some went to order food. Except for one or two people who went into a theater, everyone milled about. *There must be a glitch in the system*, she thought. No one seemed in a hurry to see their movie. A lot looked hesitant about going in, hovering by the doors without entering, talking to their family or friends instead, reading books, or playing the arcade games.

Melanie pushed her curly hair out of the way and pointed at the *Slot of Life* game.

"I want to check that out. No one's touching it."

"Sure. You feel better?" Cynthia asked, her blue eyes wide with worry.

"Yeah."

The game called to her. Before getting food, before seeing

the movie, she had to play. There was no explanation for it. It felt like a duty, a checklist she must complete first. She gazed at Cynthia, worry still in her face, and she was hit with a flash of Cyn in another time: her friend bent over patients in bed, talking soothingly to them while she tended them. Of course. Cynthia had become a nurse soon after college. And she'd retired at sixty-five sharp, having exhausted herself in the medical system, but she had cared for a great many patients.

Again with the conflicting memories and poor continuity of time. They really must not drink so much next time.

Melanie pushed the start button on the game and a menu appeared, with some fanfare music.

"Welcome to *Slot of Life*! Where you play slots of your life. Want one specific memory? Insert a quarter. Want one summary of your entire life? Insert a dollar."

Melanie laughed. "What game is this? It's supposed to take me through my life? No game does that."

Cynthia tried talking to the other gamers to see if they knew what this game was. But they were engrossed in their own games.

"Fine," Mel said, removing her bonnet. "I'll play. But what if I only want three memories, huh? And I want to take you with me," she gently pulled on Cyn's sleeve.

Melanie put in three quarters and added a dime just as a joke.

Two handprints appeared on the screen.

"Ready?" she asked Cynthia.

Her friend nodded and they placed their hands on the prints.

Their palms tingled, and they both pitched forward into the screen, a bubbly eight-bit jingle reaching out to welcome them.

Falling into the game felt like those precarious moments right before vomiting and passing out after a night of boozery.

The world spinning, senses in limbo, reality not making sense. Melanie skimmed by her younger self, and Cynthia's too. Both of them meeting in kindergarten, hogging the Play-Doh centers; going to Christmas workshops and creating cotton snowmen, pinecone reindeer, Christmas light earrings. Meeting Matthew in third grade, a newcomer from New York; defending him from the wrathful teacher as he became the class clown; multiple themed birthday parties at each other's places, dressing up as superheroes or Alice in Wonderland characters; going to the mall and movie theater for the entire day, getting sick on one too many bags of popcorn.

Melanie tried to snatch at the memories, but they flew by, ephemeral and bubbly, winking out. Her feet finally touched the ground and the scene around her changed. Her heart thudded, a lump forming in her throat. She had hoped to never see this place again.

Her childhood home. Home to too many good memories wrapped in rotting layers of suffering. She was in her bedroom, boxes piled up high, curtains ripped to the side, toys in a bin to sell. This was the night she'd said goodbye. Having just gotten her emancipation papers, after she decried her father's neglect and his habit of dating women who wanted nothing to do with Melanie. When the last one karate kicked Melanie in the face, that had been the last straw.

Melanie traced her hands over the worn wallpaper, the retro shelving, the doll collections scattered on the floor. Books, ornaments, photo albums lay in boxes, waiting to be rescued. All this would remain with her. Cynthia watched her, biting her lip.

Cynthia and Matt had pitched together to store her belongings until she found a new place. Waited until she graduated from high school and found a job, until she was finally able to afford her first home.

Melanie had never gone back. In all her life, she had never

spoken to her father again. Or seen her childhood home ever again. But how did she know this information from her life? That drunk feeling swung through her again. Cynthia grabbed her arm.

"Mel. This is the night you packed, right?"

Melanie nodded mutely.

"What are we doing here?" her friend asked.

Melanie shrugged, blinking away tears. She thought she'd done a good job of walling away that particular memory.

"I don't know. Out of all the memories, *this* is what I get?"

They stood there, contemplating this forlorn shell of a memory.

"I overcame. I worked so hard, I became happy. I never looked back. Why then am I feeling this wretched?"

It took a while for Cynthia to respond.

"Maybe you never processed your grief. You lost a lot that night, Mel. Your family, your home. You were young. So young. You found out the people who should have had your trust were incapable of protecting you. Maybe you're here... to make peace with that."

"Since when did you get this wise?" Melanie sobbed, trying to laugh too. Wise words for the twenty-one-year-old kids they were.

Or were they?

Whatever it was, she hugged Cynthia and sobbed, soaking in the last sight of her childhood home, letting the good memories travel through her mind once more, pushing away the sorrowful ones. As she cried, her cheek burned; the bruise from that kick still hurt.

Melanie and Cynthia lurched out of the game, faces gray, panting.

"What was that?"

"It showed me exactly a portion of my life. This thing wasn't kidding."

Cynthia frowned. "This is too strange. Gotta show Matthew." She turned to look for him.

"Matthew? Matthew!"

He was beside them, on an arcade game, playing away, his fingers blurring from his exertion.

Cynthia rolled her eyes. "I'll be back. He probably forgot our food, the big lout."

Melanie nodded, throat still constricted. She glanced briefly at the room. There was still the same number of people, but they were different somehow. Yes, they were. Some adults were now children. Some older people loitering near the bathrooms were now young adults, switching seats at their arcade games. With a start, she focused on Matthew, and he too changed; his mullet hair changed into a sensible short cut, his belly stuck out now, and he wore glasses. He'd never needed glasses until he hit middle age.

Goosebumps traveled up her arms. What was going on?

The fuzziness curled up in her mind again, and lazily, her finger pushed the button on her game.

"Memory number two!" it announced happily.

Melanie pitched forward again but this time she was ready.

She trickled into existence from a dimension of pixels and erratic memories.

She materialized as her fifty-year-old self, speaking at a writing conference about her latest historical novel. It had just become a #1 New York Times Best Seller.

Melanie gazed out at the crowd, their eager eyes lapping up every word. A stack of her books lay beside her, a mountain of success, waiting to be signed. Fellow writers sat on the panel next to her, at varying stages of joy or discomfort. The smells of unsweetened coffee, of freshly printed books permeated the air. She had done it. As she wove her speech of gratitude, of bewilderment and pride at this latest achievement in the writing world, her younger self remembered the years of unrewarded labor, the weeks of research, querying agents to the endless tune of rejection. Skeletons of manuscripts abounded in her closet and filing cabinets, much to her husband's exasperation.

Husband. She had a husband? She was fifty?

Of course she was. People always said life started at fifty. Her first literary success. She had flitted from day job to day job in her earlier years, picking up whatever she could find as she worked on her books: waitress, secretary, teacher, coach. On the side, always researching, attending writing workshops and conferences, improving her craft until she wrote her mastodon. Her two-thousand-page historical saga covering a family history from the 1400s to the 2000s.

She didn't think she could have done it without her husband's support, or Cynthia's, or Matthew's. Her childhood friends had talked to all their own friends, their professional circles, and gone on social media to garner as much attention as they could for her book.

Melanie detached herself from the avatar of herself. It continued speaking, and she roamed the auditorium looking for her friends. There they were. Front row. Beaming at her. Her husband, Nicholas, sat next to them, pride shining in his eyes. They couldn't see her, of course, her teenage form. Why she was stuck in this form tonight she did not know. But gratitude poured out of her at the sight of them. Her friends had stuck with her through thick and thin. If her memory was right, despite the difficulties of their jobs, her friends had requested time off to be here with her. On whatever day that conference had been.

Slivers of anxiety wormed their way in. Melanie recalled going home that night and facing the terrible question: What if this was doomed to be her last great creation? To be a rising star only to fall brutally back to Earth? It had taken half her life to get to this point. Would she do bigger and better things? Could she challenge herself to become even more reputed, even more sharp?

In the end, what did it matter? Shouldn't a happy personal life matter more than anything else? A loving husband, devoted friends, work colleagues who helped bring out the best in her? A far cry removed from the miserable teenage years she had spent and worked so hard to overcome. She should be happy. The fifty-year-old had been happy up until the doubts crept in.

A stabbing pain lanced through her brain. Melanie grasped at a seat, bumping an audience member. They didn't notice. She gasped, and she was ejected from the game.

She came to, gripping the console on the arcade game so tightly her knuckles hurt. Her heart pounded for every doubt, every dubious memory racing through her psyche. She looked at her hands. They were thicker, a little more wrinkled, a wedding band on her fourth finger. She panicked, searching for the nearest bathroom.

"Mel!" Matthew called, except was it Matthew? An old man stood looking at her, blocking her way to the bathroom. But it was his smile, his slouched pose. No walker though.

"Matt?" she breathed, anxiety clawing its way through her guts and throat.

"Mel. You look like you need some food. Or a hug. Or both," he chuckled.

Melanie wanted to throw herself in his arms for a Matt bear hug. But she didn't trust her eyes, her mind, or anything else.

"We all look different. We're all changing. This isn't normal. What is happening?" she croaked.

His face softened.

"Mel, this is us. Us as we are. The compilation of all our experiences, our memories. I think this place shows it all at once. It shows what we need to see. I've been having a blast all night."

Exasperation pushed out the existential fear that threatened to encroach her sense of reason.

"You've been playing that stupid *Asteroid* game all night. Don't pretend you've been having doubts about everything—"

"Mel. All the machines are *Slot of Life*. They just look different for all of us."

Words died in her throat. She searched for a twinkle in his eye, some twitch of the mouth to indicate a joke, but he stood there, calmly eating chicken tenders.

"Where's Cyn?" she asked.

He pointed. She was playing a black arcade game, fingers busily handling the joystick. She was a little girl now, two braids poking out.

"What is the point of all this?" Melanie waved at everything. "The games, the movie? Showing our lives all at once? It's depressing."

Matthew's eyes widened. "It's not depressing. It's a celebration. Well, celebration for most people," he whispered, avoiding the gaze of some groups hesitating outside the movie theaters. "Not everything has to mean something. Existing is a gift in itself. Life is. I'm not sure you truly learned that, Mel."

Melanie rubbed her arms, feeling a chill. For all the warmth in his voice, the welcoming glow of the lobby, the tasty smells, it still felt like a ticking clock was running somewhere. Somewhere against her. She decided to stall.

"Did you share some of your memories with Cynthia?"

"Yeah, of course. Remember that time in our thirties, we went to Italy, and we didn't know the language at all?"

"Oh yeah. You said a few swear words without meaning to. It's a wonder we didn't get kicked out," Melanie laughed.

"Or when my son was born and I was so nervous I was in the bathroom the whole time?"

Melanie roared with laughter, the memory vivid as Matthew painted it sheepishly with his words.

"Yeah. I don't think Lyel ever forgave you for that."

Matthew downed some Coke and continued. "Or when you got married and got lost on your way to the reception because Nicholas refused to use Google Maps?"

Melanie growled playfully. "Up until he died, he refused to use Google Maps. To be fair, we should have done a rehearsal, but as we chose the reception hall last minute..."

"Still. We had fun, didn't we?"

Melanie nodded. Too many memories to retain. Matt had always had a knack for focusing on the positive ones.

She frowned. Nicholas was dead. She was sure of it. He had only been seventy-five, a year younger than she. What did that mean for her?

Matthew regarded her with somber eyes. "You overthink it, Mel. Just enjoy it. Go with the flow. Don't block it or you'll make it worse."

He may as well have been speaking Angolan to her. But she'd learned a long time ago to let go and coast, whatever mood Matt was in.

"Cyn is almost done with her experience. You're almost done too, right?"

Melanie shook her head. She heard the screen beep and the announcement, "Memory number three coming up."

A sordid terror blossomed in her. Once that was done, then what? She noticed a few of the people who'd put off going in the theater sigh and finally make their way in. No trailer music, no dialogue. Only silence.

"Can you come with me?" Melanie asked in a small voice.

Matthew nodded. "Sure. But you need to eat."

She half-heartedly smiled, taking a fry, then, too tantalized by the popcorn, she took a big handful of that.

Matthew accompanied her to the arcade game. Like with Cynthia, two handprints appeared, allowing them to press their hands.

Again that tinny music resounded, merging with the sound of their gasps.

When they materialized, Melanie's heart dropped. They were in a nursing home. Her nursing home. That incense smell, the cardboard-thin tables, and uncomfortable chairs. The professional and brief kindnesses from the staff who milled about, ready to rein in forgetful residents. Yes, she had been here before. After Nicholas's death, about a year after his passing. She'd broken her hip fumbling around in the dark to use the bathroom. Her friends had pressured her to go to a nursing home. She had the money, though most of it had gone to charities and writing workshops and scholarships around the country.

The residents here. All old, relatively sane, but alone. Bickering over food, bickering over tv shows, bickering over rumors. In many ways, exactly like high school had been. A few were gems, with lives as expansive and intricate as the sweaters they'd knitted. But after a few died, Melanie had walled off her heart to sympathetic strangers. She knew her time would come soon.

This memory, though, it shifted. A child burst into the nursing home, followed by a huffing mother.

"Adrian!" she called, apologizing to the residents with an embarrassed glance.

The little boy skidded to a halt, but his entire body vibrated with excitement. "Mom! Melanie is waiting for me."

"Yes, yes. But you'll bump into somebody here and hurt them. Slow down."

Adrian, of course, being Matthew's grandson. Melanie's heart warmed at her godson and his mother.

She knew what came next. Melanie followed her godson into her room, where another version of her sat in a velvet armchair. She lurked as he threw open the door and bellowed, "Happy birthday!" while his mom flinched.

Melanie watched as the other her opened his present carefully, unravelling a music box. The tinkling, oddly melancholic tune of "Greensleeves" poured out. Melanie sighed, absorbing the stains on the walls, the wooden ornaments Nicholas had made, the walls of pictures arranged crookedly on the lemon-yellow surfaces. She sat on a pile of her own published books. "Greensleeves." It brought back memories of her great-grandmother playing it on an antique harpsichord before she passed away.

Adrian started singing the words to the song, in a clear treble tone that impressed her now as much as it had when he'd come to visit. Dutiful cyan eyes flared with concentration as he maintained himself straight, clasping his hands together in front of him. His dirty blond hair, like his mother's, like Matthew's, tumbled in a messy aura around his head.

"That boy is going to do things with his voice," Matthew said, puffed up with pride. "I wish I'd had his voice."

Melanie nodded. Adrian had perfect pitch and an earnestness that lent a crystalline quality to his voice.

She and Matthew kept watching as Adrian prattled on about choir, about school, about his friends. Melanie wanted to lose herself in the moment, but she couldn't. Her mind kept jumping ahead. Why could she not remember anything after that visit? After that afternoon, she'd gone to bed and read new historical articles. She'd woken up the next day, made coffee, then... nothing.

As if reading her mind, the game's music blasted, interrupting the memory.

"End of game. To complete, select one. To continue, select two."

Melanie gurgled as she and Matthew were expelled from the game. Her watery eyes contemplated the flashing buttons on the screens. *End Game. Continue Game.* Then what next?

She hung onto Matthew and he gave her a gentle shoulder-squeeze.

"I think Cyn is waiting on us."

Melanie fiddled with the buttons on the game but didn't press anything. Cynthia stopped texting on her phone and looked up. She was standing next to a room labelled *A Spot to Play In*. She waved, a bright smile on her face.

"These games are amazing! I couldn't remember half the stuff they showed."

"You saw your life too?" Melanie asked.

"Of course!"

Melanie lapsed into silence. She watched other gamers stand at the arcade games. Those who finished walked pensively to a theater room. Some went right in. Others waited.

"We can all agree today's been a heck of a day, right? My memory is like scrambled eggs. Nothing is making sense," Matt said.

"Yeah. But life is always kind of like that," Cynthia said, reaching in Matthew's pockets to hunt for errant fries.

They were all teenagers again. Melanie breathed a sigh of relief. Some normalcy at last, perhaps.

"We should probably go inside," Matthew said, ducking as Cynthia grabbed some chips from his shirt pocket.

"We're not even at the right room," Melanie said.

"Since when do we do as we're told?" he said, raising an eyebrow.

"Oh, gosh, that game reminded me... Remember when we snuck on that cruise ship at sixteen and we pretended to be guests for an entire day? We even drank some margaritas."

"Yeah... Oh, remember when you tried to drive your grandpappy's tractor and it got stuck in the stream?" Matthew laughed.

"Oh. This! I parked in a no-parking zone in Boston, and we didn't get towed because I read one of Melanie's stories in my most dramatic fashion. The tow truck person recognized Mel's work and took pity on us." Cynthia flicked her hair.

Melanie had one. "Remember when we substituted glitter balloons for water balloons? They exploded at the pool party, and we had glitter in the pool for *years* afterward."

They chortled. They could reminisce all night. But more and more people were heading into the theater room. It must be time.

Matthew settled down first.

"It is our time. We spent money and time to come here. Let's go in."

That soul anguish clawed at Melanie again.

"What is your last vivid memory?" she asked, her voice trembling. Why couldn't she remember what had happened the day after Adrian's visit? She prided herself on her memory. It was how she'd been able to write such detailed, lengthy novels for so many years. Even historians and biographers found little to criticize in her manuscripts.

"I don't know. Putting salt instead of sugar in Matthew's milkshake," Cynthia giggled.

"Hmm. My last memory... I don't know. Mowing the lawn?" Matthew offered.

"My last clear memory was when Adrian visited. The next day starts... and then nothing."

Matt and Cyn looked at each other.

"I was looking at my great-grandchildren's school pageant on my tv," Cynthia said slowly.

"I was getting a nap," Matthew said, frowning. "Lyel was supposed to wake me up, but I don't think that happened."

"We are old. Were old. Weren't we?" Cynthia asked at last. "And this..."

Melanie choked down a sob. "I am not ready."

"Why not?" Matthew asked.

"Because. It was a good life. I had you guys. My husband. All my readers." She faltered, staring at the ominous, so easy-to-open theater doors.

She liked to think she'd led a full life, living it out to the max, enjoying it, being the best person she could be. But a part of her worried; what if she hadn't? What if she'd missed a crucial detour? What if she'd forgotten something? What if she could have done more? Sure, in this lifetime she'd managed to become a best-selling novelist. She'd been a loving, devoted wife. But she'd chosen not to have children. What would be her imprint on the world once she passed? Would her petty attempts to leave a mark amount to anything? Or would she be forgotten within a century, a footnote, lost in the dust of humanity's library?

She couldn't bear the thought. If she'd squandered her life...

Matthew and Cynthia both whacked her upside the head.

"Stop it," Matthew, said, for the two of them. "Existence is not a contest. We are not scoreboards."

"I still feel like there's more I could have done," Cynthia added. "But in the end, I'm happy with my life. It was mine. Will I get a crappy life next? Does it matter? Every life matters. Every life is worth living."

Melanie nodded and wiped her sweaty palms on her sweater. They were right. She had done her part. She wouldn't take back anything she'd done. Even her mistakes. They had schooled her in patience, trust, friendship.

The music swelled behind the doors.

"Looks like we missed the ads," Matthew said, crunching on a chicken tender.

"Let's go in," Mel said. "Together."

"Of course. Don't we always do every sodding thing together?" Cyn said, trying to hook her arm around Melanie's.

But Melanie quickly dashed back to the arcade machine. The screen choices still blinked. She pressed the number one button. The dread molted from her like snakeskin. Then she rejoined her friends, swinging her arm in Cynthia's, and opened the door.

Matthew joined them, pushing them through the open door, before leaping after them with a shriek of delight.

"You jerk!" both girls cried happily.

Embracing their last celebrations of mirth, the darkness of the theater claimed them.

THE SEA PART I

I am dreaming, again. I am walking barefoot along the oceanside, wearing pants that miraculously don't get wet. I realize I am nine years old and I am splashing water at my sister. The sun is at its zenith, scorching our backs and our scalps. We take turns splashing each other and I reach out for the dilapidated sneaker we are using to collect seashells. I throw in seashells whose names I don't remember, and I look up to see jolly people running into the surf, screaming their heads off. A few of them have candy wrappers in their hands, and just drop them into the water.

I sigh sharply as the waterline suddenly shifts from lapping softly at my feet to roaring halfway across the beach. I have suddenly been transported onto some nearby dunes, and I can see how high the tide has gotten. I stare in consternation at the people in the water, still laughing and talking and playing, though should be underwater and drowning by now. Miraculously, they still bob on the huge waves. I back away, thinking to myself how stupid these people are; can't they see the danger? They must go, now! The tsunami will come, as it always does, and it will destroy everything in its path!

As if listening to my thoughts, the waterline gets closer to me and I back away, dread churning in my gut. I am an adult suddenly, dressed in a business suit. The sky is darkening, the previously bright noonday sun now a leering sunset, the sky a red-veined eyeball, leaking shades of gray. I race away from the beach, passing by tiki bars filled with laughing drunk teenagers and incoherent snowbirds. My feet slide as I transition from sand to cement, and I run to a hotel which seems as familiar to me as the palm of my hand. Its sleek fancy facade glitters red as I rush in the entrance, past an astonished bellboy and oblivious guests. I post myself in front of one of the glass panes and look out at the sea. I can hear the sea's infernal cries through the glass, panting and hissing like a cat in heat. I look around in bewilderment. Can no one hear the approach of impending doom?

Don't hurt these people. They don't need to die.

The roar becomes louder, and I see the white crests of the waves approaching, the maw of the tide advancing, darkening everything across its path.

Please recede and leave us all alone. I love you, Sea, and you have been my companion since I was a kid.

The sea, that merciless bitch, keeps advancing, and I tremble. Of course, she picks up on the "b" word, and advances furiously. I can smell the foam and the brine. Nobody is laughing anymore; people are shrieking and rushing around. I can't see the sky anymore; it's a watery hell disguised as heaven.

Maybe flattery will work.

You are a formidable dame, Sea. Your power is astonishing. But you must control it and not kill us all.

Why? she asks, her roar so fierce I can barely make out the question.

I want to answer her. Because... Because... But now the tsunami is directly above us, and I close my eyes. I cannot think of anything. I am deafened and the world is dark. I can feel the impact of the wave crashing on the hotel, water bursting like a disemboweled force through all the windows and doors. Glass shatters everywhere, my feet are getting wet, and all at once I am picked up and thrown by a cold, cold violent arm. The sea has slapped me in the face with death.

I wake up shaking. I put my hands on my knees to stop the tremors. I'd felt my death coming and there'd been nothing I could do. So powerless...

I stand up, groaning as my hands come away wet. The skin is pruney, and I smell like salt. The sheets are soaked, and a puddle is forming on the floor, spreading into the rug. The trickle of the pooling water is maddening. This is the reason I have barely any furniture in my bedroom. My messes would ruin everything in a matter of days.

I feel chilled. My pajamas are sticking to my skin, gross and cold. My eyes are burning, like I've been swimming. The same old shit. Why, oh why am I cursed with this? Why can't I have peaceful dreams of going for a swim and hunting seashells? Or snorkeling contentedly? Why does the sea in my dreams always seem so set on killing the human race?

No, instead, when I dream, I fear the rising of an ocean-front, and the annihilation of my world as I know it in a watery apocalypse. I've been having these strange dreams as far back as I can remember. Not just the usual flying, losing your teeth, being chased sort of things, but intense dreams that almost always follow the same pattern. Dreams where I am at the seashore, the sea is raging, and she is out to obliterate the world for no apparent reason. I hate those. They leave me shaking hours later. They make me feel something other than crushing boredom: fear. The fear never truly goes away; it is the stepsister to my apathy.

When I was a kid, my parents and sister thought I wet the bed. But I didn't smell like pee; I smelled like the ocean. None of them ever caught on to that. I never insisted on that point either, because I didn't want them to be stuck with *two* kids who had something wrong with their heads.

Don't get me wrong, I had ambitions as a boy. I wasn't always this empty. I guess in our society that's a good thing. Back then, I was a model kid, doing my homework every day, running to the TV and watching *National Geographic* specials and *M*A*S*H* with my dad when I was done. I was even nice to my sister. My favorite class was when Mrs. Walker talked to us about the natural disasters. I loved them all, from the earthquakes to the hurricanes. The formidable forces of nature at work. Back then, I didn't fear anything.

That was before my sister's diagnosis. That was before *her*... Ciara.

Having those crazy ocean dreams while sharing a bedroom with my sister didn't exactly help. She couldn't understand why sometimes the floor would be sopping wet. Thank goodness we didn't have bunk beds. It wouldn't have helped either if I'd told her that the water would whisper to me, or refuse to completely come off the sheets, only doing so after much coaxing and hair pulling. But I think my secret was safe. My sister never caught on to my problem, even though I'm not sure my waking up soaking wet all the time didn't mess her up further.

My dreams are the main reason I don't have women come over for romantic encounters. Nope, it's not the emptiness, just the fear that I will sleep with a woman and dream. And my dream will drown her with proof of some insane reality. I don't need that drama in my life. The last time I thought I had something with a woman, it had gone badly. Three years ago...

I looked into Marion's eyes as she ate her lamb kabob. She winked at me, downed the meat in one gulp and the vegetables the next. We were in Shanian Cafe, my favorite Lebanese restaurant. I'd offered to share my table with her since she'd looked so alone sitting at the bar, her body turned away from the others seated there. The flickering light of the candle cast reddish highlights on her dark wavy hair. We hadn't talked so far; I find it rude to talk when you're eating, plus it slows you down. She initiated the conversation.

"Do you come here often?"

I liked her voice. It was low and had a hint of vibrato.

"Every so often."

"What do you do?" she asked, the bracelet on her wrist tinkling as she brought the glass of wine to her lips.

"I do nothing."

She shifted in her seat, smiling nervously.

"Surely there must be something."

"No, I'm serious. I have a contractor job as a data entry coordinator. It's so insignificant it's nothing. I spend my days doing nothing."

It was true. I was simply weary. I was tired of living. I felt like a cog turning for nothing in the machinery of this equally tired society. Life sucked because it simply was.

Occasionally I'd find myself wanting to turn off a switch to a power outlet that wasn't there. There it was, the inevitable fact. I was alive, and there was nothing I could do to change it. It would have been a waste of energy to end my life, as diverting as that would have been. I was brought into this world without my consent. But I was so, so, so, *so* tired of living! What is living, after all, if not just breathing and going through the motions? What makes living so special? Why are people so afraid of *not* living? Death is but a state of endless apathy that one never feels. Well, life felt like the same thing. Of course, people would have said I was suicidal, or antisocial, or any one of those overused psychological terms people only have a general concept of.

I masked my thoughts with a sip of wine.

She picked up her fork and started poking at her tabbouleh.

"There's got to be something that fascinates you. Politics maybe, or food, or books, or something." She winked at me again.

I started laughing. Heaven forbid if my interests actually lay in what she mapped out. Did people truly find passion in these things?

"Politics disgust me. I don't pay them the slightest attention anymore. I cook my own food, but although it keeps me busy, it doesn't fascinate me. Books, eh, any old fart can write anything. I am not impressed."

I bit into a falafel, the chickpea flavor unexpected. It was as good as, if not better than, your average meatballs, with more spices.

"Surely there must be something you were fascinated about in the past," she stressed, raising an eyebrow. She gulped down her wine, choking a little as it caught in her throat.

"I suppose. When I was a kid, I loved the sciences and the natural disasters. I guzzled disaster films like *Airport 1975* and *Poseidon Adventure* like there was no tomorrow. Every time there was a storm, I expected a tornado to pop out. I waited many a time with my camera to capture one."

"I like the sciences too," Marion said, smiling at me.

"What do you like about them?" I asked.

"Uh...their uh... the... the natural disasters like you said. They're... formidable."

She was more drunk than she thought, apparently. She couldn't keep her thoughts together.

"Did you like the volcanoes or the tornados, the hurricanes or the tsunamis?" I pressed on. It was an old passion, but I was glad she seemed to share my former interest.

"Um. The... the hurricanes," she said.

"Yes, but what exactly fascinated you about them?" If one had to have an interest, one had to wholeheartedly know why.

"The winds, the power, the, oh, I don't know!" she frowned.

I expected more, but she glowered down at her plate.

"Goodness, your sister said you could be annoying sometimes," she put a hand over her mouth.

I recoiled, the stuttering, the halting pauses and awkwardness suddenly making sense. She'd been faking me out all along! What the hell?

"My sister?! How do you know my sister?"

Marion refused to look at me, but I pressed on.

"Tell me."

"She... well, we met at work and she thought I'd be a good influence on you. I mean, it was her plan. But I do sort of like you! I mean, you're weird. But—"

"I'm weird," I said flatly.

"Yes. I mean, in a good way. I mean I didn't know what to expect. Your sister—"

My heart pounded so hard my vision shimmered. My sister. My bane. And this fool was her puppet.

"She wanted you to date someone. Anyone. You're a loner. I can see that but—"

"She set you up with me?" I said glacially.

"Well, yes," she said, cocking her head.

I stood up and the napkin on my lap tumbled to the floor. I tipped the waiter and walked out of the restaurant, slamming the door and almost tripping over a parking meter.

I drove home in silence, my chest heaving, as I struggled not to lose it. Breathe. One. Two. Repeat. Tivana... I missed a green light as I composed myself, trying to breathe and evade the lightheadedness and sense of suffocation. She'd tried drowning me so many times in the bathtub, in the pool, at the beach. She'd say it was fun. Our parents had to separate us whenever we were around water. I have tried to forget that sense of suffocation, the blackness shimmering in my vision, that strange feeling of peace and terror intertwined in my gasping lungs. I have tried to forget that surreal whispering of a woman, that sense of intangible hands scooping me and pushing me to the surface. It was back. And my sister was going to know how I felt about it.

I called my sister as soon as I got home. I paced the kitchen like a raging wildcat, waiting for the infernal ringing to stop. Oh boy, she would not want to hear my voicemail—it would be worse than what I'd say to her in person. Finally, she picked up.

"Hello!" I shouted, cutting through her first syllable of hello.

"Amos? What's up?"

"You're asking me what's up? You know full well why I'm pissed at you, Tivana!"

"Dude, chill. What's your problem?"

"You set me up with this Marion chick! How dare you?"

"I didn't set anything up."

"Don't lie to me. I've always been able to know when you lie. You suck at it," I replied, clenching my jaw.

"Well... My husband and I thought you needed a companion. A friend of sorts. To help. You know..."

She didn't even sound apologetic.

"To help? To help! Is it any of your business?" I shouted anew. I could feel myself getting light-headed.

"You do nothing all day. Nothing holds your attention anymore, you just stew and sit in your freaking mobile home and don't see anybody. A woman would put you on the straight path again!" Now it was her turn to shout. She wasn't a good shouter either. Her voice got reedy and high-pitched when she yelled.

"You talk about putting me on the straight path?! Me? What gives you any right to judge? What gives you any right to meddle with my life?"

"You—"

I didn't let her finish.

"I didn't fucking judge you when you hung out with druggies in college! I didn't take away your precious LSD and coke even though I wanted to! I didn't intervene when you were dating Isaac and you were promising to stop even though you didn't for another two years! *You* were the one who tried to blame me for everything when our parents called, so freaked out about you. *You* lied to everybody about how great you were, when instead you were falling apart. *You're* the one who covered up your psychotic breakdown and paid the price for lying about it. So give me a break, Tivana."

I was surprised by how angry I felt. I hadn't felt this angry in years. But I liked my life, and it was nobody's business to patch me up, family or not. And it was true, everyone knew I had to be "fixed," yet her stint with drugs was hushed up. But talk about not wanting to be a part of society anymore and wanting peace and quiet, and that's not okay. I heard Tivana gather herself and speak hoarsely into the phone.

"Okay, you got me. But I stopped my drug use. I've been clean for eight years now. Please don't bring my past issues into this. You've got a problem and it's a 'now' problem. You're a hermit! I thought a girl in your life would motivate you to care about things, to enjoy this world we live in, instead of sitting on your ass all day! Move your bones, Amos! Just because you were with that bitch Ciara, who treated you like shit, isn't a reason to give up on everybody."

Ciara. I hadn't thought of *her* in a long time. It did nothing to help me calm down. On the contrary. Ciara, advancing on me, her tiny fists raised, ready to leave another bruise on my ribs, her mouth open in a maw of hostility...

"I have no obligation to you. Don't ever do something like that again," I replied, feeling my pulse accelerating.

"I can't let you do this to yourself, Amos! Live, love, laugh! Come on!"

I scoffed. Seriously, she was going to low depths to bring *that* up.

"You're bringing up a botched version of Coca-Cola's motto to motivate me? Are you serious?"

My sister sounded sheepish.

"It was as good a try as any. You need help. Try going to a therapist!"

I sighed, feeling the anger receding but not the amused disappointment.

"And tell me, oh wise, life-loving Tivana. Do you think a therapist will be able to fix me? Why should I? It took years for the psychologist to get through to you. Besides, what do you care? You're the one who kept trying to drown me as a kid."

My sister stuttered, muttering platitudes under her breath. She might have sounded apologetic, but I didn't want to hear it.

"If you can't explain to me why I can't be the way I am, at least stop fixing me. I don't want to talk to you until you explain what is so great about life and until you promise to stop meddling in my affairs."

"But—but it's normal! You've got to love life! If you can't, you've got no purpose! Believe in God's plan!"

I hung up the phone. The nerve of Tivana. My sister, my perfect sister who could do no wrong in my parent's eyes. She thought I had psychological issues? She had major psychological issues. I first started noticing something wrong when she was in her early teens and she'd burrow in her room, refusing to talk to anyone, even her best friends, even me. The rare times I got something out of her, she thought she was a failure, a scarecrow for the whole world to see. And then, when she got out of those funks, she bounced back, thinking she was the coolest kid in the town, that she was *the shit*. I noticed when she ripped all her prized Star Trek trading cards and stickers to pieces after a fit of rage, because one of the cards didn't fit well into her binders—and then later she cried and wondered why she'd done it. The last straw was when I saw her throwing her schoolbooks at the family dog, as it whimpered and growled fearfully at her. All she'd said, while backing away with shaking hands, was, "It wasn't me, it wasn't me, but he looked at me funny." Then the psychologist visits started. Eventually a psychiatrist put her on mood stabilizers.

Now, she's drunk the Kool-Aid of life and has the nerve to meddle with mine.

So we didn't speak for three years, despite her voicemails, despite her emails, despite her letters. Her son tried to call once or twice, and sent letters, but I didn't open them.

Today is my day off from work. Thank goodness. Now I have time to clean the mess my dream created. Usually, I would peel my butt from this mucky beige sofa, and go to my tiny bathroom where I always feel that if I were to sit down on the toilet too hard, the wooden floor would cave in. The bathroom would gaze at me passively with its sun-faded light blue walls as I shave and groom my goatee, shower with water hot enough to scald, and then comb and part my long sandy hair. Men's Sea and Sand would fill my nose as I make faces at myself in the mirror. My bangs would hide my left eyebrow, where years of plucking out extraneous hairs has messed up its shape. I would then stalk paranormal message boards and see if anyone has experienced what I have experienced.

No, instead, I am cleaning my bedroom. Again. I take the mop and drag it across the floor, where scratches and dings abound from previous, more drastic attempts to clean.

My mind jumps ahead. Why me? I haven't read about or met another soul who suffers the ailment I have. I go through waves (ironic, I know) where I do want to see what's wrong with me. I can't use a mental illness as a logical explanation. The water is too incriminating and too tangible. Is it a physiological thing? Is it a psychological thing? Is it a curse? It definitely isn't a blessing. All it has done is make me avoid the beach and become a recluse. No positives come from these dreams. Once, just once, I would like to see something substantial come from these dreams. I want answers.

The phone starts ringing, my obnoxious ring tone setting my teeth on edge. I stop in the middle of my bedroom, closing my eyes in exasperation. I sneeze twice. The smell of salt burns my nose. No one has called me in ages. I've scared off all the telemarketers by answering their calls with heavy breathing and nothing else. I wait for the ringing to stop. I watch the lime green phone shudder on its charger as it rings again. Well, no peace this morning, that's for sure. I approach my cell phone and recognize the number. It's my sister. I do *not* want to answer. Hasn't she gotten it yet that I don't want to talk to her at all?

Maybe something is wrong and she needs my help. I sneer. That's doubtful. But then again, her calling is uncommon and unusual, and *that* piques my interest.

I answer curtly.

"Hey," she replies, obviously stunned but happy to have snagged me. She'd better not push her luck and start prattling on about life's inanities.

"So, I know you told me to not call again..."

"Glad to know you remember that."

"But I just wanted to invite you over. Steven is turning ten years old today. It's special."

"You called me for this?! I don't want to be stuck in a room full of hyper kids with you! That's not going to happen."

"Please, Amos! You haven't seen him since he was five. Cheer up, will you? Can you at least do it for him? It'd be nice for Steven to see Uncle Amos for his tenth b-day."

I grumble.

"Stop being a selfish prick! Come or don't come, at this point I am done with you!" she shouts.

"Fine." I hang up.

I feel a queer sensation going down my body, down my legs. I look down and see water sloughing down me like a sullen caterpillar. It spreads out into a puddle on the floor. I throw up my hands and get a towel, and I wipe the floor. The water plays games with me. The towel absorbs the water and as I turn to avoid slipping on remaining streaks, the water dribbles down the towel all at once and crawls hastily along under the bed, the streaks following suit. I glare at the towel, then at the space under the bed. If this hadn't happened so many other times before, I would be calling Tivana's psychologist right about now.

I glare at my bed and rip off the sheets. The water snakes up and dumps itself on my sheets and bedspread. Droplets fly in my face, and as I ball up the sheets to put them in the washer, the water does something it has never done while I was awake: it calls to me. So softly I cannot hear it at first. Then the fricative voice tries again.

Amos, leave us.

I shake my head.

"I want to stop having these dreams," I cry. "I'm going to go mad. I don't want to be like my sister!"

A wetness seeps onto my side, the ocean water pools into

my clothing. Now, the sheets are dry. The water has never done that before. I am soaked again, and I start shivering.

Why? the water murmurs, and it slides to my face, around my neck. I close my eyes and relish the scent of salt and brine.

"What kind of question is that?" I yell. The water lazily travels down my body and splashes on the floor, increasing the size of the puddle there. Screw it. I throw the sheets on the floor and undress. I can't deal with this. I must go to the party. Anything to distract myself.

I call back. Surprisingly, Tivana picks up. Her angry breathing greets me.

"You can stop getting your panties in a knot. I'm coming. There. Happy?"

Another realization flares to the surface. Tivana lives near the beach. If the water is responding to me... Perhaps if I go to the source, I will finally get answers.

Plus, a small part of me does feel bad about missing the kid's birthday. For all my annoyance about kids, Steven isn't responsible for his mother's decisions. A tenth birthday is special, after all. What else do I have going on? Clean the mess on the bed? Sit on the misshapen sofa with its flattened cushions until I go to work? Then go through the motions until lunch break, where I play mini chess with myself and eat P.F. Chang's? Then come back to my dark mobile home, tripping as always on that uneven step to the front door? Even for me, that is way pathetic.

While I hadn't spoken to Tivana in the past few years, she'd left voicemails which I'd sometimes listened to, sometimes not. I remember one in particular where she said she'd taken Steven to a therapist because she was afraid he also had borderline personality disorder. The kid was acting out in school, closing himself in his room every night, and having crying spells at the weirdest times. It turned out he didn't have his mom's disorder, the kid had just been under a lot of pressure and had been bullied a lot at school. Even though I'd still been angry with Tivana, I knew I was scared too of the possibility of BPD. It is most likely a genetic thing. I'm surprised *I* don't have the disorder myself. I always wondered if the BPD that runs in my family was somehow replaced with my freaky sea dreams. I don't know whether to be relieved or not.

I find myself moving to the pile of mail stashed in the corner of my living room, where I keep my junk DVDs and cables. Most of it is my sister's and nephew's letters. I decide to open them. Might as well be on top of the family situation if I am going to this party. I open Steven's stuff first, evidenced by the large, slanted writing in blue gel pen, and am greeted with various goofy cards, stickers and Marvel cartoons. I go through card after card, skimming past the *I miss yous, Here's what I'm doing in schools*, and *I love farts*. He is one zany kid. He loves Aquaman and Storm and Wolverine. He does indeed love farts, and does okay in school. I pause on one card where he wrote: *I learned how to swim today. Mommy says she doesn't want me to drown. She says you used to drown a lot. Do you know how to swim? I hope so. I can teach you. Drowning is bad. I wish we could all be Aquaman.*

You and me both, kid, you and me both. We have some things in common, I think, smiling a little. Maybe this party won't kill me.

I step out in front of my sister's home, my legs aching from having had to park a few blocks down. Her driveway is cluttered with cars parked in ways I know will make their owners curse when they come out later. The sight of my sister's home, well-kept and so much fancier than mine, makes me drag my feet. I don't want to be here. But I certainly don't want to be at home either. I'll talk with Steven for a while, hang out for no more than an hour, and then I'll leave. Maybe take a detour and go visit the ocean. I look up at the brand new palm tree swaying in the breeze, scraping against the roof. My sister had gotten a paint job done on the house, and instead of a flashy coral peach, the wooden slats of the house are a modest white. The smell of the surf tickles my nostrils and I feel both an excited leap and a dreadful cramp in my stomach. The seawater... I grunt as something, someone, squeezes my waist.

"Uncle Amos! You're here!"

"Yes, yes, I'm here," I grumble.

Steven looks at me with a wide smile. He has all his teeth. The last time I'd seen him he'd been missing a few of them. He has impressively high cheekbones. His knobby knees make me smile. His eyes are green like mine, though. I don't say anything, but he straightens and tries to look less bouncy.

"I'm glad you came, Uncle Amos," he says gravely. "Why don't you come over more?"

I stare at him a little shamefacedly. I can't reply. Thankfully, I don't have to. He beckons me into the backyard and to the open pool deck. Why my sister has chosen a house with a pool when she lives five minutes away from the beach, don't ask me. I follow Steven's bobbing head with its lopsided violet party hat. I hear the bubbling of the pool fountains before I see them. Steven dashes ahead, yelling, "I'm coming, guys!"

I finger the makeshift card in my pocket, I put it together for him last minute. As I round the corner and see the mob of kids jumping around, blowing party horns, and chatting their heads off, I cringe. In the pool, another group of kids is playing with balls and paddles, making up rules. Balls are flying everywhere in a flurry of chaos. One of the balls arcs toward me and I duck. The smell of seawater hits my nose. Confused, I go to the pool and dip my fingers in. Of course Tivana would have a salt water pool. Why not? I resist the urge to start laughing hysterically. This is going to be a long day.

I am rubbing my face in exasperation as I hear the little buggers screaming around me, splashing into the pool so hard the deck itself looks like a Jacuzzi. I am wet and I haven't set foot in the pool. I look around. There should be more adults here. Only a soccer mom here, a deadbeat dad there, both on their phones, they can't possibly keep an eye on the kids. Tivana hasn't assigned me to guard duty, so I'm enjoying that freedom. It would be even more enjoyable if the adults who were assigned to watch the kids were paying attention. Tivana's rhododendron bushes bend down, wilted in their cracked hanging pots. Colorful South American mosaic fishes with over-exaggerated lips jut out pretentiously from the wall. A dark blue plastic table is covered with a weather-worn vinyl tablecloth, the kind that sticks to your arm hairs even after multiple attempts to dislodge it. Matching chairs are strewn about. Mangled party hats and trays of half-eaten chocolates and blueberry muffins sit on them.

Music is blasting, and all at once I recognize the cheesy sound of Charles Trenet's *"La Mer."* That damn bloke always sounds so happy. Granted, it is an idyllic love song to the , but still. It used to be my childhood soundtrack, though. My father used to put on old records on Sundays. One of his favorites was *"La Mer."* I used to love it. But as with everything else, I became jaded.

"Hey! Excuse me! What is this song about?"

I turn my head and there's this girl bobbing in the water, her eyes wide and red. The ever-present fragrance of the sea make my nostrils flare.

"I don't remember exactly. Sorry," I say nonchalantly.

"You sure you dunno? What language is it anyway?" she asks, her arm floats bobbing up on the surface.

I sigh.

"It says something about loving the sea. It's French." I could say more if I tried, but I really don't want to expend the effort.

The girl gives me the stink eye, her dark hair floating around her as a belly dancer's shawl. She has a slight accent, and I wonder if she is Indian, even though her skin tone is quite fair.

"You don't know much, do ya?" she pouts. "Martin at school knows some French. He says he knows twelve languages!"

"And you believe him?" I ask witheringly.

She frowns, splashing her hands in the water.

"Well, I didn't believe him when he said he went to Pluto and died and came back again. I mean, wouldn't that make him a zombie?"

I stifle a laugh. She at least is funnier than some adults I know. I nod my head in assent.

"Do you have friends that make up stuff?" she asks, fiddling with her arm floats.

"I don't have any. People don't like making stuff up anymore," I reply truthfully.

"Well, I have lots of friends, and they make stuff up with me. We watch the same movies, we drink the same soda, we like—"

I turn my head when I hear Tivana calling me for help. I get up and start walking away from the girl.

"You're not listening!" she shouts, pointing to her sopping head. "Friends are important."

I shake my head and observe Tivana racing around trying to organize the party decorations, which are falling everywhere on the pool deck and inside the house. A few other adults help, and I stumble forward to pitch in. It's easier than saying hi and having a whole conversation. Tivana raises an eyebrow at me, but I don't acknowledge it. I grab a wayward muffin wrapper and start cleaning up the place, adjusting banners, blowing air back in balloons. The whole place smells like pizza and Doritos, mingled with the salt. It's a gnarly combination.

It's grunt work and it's time consuming, but eventually we manage to tidy things up while stepping over and around hyper bouncing kids. I nearly slip on tacky soda stains once or twice. Several times I think Tivana is about to talk to me, but I don't encourage her. I don't have her husband Isaac as a buffer between me and her. I guess he's too busy putting in overtime so he and his family can maintain their lifestyle.

Finally, we go back out on the pool deck and I resume my position on the wet deck. Still the adults are on their phones. I swear they haven't changed position since I left. The girl is playing Marco Polo with the other kids. Some are doing raspberries underwater, and others time them to determine who's the champion. I haven't blown a raspberry in years! Elton John's "Bennie and the Jets" is playing now but I find myself thinking back on *"La Mer."* For all its cheesiness, it is a reminder of a shadow of myself, a shadow that used to feel joy and other confusing but vivid emotions.

I stare over at the pool, not really paying attention. The kids are splashing around. Steven is somewhere in that mêlée, holding onto his noodle for dear life. I don't see the girl right away, then I spot her underwater, still holding her breath. What a trooper. The kids don't seem to be paying attention to her anymore, though. Then I see her kick out with her legs, and her arms start flailing. The kids around her laugh, they almost swim over her. She is moving and twisting almost as in a dance. She's been under for a while, I think. I lean forward. She's really acting it up. The kids swim around her. She raises her arms and keeps sinking. Her hair whirls in a bubbly mess. Then it hits me. Where are her arm floats? I look around and see her neon yellow Spongebob floats in a crumpled heap on the steps. I look back at the pool and her flailing is weakening.

My God, she's drowning and everyone thinks she's playing! I dash out, shirt, cargo pants, flip flops and all, and dive. I reach her, my eyes stinging like hell, and grab her by her tiny waist. I float her up to the surface, where she is now choking and retching hard, her skin camellia white. Water and drool trickle down her chin as she coughs and chokes. Her eyes bulge and her face turns red as she hacks out the water from her lungs. Her body is trembling so hard she is making waves which splash over onto the pool deck. The kids have stopped playing, and are now encircling us, befuddled.

"You okay?" I ask.

"I guess," she croaks.

"Why'd you take off your floats if you don't know how to swim?"

She bows her head and then glares at me, although she quickly drops her gaze. "I thought I could!"

Behind me, I can hear Steven climbing out of the pool, yelling, "Mom!"

I don't want a fuss. I know how drowning feels all too well. The last thing you want is a suffocating tide of people around you; all you want to know is that you're breathing, you're alive. I steer the girl to the shallow end of the pool and place her floats back on. They are partially deflated, but they're better than nothing.

"Did no one realize what was going on?" I ask quietly.

The kids blink at me, but I can tell they are shocked. I look at the adults on the deck, now staring at me, chagrined. "You didn't see this, did you?" I shout.

I ask the girl gently as she wipes her streaming nose, "What's your name?"

"Adi," she mumbles.

I look up to see Tivana hovering over me. Steven looks as guilty as if he'd drowned Adi himself.

"Amos, was she really drowning?"

"What a question! Of course she was drowning! She was under for a few minutes without her arm floats, and nobody saw what was going on!"

Steven speaks up, somewhat embarrassed. "I thought she was playing."

There is an awkward silence. I could be sarcastic, but it's the kid's birthday. Tivana whips out her cellphone and starts dialing.

"Hello? Hello? Mrs. Schraff? Yes, hi, it's Tivana. Um, I just wanted to let you know your daughter had a little incident in the pool. Nothing major. Her arm floats got lost in the pool. My brother took care of her. She's all right. Here, let me put her on the phone."

Tivana holds out the phone to Adi. Adi looks fragile holding it to her ear. She's still shaking. "I'm fine, Mom," Adi says. "Mom, I swear I am fine. I took off my floats... I thought I could do it. No, I won't do it again. Mom, I'm fine, I pinky promise! Mom, really, I'm ok." Adi hands the phone back to Tivana, who mouths to me, *She wants to talk to you!* I raise my hands, mouthing back, *No! Not happening!* Tivana insists, even going so far as saying, "Of course he'll talk to you, he's right here."

I give her a stare of pure loathing and take the phone.

"Hello?"

"Amos, hi, I'm Adi's mom. You took care of her? Is she really ok?"

"Yes," I reply curtly.

"Oh, thank God! Thank God!" She starts crying, ugly crying by the sound of it, but it doesn't annoy me as much as it should. "Adi doesn't swim yet, you see. I give her floats, but she doesn't always keep them on."

"I noticed."

"It's so rare to find Good Samaritans these days. I can't

thank you enough for saving her! She is my life, my everything. Is there anything I can do, anything at all, to repay you?"

You could hang up the phone and leave me in peace, but instead I say, "Nothing."

"Oh, surely there must be some way I can repay you. You've saved my daughter's life. I can't just let you walk away after doing something like that—"

"No, nothing at all," I reply and quickly hand the phone back to Tivana. I ignore her glare and walk over to Steven. He is shaking, biting his nails so hard I see blood.

"Don't beat yourself up about it. It's ok."

He looks like he's about to cry. "I swear I thought she was playing. We all thought it. She could have died. Oh my God, she could have."

"Steven, breathe. The adults assigned to watch you are to blame. It was their responsibility. They shouldn't have been on their phones at all. In the future, though, even if you think someone is playing underwater, if they're holding their breath, it's better to make sure they are okay, if they've been under for a while. All right?"

"Thanks, Uncle Amos," he murmurs.

I look over at Adi.

"You sure you're okay, kid?"

She nods, trying to play tough by crossing her arms and legs. Well, there it is. This party has gone on long enough and I'm tired, annoyed and soaking wet. I get up and wave good-bye. Tivana, still on the phone, mouths, *Where do you think you're going?*

I shrug. "Thanks for inviting me, Sis. Maybe pay more attention to the kids swimming and drowning in your pool, especially in front of Steven?"

She pales, and I feel genuinely bad. I hope that comment won't bring on an episode.

"I'm sorry," I murmur, and start walking away. I can be a jerk sometimes, but even for me, that was going over the line.

"Wait," she says, and as she flounders to end the conversation, I hightail it, leaving the pool deck, going through the screen door, walking around the elaborate shrubbery. Tivana catches up to me as I walk out of her driveway. Out of breath, she takes me by the arm. "Before you go, I'd like to tell you something. I wanted to invite you for Steven's birthday, yes. But I also wanted to see you, and... and..."

I wait for her to continue. Her face is going through a palette of reds and whites.

"And apologize to you."

I step back, not believing what I'm hearing.

"I'm sorry, what?"

"I've been thinking a lot lately, and I've been really opening up to my therapist. I feel guilty all the time, Amos. I feel like I've ruined everybody I care about, hurt so many people, because I was selfish. Because I let my BPD take control of me. It's not cool."

I shake my head. Indeed.

"I've been doing much better, but every time I look at Steven, I think about how much of a wreck I was the first few years of his life. I hurt him badly. And Isaac, too. Lately, I've realized I've hurt you, too. Steven doesn't see you because you don't come. And I know you don't come because you don't like me. I don't blame you. For Pete's sake, I almost killed you multiple times!" She runs a hand through her tawny hair, and I reach out, gently patting her thin shoulders. I don't want her to have an episode while she is beating herself up about what she's done during her episodes. That would be ridiculous.

"Tivana, say no more. You know I'm not a fan of saccharine statements. You've said enough. It's true, I don't like you. But you're my sister. You *have* gotten better. I am happy for you. In fact, I am *proud* of you for it. You've grown up," I say, realizing it as I'm saying it. Gone is the girl who'd blame every-body else for her actions, gone is the impulsive, fearful brat who'd throw tantrums when things didn't go her way. She *has* grown up, even if she still relapses from time to time.

Tivana looks down at the pool deck.

"Thank you for coming. It means so much to Steven. He really likes you, you know."

"Yeah, yeah," I grumble. But I can't hide the fact that it's more of a show. I truly like the kid.

"By the way, Steven has been waking up from intense dreams these past few years. He won't shut up about them. When he wakes up, I've noticed there's water in the bed. It doesn't smell like pee. It smells like the ocean."

I blanch.

"It reminded me of you, when you'd wake up as a kid. Mom and Dad never caught on. What was the deal with that? Were you trying to prank us? Why would there be saltwater in your bed? I ask Steven how he does it, but he won't tell me. He swears it's already there when he wakes up, although it wasn't there when he went to sleep."

"I need to get going," I say hurriedly. "I'll keep in touch, bye!"

"Amos! What is it? Do you know? Please tell me."

"I... I can't. I don't know. I... don't want to think about it. I didn't know you knew. I... It's none of your business! I have to go."

And I jog away, taking the road that leads to the beach.

———

That was close. I'd never realized Tivana knew my secret. Part of it, anyway. Apparently Steven has the same shit happening to him. I truly don't know what it's about. I've spent years trying to research it but have never found anything. I know I am not crazy. I know Steven isn't crazy either. It's frustrating, but there's no use being angry about it. If the kid is smart, he will do what I did and soon shut up about those dreams, clean up the mess, and deal with the burden.

I think back on Adi and shudder. Poor girl. It's a young age to feel your death coming, even as you struggle against it. I just hope she doesn't fear water from now on. I am still amazed people didn't realize what was going on. People pay attention to all the wrong stuff.

I'm walking to the beach now, it's so close to my sister's house, going through the cheesy streets named Siesta, or Sun Dance or Blue Waves. Seriously, Florida? Couldn't come up with anything more creative? But I know these streets will take me to an isolated part of the beach where tourists don't like hanging out because the sand is much rougher and the dunes are rockier. The hypnotizing roar of the surf is soothing, and I reach the boardwalk, where I promptly throw away my shoes. The pool water ruined them, but to be honest, those shoes were old anyway.

The sand scrapes against my feet, a blend of dry and wet paste eventually squishing between my toes. Ah. The hot, coarse sand. It brings back the sweaty heady days of my childhood, as well as the shadow of the terrifying dreams I've had since my teenage years. Although it is midafternoon now, the sand almost burns my soles as I walk on its gravelly surface toward the water. The Sea is a muted emerald hue interlocked with moody indigo, a lazy coupling that inspires fatigue and melancholy. Funny, the sea. I used to bound and leap in it like an orca, with no respect for the ocean's grandeur or stateliness. But it's been years now that I haven't set a foot in the water because of those nightmares.

I want answers. *Come on*, I think. *You talked to me earlier. Can you hear me now?*

My breath catches as the waterline suddenly rises, slow and

gentle waves now sharply lapping almost at my feet. I am halfway down the beach, and a few minutes ago, the waves were a good distance away. I shudder. Maybe the heat is affecting my vision. The sea is still her morose shade of indigo green, though now she is speckled with sunlight, sequins bobbing on her back like a gaudy cloak. I feel a faint viciousness in the air, like someone cracking their knuckles, getting ready for a fight, an agitated tingling that is about to come at me. I brace myself. I expect the sea to talk to me in that strange, intimate whisper she spoke to me in earlier.

The water rushes once at me, then again, knocking me off my feet. I land facedown in the waves, and it feels like I've been boogie boarding and missed a wave. I scramble for footing and I grab at whatever I can to stand and breathe. I look up from my watery muzzle and realize the waterline is almost up to the dunes. I swim awkwardly to shore, although I'm not sure it can be called a shore now. I can barely see the sand. I keep slipping and sliding until finally I hook my elbows into some bedraggled dry grass and hoist myself up. Holy shit! This doesn't make sense. This is like my dreams. A watery apocalypse rising and rising, ready to sweep away everything in a heartbeat. I can barely breathe. I pinch myself to make sure I'm awake. Unfortunately, I am. The waves are roaring now, crashing into each other like animals, foam flying like spit from angry mouths. What devilry is this? What the bloody hell?

I never know what triggers the sea to rise in my dreams. She just does, a lone, immensely powerful being suddenly turning on humanity. Maybe, like in my dreams, I can try talking to the ocean. A wave rushes over me, chilling me again and invading my nose and mouth. I gasp and cough, the nauseating amount of sea salt I've ingested sure to give me gastric troubles later. That ruthlessness around me I sensed earlier is replaced by a feeling I know well. A grinding, seething age-old anger that is waiting to be unleashed. I really don't want the sea to be any angrier than she already is.

I grimace as I feel sand rasping against my teeth. *Why?* I start projecting my mind and I fall flat on my back as another wave rolls over me commandingly.

Damn it! WHY?! Stop freaking trying to drown me and explain to me what's your damned problem!

I cringe. That's a sure way to piss her off. Great, my life will end shortly in whatever twisted reality I am in right now.

Surprisingly, the sea seems to recede a tiny bit. At least, enough that I'm not floundering like a beached dolphin. The hiss of the tide whistles in my ear and it tunes in and out, like a dying radio. Then I recognize the sea is trying to talk back to me. The static becomes louder and it makes my head buzz.

Listen, it rasps, the waves now trickling tranquilly over my body.

"What for?" I answer back. "Why should I listen when you're trying to kill me?"

The sea roars, foam slamming me in the face. I can feel the water rising and my heart jumps. Oh no. I am not getting drowned this easily. I can't talk, so I project my thoughts, hurling them at the sea like pellets.

Stop getting pissed already! Just explain why you rise like this, in my dreams, and now. You are angry. Why?

For a moment I think the sea is going to drown my miserable self in rage, but the waves recede ever so slightly. My skin is going to be wrinkled like a prune later.

Because you keep trying to kill me. And you do not care, repeating mistakes over and over, eternal as my curse, to watch you fall, again and again...

The waves roll over me, up over the sand and back. Her feminine echo is in my head, and I feel nauseated, the incessant echo overwhelming.

"But I'm not trying to kill you. I don't even know what you are talking about."

Now I think I've done it. I brace myself for a watery death, expecting the sea to cast the vast expanse of her limitless girth over me like a bitter lover. But she doesn't. The water curls around me like a comforting arm, soothing for now, but with restrained power behind it. The waves surround me, way too close to comfort, but for now their frothy anger is abated.

I am a force. A force has power and energy, just like you. I am a force in tandem with the force of the sky, the earth, and the intervention of you humans. You, my children, my ungrateful, destructive children, come from my loins. You started as a microscopic species, able to do nothing but eat and wriggle around. Then you learned to swim, you became different creatures, you discovered land, you were able to move, to survive, to evolve. You are a strong force too. You were given a great gift. Your mind and your mortality. But you squander the opportunities given to you. Again and again you use me, not as an instrument of harmony, of abundance, of love, of communication, of protection. You use me for your petty wars, your avarice. You satisfy the most base desire, eating, by murdering my other children in ways that should not be possible. You are the oil spill to the rest of my children, a vast, putrid cloak choking and suffocating them into nonexistence. I regret ever bringing you forth from my womb. Your small lives should be revelations. Instead, they are a curse.

The sight of nothing but water makes my teeth clench. She has me cocooned like an infant, obscuring my vision of everything but herself.

I still don't know what this has to do with me. I haven't done anything to her. She is talking about other people, so many other blasted members of my race. Why is she talking to me?

"Why do you speak like this? Why speak to me?"

You are my child. We have a bond, a bond you cannot escape. Cease trying to disbelieve it.

"No, but why *me*? I'm just one person. We are not all alike. You cannot judge us based on the actions of a few. Why tell me all this? Now, and in my dreams?"

It is the only way I can reach you. Man has become blind to the reality in front of his eyes.

My heartbeat slowly matches the frantic rush of the water around me. I try to understand but find my inability to connect with her, the same problem I have with my fellow human beings, impeding me. Yes, she is right, mankind makes mistakes. But we learn. It's just a part of life. To get so angry about it is futile. Things will resolve themselves over time. She should understand that.

A guttural growl ripples around me, and I realize she is latching on to my every thought. Waves sting me in the face like slaps. They course higher and higher on my face until I'm having trouble breathing again. I start gasping.

You have the gift! she roars. *And you squander it. You are just like your brothers and sisters. Uncaring, apathetic, blind to a problem until it affects you directly. I should let you live and see what happens during the rest of your puny lives, after you have poisoned me more than you already have. Once you see the children in my depths die one by one, once you see your own race starving and dying from pollution, you would see the misery you have brought on yourselves. A hell you cannot repair, a hell that will take lifetimes to reverse, if it can be reversed at all. But I shall be merciful. I shall kill you now, and put an end to it once and for all.*

I can see the sea rising above me, a feral wall of frothy tomb-white water looming above me, exactly like in my dreams. I don't want to be pulverized like an insect under her furious hand. My panic rises, and I frantically shout in my head, *Please don't kill us! Please don't; we can change,* I plead.

Remember when we used to be little worms living in you? And now we are where we are? We have changed. We can still change.

The sea is still agitated, but at least the waves are lapping around me instead of on me, slowly withdrawing from my face. The water is now a sickly pale green, a faded teal bed frothing madly around me.

Why should I believe you? she whispers, coldly.

You might not believe the human race. But you can believe me.

All of a sudden, I am thrown back into memories, memories I'd forgotten: reading the news, hearing my former friends talking about various ocean disasters in the past few years. I am caught unaware, as disaster after disaster rolls through my mind: the waste patch covering the majority of the Pacific Ocean, millions of square kilometers of garbage in some areas; the *Deepwater Horizon* oil spill, originating in Mexico but spreading like a cancer to all parts of the globe, killing and poisoning so many species, causing mutations in so many others, for years afterward, to say nothing of its effects on the beaches themselves. I remember my parents talking about the *Torrey Canyon* oil spill and the Runit Dome construction in the Marshall Islands when I was a child, and then promptly forgetting about the events soon after they happened. Facts I'd forgotten race through my mind: billions of pounds of trash dumped in the ocean every year; runoff, toxic chemicals and sewage disposal, all enthusiastic harbingers of eutrophication. Climate change and pollution steadily depleting the ocean's oxygen, leading to eventual mass extinction of multiple species, possibly even including ours. In the near future, our Earth could be completely overflowing with microplastic and toxins.

For the first time in a long, long time, I feel emotions. Exasperation. Anger. Fear. Fear of the world we are creating.

Fear of the legacy we are leaving behind. And disgust. Raw, unadulterated disgust at what we are doing to ourselves and the sea. The human race sure has a poor way of repaying favors. Killing the mother source of our existence takes the cake. Why do we keep doing this? Why do we resist change? We must be able to change. There must be something we can do.

How to change? How?

The sea rushes around me, rising higher past my vision. But the water cushions me in an empty space.

I think of Tivana. She wasn't able to do anything to change and improve herself until she was willing to find out the root of her problems. The first step was seeing a psychiatrist, the second and third were getting a diagnosis and working on treating her problem. But she resisted the first step. Because of fear.

I gasp as the realization hits me. Why does the human race repeat mistakes over and over? Fear. Greed. Lack of empathy. Without knowing it, I had been part of the problem, by not caring, by turning a blind eye. The way to fix the problem is to be aware of it and act on it. You cannot act if you are imprisoned by apathy.

I feel a weight lift from my shoulders, even though I am still encased by water.

Don't kill my kind, I think at the sea. *Hear me out.*

Oh, how I wish I were back in my normal life, or even back at the party with Steven. That at least was manageable. I am almost appalled I am making excuses for my fellow men. They don't necessarily deserve it, in my opinion. But I don't want to see them die either. *I* don't want to die. If we die, we can't fix our mistakes.

Why? Why should I believe you will change?

I swallow hard, measuring my thoughts carefully.

Because we are your children, with diversity abounding.

Because we are not great forces, but individuals who have choices to make. We make mistakes. But we learn too, even if it takes longer than it should.

I pause and hurry to finish my point, struck by another realization.

Because we live for so little time, we try to conquer our fear of death by doing stupid things. It's a stupid reason, but it is a reason. We get bored. Boredom lends itself to mistakes. But boredom also gives us creativity. We can harness that creativity to fix our mistakes.

Some humans are bored? the sea asks, and for the first time I feel a hint of doubt, a lessening of weary rage.

Yes, I sigh. *It's just that some of us don't like to admit it. Existence is tiring. Some of us clutter our lives with meaningless junk to give ourselves purpose. Some of us try to use religion, or the spiritual. Some of us live for something that arouses passion. Some of us are already broken, trying to function even though the world makes no sense. I found my existence by denying its validity. But that is not a way to live. That is a lesson we need to find out on our own.*

You humans have to live. You must. You have infinitesimally small lives. You have such a short time to fulfill the purpose of your existence. You should not waste it.

All of a sudden, I feel a great sorrow for the sea, deep and ponderous in my gut, even though I wish I could give her a soft slap on the shoulder, like I used to give to Tivana. All my childhood memories I took for granted, playing and frolicking in the waves, having fun, while the sea endured and endured mankind's mistakes, for millennia perhaps, seemed so shallow now. I'd be ashes in the earth in epochs, but she would still be here, our ever-watchful mother unless our planet exploded. It is a misery for her to see us stumble and fall so many times. I can finally understand that a little. We both give ourselves legacies of pain and sorrow, when you think about it.

A memory floats in my head of lazy English III classes during high school with Mrs. Greylda. I didn't learn anything useful from her. But she loved teaching poems, and those were my favorite part of the class, the only part I liked. It's been fifteen years, but I remember a few. A poem comes to me now, *The Triumph of Time* by Swinburne, fragments of its rich verse coagulating in my mind:

"The sweet sea, mother of loves and hours,
Shudders and shines as the grey winds gleam,
Turning her smile to a fugitive pain.
Mother of loves that are swift to fade,
Mother of mutable winds and hours.
A barren mother, a mother-maid,
Cold and clean as her faint salt flowers..."
My memory falters, but then I remember a little more.
"The loves and hours of the life of a man,
They are swift and sad, being born of the sea."

We are both the same, deep down. It is ridiculous to give each other such legacies. We need to both stop taking things for granted.

For me, I can't keep wasting my days, frittering away my life. I need to raise awareness somehow to the grave rape of the sea. Maybe I can get a degree and start a career in marine biology, creating opportunities to engage people and have them fight the corporations that keep polluting the sea. Maybe, who knows, down the line, I could use my gift to scare people, to convince people of the disaster that lies ahead if we don't change. To resist living is an exercise in futility.

I suddenly am aware of the sea reaching into my mind, her cool touch making my very innards shiver. It's too much. If she doesn't stop, my brain is going to burst. Thankfully, she recedes, and I can sense her mulling over that poem and my decisions.

Please don't kill us, I murmur. I feel chilled to the bone.

Please stop killing me in my dreams. Be patient with us. I know it must be hard. Watching us fall over and over. But you are infinite. We are ephemeral. We need to bridge the gap in time between us. That itself will take time. Remember when you gave birth to us, the hundreds of millions of years it took for us to reach land, and the hundreds of millions after that it took for us to create civilizations. It will take time.

I can feel the sea ruminate, her waves getting smaller and smaller, less and less jagged.

I am a part of you. Always have been. That will never cease. You will keep seeing me in your dreams, others in your line will bond with me too. They, too, will dream of me. You can do much. Remember you are a great power. I will wait and abide. I will not kill you. But remember, do not lapse back. Or I shall be forced to do what I set out to do today, the sea whispers as she starts receding, her infinite robe tucking back in where it should.

The sea withdraws, the foam glittering impishly farther and farther down the beach. The water is a brilliant turquoise, so bright and vibrant it's like nacre amplified to supernova limits. The sun isn't shining anymore; it looks waterlogged in a hazy, uncertain cloud. But the sea is back in pattern, the moan and roar, the snarl and murmur, the low and lament, the scream and miserere, the exultation and triumph of life, of her waves, echoing. She waits. I walk to the edge of the shore, looking for seashells, parting the wet sand with my toes. My whole body is soaking wet and the wind makes me shiver. I do not want to think. It is time simply to feel and act. The waves lap at my feet, ebbing and receding, ebbing and receding, again and again and again.

THE SEA PART II

Twelve years later

I am finally here. Good Harbor Beach's salty air slaps me in the face like carbonated soda. I take out the map and observe the geography of the area. A few hours earlier, I had compared maps with an oceanographer at the Woods Hole Oceanographic Institution. The drive had been stressful. It was what I'd thought. The sea levels had risen considerably in the past decade. Enough so that they'd had to relocate and rebuild the Good Harbor mansion farther away from the beach. The mansion wasn't the only thing, of course. Most of the town had had to be relocated as people lost their homes.

Steven is going to meet up with me here. I am nervous and excited. He is technically a grownup. But I know his mom stills calls him a child behind his back. I am so proud of him, going to college and choosing to major in marine biology. If I were him, I would have chosen anything else. But I'm a big old hypocrite. Here I am, a consultant for private geological oceanographers who have been fired from their jobs. Climate change is real. The world around us is a constantly evolving warning sign. The ocean levels are at an all-time high. Some islands have disappeared off the map. Cities have been swallowed up by the rising waters. Debris from the ocean is making its way into the dry parts of the cities. I still have my nightmares, but since I've started this job, they are becoming fewer and fewer. I don't need those dreams anymore. The Sea's threat is becoming more and more tangible every day.

It is my job to record and confirm what the oceanographers suspect is happening. They can't be too much in the public eye. The last ones I worked for, under the table of course, were heavily fined for spreading "misinformation." The next step would be jail time. The oceanographers and I meet in private and conduct our business through coded postal mail. I am still in shock about it. I never would have imagined I would skirt the law for a good cause. It means I am losing my selfishness. I am not old enough for that yet.

As I roll up the map, Steven walks across the dunes, all 115 pounds of new adult swagger and concealed guilt in his shifty eyes. He is also the reason I am here now. I still have the letter he'd sent me in my wallet.

Dear Uncle Amos,

I miss you. I do. Really, though, Mom is making me write this so you can "talk some sense into me." I don't know how else to say this. I'm dropping out of college. Mom is super mad because I am over 18 and she can't do much about it. I don't want to continue. It's overwhelming. There's more, but I'd rather talk about it. If you can come see me, I want to talk with you soon.

Steven's one of those freaks who prefers calling over texting. He loves calling people. But the fact that he wrote a letter and wants to talk in person troubles me. His lanky frame approaches me languidly. As he waves, the awkward hand gesture morphs into a hug, but then he stops and pulls back. He's too cool even for me apparently.

"Steve. Hey," I say, mimicking his gesture.

Steven blushes and recovers quickly. He clasps his hands behind his back, obviously awaiting a sermon. I shake my head.

"Walk with me," I say, heading off along the mucky sand, and Steven eventually follows me, his eyes like saucers.

We walk in silence. The water creeps to my toes and recedes. I eye it like a hawk, but it just continues its innocent game of ebbing and flooding, whispering nonsense that gets jumbled with the sounds of the wind and my stumbling footsteps on the sand. It is bumpy terrain and my hips are starting to burn when Steven finally talks.

"Uncle Amos, you're not mad at me, are you?"

"No," I say.

"Why not?" he asks, pushing his rugged hair out of his face as I turn to face him.

"Because it's not my life. Technically, you're an adult. I just want to know your reason for dropping out. You really wanted to go to Boston University. You really liked their program. What changed?"

Steven's face scrunches up, like he is about to cry. I turn away, not wanting to embarrass him. He unloads his reasons so quickly I have to strain to hear him over the quickening beat of the tide.

"Amos. It's all too much. It's not like I don't know what I want to do. You know that. It's just too much! I hear them. The animals. From the jellyfish to the clams. I hear their thoughts. They talk constantly. When they are suffering, I hear them even more."

I cross my arms. It's one thing to hear the ocean. To dream about her, to wake up soaking wet from those dreams, sure. But to hear the animals? That is right out. Not once have I been able to understand sea life. I can't begin to envision how that would be. Is it a voice in his head? Do they actually talk to him? No, surely, that can't be true. It's too fantastical on top of everything else. I don't want to call him a liar, though. He is confessing to me, after all. But I can't help blurting out, "Steven. Really? You hear their thoughts? That's something I thought you'd say when you were eight. Not twenty-two. It doesn't work like that."

For a second, I think my own nephew is going to slug me. The color drains from his face and his eyes narrow to slits.

"You seriously don't believe me? Fine," he grits out. He wades into the water and fishes through handfuls after handfuls of junk and cigarettes. He manages to finally scoop up some crabs. He cocks his head and brings them up to his ear. A concerned look washes over his face. I stand there like an idiot, my hands hanging like drying sausages. I am obviously missing something.

"You can't hear it, can you?" Steven asks, his anger melting into disappointment.

I shake my head.

"They can talk. And I can understand them. They are in pain. The sea is becoming uninhabitable. They are the last of their kind. And soon, we will be too."

The Sea's deadly warning floats into my head. If nothing is done, she will kill us all. I turn away from the Sea, facing the tired landscape, staring out into the permanently ashen tone of the sky. Lack of regulations has loaded our clouds with bloated carbon and coal weights. It's not just the Sea. The entire earth is suffering. I take a deep breath and find that I can't without coughing. It's not new. But it's the first time I acknowledge my body's reaction. I try again. My lungs don't allow for a deep breath.

"You know, Uncle Amos. You do, don't you?" Steven says, his green eyes intent on mine.

I sigh. What happened to the knobby-kneed boy of ten?

My nephew continues, more grown up and forbidding than I am comfortable with. "It's not just that. I'm dropping out because our program is being slashed. Our work is considered unnecessary, and in some circles, divisive. I'd rather leave now."

It pains me. His words make my stomach roil. It's not surprising. After all, why am I a "consultant" for former marine biologists? Saving the environment has become illicit. However, I did not anticipate college programs being cut down so soon. I have been too involved with my own research. If I weren't, I would have been able to analyze the exact laws, exact moments, exact people responsible for the insidious fall of environmental conservation. I am not an apathetic fucker anymore, but that comes with its own special set of downfalls.

"If you drop out, what are you going to do then?"

Steven shrugs. "There's a lot I want to do. But I'm not sure what I can do."

"What you have to do is find the right people who share a common goal. People who are willing to... bend the rules a little. Or you could start your own venture. It depends on what you want to do. I'm focusing on exposing the reality of our situation. What do you want to do?"

"I want to... to actually fix stuff!" Steven runs a hand through his dirty blond hair; I swear it gets lighter every year. "I want to go out in the ocean and clean up all the crap out there. I want to make equipment that'll do it. I want to put the remaining sea life in conservation labs so we can save the dying species by breeding them. But... but I can't do that, can I?"

I wish, not for the first time, that Steven's life and mine were switched. With his brains and determination, the Sea would perhaps be cleaner by now. I can't tell him that, of course. I also can't outright tell him to break the law either, no matter how good the cause is.

"It will be hard..."

I pause and continue slowly.

"Perhaps in really illegal territory."

"What do *you* do? Is it illegal?"

I nod. "Yep. Technically. I am savvy about not getting caught."

Steven looks at me so plaintively my spirits plummet for him.

"What's the point of doing something good if you have to break the law to do it? Do you feel you're really making a difference?"

My breath catches. I feel like I am doing a little something. It's better than sitting at home all day contemplating what it means to be alive. But really, what exactly am I doing? All the findings we uncover are published in individual fringe presses. It's all so anonymous I truly don't know who is reading our stuff. In the grand scheme of things, I am not seeing any difference. No policies are changing. Every year, the problem gets worse and worse. Are my meager efforts making a difference? No. I don't want to tell Steven that, though. His expectant glance wilts as I search for an answer. I can't lie either. I turn away, and mumble, "I like to think that I am."

Steven sucks in air through his teeth and starts walking. This time, I follow. We walk through the pained silence of anxiety too great to be spoken, until I break it with an inane question I would have slapped myself for twelve years ago.

"Any girlfriends?"

Steven's walk falters but he doesn't stop. He shoots me a sly look over his shoulder.

"You sound like Mom."

"That's insulting."

We keep walking and he kicks at the sand with his feet.

"Do crushes count?"

"I guess," I say, sucking in my breath as a particularly cold wave washes over my feet.

"I don't really want to do anything about it."

"What?"

Steven throws his hands up in the air. The sun shines almost silver and blinds us both as it emerges from the clouds. A brief vision of triumph. Then it disappears, sucked behind a mass of pollution-ridden clouds.

"Uncle Amos. What am I supposed to tell girls when we wake up and there's water around us?"

My mouth dries up. I have never found a solution to that particular problem. Feebly, I joke, "If you're in bed with a girl, you should be doing other things besides sleeping."

Steven shoots me a signature scornful look he inherited straight from Tivana.

"I'm serious, Amos. How can I have girls over when there's a chance they'll find out my secret. They'll think I'm nuts."

I don't want to admit that he's right. There has to be a positive aspect to this.

"Maybe just try it and see what they think. When I was a young man," I chuckle ruefully, "women were afraid of all kinds of stuff. Now, they might be more open-minded. They might think someone who wakes up in a puddle of seawater is like Aquaman or something." My argument sounds lame, even to me.

Steven snorts, but there is some wetness in his eyes that is not due to the sea mist sprinkling the air.

"You know that movie was banned in the U.S., right?"

"Oh." I'd forgotten. "You can still find bootleg copies, if you know where to look." *Aquaman* and many other films had been blacklisted in recent years.

"Are you going to talk to Mom?"

"No. You need to deal with this yourself. You have to explain it to her, same way you did with me. She will understand. Eventually. She's taking her meds, right?"

"Yeah."

That settles the anxiety in my heart.

"Uncle Amos? What do you do when things seem really hopeless and overwhelming?"

"Not much. I'm better about actually doing something than I used to be. But it's not great." In truth, I hole myself up and binge read on natural disasters until my eyes burn. That won't help Steven. So I say, "I drink until I feel sleepy. I'm joking," forcing a laugh out. When I do drink too much, I wake up with even more water and even more intense dreams. "I talk with someone I care about. I take walks. I read some good books that make me forget about the world around me."

I go to Steven and wrap an arm around his shoulder. "It'll be fine. If things get too crazy, give me a call. If you need more information, call me."

"Ok." Steven looks down at the Sea, the waves reflected in his eyes, miniature worlds churning in his irises. He worries at his lips with his teeth. "I will."

I fall off the bed, my butt hitting the toy balls my cats like to play with. I hit my head on the gaudy bed post and stun myself. A huge splash erupts around me. My room is flooded with about three inches of water. Spaz and Jazz are on the dresser, glaring at me. Great. The water rolls around and sloshes in waves ruining the legs of my dresser. This is my biggest mess yet.

I put a hand over my heart. It is still beating super fast. In the nightmare, I'd been swimming in a pool, surrounded by flaccid, sunburned tourists in cheap sunglasses and floppy hats. A guitarist with those corny plastic leis around his neck strummed a cheesy tune as kids screamed and cannonballed into the pool. Noodles went flying, pool jets were sliced as hurtling bodies hit the water. The first red flag that this was a dream was my being in a pool with people. The second was that everyone looked so happy. In the waking world, everyone scurries around with fatigued eyes and sunburned skin, thanks to the decreasing ozone. No one takes the time to interact with others or look too closely at their surroundings. It is like the entire world is a big taboo right in front of you. In my dream, everyone was laughing, floating along on their inflatable rafts, drinking their uber-sticky sweet alcoholic drinks, and the guitarist has people singing along, like karaoke.

Then, *she* came. A humongous shadow in the sky, a roiling mass of pure ocean rising over us all. Everyone kept laughing and swimming. I raised my voice, trying to scream, but nothing came out. She took her time, like a bird hovering over its prey. I knew it was useless to run, but I did anyway. I threw myself out of the pool and fled into the hotel. Orange-streaked walls with crummy stucco over big mirrors blew past me; tourists gawked as I streaked past the concierge, telling everyone, "She is coming! Take cover!" They just stared at me as I tried the elevator, mashing the button over and over. It didn't work. I dashed up the stairs and burst into my hotel room. I went to huddle under the bed, but a horrible part of me stopped and stared out the window.

Yes, I could see nothing but a deep, forbidding wall of gray and blue. I tried to say, "Stop." But it kept coming. I closed my eyes. A thunderous crash exploded around me. My entire being rang with the force of the blow. Then nothing. I massaged my ears, then opened my eyes. A clean, undestroyed room mocked me with its normalcy. There wasn't even wetness on the floor. I glanced outside. Debris and some bodies floated below. I pressed my face against the glass and saw nothing but rubble and rent ground.

I dashed to the door and ran out. Water sloshed as I ran through it. Every single room was no longer a room. The walls were barely standing. I raced to the staircase only to find a hole in the building. I jumped down, knowing that even if I died in the dream, I would wake up. Disappointingly, I landed, and waded my way to what had been the pool. Amorphous blobs of stuff floated here and there. I suppressed the bile rising in my throat. Everyone was gone. No building was standing, except for, weirdly, the space around my hotel room. The trees, the fences, the cars, everything was reduced to a pulp. Why wasn't I dead? Why had I been spared?

A body floated next to me, its face unrecognizable. More and more came along, and I was surrounded by this orgy of mangled bodies, all victims of the Sea's wrath. I tried to swim out of the way, but I couldn't. They bumped and jostled me and I had to look at the sky. I was trapped. The bodies pinned my arms to my sides. My legs pumped in the water, but slowly, so painfully slowly. I screamed to the Sea, "What have you gained?"

And for the first time ever in a dream, she did not respond.

My heart is still beating too fast from that nightmare. The cold water around my shins pulls me out of the remembrance of the dream. I roll the balls away with my foot and strip. I will clean the mess later. I walk to the bathroom, rip the towel from its rod and rub myself dry. My stomach growls. I head to the living room, making a detour to the kitchen. Of course. I forgot to eat dinner. I was too busy talking to Tivana, insisting that she give Steven a break about his decision. After that talk, I'd watched one television show after another, too riled up to concentrate.

I don't have much in the fridge. A few cheese sandwiches. Some rotting fruit. There are some leftovers of plant-based meat with pasta. None of it is appetizing. I peek in the freezer. I have some packets of tilapia, salmon, and shrimp, but I regret buying them. They don't taste the same since they're manufactured in labs. They are too big, for one thing, way too big compared to the originals. And the flavor is off. None of the food I have in my fridge tastes the way it did when I was a kid. All food is fake now.

I slam the fridge door in disgust. My appetite soured, I head to the living room. No. If I turn on the TV, I will either watch fragments of shows again, or lambast the news channels as they spew their inane nonsense. Instead, I take a childhood book from my sagging bookcase, *Song of Solomon*, and read it until dawn.

Two weeks later

I leaf through my reports, reciting them in my head to make sure I'll have them down pat when I call the senator, Roger Caulfield, which I am going to do as soon as I'm done editing the video I'm working on to submit to *National Geographic*—what remains of it, anyway. My scientist allies want to do an anonymous conference call with one of the youngest senators in the country. Supposedly, this senator is one of the very few who believes in climate change and the devastation that's happening around us. He could leak our reports if he believes they are significant enough to divulge to the public. The reports show approximately three-quarters of our globe has dead zones. All but a few of our marine species are gone. Sure, some of them are being cloned in labs specifically for consumption. But a lot have been killed off. If the lack of oxygen didn't kill them, overfishing, oil spills, infestation of plastic and debris, and eradication of coral reefs did. The list of islands and little nations swallowed up by rising waters fills two entire pages single spaced. There is a lot to report.

My scientist friends seem to think this senator will listen to us. I have my doubts. Blame it on the cynical part of me, but I've had my fair share of hopeful leads, from TV anchors to minor government officials to CEOs of megacorporations. Every time they've ignored or disbelieved what we've said. I have hung up more than once with a sore throat from screaming at them.

I dial the senator's number and Aaron and Xavier, my two scientists, join me on the call. *Don't be a cynic, don't be a cynic.*

Caulfield's reedy voice answers.

After a few minutes of paying the obligatory lip service, we dive into the information we have gathered. Ultimately, the senator says, "So is that it?"

"What do you mean?" I ask, as Aaron and Xavier sputter incoherently.

"That is a lot of damning evidence. It is overwhelmingly negative. But you don't offer any solutions."

"We haven't gotten to that part yet," Aaron says, "Right now, we are forced to be underground. The funding we would need to effectively tackle the problem is nonexistent. We have been stripped of any authority." Aaron moderates his accusing tone with effort. "We thought you would help us disseminate these reports to the public, give us a voice, so the government and corporations can acknowledge the problem and help. With their help, we might be able to halt some of the damage."

The silence on the end of the line doesn't bode well.

"It's not up to us to do your job," Caulfield says. "You predicted this climate change disaster, now you have to fix it. We need hope right now. Not fearmongering. I will need much more research and proposed alternatives before I promise any financial assistance or even spread the word in the media."

I suck in my breath in outrage. I knew this would happen. I knew it was too good to be true. If I didn't think senators didn't have time for it, I would have said this senator was taking us for a ride. Trolling us. I am glad we are on an anonymous call. The last thing we need on top of this would be to be ratted out.

Xavier's gravelly voice becomes high pitched in his anger.

"No fearmongering? We need to fix a problem we predicted?! Where is your common sense, man? The corporations you let run rampant! The policies you let pass knowingly destroyed any regulations to keep our air and water clean. Where were you when all this was happening?"

I think he's wasting his time. I am tempted to hang up now. In the distance, I hear my phone vibrate. At this time of day, it's probably telemarketers.

"You gentlemen are trying to blame me? You should be thankful I even deigned—"

"Yes, yes we are!" my scientist friends shout, their voices a unified front of rage. Aaron yells, "You want hope? How about if we start tackling these issues now, the Earth won't go farther downhill than it has already! How about if you—"

I tune them out. It truly is hopeless. We are back to square one. Sure, I should probably just perk myself up and try to find more people who might be willing to publish and/or broadcast our findings. But that means going through many more iterations of disappointment. At this point, I almost wish the Sea would hold up her promise and destroy us all. We deserve it. Well, actually, just a select few. Only those who purposefully let things come to such a point. They should be the first to die.

I can't help but think that if I had been invested in saving the earth while I was younger, I could have done something, something significant that might have changed the outcome of everything. I could have reached out to people who could have done something before they were silenced. I could have created my own organization. I could have gone back to school and found a way to make an actual difference. Before the world decided to shut its ears to the cries of the planet. Before jumped-up political leaders of rising countries threatened us with war and only backed off after the might of the United States threatened them back. No one wanted to risk annihilating Earth over... well, the annihilation of Earth. It's ironic, really. I have failed. I could have done something and I didn't. I can't make up for it now. I don't think the Sea will care either way. We have fucked her over.

The buzzing of the conference call snaps me back to reality. They have hung up. All of them. I check the time. Five minutes have passed since they hung up. I get up and slam the laptop shut. I have wasted enough time tonight.

I eat a miserable dinner, throwing most of it in the garbage, and continue with the video editing. It is almost midnight when I remember the missed call. I check my phone and see that it's Steven's number. There are two voicemails.

The first is: *Uncle Amos. It's me. I just need to talk to you. I think I want to do something. Not sure if it's the best choice.*

The second is: *Hey. Call me back please. I am doing some more thinking. It is the hardest thing I've ever done. I can hear them still. Now they're in my dreams. It's driving me crazy. Is there ever a point when it stops? I don't want to sleep anymore.*

I stare in frustration at the phone. Them? Who is them? Then I listen to the second voicemail again. His dreams. He must be talking about the Sea and her animals. It is concerning that he has my gift, and in a much stronger capacity. I can't help him. I can't comfort him. If he expects platitudes, he won't get them from me.

I want to call back, but it is late. If he's a sensible teenager, he should be sound asleep now. Or if he's not, he's masturbating, or at least thinking of girls. But I don't want to be an asshole. I call him back.

It rings and rings. Nobody answers. I call again. Same thing. Good. Hopefully he did get some sleep after all.

I am in California, filming the alarmingly quickening erosion of the beaches and the abundance of red tide. Through the lens it's almost as if I can see these unnatural progressions as I film them. This is the latest place Aaron and Xavier have sent me. What they hope to accomplish I'm not sure. Officially I know why we're here. But none of this will matter if the research doesn't see the light of day. Our newest plan is figuring out a way to hack into a news channel and broadcast our findings. Perhaps rally people to our cause. Aaron swears there are people here in California who have the right skills to pull this off. He's given me code names with brief descriptions. It is like some cheesy spy flick.

I find the coffee shop and I'm waiting for the hackers to show up when my phone rings. Always interruptions. The caller ID shows up as Tivana. I keep glancing up at the people around me. I have to take the call. I don't want to strain our relationship. She gets moody sometimes if I don't pick up, even though I'm not ignoring her, like I did twelve years ago.

"What?" I say.

I am astounded to hear her sobbing.

"Are you ok?" I say, mollified.

She tries to speak, but all that comes out is wretched blubbering.

"What's going on?" I say, trying to streamline her thoughts.

"St—St—St—even," she gasps.

"What about Steven?" A pooling of dread slowly creeps in my veins.

A stormy fit erupts from her. I can envision her tears splashing on her phone. Some people ugly-cry and my sister definitely ugly-cries.

"Hung himself. He hung himself," she sputters out, as if all the breath was squeezed out of her lungs.

My own lungs seize.

"Hung himself." My brain grabs on to the first wayward thought, the first raft of hope. "He wasn't successful, right?"

"Amos," she blubbers, "he's dead."

You've got to be joking. It can't be. Steven, my healthy, handsome, smart nephew? Whom I saw recently, full of hope and asking for advice? Dead? She must be joking. Maybe she was having an episode. Nothing else would make sense.

As she continues to cry, any lingering hope plunges into an abyss of sorrow. My nephew is dead. I want to throw up. I want to smash things and scream at the top of my lungs. Instead, I sit there dully and watch the people in the coffee shop flutter around with their nasty, overpriced heart-stimulating concoction, a foul result of effective marketing. Their stupid bright clothes, their stupid too-white smiles. I reel my brain back in with effort, stopping the snarl on my face.

"...did you have any idea? I mean, did he leave a note?" I ask.

"No. Nothing."

That isn't quite true, though. I don't have the heart to tell Tivana. He did leave a note, two, in fact: two voicemails on my phone. Both heartfelt pleas for help. I hadn't recognized them as such, because I'm an antisocial bastard preoccupied too much with the moment. He'd reached out to me. Not his mom, not his friends, me. And I'd failed him. He's dead because I didn't take the time to answer the damn phone when I had the chance. The time I'd spent arguing with that blasted Caulfield, or more accurately, listening to an argument during that fruitless conference call, could have been spent talking with Steven, talking him out of his suicide. He'd been so afraid of going to sleep, he chose to sleep the deep sleep instead.

I get up and storm out of the coffee shop. I don't know where to go now. I disconnect the call.

I forget to eat. I forget to shower. I don't sleep. I don't want to meet the Sea in my dreams. She might find herself facing my wrath for once. Her and her demented connection with my family, her incessant voice whispering the horrors of her plight, *that* is what drove Steven to his death. She's responsible for his suicide. Death was preferable to hearing the suffering of her children over and over again.

Why couldn't she have taken me? My life, a wasted life by my own means, a life in its middle age, a life left to sour and become even more bitter, could have been taken. But no, life is too ironic for that.

I almost forget to reserve the flight back for the funeral. It takes Tivana's frenzied calls to rouse me into action. I sit in front of the computer screen for an hour before I muster the energy to click on the necessary websites. It takes me another hour to find a credit card and plug in the information. I wordlessly listen to Tivana's endless phone calls as she sobs her sorrow out to me. When she starts screaming and shouting, I decrease the sound on my phone and leave it sitting there. I don't know what to say. He was my nephew, but he was her son. No words of mine can fix the hurt.

My anger is in there too. It is wrapped in a shroud of numb disbelief and cold resoluteness not to lose my shit. It's not like I'm getting an award by stifling the anger. I just don't want it to get the best of me. A part of me knows the Sea isn't really to blame for Steven's death. Society's lack of empathy is to blame. I cannot be angry at an entire society; it's too much wasted effort. So I acknowledge the anger like I would acknowledge a clingy ex-girlfriend and I brush it off. I have to keep cool and composed during the funeral. I cannot let myself dissolve into tears or lapse into a sudden rage. I need to hold it together just long enough to make it through the ceremony and get away as soon as it's done. I've already told Tivana that I won't be delivering a eulogy. She is pissed at me, but I hold my ground. Steven is... Steven was like me. Not much for overt displays of emotion. I don't think he'd want such a hullabaloo for his funeral.

I cannot fall apart. It is other people's jobs to fall apart at events like this. I must be the eye in the storm and passively observe while the grief, anger, chaos and confusion slide off of me. If you are passive, others' chaos cannot hurt you.

I stand on the dinky, filthy beach and raise my arms in the air, letting the acrid wind tear through me. Its bitter, violent gusts are almost enough to wipe out the memory of Steven's coffin, of the monotone chant of the *Tzidduk Hadin*, of the moist texture of the earth as we filled the grave, handful by handful of dirt. I'd been late to the *Keriah*, and I am glad about it. I'd made an ass of myself after the *Kevurah*. I'd chosen to leave instead of sticking around for the elaborate, morose process of the Comfort of the Mourners. I'd run through the procession of people repeating *Hamakom yenacheim etchem betoch shaar avelei tziyon v'yerushalayim*, over and over, as if their words truly could offer comfort. Tivana was too far gone to even shoot me a nasty look. I'd had to get away from the smell of people's grief and the overwhelming reminders of Steven's absence.

That is why I am here. This beach offers no comfort. It is a ruin of itself. Black masses of decaying algae litter the gray sand, and mounds of plastic create mountains of ugliness on the shoreline. The seawater is slate gray, a darker shade than the sand. Well, what little sand is left, anyway. I am impressed Florida isn't completely underwater at this point. It doesn't matter. I don't need beauty, I don't need cleanness, I don't need comfort. I just need a familiar chorus, the mournful chorus of the Sea as she crashes along the shore. Filthy, aggressive, monotonous, she and I are kin. I sit next to an amalgamation of debris and half-melted plastic. I don't know what to do with myself. I'm almost tempted to walk into the Sea and let her take me. Except that a part of me is afraid I somehow wouldn't drown, just to mess up my day. What is the point? All this fighting, all this emotional investment, all for what? It is useless. I don't know why I even try.

Nothing I can do will bring Steven back. I missed my window. He is gone. I am trying to save the Sea, and all my efforts are like a child's. Two epic failures, and there is nothing left to fight for. I sit and lean back in the hard sand and rest amid the stinking wreck. My eyes close and the silver sheen of light in the sky darkens. People start murmuring. Some start screaming. I open my eyes.

She comes. She comes in all her righteous fury, her encompassing girth unfathomably wider, taller and deeper than imagined. Her crest is so high it is unseen, just a blinding wall of muddy, dirty ocean water obscuring everything. The sky does not exist. It is exactly like in my dreams. All my limbs tingle. My stomach plummets like I'm on a roller coaster. She comes high over me, I look up and she is my everything. She *is* the sky and the earth at that moment. Her shadow makes it dark as night. The people around me scream and run for cover. Some start falling under her weight as the waves race terrifyingly fast up the beach. There is no sound, which makes no sense. She roars toward me in silence. I totter back, knowing I will never make it to safety. The wall comes arching down on me, tons of seawater dumping all at once and I raise my hands to shield my head.

Her suffocating grasp plunges on my head. I touch myself. Nothing. No wetness. I suddenly can't see. A sarcophagus of silence and water surrounds me. I gradually hear the churning of waves, and my eyesight comes back. The world is destroyed, everything crushed and annihilated to tiny, insignificant bits. I'm on top of the world, and everything is covered in water. No continents emerge, even the ice caps are buried under oceans of water. Then, like elastic the Sea snaps back and recedes to her normal position.

I rise up and realize I am floating. I paddle about madly and spit out brackish, contaminated seawater. I flounder as the water shifts around me and starts lowering and ebbing away. The salt stings my eyes and nose. I cough and clutch my eyes. The pain snaps me awake. Wait, I am awake. Where is the beach? I cannot turn my head, I am rocked to full awareness in a tumultuous bed of ocean water. Where am I? More seawater enters my nose and I spit and gag miserably.

I float and float aimlessly, and suddenly the water recedes and drops me down on what looks like the remains of a street, water splashing around me as I tumble. My elbows and back flare in pain and I look up at the mangled shells of buildings. Street signs are bent down on the ground like supplicating pilgrims. Immense holes decorate the street as if giants had stomped through. Floods of trash and plastic stand vigil, statues of humanity's folly standing at attention. Some of the trash heaps are higher than the buildings used to be. Some furniture is strewn in the street, cars are wedged into each other firmly, shopping carts lay upside down, their contents nowhere to be seen. Most importantly, I don't see anybody.

"Hello?" I call out.

My voice is swallowed by the silence. I keep walking. There is nobody, just wrecks of former homes, former business districts, walls and billboards standing pathetically before tumbling to the ground in a sodden mess. Entire foundations have been razed away. I see smatterings of clothing, ripped apart fragments of cloth so thin and small they could be confetti. I still see no one, as I continue my lonely sojourn through the ruined city. If the clothing is that destroyed, I cannot imagine what happened to their owners.

I finally find a motel that has some walls standing. The rooftop is gone, the whole façade sags like a sullen child. I go inside, stopping in horror at the heap of soaked, dead bodies strewn in the lobby like broken marionettes. I stumble over one of them, its sneaker-clad foot the culprit. Its face is turned upward, the livid face of a young boy, his mouth still open in a scream. A lightning bolt of wrath singes through me and I wheel out of the motel, swinging my fists and stomping my feet in the flooded sections of the crumbled streets.

I head east, until I am roughly where the beach used to be. The bar and chairs that used to be there are gone. The Sea rolls in, sneakily gentle as if I don't know what she has done. Gray clouds streak quickly across a watery sun. Everything is wet. Everything is destroyed. I am soaked from head to toe as I angrily march to the new beachline. I stop and kick at the water. Once I start, I cannot stop. My leg is burning from the effort of kicking, but I keep doing it.

"You killed all of them. Men, women, and children. You killed any family I had left. Is this your idea of revenge? Is this your idea of *justice*?" I scream, my voice so loud it tears my throat.

The Sea increases her rhythm, and I know she is listening. She doesn't reply, though.

"Answer me. The whole world is dead. Happy now? Does that solve anything?"

When I kick my leg this time, the water wraps around it and yanks. I hit the ground.

"Why didn't you kill me?" I croak, tears in my eyes suddenly, and my throat closes up.

The Sea pulls back and rises above me, not threateningly high, but enough to remind me of her threat.

Amos, Amos, she whispers, a fierce whisper. *Have you lost all reason? I cannot kill you.*

"You should have. I lost my nephew. Now I've lost everyone. How am I going to survive in a world devoid of living humans? I've never been a social person, but the complete absence of people is a different kettle of fish. Without humanity, nothing is going to change. My existence becomes a superfluous point."

So much sorrow in your heart. This is new for you. When did this empathy come to exist?

"When you decided to wipe out humanity! How dare you? You act as if you've done nothing wrong, as if everything is fine and peachy. If anyone should feel sorrow, it's *you*," I shout, pointing accusingly at her.

The Sea flexes, and her mighty wall of water shakes a little. She rises higher, so I can't see the sky at all. For a moment, she looks like my mom did when she thought I'd cussed at her as a teenager, imposing and ready to cuff me around the ears.

I have done what had to be done. What have you done? Some but not enough. Nothing of what you promised came to pass. I fulfilled the promise I made to you. I destroyed a world that had forgotten about me and would continue to destroy our home. I had to do what was necessary. What have you been doing since we last spoke, twelve years ago?

A flush inflames my face and I puff myself up.

"I have been working to bring your plight into the public eye. I did illegal things to try to help you. I traveled everywhere to report on the crimes being committed against you. I tried everything I could think of. Nothing worked. How is it my fault?"

You speak of doing illegal things as if it is something

commendable. When you are doing the right thing, it does not matter how you do it. It is something that has to be done.

"That is not the point. The point is that you wiped away my whole species!"

You were killing me much more cruelly.

"Granted, we were killing you off. It is what we do best, decimating things at a record rate. Now how can we learn? How can we do better?"

I extended more than enough patience toward your kind, the Sea roars.

"And you should have done more yourself instead of relying on me," I shout back. "Why didn't you present yourself to the world and speak about what was going on? Why didn't you give your gloom and doom predictions to mankind earlier? It would have been nice to see you show yourself at all those U.N. meetings when they were discussing whether climate change was real or not."

The Sea's color darkens. She inches closer but I don't budge. She is crazy if she thinks she can intimidate me.

Because, you reckless foolish child, humanity could not understand me. I tried. Only a precious few could understand me. They usually saw me in their dreams. Otherwise, I could roar at them and all they would hear was the lapping of my waves on the shore. I sent warnings throughout time to your kind. I was ignored. There was only one who seemed to understand me even when he was awake. I do not sense him anymore.

My throat constricts once more. She can only be talking about one person. Steven. He could hear her. Too much, all the time.

"He's dead," I state. "He killed himself because he couldn't handle your distress."

It should have been me. Steven could have done so much more.

"You should have killed me. Why don't you?" I ask,

wearily. All I want to do is go back to sleep. Sleep and forget everything I have just been through in the past seventy-two hours. Sleep and float away, in a vacuum of absolute uncaringness. The Sea recoils then rushes toward me. I cross my arms.

Do you desire that I kill you? Then I can kill you here, now. Utter the words, mortal.

I start laughing. "You can't. You can bluster all you want. I can see through your b.s. You could have killed me earlier when you drowned everyone else. The question is—" my laughter dies. "Why *can't* you? Why can I understand you? Why is it that I and a select few are able to hear you?"

The Sea droops, her foamy crest finally coming into view again. I can see the sky again. The clouds are still racing.

I do not know. You have the gift. I was unaware of the gift until you appeared to me, until you dreamt of me. More than that, I do not know.

A crooked smile breaks across my face. I have the gift, whatever that means, and even the Sea doesn't know how it works. It just happens. What freaky gene in my DNA is responsible for this? Will I ever know?

Come to me, the Sea says, in a purring voice. Echoes of her voice tinkle all around me like a nonstop waterfall.

"Why?"

So I can show you.

I am tired of bizarre circumlocutions. I am tired of speaking. I don't know what she wants to show me, but I go to her and gently step through into her depths. She washes over me and scoops me up like a child. My legs go flying. She swallows me whole and I am swept inside of her. I tumble and flounder in her entrails for a while. It is unbearably hot. I recognize it's an unnatural heat. It burns, it stokes fires of anger and hopelessness. If she suffocates in this heat, no wonder the wildlife inside of her deteriorated so fast. Somehow, I can breathe. But my breaths are short and painful. The water is so *thick*, full of oil, tar, and other filth. How can she breathe? My vision is speckled with ghostly floating objects. Mockeries of jellyfish, deformed bits of plastic everywhere, filling the waters with their ugliness. A long strip of plastic wraps around my neck like a noose and I wriggle around trying to unclasp it from me. My eyes, my lips, my ears burn. Random acrid tastes dance across my palate as I open my mouth to breathe more deeply. It is true. All the reports we tried to disseminate to the public: the excess of chemical nutrients, the acidification of the sea, the sheer amount of toxins and the mutation of life forms, these and more are all around me in their lugubrious truth. The human race definitely screwed up the environment. It is gut wrenching to experience. Perhaps the Sea was right to destroy my kind. We'd been piling on, a snowball effect, far too fast in too little time.

"I wish there were something I could do," I murmur. "There is so much. Is there any coming back from this?"

The Sea is silent for so long I assume she doesn't hear me. I continue to float in the embryonic slime. Then she says, "If we have children, we can finally remedy the problem. Our offspring will do what by ourselves we could not."

She is jesting. Children? Has she gone bonkers? A man and the Sea cannot have children. It is physically impossible. I shudder to think what any possible offspring might look like. They'd be mutants. The whole thing is preposterous. The Sea cannot be impregnated.

I never get a chance to ask how. She scoops me up once more and spits me out onto the beach where the hotel used to be. I land with a thud, my lungs contracting painfully as I adjust to the oxygen on land. I gasp for breath, my eyes still stinging. The sopping wet sand cushions my head in its muck. The Sea rises in a funnel, then drapes over me like a mother gently placing a blanket over her child. She covers my entire body in a thin layer of water and starts trembling. As she trembles, my limbs start to tremble too.

"What are you doing?" I croak, my lips suddenly devoid of any moisture.

My eyes sting even more. The Sea lovingly laps over me, up and down, up and down. She rises straight into the air, a thin sheet of water tugging something brilliantly pearlescent from me; a thin stream of... something. A lacework of light emanates from her and joins the thread of whatever she is pulling from me. It is a disconcerting sight. But she continues her strange dance above me, rising and falling, pushing and pulling, and calmness washes over me, as if she is caressing me like a lover. The coldness of her touch sprinkles on my cheeks. A surge of fresh energy traverses from the top of my head to the tips of my toes and back again. I feel so dry... I do not have the energy to even lick my lips. My eyes are drying out so badly I can barely see. I close them.

Her touch fountains over me once more, and it is a swirling abyss of pleasure and bliss, agony and pain. The prickling sensation mounts and mounts, becoming untenable, as if my skin is itching to slough off. Tremors wrack my body. I feel less and less human. I feel my body so much it becomes alien. Something is being drained from me. What is she doing?

My mouth opens futilely. I open my eyes, and they flutter painfully. A huge ball of water spins above me, wavering in and out of focus. That orb, I want to touch it. It's as clear as glass; if I could touch it... The Sea pushes and the orb explodes, thousands of droplets scattering in the air, sprinkling impishly down to the ground, over my face. With effort, I turn my head to see the droplets of water twisting and turning, coalescing into bigger, writhing globs. The orbs elongate into slug-like creatures. Crystalline sparks blossom from within, and they wriggle out, flashing and expanding into little legs. One that lands on my face slides down to my belly. More legs keep sprouting from it, in a pinwheel fashion, and they all wave about as if greeting me. The legs retract and a tail begins to emerge, long and forked. Before my astonished eyes, the tail melts into tentacles, which melt into spikes, which melt into a spacious carapace.

"Please," I whisper, wishing for any shred of normalcy. I sense movement all around me, and I catch flashes of dancing creatures leaping and twirling about. The one on me bounces up and down, a face emerging from its constantly shifting surface. Multiple eyes pop out and blink at me, all kinds of colors, and a mouth with a baleen plate opens. It looks horrific. I can't look at it anymore.

If this is what my offspring are going to look like, I don't know if I can face it. It's like the Sea herself doesn't know what she wants our offspring to be. How can a child born of a man and the ocean even begin to exist and function in this now defunct society? I am living in a demented, upside-down reality. Perhaps I am dreaming a terrible nightmare, perhaps I will wake up and still be on that conference call, answer my cell and find that Steven is still alive. Steven's voice, his velvety timbre and playful eyes, his crazy hair that doesn't want to stand still, I want to experience all of that, just one more time. To be able to hug him, to cuff him gently on the cheek, to shoot the breeze with him. I would give my life for that.

A heavy pressure builds on my chest and when I open my eyes again, the crystalline ooze becomes opaque and flesh-toned, materializing into familiar body parts which writhe uncertainly until.... a young Steven forms in front of me. Dark green eyes regard me keenly, as a mouth twists into existence, etching itself into the tentative grin he sported nonstop up until puberty. The rest of his body fleshes out, becoming a jumble of knobby knees and elbows. No, no, this is too much, too strange, too... everything. I lurch to my feet, only to stagger and fall back on to the sand. When I straighten my aching back, I'm met with frolicking, leaping water-creatures gallivanting all over the beach. They look vaguely humanoid, but there are no eyes, no mouths, no hair. They're a rough sketch of humanity.

"What are these?" I ask, my throat so dried out I'm concerned the Sea won't hear me.

She responds immediately.

These are our children.

I observe them again, these floating, cavorting creatures blissfully dancing on the beach. Some doing what seem like cartwheels. Some of them bump into each other and roll around. A tinkling fills the air, like laughter; streaks rainbow hues glow and bounce off the creatures' constantly shifting bodies. The birthday-party Steven-spawn runs to the other creatures and throws himself on the sand, droplets of himself flying out from him before zooming back to maintain his form. He laughs, and it is truly Steven's laugh, high, stuttering, unappealing. But my throat locks tight.

"Our children," I whisper, a grin tempted to come out, watching them play. They might look odd; some are definitely hybrids that could only have come from H. R. Giger's mind, but they are innocent, unaware of the destruction all around them.

"Are they humans? Are they animals? What are they?"

They are our children. Does it matter?

Sheepishly, I shake my head.

As I continue to watch them flittering about, their forms become other people. One the mailwoman who always delivered the mail with a scowl when I was a kid. The laid-back math teacher I had in fifth period in high school, the one who let us watch videos the whole time. Adi, the little girl who'd almost drowned. Another becomes my sister, before the vitality and color left her soul and skin.

I flinch in revulsion; the children's faces continue

morphing into more people I'd had the bad luck to meet throughout my uneventful life. Adults, children, friends, enemies, all shifting more quickly than I can blink my eyes. They all have one thing in common: the pure smiles on their faces. The Sea whispers to me once more.

What do you want them to be?

"What kind of question is that?"

You know, Amos.

They are our children. Somehow. I am a father. One of the hybrid creatures bounces forward, jumping at me. By instinct, I spread my arms. It bounces on my chest, leaving a sizeable wet spot on my shirt before flopping to my feet to rub against them as only a cat could. I never thought I'd be a father. The thought of children always made me break out in a nervous sweat. Everyone in my life always told me I'd change my mind, when the right person for me came along. I am a father, suddenly, to what looks like dozens and dozens of strange hybrid beings. As I scan the beach, I see more and more popping into existence. In the Sea's depths, I see ghostly outlines of amoebic shapes sliding and rolling around, their creepily human laughter echoing around me. Like everything else in my life, I am a freak and I have somehow fathered freaks.

As they keep dancing, one leaping at my head and sliding down like jelly, surprisingly light, deliciously cold, one tumbling around in a circle around me, their faces half-morphing into people I know, it hits me. They are our children, yes. As bizarre as they are, they are hope. Who knows what power they may have? Who knows what they can do? They could be a thousand mes, a thousand Stevens. They have the Sea's genes in them, and mine.

Yes, they can do so much. More than you know, more than you can dream of. Alone, we could not cleanse what has been done. Now, we have an opportunity.

"What are they exactly? Are they human?"

They are better than that. They are a mix of us, and more.

If the Sea could smile, she would. A warm tone infuses her voice. She truly believes they will make a difference.

I'm not sure I want our children to be hybrids, these spawns. Being half human, half ocean, how the heck are they going to help clean the sea? What strange powers are they going to have? What can they do that we can't? I am missing something. Or the Sea is crazy. She did choose to make children with me. Only a woman of unsound mind would want that, right?

The Sea calls to the children. Our children.

Come. Come home.

They are the only hope. There is no one else. The chances of any survivors are slim to none. My children. Everybody else is gone. There *is* no home anymore. What am I going to do? What is left to do?

The wiggly creatures slink down the shore and jump right into the waves. Before my eyes they transform into little boys and girls, shadows of Steven and Adi, and other faces of bygone childhood friends. Their amorphous shapes a flurry of skinny legs and flailing arms and wild hair. Their laughter continues even as they plunge into the Sea. I can't call them spawn or hybrids. They are more than that, a thousand times over, no matter their shape. They are elemental, primal. They are my Primals.

They will keep whatever form you want them to, Amos. Come home, the Sea says. She tugs at me, her cold touch cocooning me.

I will not repeat the mistake I made with your kind. You left me too early. This time, I will keep you and teach you how to take care of what is given to you. May you always remember.

She drags me forward and I'm swept inside her again. I tumble and roll uncontrollably. The cold becomes a searing heat and I howl. Tendrils of agony snake their way inside me. My skin glows, a fierce turquoise that leaves shimmering spots in my vision. The light travels from me and spiderwebs into the Sea. It flares but vanishes as the pain becomes too much for me to handle.

"What is this?" I ask, my skin slowly reverting to its normal color. One of the Primals comes and brushes against me. Its touch relieves any lingering pain.

You will discover what you can do soon. Be patient.

I learn... I learn that I have powers above and beyond what I ever imagined. The strange light that traverses my body leads me to oil spills, to plastics, to chemicals of all kinds imaginable. With my kin, we are able to swallow it all and digest it. All the toxins get destroyed in our bodies and what emerges are new forms of life. New corals, new plants.

I learn... that my body transforms according to where we are and what needs to be done. In the deepest recesses of the Sea, I become a tiny microbial being, capable of navigating with only a quarter of the senses I had as a human.

Sometimes, I become part of the Sea herself, a vengeful sprite during a thunderstorm, striking and fountaining up mighty swaths of ocean water violently across kilometers and kilometers, as I... we... struggle to purify the waters. Our children roll inside of us, sucking all the toxins out as best they can.

I learn... I learn that the Sea has given birth to new species as more and more of her depths are cleansed. My brethren begin to mate with those new species. Species with human heads and limbs, but also tentacles and fins, gills and spouts, air bladders and roots. There is every variety. They grow, bit by bit, developing and morphing into their ideal evolutionary form according to the location they choose to stay.

Half humans, half everything become my grandchildren. They become the Descendants. My kin never lose their mirth, their dynamism. They teach their own children. They help me and cuddle up to me just as much as they did that first day. But now, they are teaching me too.

I learn... I learn that slowly, I am losing what makes me me. My mind, my thoughts. My human form. I am a super-charged powerful being and I am purifying the Sea. This is not Amos. I am flawed, I am adrift, I am sardonic. I am human, burdened with the knowledge that my species was imperfect, but incapable of doing much about it. Now, the Sea and my children's thoughts float into my head more often than not.

So many friends, so much family. Our next stop is the Great Barrier Reef. It should only take a few more years to restore.

Silly humans. They didn't know what they were doing.

Are there any humans left at all on the planet? If so, I will have to find them and give them the gift. Maybe then I can stop their folly.

Steven... We miss Steven. His kindness, his dedication. His death even now is a gaping hole of absence. With the gift, he was mighty. Without it and gone, he is insurmountable. We drove him to insanity. We should have guided him better, taught him to use the gift and not succumb to it.

The Sea's or my thought, it doesn't matter. We both agree, in essence.

The Sea is teeming with so much life. We can all breathe. The Sea's color is becoming limpid again. We have started to cleanse the glaciers at the poles. Everything is good. I should be happy.

But I am deeply unhappy. I want my thoughts back. I want my body back. This is home, but it's not. My place is on the land, surrounded by people struggling like me. I am a fragile human being. Here, I am losing everything that defined me as an individual. I dislike that I can hear everybody's thoughts so easily, an instantaneous web of emotions and talk. From hemisphere to hemisphere, from pole to pole, I see and hear my brethren, in my mind, as they mate and clean the remaining impurities in the water. Likewise, they see and hear me.

How long has it been? I ask the Sea.

Ten years, she replies.

I am both unimpressed and shocked. Ten years... An eternity and a breath. Like it was millions of years ago when she took me and created our children. Like it was yesterday when my children and I roamed every ocean cleansing it. Ten years.

I want to go back.

But this is your home, Amos. There is still more to be done.

I know. But we are not alone anymore. I want to see the skies, the land again. The earth is my home. To continue to clean you, we must go on land. The pollution, deforestation, global warming, all of them have to be fixed up there. Please let me go back. I need to go back.

If you go back, you will lose what you have gained here. You will become more a mortal being again. You will lose the universal connection that you have now. Are you quite sure you want to lose that?

Yes. But I want some of our children to come with me. They can help me with their powers. If they can survive.

Of course, they will. They are yours. They can survive on land.

A point of wistfulness fills the Sea's voice. If I didn't know better, I would say the Sea sounds anxious about my departure.

Amos. You have been a father. A grandfather. A child. What will you be on land?

"I will be me. Amos. That is enough."

I am pushed and pushed until I am deposited on the same beach where I'd been scooped up a decade before. I smile. The sand is clean. The algae is gone. There is still debris. But as I look to the former cityscape, I see tall grasses, tangled weeds and green saplings poking from cracks in the cement, climbing on rotting bridges, snaking up crumbling facades of buildings. My children hold my hands and giggle.

"Are you ready?" they ask. Their wide eyes soak in the sights around them. "This will be easy."

I nod, a tightness in my chest. I touch myself. Long gray hair brushes my chest. My nails are obscenely long. I feel old inside. But my skin looks younger than ever. No wrinkles, no flabbiness. There should be. By my calculations, I am sixty-two years old.

Once we finish our work, the earth will be clean. But it will not be repopulated. What is left for me to live for? My children? They are all equally connected to me. Just as they are connected to their mother. They cannot go to school, have jobs, grow old and die. They are more than me. They will never be normal.

Behind me a gurgling sound splashes in the air and a woman walks out of the ocean. Her white-blue hair cascades in waves to her feet. She is beautiful. Her almond-shaped eyes sparkle with ultramarine, violet and indigo shades. Her thin lips smile at me. Scars and burn marks litter her body. It doesn't matter. The affection and worship in her eyes astound me. She walks up and embraces me, nude as I am. Sea brine is on her skin, in her hair.

"Who... Who are you?" I stutter, releasing her.

"You know me."

Her voice. Identical to my dreams, identical to the essence that coursed through me for all these years.

"You're human?"

"I am your other half. I have to take a mortal form. To be

with you. To help you. It was foolish to expect you to do things alone."

I point to the crashing waves.

"Are you... not going to be in there anymore?"

She laughs, the sound tinkling and ferocious all at once.

"Oh, I am. But I will be here too."

I want to bombard her with more questions. But I just want to enjoy this. She is as tall as I am. Her arms are smooth and her breath sends shivers in my face as she breathes at me. She smiles at our children.

"Let's go."

She takes my hand. Her long slender hands are perfectly cool. Where she touches me there is a faint wetness.

About the Author

French-Venezuelan Sophie Jupillat Posey wrote a poem about spring in the 4th grade and started a mystery series a year later. She's been hooked to creating stories ever since. She studied writing and music at Rollins College, and has had numerous short stories and poetry published in literary magazines since 2014. She enjoys reading and writing anything from science fiction and fantasy, to paranormal and mystery novels. When she isn't writing, she is composing music, creating albums, and teaching students in France. You can reach her on Twitter, Facebook, and her website.

Social Media Links:

Website: www.sophiejposey.com
Facebook: Sophie Jupillat Posey Writer
Twitter: @JupillatPosey
Goodreads: Sophie Jupillat Posey
Bookbub: Sophie Jupillat Posey

ACKNOWLEDGMENTS

As always, there are multiple people to thank for a project such as this. I am deeply grateful to Danita Mayer, for being my steadfast editor and always pushing me to dive deeper into my works. Thank you to Swati for editing my earlier stories, Christopher Posey for dissecting them all, and David Curran for cleaning them up over and over. Ira-Rebeca designed the amazing cover.

Afterword

Thank you for reading The Inside Out Worlds: Visions of Strange! If you enjoyed it, please consider leaving a review on Amazon or Goodreads. Reviews are incredibly helpful to indie authors in getting Amazon in particular to recommend their books to other readers.

If you'd like to read more of my works, receive news of my writing journey, and occasionally get some freebies, please sign up to my mailing list at www.sophiejposey.com.

Pop in your email and you will be subscribed. You will get updates on future novels, and story and poetry collections as well as any promos for my books or fellow authors who are running giveaways of theirs.

Of all social media channels, I am most active on Facebook and Instagram.

Thanks again for reading my first magical realism/science fiction story collection. More stories are sprouting in my head every day. Another collection is already forming, but it might take time to complete and publish. In the meantime, I am working on my upcoming dystopian science fiction novel *Thou Shalt Not Dream*.

Take care !

Lightning Source UK Ltd.
Milton Keynes UK
UKHW012210230822
407726UK00002B/584